THE

GREY HORSE

LEGACY

THE

GREY HORSE

LEGACY

BY

JOHN HUNT

New York / Alfred · A · Knopf

1 9 6 8

THIS IS A BORZOI BOOK
PUBLISHED BY ALFRED A. KNOPF, INC.

First Edition
© Copyright 1968 by John Hunt

Library of Congress Catalog Card Number: 68-14884

Manufactured in the United States of America

FOR MY FAMILY

ALL OF THEM

WHO HAVE GIVEN ME SO MUCH

AND MORE PARTICULARLY

FOR DIANA AND MEAD

FOR REASONS THEY KNOW BEST

Author's Note

THERE IS A TOWN BY THE NAME OF GREYHORSE IN NORTH-
ern Oklahoma, but it in no way resembles the town of that name
which I have here imagined.

If by inadvertence I have used the name of any living person
or Indian family, I ask their pardon and understanding. My
Indians belong to an imaginary tribe and live in a mythical
county, even though my version of their history may at some
point or other seem dimly recognizable to anyone who has ever
cared about what happened to the people who were removed to
Indian Territory.

Then, too, in my part of the country, where the myths are
as violent as the weather, the story I tell may in some unintended
way recall events which resemble those that I relate. But my purpose is a special kind of history, and my tale has happened mainly
in my mind. If someone should imagine that he sees here the
features of the living or the dead, let him put it down to sheer
coincidence.

J. H.
Paris, 1967

Contents

PART ONE

In My Beginning

Grey Horse, Oklahoma,

in the Twenties

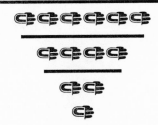

1

"I SUPPOSE YOU'RE WONDERING WHY I'VE ASKED YOU TO come here." Andrews Thayer stood beside the open window of his office and watched the town blur into night. "Things are happening that you haven't heard about yet, Cody—things that have a lot to do with you." He looked out to where the twilight spread like oil, his face controlled, his body as casual as he could make it. Then he turned away abruptly from the window and stabbed his finger through the silence. "You're going to need whatever help you can find."

"Ain't no trouble that I know of happening to me, Mr. Thayer." Cody scratched the back of his neck and leaned forward in his chair. "Not that that's saying a hell of a lot, but . . ." His smile seemed no more than a kind of nervous tic as he looked down at boots polished to the sheen of varnish. Then his face came up again, closed and secretive, the eyes vague and restless. "What kind of things are happening?"

Andrews stared at him contemptuously. "I don't suppose you have any idea."

"Well, you said yourself I hadn't heard."

He looked at his watch. It shouldn't be much longer now. And he wanted to tell Cody himself, just to see his face when he told him. Because he would have to hit him hard and keep on hitting him until Cody threw in the towel. "I ought to be getting a phone call any minute. Hold on a little. I want you to have it, so to speak . . ." and he hesitated momentarily, his lips pursed, his eyes hard with irony, ". . . straight from the horse's mouth."

Cody pushed the broad-brimmed cowman's hat away from his

forehead. "I got a considerable amount of business to attend to before I go back out to the place, Thayer. Unless there's something real pressing . . ." He licked his lips and took a deep breath. "I'm hauling feed already," he said, and then his face lifted pompously. "I don't want to get caught again like I did last winter. We only lost five head at that, but Clay—Mr. Carter don't take kindly to loss. Man lose something of his, cross him some way or other, he's gonna want to know why." His face folded into a smile of something like complicity. He rubbed the knob of his wrist across his jaw. "Maybe it can wait until tomorrow."

Andrews took a cigarette from an embossed silver case and turned it slowly in his slender fingers. "How long have you worked for Clay Carter?"

"Best part of my life. So what."

"Been with him right from the start—all the way through?"

Cody sat without moving. "Depends on what a man would call the start, don't it. Now look—"

"He's in trouble. I'm talking about real trouble." Andrews dropped his voice to the threshold of a whisper. He leaned against the window sill, his knuckles showing white where he gripped the edge. "You're going to have to do some tall thinking about who your friends are before this is over. You're going to have to figure out whose side you're on." He scratched the match and narrowed his eyes behind the smoke. "God helps those who help themselves, Cody. The best way you can help yourself is to open up. Talk. Now. Tell me everything you know, whatever there is left to tell that I don't already know." Coils of smoke spun slowly to the light. "It's been a long time coming, but Carter's reached the end of the line. There's no way out for him, Cody—he's finished. But for you, just maybe—"

And then the phone rang, and without taking his eyes from Cody's face, he went to the desk and picked up the receiver.

"Yes. Thayer here. You'll have to speak louder—I can't hear you. What was it again?" Then, as though it were a pistol, he pointed the receiver straight at Cody.

"I said we've picked up Clay Carter, damn it." The words

came through urgent, harsh, metallic. "We've got him down at the jail. He's asking for his lawyer. Thayer, I'm getting the hell out of here until Monday. You've got that long to get enough on him to make it stick. And you better goddam sure have produced something by then or we'll both . . ."

He brought the receiver quickly back to his ear. "Yes. That's right. Good. I've got the weekend, then. I understand. No, no trouble. Like we agreed. All right."

"What the hell's he talking about—jail?" Cody was rubbing his hands hard back and forth along his pants leg.

"Murder." The word was eager in his mouth as an ax stroke. "Murder." He could hear Cody's breathing, could see the muscles in his jaw bunch like a fist. "That's what I mean by trouble."

Cody rose and shoved his hat down on his head. "I don't give a good goddam what you say—Clay Carter ain't killed any— You haven't got anything on him. What proof is there, just tell me that?"

"We've got what we need. You better start thinking about yourself, Cody. Right now. There'll be questions. Lots of them. I want to help you. Remember that. I'm ready to help you. There's not much time."

His words, louder now, followed Cody through the office door and down the dusty, echoing stair well.

"You know where to find me. I'll be waiting for you. You're going to need me, Cody. A lot more than you ever needed Carter. You're going to need help, brother, all the help you can get."

He was shouting when he heard the slam of the street door downstairs. Then he leaned against the wall, his head upon his arm, his hand moving roughly across his face. His breath came painfully in gasps. For a long time he fought the thickness in his throat, until the sound of someone's laughter outside made him turn back to the window. The street was empty, the town a haze of dusk, silent as though drowned beneath the film of night.

He leaned limply against the window frame, the strength drained suddenly from his body. He had made his opening gambit, and it had gone as he had planned, and there was no turning back. Yet, behind the abstract symmetry of the case, whose moves he had worked out as deliberately as a problem in chess, was the tormenting uncertainty of so much that he could not control. Because everything hung now on Cody, on Booth, and on Rita, Carter's wife. Without a statement by them, without their bearing witness, no amount of circumstantial evidence could wring a conviction from a jury whose sympathies would be with Carter from the start. And given the situation, it would be far more than a mere matter of sympathy. Those twelve men in the jury box, Clay Carter's life in their hands, would each of them be standing at the bar with the accused, each of them accused too, judged, reliving painfully the pity and the terror of their own lives as they tried to find the measure of a man who all unaccountably had found himself fixed in the gaze of God. Because it would not be just Clay Carter in the dock, or twelve men caged in a jury box, or the exhumation of corpses from a man's past, or even a trial, properly speaking. Rather it would be, in one man's history, the stylized rendering of a town's ripeness and decay and death: the solemn telling of the tale of how they all had died. And the evidence would have to be beyond question, unimpeachable, a kind of Gorgon's head upon which they would all be afraid to look. Evidence, in short, which would stop a man's ears against the paralyzing *There but for the grace of God go I*. And what more calculated to achieve just that than sworn statements, witnessing, testifying, damnation by those people closest of all to Carter—Cody, his friend, foreman, constant companion; Booth, his brother-in-law, his befriender; and Rita Carter, his wife.

You're just a little premature with that prosecution rhetoric, he said to himself. You're not pleading that case yet. But it wouldn't be long now. Cody would be frightened after tonight, wondering who else knew and how much had been uncovered. The way he had shifted there in the chair, moving his hands clumsily as though trying to hide them from sight, with guilt like a birthmark on his face. Was there blood on those hands? Andrews took another cigarette from the case. They were all guilty. Guilty as hell. It was just a matter of finding the plague spot. And very likely Cody would be willing to put the finger on Carter now that he was safely locked up. You didn't work for a man like Clay Carter for over twenty years without scores to settle, and Cody would know, too, that the hand that had reached for Carter could settle on him next. God helps those that help themselves. Let him meditate on that homely New England truth for a while, and then ask himself once and for all: What price loyalty?

And Cody would talk all right. Sitting there in that ridiculous Buffalo Bill outfit, spinning out his evasive country nonsense—just the kind of clod who would be crushed by the first sign of strength. Yet he would never abandon Carter without someplace else to go. Some kind of haven—of acceptance, of understanding, of forgiveness. He knows not what he does. A judicious mixture of mercy and terror . . . help him wash the blood off his hands . . . hold those whitened fingers while he prays . . . but sternly, sternly . . .

And Carter? Andrews's eyebrows raised a little. He considered how it must have been when Carter had opened the door to the sheriff—the long, narrow-nosed fox face alert with surprise, the soft voice wondering, the terrible race of thoughts behind the deliberate movements of his lean body, the trembling in the knees at the thought of . . . what? Betrayal? Ghosts risen and walking abroad? Some simple oversight compounded by the chancings of fate into a fault as fatal as a corpse before his door? All of these and worse—the fog-enshrouded vastness of ignorance and surmise through which his mind must search furiously while he stood there at the door, bending his height slightly to seek the sheriff's troubled, almost apologetic eyes, his quiet voice sharpened with just the merest edge of anxiety. Gentle, courteous, elaborately assured to the last. A disguise as intricate as medieval armor to protect the ugly man inside.

Clay Carter . . . Andrews reflected grimly that following his trail had led him through the desert of a lost past where the few discoverable facts of Carter's existence, gleaming hard and white like the scattered bones of a skeleton, had only deepened the mystery of what the man had been. Born in West Texas (the records in Austin showed March 23, 1880, as the date of birth—but the birth certificate had not been registered until 1883, the first time the father, Jackson Carter, had "had the occasion to get it down on paper," and therefore the word *uncertain* appeared on the record, and "Carter ranch south of Midland" as the place), in what was probably an earth house or at best an adobe hut, Carter had crossed the Red River into the Territory in 1889, come as a boy with his people for the April Rush into the old Creek and Seminole reservations. Jackson Carter filed a homestead in what became—between high noon and sundown of the twenty-second day of April, eighteen hundred and eighty-nine—Oklahoma City, but later the claim was sold and the Carters, some or all, drifted southwest again, looking for whatever it was that in the first place had made them follow the sun from the blue-walled tidelands of Virginia to this wind-haunted, last-chance land.

It was 1908 before Clay Carter left tracks again, at least that the law could find. It was a matter of court record in a dusty, sun-hammered county seat in the southern part of the state, but no one seemed to remember just what had happened beyond the fact that this young man (*Said he come up here from Texas—I don't know, maybe he did—but what in hell did he come for?—wasn't Texas big enough and windy enough and ugly enough for him? I would figure that in a place that size there'd be plenty enough of dust to go around—*) had lived in a place outside of town, married to an ailing Indian woman who held the deed. One day he showed up at the Court House to file probate proceedings on the property—the house itself was gone, burned down in a fire that had finished the house as well as Carter's Indian wife, who, being badly crippled, had been trapped inside. (*Nope. Nothing left to investigate. Poked around in the ashes some. No witnesses. Woman had no kin that anybody could locate. By the terms of the will it all went to—how'd you call him?—Carter. Clay Carter. Anyone else, you say? Well, there was a hired help on the place. Can't recall his name. He stood back of Carter on the thing—how*

*they got to the house too late and all. No, nobody asked. Start
asking questions like that around here, where would you stop? If
you ever got the chance to ask the second one, that is.*) And when
the title was cleared, Carter sold the land and disappeared. The
next place he hung his hat was the State Hotel, Grey Horse, Oklahoma, April, 1909. Traveling light, but not alone. There was
someone riding with him. A man whom he could count on to
stand at his back.

So it would end as it had begun, Andrews was thinking, as he
watched the town disintegrating like a sand castle in the night. A
Southern family, worked out and fallow as the land they had
settled four generations back, following the roll of the dice westward; Carter himself bred in an emptiness of prickly pear and
mesquite trees and honed by sandy winds to coyote sharpness; the
insane greed of the Land Rush, sucking inexorably into its vortex
all of the floaters, the failures, the drifters, the scum—the refuse
of civilization; the Carters, no more able than a tumbleweed to
take root in this final, dusty, scrub-oak and short-grass denoue-
ment of all that was left of the old dream; and Carter himself,
following the trails of his blood, coming at last into his legacy of
wandering and violence—a clearing in the red clay country of
southern Oklahoma, a soft pine shack cupped in a wind-whipped
flower of flame, staccato screams choked in smoke, and at last, in
the silence, a shifting heap of ash beneath the sun's dead stare.
Then moving on again to where a man could see for thirty miles
or more and go as far as his stake and his guts could carry him, so
long as his luck held out.

And for all of Carter's quiet arrival in Grey Horse, the years
had seen him close the town inexorably in his fist. Some said he
had been lucky, that with Clay it was just seven good years all the
way through and the lean years he divided up among his friends.
Others—the few who would talk—linked him with the early-day
killings of several tribal members whose insurance policies had
reportedly borne his name. And more recently there were stories
about the Red Hawk family and the mysterious wave of murders
that brought Clay closer, corpse by corpse, to all the family's

headrights and an annual government payment against oil rights that would make northern Oklahoma a kind of Carter barony. But however he had done it, a well-stocked fifty-thousand-acre ranch made his voice loud in cattle councils; in Grey Horse itself he owned a dry-goods store, an automobile agency, a funeral parlor, a pool and domino establishment known as the Smoke House, and a grocery; in addition, he controlled one of the town's three banks. As the whittlers who enjoyed squatters' rights on the hotel steps put it, there wasn't a whole hell of a lot a gent could do in this man's town without putting money in Clay Carter's pockets, lessen it was to take a piss. His rise had been, like himself, quiet, steady, and relentless; he had put the place in his hip pocket piece by piece before most people knew what had happened. A good part of the town still thought of him as the rich cattleman who lived in the vast, rambling Spanish-style house that overlooked the valley in which the town was built. But he was much more than that; in some important way, Andrews reflected, Clay Carter was the town, what had made it, what was wrong with it, what would kill it. Rancher and merchant, banker and politician, a feudal lord in Stetson hat and Fort Worth boots, married to an Indian girl half his age who had been a celebrated dancer until Carter brought her back all improbably from Paris and who as much as said, at least to Andrews, that Carter had systematically killed off her family until only she and two sisters stood between him and the handful of headrights that could finance him to anyplace short of the moon he felt like going. This was the man, in flesh, in history, and in simple ownership embodying the town, whom the sheriff had arrested just some two hours ago now as he sat down to dinner in the long, high-ceilinged dining room of the house that loomed above Grey Horse like a palace. And so it was that the cell door, closing upon Carter, had closed in fact for the time being upon the very town itself, locking each man fast into that cube which is the shape of his past. And for me, too, Andrews thought suddenly, lifting his face to the vast obscurity of the sky. For me, too. That jail door has closed upon us all.

Outside lightning broke across the night like phosphorescent waves upon black beach. Late autumn; dog days drowsing like a

drugged patient waiting for the knife; the last of the locusts ringing in the elms; night infiltrating the town like a guerrilla army.
He stood there partially concealed in the wind-stirred curtain,
breathing heavily, knowing that the swinging to of that door had
been for him no end but a beginning. For Carter, perhaps, it was a
termination of sorts. Walking into that washboard-grey, iron-
barred-and-bedded cell might conceivably mean a paradoxical
kind of freedom; in his cell he was perhaps in some ambiguous
way a freer man than those who were left with the need to keep
him there, as though his ritual imprisonment could lock up forever the fears that plundered their days and destroyed their
nights. But for Andrews it was all too clearly the beginning of a
journey toward an unknown destination across a parched land
where dust devils writhed in spinning fury, beneath a menacing
sky hovering overhead like a vulture. And yet this hush, this
expectant silence from which the very air seemed to flee—what
did it prefigure if not that Judgment Day which would ride down
tornado tall and terrible upon the prostrate town?

Oh God of wind and water, fire and earth, in whose eyes this
town is an abomination, in whose nostrils this town stinks of
death, let the heathen be judged in thy sight. And to Andrews, his
face straining avidly through the darkness, there came with jolt-
ing suddenness a fiery vision of the necessity of it all. Water
sprang to his eyes, his mouth sucked for air, his bones melted into
rivulets in the clay of his body. And all around him he felt God's
will turning through the heavens like the slow cycle of the seasons: birth, copulation, and death; innocence, temptation, corruption, and the avenging angel. The vision flared before him like
a flame. He nodded his head, no longer fearing where his journey
might lead him, smiling as though in assent to angelic tongues
heard somewhere in the night. Through him surged a sense of
inevitability; purity burned in his breast; he was a knife in God's
hand. And deeply he knew that this was what he had always
sought—the stripping away of his own flesh, too merely and
grossly human, and the armoring of his bones with the hard purposes of God.

The blood sang in his ears like the trumpets of angels, and his eyes glistened with triumph as he looked down upon the cowering town. I'll get him, he thought benignly. I'll get them all. Thy will be done . . .

The jangle of the telephone was as shrill and unpleasant as an unloved voice calling him back from sleep. He closed his eyes and rubbed hard at his forehead, then lifted the receiver.

"Yes," he said abruptly, half expecting the county attorney who would be drunk by now and afraid and looking for someplace to hide.

"It's Rita, Andrews. I had to call you."

For a moment his eyes closed again; then his lips curved down into a smile his mouth had never really learned to make, as though he were mocking his own happiness and relief. His body relaxed against the desk, and he stubbed his cigarette slowly against the ash tray.

"Hello, Rita." And then he knew that he had been waiting all along for her to call.

"The sheriff was here—they took Clay—the sheriff and Hub Prudom and somebody I didn't know. They've taken Clay off. Oh, Andrews, I'm afraid. What's happening? What are you trying to do? It is you, isn't it?"

Her voice was a tissue of apprehension, of joy, of something else softly and seductively secret which he tried hopelessly to pretend he did not hear.

"I wonder . . ." The words fell soft as mist upon his ears. "Couldn't I see you? I realize—well, you may not want it this way right now. But I'm afraid—for both of us. You don't know Clay. Didn't you understand what I was trying to tell you?"

As his mind worked frantically, calculating the risks of compromise, the dangers of being seen on this particular night with the wife of the man whom he had finally succeeded, for the moment at least, in placing behind bars, her image gradually took shape in the darkness before his eyes. Her coarse hair pulled to a black knot at the back of her too slender neck; her heavy-lashed eyes that always seemed a little too bright; the fragile flower of her body poised like a tiger lily on legs too long to be strong, yet hard as cables; the carelessness of her sudden movements, clumsiness in other women, lynxlike grace in her; a bronzed, queenly woman upon whom the haphazard combinations she wore of ephemeral Paris dresses now out of style and dusty Italian shoes run over at the heel and Indian beads and ceremonial ornaments and a somber woolen shawl found somewhere in Spain lay like a cunningly draped mantle of studied order. And withal, indistinct and clinging as her shadow, an aura of doom—a desperation that made her laughter sharp with scorn, that made her eyes too wide, too free, that kept her hands moving like bats. All too often her own particular scent was bootleg whiskey.

"Of course if you can't make it tonight—it's just that we have so little time . . . to decide what to do," and in her voice was that curious intimacy which had established itself so quickly between them.

She had sensed his hesitation, and now Andrews knew that he must see her. She was essential to him, to the case he had built, and in some more profound way, to his life, or to a life that was struggling almost against his will to be born within him. Suddenly he realized how completely all that he had come to be now rested in those unpredictable hands. A cold sweat broke through and chilled the surface of his body. He slid the desk drawer open and looked down at the typed foolscap:

I, Rita Carter, wife of Clay Carter, *do hereby swear that Clay Carter, acting in league with Blair Booth and William Cody, did knowingly and deliberately plan and carry out . . . remaining members of my family . . . overheard discussions between him and Booth . . . premeditated murder . . . title to headrights . . . unusual intensity of interest in the details of death to the point of obsession . . . referred to Cody in my presence as an Indian killer to which Cody replied that Clay knew more about killing Indians than any man in Grey Horse . . . total inheritance . . . Item: Jimmy Red Hawk . . . shot to death in Cedar Canyon, Carter and Booth both present; Item: Frank Red Hawk . . . shot to death in the Carter pasture north of Choctaw; Item: Kenneth Red Hawk, beaten to death in the Smoke House in a fight with William Cody; Item:*

Jewel Red Hawk Gunn . . . killed when her home was dynamited, Booth present shortly before the explosion; Item: Ruth Red Hawk Pinto . . . killed by strangulation, the body found and brought to town by Carter . . .

On and on it went, chilling, horrible, a morgue with all the mangled bodies laid out for identification. It was all there, as perfect in its icy clarity as a geometric proof, awaiting the Q.E.D. of her signature. He hadn't wanted to rush her too fast after the arrest, to make her frighteningly aware of just how much this particular piece of paper meant. Yet he must get her name on it tonight. . . . Because Clay would be free on Monday. The county attorney, Dickey, had given him the weekend, and no more.

For it was just three days ago that he had gone to see Dickey in his office at the Court House. The ceiling fan had whined overhead, stirring eddies of acrid cigar smoke, while Dickey read through the statement he had prepared.

"Well," Dickey had said speculatively, looking out from behind his cigar. The sweat glistened darkly in the pores of his whiskers; beneath oiled black hair parted in the middle, his eyes were wary. "You've got quite a bit of paper here. Where do you want me to file it? Unsolved cases? Got lots of paper in there already. Crapper reading, maybe."

"You're not going to file it anywhere, Mr. Dickey. You're going to act on it. I want you to get out a summons for Carter's arrest."

Stud Dickey winced, and the swivel chair squealed under him as he shifted his weight. Probably nobody had ever called him anything but Stud in his whole life, except the preacher at his wedding.

"Charge?"

"Conspiracy to commit murder."

"Shit, Thayer."

"I mean it, Mr. Dickey."

Dickey turned sideways and looked at him from the corner of his eye. "I admit it ain't saying a hell of a lot, but we both know that you know a damn sight more law than I do. You can't expect this thing to stand up. Even as an informational document, which is the best we could hope for—my God, it ain't even signed."

"It will be. Once Carter's in jail."

"What makes you so sure?"

"That's my concern, Mr. Dickey. I'm only asking you to lock Carter up."

"Who's making the complaint?"

"I am. Get it typed—I'll sign it right now."

Dickey fished for a match in his shirt pocket, then lit the dead cigar stump. He was scowling, half mad, obviously not liking what he heard and yet needing to hear more. "Isn't there some piece of this we could get a corroboration on, Thayer? Hell, I'm the one that's on the hot seat; I want to clean it up every damn bit as much as you do. But God Almighty, man, look what you're asking me to do."

Andrews got up slowly and closed the office door. Then he hitched his chair a little closer to where Dickey sat, took a cigarette from the thin silver case, and scratched a match on Dickey's desk. "Mr. Dickey, I'm asking you to take a good hard look at your situation. You've been in public office four years. You're coming up for reelection. Your term has been chiefly characterized by the number of unsolved murders committed during that period. Some people call it corruption; everybody thinks it's a scandal. The circumstances of some of these killings have been such—and right now I'm thinking of the Red Hawk family—that even the national press has seen fit to draw attention to the crimes for which Grey Horse has become notorious."

It hadn't been too difficult to bring Dickey around. He gave it to him hard-nosed and arrogant, looking down at him from a long way up. And he had the book on Dickey—a man who had played guard during six years for two Southern Bible colleges before scraping through with a physical-education degree, then a night-school law diploma from one of the smaller Southern legal factories, then wandering west to Grey Horse, where a man with nothing to go on could at least start even, then politics because he took easier to people than he ever did to law. Useful to the back-room boys because he had always left the thinking to the quarterback, and because he was rednecked and country Southern, and because he could always draw a laugh when the thinking got a little fancy for him.

"If you've been protecting Carter, then Carter hasn't been helping you much."

"Carter? All I am to him is the man he hires to keep it reasonably clean over at the Smoke House. Now look, Thayer—"

"No, Mr. Dickey. Don't waste your time on me. I have no stake in this town beyond doing what I came out here to do."

"Namely?"

But Andrews had shaken the question off. "I can promise you that this place will be overrun by federal law inside of a month. If you've been cooperative, then everybody will stand to gain by being with you. If not, you may find yourself in the bullpen with the big losers. No job, no prospects—maybe worse. You're not that young, Mr. Dickey. Take it easy on yourself. Politicians don't like losers. And if Carter gets wind ahead of time that we're after him—well, I wouldn't lend you a dollar. The odds would be too great against ever getting it back."

Then he had leaned forward and put both hands down flat on the desk. "Mr. Dickey, I am asking you to instruct the sheriff to arrest Clay Carter on a charge of murder. I guarantee to have Rita Carter's signature on this statement twenty-four hours from the time he walks through that cell door. In another twenty-four hours I'll have detailed statements from Booth and Cody. From there on in it will be a federal case, since the murders were committed on Indian Trust land. You'll get the credit, Mr. Dickey. All I'm asking for is a warrant and forty-eight clear hours."

A wasp beat at the window screen and the overhead fan went on silently churning the smoke.

"Mr. Thayer," Dickey said, and then waited as though hoping to be interrupted. "Mr. Thayer, as a lawyer, you make one hell of a preacher. When you say federal, I reckon you spell that Washington. No locals. Professionals."

"Mr. Dickey, we have understood each other perfectly."

Dickey bowed his head then so that Andrews could see the

ivory part running all the way back to the folds of his neck. "If you, sir, will sign the complaint under oath, I will send it on down to the justice of the peace. But let it be said once and for all, Thayer, that if you are shitting me, then we are both up the creek. Now the calendar says Tuesday. The arrest will be made on Friday. I won't be here on the weekend. You'll have until Monday. Goddam you if you make one false move. God help us both if you're wrong."

"Andrews—are you still there? Answer me, please answer. I'm afraid to be alone ... please ..."

He trembled as though trying to awake from a nightmare that he was sure must be only a dream.

"Yes," he said loudly. "Yes, of course I want to see you, Rita. There's nothing to be afraid of. Clay can't hurt you where he is. Come on down to the office. I'll tell Emily I'll be late for dinner and wait for you here." As though part of him were in the pulpit, hand upraised, and the other part down kneeling in the dust, praying *not now O God not tonight not ever again until all the darkness goes away.*

And even as he spoke he knew it was wrong. He could hear something like laughter, could imagine that strange blend of pity and scorn that came so often to her eyes. Yet he could not stop himself. "I want to see you." A sudden thrust of despair made him turn hard into the desk; he reached for her with his voice. "Come now, Rita—as soon as you can. I'll wait here. . . ." His voice was soft now with wanting her, and her answer was laced with laughter.

"I have to change," whispered, assured. "It will take me a little bit—fifteen minutes or so," and then for a moment she was silent. "Is the front door open . . . or should I park in the alley and use the back?"

"Yes," he said urgently. "Yes, the alley. Put the truck there. It's better that way."

"Yes," she said, and the word had a strange finality about it. "In a little," husky, coarse, and then her voice was gone.

He heard the click of the receiver, held the phone for a moment longer in his hand, then slowly replaced it on the hook. His desire had faded into apprehension; he had the impression of entering unwillingly a field of force against whose blind pull he would be helpless. The taste of fear dried his mouth and drew it tight against the bone, and in the emptiness of her going he felt his stomach twisted by the grim suspicion that he had spun a world of gossamer and hung it by a thread from her heart.

He hesitated, then shifted his shoulders awkwardly. Through thin lips he asked the operator for the number of his home.

The phone rang several times before Emily answered. Her voice rushed with relief when she heard him speak. "Oh, Andrews, I'm so glad you called. It's Amory—he's flushed and terribly hot; red all over. I'm awfully worried; nothing I do seems to help. I wanted to call you but with all this—I knew you'd be busy—"

"I'm never that busy, Emily." He spoke calmly, his words as precise as a palisade of stakes set against her need. There was something these days about her simple emotional responses that set his teeth on edge, so that he always seemed to be put in the position of admonishing her. And yet surely it was this very simplicity, this innocence, this uncomplicated goodness, damn it all, that had drawn him to her in the first place. Or had it been that he was simply seeking a pupil or, more aptly, a congregation. I've never loved her, he said to himself suddenly, accepting the fact of it now without emotion, as though he had finally grown accustomed to those sad words. But where was all this taking him? "You should have called."

"Oh, you know," she hesitated. "All this business about Carter. Blair Booth stopped by; he's out in the garden. He says he has to see you—tonight. What's happened, Andrews?" She asked the question as though merely looking for a way to call his name, as though no answer that he would ever give could answer what she could never ask.

"Carter's been arrested. They've got him down at the jail. Jack Bird will have him out on bail by Monday at the latest. I've got three nights and two days, Emily, to get enough on him to keep him there. That's what I came here for."

"For Carter?" shyly put, already in retreat before the reply.

Andrews's jaw set hard, the blood beat at his temple, and his words were as harsh as a slap in the face. "For Carter, Emily—and the others—anybody who's got blood on his hands."

"Oh, Andrews, be careful. You know how these people are . . . they're just not the same—they're not like we are. Can't they keep him locked up? Oh, this town . . ." Her voice broke, and for a moment the phone hummed silently. "I'm sorry. Forgive me. I'm so worried about Amory. He's never been this—"

"There's nothing to worry about, Emily," he said with finality. "You stay right there and look after the boy. Don't do anything until I get home. Then if he's really sick, we can take him to the hospital or get Doctor Cooper. He's probably eaten something that doesn't agree with him—remember the Fourth of July, after all that watermelon?" He hesitated for a moment, his eyes suddenly reflective. "Does Booth want something special? Has he told you anything?"

"Just that he wants to see you right away. He seems upset." She waited for a moment. "What would there be for him to tell?"

"I imagine he is," Andrews said curtly. "Now you go ahead and eat. Don't wait for me. I'll have to stay here for another couple of hours—maybe longer—and I don't want to be disturbed. Look after Amory and don't worry—as soon as I get home we'll find out what's wrong." His voice was commanding, but weary of command, as though he spoke to a servant or a child.

"All right," she said faintly. "If you think that's best . . ." She was silent again. "Andrews?"

"Yes," he answered impatiently.

"Is Booth—well, really mixed up in this?"

He smiled bitterly. "Blair is into it over his head. Way over his head. Tell him Carter is in jail. He'll know what's happening."

"Promise me you'll be careful." Her voice trailed off into a dry sob. "At least think of Amory, Andrews."

"For God's sake, Emily, get a grip on yourself. Pour yourself a drink or something. Carter can't hurt anybody where he is, and if they let him out on bail, I'll be the last person he'll want to see. Look after the boy, Emily; do what you can for Amory. There's nothing you can do for me now."

When he replaced the receiver, he could hear the sound of his own breathing in the silence. So now the boy was sick. He put his fist against his forehead and closed his eyes. Somehow the pattern was beginning to fray around the edges, the pattern he had so deliberately woven and which was now so close to fulfillment of a kind—his marriage to Emily, then the coming of his son, Amory, then the Indian Service, then the call, seemingly providential, to come to Grey Horse—a life of planned, willed sacrifice to ideals handed down through his Massachusetts family like heirlooms, seeking always some continuity with the rude integrity of his family's past. And now Rita, risen like a phoenix aflame into an existence become dry and explosive beyond his imagining. He stood there motionless as though listening for something he could barely catch down the distant corridors of his mind. Some dimly remembered voice? Some whisper of warning? Or just the furtive rustle of betrayal?

He stood again by the window, hearing the fitful wind lifting the leaves to the crest of a moan, then letting them down once more into a trough of trembling silence. Night had overrun the town; like powder smoke the smell of autumn drifted on the air. But in this country of extremes there would be hardly time for the land to recover from the devastation of summer before the probes of early winter would once again reduce life to a holding action, this time against the cold. And always, whatever the season, there was the wind, flowing like blood through the body of this chilled and fevered town.

For the space of a cigarette, Andrews felt himself momentarily becalmed in the lassitude of this season and this hour, in the peculiar suspension of will that followed the closing of that cell door. Between the replacing of the receiver and the sliding crunch of Rita's tires in the gravel of the alley, there was only dead space, an extended emptiness during which his mind lay still as though stunned and he felt no longer involved in what he had wrought. He was the unblinking eye of silence at the dead center of the tornado's furious cone. As though I were merely along for the ride, he thought ruefully.

And as he thought about it all—these people, strangers to him less than a year ago; this town, not even a name then on any map he had ever seen—he felt again as though he were caught in a dreamlike web from which he could not free himself, suffering from a peculiar kind of anguish as unreal as someone else's pain.

For dimmed in depths of darkness, the town had taken on a sudden temporary quality, as though it were merely scenery that could be moved at will, as bare and elemental as the settings of ancient tragedy, against which he must act out that drama in which he was both author and player. As though the town and the people in it had come full-blown into being with his arrival, only to disappear again when he would leave. And he asked himself how real any of it was beyond what the imperatives of his destiny required.

Rather what God requires, he murmured to himself. For this was all God's doing, whether he now shrank from it or not. Even in this momentary drift, as in all the rest of what was happening, there was that iron inevitability that he could feel as clearly as he felt the cables of command strung between mind and flesh.

And if he should start asking for reckonings . . . It was very late in the day to be seeking explanations, he who had never asked more than to feel that his own will had been dissolved in that mysterious continuity of things wherein he believed somehow the meaning of his life to lie. And yet in this hiatus in time's flow, he felt an urgent need to be once more as sure as possible of where he was going. It was as though he had reached the last marked water hole on the edge of a smoldering desert which he must cross, putting himself face down for a last long drink from the revivifying springs of the past, taking last readings with his compass from the few fixed points he knew.

GREY HORSE, OKLAHOMA. Just a name to him at first, a strange and lonely name, until after long nights of reading from the dust-covered files, the faded reports, the Agents' correspondence, the travelers' accounts, it had become a place as well defined in his mind as Concord or Groton. And like them, lodged in some earlier strata of time, so that its present inhabitants seemed impermanent and unimportant when set against the town's historic life, as though it were the town which gave them life and not the other way around. And yet not the town, either, at least not in the sense of the New England towns he knew with their black-shuttered white frame houses trim as clipper ships anchored forever in the tranquillity of soaring elms and solemn churches and broad reaches of undulating lawn. Rather the land, the last leveling off of that vast upthrust of rock which crested far away to the east, the furthest line of advance of the trees right down to the shore of the great prairie sea which rolled westward to the Rockies. Land that had been the Chetopa's beyond any reckoning, much more than the eye could cover in days of riding, as much as they could defend from any challenger, Indian or white. And more particularly the valley of the last encampment, the sandstone and timber Agency building, the buffalo-hide lodges, beef drying on hickory racks, wood smoke veering crazily in the wind, dogs curled up in the shade and babies playing in the dust and ponies wrinkling their noses against the wind, their hind hooves cocked, their tails lashing at the flies—all the drowsy sun-filled life of a people vanquished, exiled, driven by the relentless pressure of the settlers to this last retreat, to this lost corner of their great hunting grounds, in this capricious land of wild winds and deadly sun and stunted trees that seemed to writhe in agonies of death like men lost in a desert. Hemmed in by alien tribes against whom they could no longer fight, by aggressive whites who owned the law, their heritage traded for ten dollars a year per man and their rations.

No, for him Grey Horse could never mean the town. It meant

the Chetopa reservation and the United States government—the Tribe and the Agency. For the town itself, the merchants and bankers, the lawyers and grocers, all those who catered to the appetites of the tribe and who were always there in triumph or disaster to claim their percentage and who had gradually spread their places of business and domicile throughout the valley and onto the hills that surrounded it so that now the dwindling remains of the tribe occupied an area of ground in the flat lands to the north of the town commonly known as Indian Camp—for what had come to be known as Grey Horse, he felt nothing but contempt on those occasions when the town as it existed today imposed itself upon him. Grey Horse as it was, and as it would always be for him, was fixed as precisely in his mind as some early geographer's rendering of the world, the wonder and simplicity of which later knowledge could never diminish. And so it was with that land that lived inside him with all the felt existence of his own spirit, as though in some curious way it were a part of him. That last, lost valley, the creek which could flood in June and be nothing but drying mud flats by August, the hills which made a cup of the horizon, the Agent's house on the rise to the north of the creek and the barn where the mules were kept, the camp for the freighters who hauled in the rations from the States, the traders' stores, the old flour mill, the sandstone school established by the Catholic Church for the girls of the tribe, the roads leading out to Elgin and Coffeyville and Arkansas City—all of this fixed once and for all with the hard clarity of an ancient daguerreotype. These were the last dwindling hours of the Chetopa's heroic age, before their minds had begun to grow troubled and their bodies sick, when the sounds of the land were still the booming and the whistle of the prairie chicken and wild turkey and quail and the clatter of deer in the blackjack thickets, when clashes with the Cherokee, themselves at the end of their long and tragic trail, could for a brief moment make the blood race again. They were a warrior people; he would always think of them thus. And he felt for them a strange kinship, perhaps because they too represented something so much older than the rootless hordes which had swept across the country, wandering westward like the

Carters, clamoring for land until even in their last refuge the vanquished could know no peace. Perhaps it was a kinship in a lost cause, just as for him early America, with its strange mixture of Yankee merchants and Southern planters whose profound English conservatism had led them to revolution, was so different from what the country had become. Colonists and Chetopa both, washed out by wave after wave of the dispossessed. And just as the New England he cared about existed for him only up to a certain point just prior to the Civil War, so he had not really wanted to look too closely at what had happened to the Chetopas after the turn of the century, once the old communal holdings were broken up and the land divided and Indian Territory had become part of the States. Because for him something essential had been lost when the Territory was put on the auctioneer's block in the name of civilization—something that had to do with the country's very soul, its inmost conception and sense of itself. Some last tenuous tie with history had been cut and that part of the ledger which read LOSS was torn out, leaving a set of books that could never be balanced. We are doomed to the emptiness of occupancy, was the way he thought about it. Something more than mathematically defined, fenced acreage and cash should have been provided for that which should have been part of our past, too. As it was, the whole country had been turned into one vast tract of real estate.

So the Territory was gone, and the land was bought and sold and claimed and fenced and fought over and abandoned. Impassive spectators, the Chetopa had watched them arrive, the lawyers, doctors, bankers, merchants—mountebanks in a traveling show for all the world like a carnival. Except that this particular carnival had never moved on. It had set up its sideshows and booths and rides and acts in the very center of the old encampment, and these turned out to be the courthouse and the jail, the bank and the hotel, the lawyer's office and the title and abstract office and the insurance office and the funeral parlor and the drugstore and the grocery store and the gentleman's furnishings— all the portable properties of civilization, somehow a bit tawdry in spite of their newness, as though they had been hauled into town in a van and nailed up over night in the rain.

It was a world so insubstantial that the very buildings seemed to shake like canvas in the wind, and yet against it the Chetopa could place no barrier save the felt weight of their own past. And reading the reports down through the years he had watched with melancholy how their hold on their heritage had slowly slipped away. The old men gradually died and the young in their bereavement chose the road of forgetfulness. The roach and eagle-feather headdress disappeared, then the long black braids and blankets, the moccasins and claw necklaces, the hunting parties and the burial rites—gone, gone like the ghosts of their fathers and grandfathers to a heaven which in its turn had ceased to exist. Vanquished, all gone, even the dreams; no road left but the white man's road.

But perhaps the most incredible of all was some town historian's compilation of news items—often retold in his own way, the ironic moral drama, the sordid dirge raised to a kind of Homeric hymn—which Booth, the resident Agent, had sent back with his reports, sardonically recommending it as essential reading for anyone contemplating a tour in Grey Horse. Here was the town's most recent past, told with all the rhetorical innocence of the dime Western, pages redolent of blood and whiskey and oil, a sordid chronicle of robbery, murder, and degradation, the story of a people eaten to the bone by a kind of leprosy.

CRIME OF A BRUTE

SATURDAY NIGHT, *May 7th, 1904, the citizens of Grey Horse were thrown into a frenzy of excitement over the report that Dorene Catlin had been assaulted by Henry Del-Sevier, a member of the Chetopa tribe. Investigation proved the truth of the report and a warrant was issued and search for the rapist begun.*

He was arrested in the next morning near the mill and taken before the United States Commissioner for his preliminary. At this hearing he pleaded not guilty and waived examination. His bond was fixed at five thousand dollars which he was unable to give and on the next Monday afternoon he was taken to jail at Pawnee, O. T.

All day Sunday the excitement was intense and for a time it looked as if the crowds would take the law into their own hands and avenge the brutish crime by mob violence, the only thing preventing it being the lack of a determined leader.

The facts are as follows: The young lady was a niece of Dell Snead, who lived across the ravine in the northwest part of town. She had no mother and had been working for Will Reardon, and during the absence of her uncle, who was in Pawnee, had been going over to stay at nights with her aunt. Usually she went before dark, but Saturday evening she was delayed until a few minutes after eight o'clock and as she passed the State Hotel Del-Sevier accosted her saying "Good evening." She made no reply but went to one of the stores for above five minutes, then started for her aunt's home and as she reached the middle of the ravine, Del-Sevier standing partly behind a tree ordered her to halt and with a revolver over her he compelled her to accede to his demands.

She made her way to her aunt's home and then reported to the officers. The victim of this fiend in human form had no mother and had been making her way in the world, but had always conducted herself in a manner to avoid censure or reproach and had won the love and esteem of all who knew her. As for her assailant, the English language is devoid of words expressive of the hatred and detestation the people of Grey Horse had for him and his crime. For some time he had been trying to pose occasionally as a "bad man" but none thought he was the moral degenerate he proved to be. For his relatives there was sympathy in the disgrace and humiliation he had caused, but for him there was no sympathy, but instead the desire was expressed on all sides that he should pay the extreme penalty for the awful crime he had committed.

A few years later, and after spending a short while in jail for this crime, Del-Sevier died upon a bet that he could drink a pint of whiskey each hour for four consecutive hours. He never finished the last pint.

CARNIVAL GROUNDS SCENE OF KILLING

CLETIS BERRY SHOT HIS WIFE *about ten o'clock Wednesday night, April 6th, 1921, from the effects of which she died a few* minutes later. *The shooting was done when the two met on the carnival grounds in the eastern part of Grey Horse. The wounded woman was rushed to the hospital, but died a few minutes after reaching there.*

Married life had not been a bed of roses nor a dream of bliss with the Berrys. They were married some time in 1919 or early 1920 and trouble soon arose. Berry, it was claimed by his bride, was unfaithful to his marriage vows and put in too much time with women of bad repute. After protesting with him over his action with a character known as Mae Hartshorne, Mrs. Berry equipped herself for action and one day as she caught them riding together waited until they parked their car to alight. The two women met face to face and Mae Hartshorne fell mortally wounded by a shot from a six-shooter in the hands of Mrs. Berry.

Cletis Berry is a Chetopa Indian and as such has a large estate. It seems that a child three or four weeks old of which the Berry woman claimed to be the mother entered largely into the trouble which caused the killing. Berry's contention was that the child did not belong to the woman and that it was being palmed off on him for the purpose of getting maintenance and a part of his property. Following this contention his attorneys, England & Biggs secured an order for a post-mortem examination before the corpse of the wife was taken away. For this examination the state selected Dr. Handler, the defendant Dr. Kelly, and they in turn selected Dr. Banks. Their unanimous report to the examining magistrate was that the Berry woman had never given birth to a child.

THE MYSTERIOUS DEATH OF TWO WEALTHY CHETOPA INDIANS

THE DEAD BODIES *of Walker White Hair of Grandview, a small town twenty-two miles south of Grey Horse, and Ruth Pinto of this city were found about ten o'clock Saturday morning, January 28th, 1922.*

The body of White Hair was found in the timber on what is known as Cedarvale Hill just north of the city of Grey Horse. It was in a bad condition and identification was made only by means of a letter found in his coat pocket. Two holes were found in his forehead indicating that he had been shot. The body was discovered by Skeet Grubbs, an oil worker, in a cluster of timber and brush near an oil derrick on the Garnett oil lease. White Hair's home was at Grandview, but he had not been there since coming to Grey Horse some three weeks prior to this tragedy.

The body of Ruth Pinto, also a Chetopa and, like White Hair, a member of the well-known Red Hawk family, was found by Clay Carter, prominent local rancher, in a pasture near Choctaw. She had been dead several days. No marks indicating violence were then found upon her body and an empty whiskey bottle nearby led to a suspicion that she had been drinking poisoned liquor. Yet she, too, had been murdered, by strangulation.

SHOOTS HUSBAND'S COMPANION

WEDNESDAY AFTERNOON, June 28th, 1916, Mrs. Virgil Espey shot Miss Lu Jean Wentworth. The shot took effect in the back, just to the left side of the spinal column and about on a level with the kidneys.

Drs. Banks and Hoad attended Miss Wentworth and reported the wound was not necessarily dangerous.

Having reason to suspect her husband's infidelity, Mrs. Espey followed him and came upon him seated at a table in the Midland Valley Cafe, enjoying luncheon with the victim of the shot. She immediately opened fire with a .32 bulldog and but for the interference of a conductor on the Midland Valley would probably have got both of them.

After the shooting Mrs. Espey went to the courthouse and swore out a warrant for her husband charging him with adultery and he was placed under arrest.

Miss Wentworth had just returned from Riverside, California, where she had been in school. Sympathy and sentiment seemed to be entirely with Mrs. Espey. That she had been humiliated beyond a point of endurance was the general opinion. Only a few months previously Mr. Espey was tried in the district court on a charge of statutory rape.

Mr. Espey was, and had been for a long time, guardian of Lu Jean Wentworth, who is a Chetopa Indian girl, and no doubt thought he had a very good reason as well as an opportunity to lunch with his ward and discuss business matters with her.

FROZEN BODY OF FRANK RED HAWK FOUND WITH SHOT THROUGH HEAD

THE DEAD AND FROZEN BODY OF FRANK RED HAWK, *fullblood Chetopa Indian, was found between five and six o'clock Tuesday afternoon, February 6th, 1921, about six miles northwest of Choctaw, in the Chetopa Hills, in his car in a lonely and isolated place off what is known as the old Burbank road. The body had been there for days. A bullet through the head from a .45 caliber revolver explained the cause of death and opinion here was to the effect that Red Hawk was murdered.*

The body was found by two hunters who were passing up the unfrequented place and noticed the Buick standing among the trees. Examination disclosed the body of Red Hawk sitting at the wheel and leaning over to one side with his head resting on his hat, in which position he had apparently been placed. The body and the car were found on what is known as the old Ben Jones place.

Red Hawk had had no trouble, as far as found out, nor had he any enemies that the people of that vicinity knew of at that time. He lived at Choctaw and had lived at Grey Horse for a number of years. Red Hawk was missed from his home, according to his wife, since January 30th of the same year. The condition of the body showed that the shooting had been done prior to the coming of the cold spell that existed at the time the body was found as partial decomposition had set in before the body froze.

BUCK MURRAY KILLED

A FEUD OF LONG STANDING *was settled in front of the Court House at Grey Horse, Tuesday morning, March 5th, 1923, shortly after ten o'clock, when J. C. Kincaid shot and almost instantly killed Buck Murray, his father-in-law.*

Kincaid surrendered to the officers immediately following the shooting and claimed self-defense.

The deceased was the founder of Roan, a small town in the Chetopa Hills some twenty miles northeast of Grey Horse.

The shooting occurred in front of the Chetopa Court House. Eye-witnesses to the shooting say that Murray started out of the front door of the Court House at the same time that J. C. Kincaid and other members of the family were approaching the building after parking their car nearby. Those who saw the tragedy say that as Murray stepped out of the building he drew two large guns, one being a German Luger, and dropped to one knee. They say that Buck fired at Kincaid and the members of Kincaid's family scattered. The shot went wild, and Kincaid went running across the street in the direction of his car. Murray started down the Court House steps and fired another shot at the running man. This bullet also missed its mark and by this time Kincaid had reached his car and brought a .40-.40 Winchester into view. He took aim at Murray and fired once. The bullet struck Murray in the left breast near the heart, penetrated that organ and came out of the body just below the right shoulder blade. He fell to the pavement, dying almost instantly. Kincaid was lodged in jail pending a hearing.

Both men were witnesses to a lawsuit scheduled for trial in the County Court to determine the competence of Eastman Murray, son of the deceased. The feud dates back for several years. About two years prior to this tragedy, trouble occurred between them and a shooting followed at the Murray place at Roan. Reno Kincaid, a brother of J. C. Kincaid, was shot and killed and J. C. was wounded. Buck Murray was later exonerated of this shooting in the Courts at Grey Horse. Trouble over money matters and quarrels between the families was said to have started the feud.

Murray was fifty-six years old and resided in the Chetopa Hills practically all of his life. He was a well-known ranchman and stockman and was survived by his widow, Marcelle, and eight children.

Buck Murray was one of the old time residents of the Chetopa Hills. His home in Caney Township was long one of the landmarks of the reservation. It sat on a hill and could be seen for miles in all directions. His house was a large two-story rock building and was built a number of years before the Chetopa allotment of lands. He was an intermarried citizen and when allotment came, he selected a large body of land surrounding the home place and plocked out one of the best ranches in that part of the reservation. His wife was the daughter of Angie Lovelady and is on the Chetopa rolls, as are all the children of the couple.

THE TRAGIC DEATH OF TWO WOMEN AND ONE MAN

CHOCTAW, *a small town twenty-five miles southwest of Grey Horse, was thrown into consternation about three o'clock Saturday morning, March 13th, 1923, by a terrific explosion which totally wrecked the home of J. B. Gunn and family, causing two deaths outright and placed another in the hospital badly shattered, damaged a number of residences in adjoining blocks, and was heard in Ralston ten miles away.*

The killed were Mrs. Jewel Gunn, a fullblood Chetopa woman and her housekeeper, Moselle Patterson, a white woman. Mr. Gunn was badly mangled and lived but a short time.

The body of Mr. Gunn was found some distance from the house wrapped in a mattress with the dead body of his wife lying across it. The bodies of both women were badly mangled when found. The home of Clyde Kerr, across the street, was completely riddled and the furniture blown away. The home of O. T. Stephens was badly wrecked, both windows and doors being blown away, and a number of others were seriously damaged; remnants of the Gunn house which was a large eight-room building took fire from the explosion and was totally destroyed. Clothing and bedding was lodged on the trees and telephone poles and wires for a distance of two or three blocks.

Mrs. Gunn was a daughter of Minnie Kaw, and a sister of Ruth Pinto, whose dead body was found in a cow pasture about a year previous to this occurrence near Choctaw, and made the third member of the Chetopa tribe to meet a violent death near Choctaw within two years. The two sisters and Red Hawk, whose dead body was found in a draw a few miles out from Choctaw. All were related.

Expert chemists were called from the A.&M. College at Stillwater to determine if possible the explosive used. At the time of the explosion no tangible cause was discovered. And the Chetopa Council was asked to bring about an investigation.

He had read as much as he could stomach, then thrown the clippings aside. It seemed that wealth, sudden, unlooked-for, uncomprehended, had done to these people what decades of displacement and near starvation had not. With their heroic heritage lost in a fabled and fading past, the Chetopa had had at least their poverty, which could maintain a wall of dignity and bitter pride between them and those who had set up their noisy midway in this ancient valley. With poverty there had been suffering, but peace of a kind as well. Now lost on a road they had never wanted to take, immensely enriched by the discovery of oil beneath the old reservation to which, by some blessing or calamity, they had managed to retain the subsurface mineral rights, they lurched stoically from disaster to disaster like some prehistoric hero whom time had outrun.

It was a sickness unto death which, like Sodom and Gomorrah, must finally call down the fire of heaven. And one of the last reports he read was the request by the Tribal Council, forwarded without comment by the local Agent, asking for federal help in bringing to an end the seemingly systematic murder of the members of the Red Hawk family, known throughout the reservation and beyond because one daughter had married the local Indian Agent, Blair Booth, and a second, Rita Red Hawk, internationally famous as a ballet dancer, had come home to marry Clay Carter, rancher and leading citizen.

So he had come to love them in a way, plowing through hundreds of pages which somehow and most improbably had succeeded in bringing them to life in his imagination—a heroic people upon whom had fallen an age of Iron, a warrior people stunned by too many blows so that, like an aging boxer, they fought on only from memory, a vanquished people whose very dreams had been stolen. He loved them, and hated what had been done to them; yet he had known that he could in no way restore their greatness, nor even their dignity. Their age of heroism was past; the war dance, the coup party, the buffalo—all gone, almost forgotten. But justice he could bring, sharp and glittering as a sword, to redress the balance just a little for a hundred years of treachery.

And yet he could not help but wonder, why me? How was it that all those separate paths taken, rejected, followed, and abandoned had led so unerringly to this window, this night, this town,

which he no longer even saw not only because of the silent destruction of nightfall but because his eyes stared blindly through
the dark, straining to catch the flicker of campfires lost from sight
now and forever somewhere down there in the valley, to see again
the blanketed figures which had moved tall and silent among the
buffalo lodges, to hear the lean dogs' high-pitched barking at the
coyote's song while high above the darkness rode a hunting moon
white and cold as ash in the smoky drift of cloud.

And how much of his course had been charted by those frontier preachers and whaling captains whose names he bore and
whose portraits, Bibles, rifles and pistols, brass-bound sea chests
and hand-cut walnut furniture cluttered the family house by the
Common and made a kind of museum of the New Hampshire
farm? The room one entered through the jawbones of a whale,
harpoons on the wall, carved teeth and bones on the tables; in the
barn an oaken pew, the last that remained of a church built,
burned by Iroquois, built and burned and built again; commodes
embossed with Chinese dragons, precious jade, books on the
moral order and man's corruption, charred pipes and compasses,
charts, lacquered trays, tracts secular and spiritual—guides to
man's earthly journey among treacherous seas. A harsh, vigorous,
comfortless, unabashed and occasionally heroic mixture of stubborn propriety and unalloyed profit, now run to ground on the
dry sands of a prim and priggish conservatism. Silent houses
moldered in the shaded backwaters of history; from generation to
generation names and fortunes were scraped and revarnished
against time's rot; genteel societies banded together for the preservation of an embalmed past as anachronistic as a meticulously
reconstructed whaling vessel. And over it all hovered the palsied
hand of the curator, Wrathful Jehovah become a kind of Keeper
of Antiquities. And if these had been the early weathers of his
soul while he had drifted as though at anchor through his youth,
he had yet always hungered to cut loose and head for deeper
waters. Above all he wished that like the Word, these bones
should take on flesh and live again and sing and suffer and bear
witness to those who had come too late of something harpoon-
fierce and Gospel-pure which had been lost, so long ago.

Long ago . . . There had been a grey afternoon at school, late November, the sky swollen with snow, the goal posts pale in the liquid gloom of early winter. Beneath the cleats of embattled heroes the frozen ground lay broken into shards; on the bench the subs shivered beneath their blankets, blowing on their fingers, calling hoarse encouragement, praying to get into the game for one play in order to letter, yet terrified at the thought of setting an unworthy foot on that consecrated soil. The Game. Raucous supporters come by hundreds from the other school. The crowd a bouquet of color spilling over from the stands and strewn along the sidelines. The swollen air jarred by the crack of pads, the rapid drumming of feet on the iron surface of the turf, the gasping grunts when someone was hit, the shrill rattle of the whistle, disjointed cries from the stands followed by a swelling roar that subsided into a clatter of applause. And through it all as though from underwater he heard his name being called. He looked down the line of faces, then picked up his helmet. Someone pulled the blanket from his shoulders and then he was down on one knee, listening to the coach, looking into that familiar stubbled face so close to his own now that he scarcely recognized it. Around him were the faces he knew, envious, aghast. "Thayer, you're going in for Ross. You know the plays. You set?" The plays fell through his mind like the tumblers of a slot machine. He nodded. "There's the whistle. Get your tail out there, boy. Give it all you got." He reported, then joined the huddle. Their faces were down, and he heard their breathing, and then the quarterback called the play. Fake the reverse, then block the charging end. He knew the plays all right. Three years of working with the scrubs, running against set defenses, honing the first string's skills by hurling himself hopelessly into holes that gaped like tragic mouths in the line. Three years of sweat and bruises and a face full of dust, always in a losing cause. So that even failure, by its very familiarity and by the permanence of hope that it inspired, came to hold a certain weary satisfaction. But The Game—he had never hoped that high. He pivoted to his right on the snap and the raised knee caught him straight in the face. He rose through a silent galaxy of bursting stars and felt his way back to the huddle. His nose was running—the sleeve he wiped it with turned slowly dark with blotted blood. He called aloud coming out of the huddle, more to himself than to his muddy teammates who seemed to look with grim disgust at his clean uniform. He caught the opposing guard waiting on the play, blocked him cleanly to the ground, then rose and sprinted back to where the huddle slowly formed. He checked signals on the play. A punt? He wondered why. They were going good. He talked it up again, breaking from the huddle, looking across at the enemy line, most of whom knelt on the cold ground, their faces drawn, dirty, silent. The stands were a hushed, suspended burst of color and he heard only his own voice, strangely distant as though it belonged to someone else, and then the count. He made a sliding block on the end, then started down the field, but the sounds and the faces and quick change of directions told him what was wrong. Blocked punt, their ball. Five yards away from a touchdown. He talked it up steadily, wiping the blood from his face, his voice catching in the thickness of his throat. He seemed to sense where the plays were going and he was in on or close to every tackle. By now the tears were running freely through the blood and he was hitting his linemen on the rumps, begging them, exhorting them, trying to lift them into that state of rarefied frenzy where he suddenly found himself. Their last try came right over him, knees and cleats and elbows and smothered curses and then a long way off in the silence the flat pop of a gun. Players unpiled slowly; the ball was a half yard short. He lay there looking at it and then the referee picked it up and tossed it to the opposing quarterback. "Game ball to the winners," was what he said, but to Andrews it seemed a foreign language. He got shakily to one knee, then rubbed the sleeve of his jersey across his nose. "But we held them, goddammit," he said aloud, looking up at the players filing slowly past him toward the gym. "We held them—it's our ball."

"You all right, Thayer?" One of the regulars ran his hand along his shoulder and then went on.

He rose and looked around him. He was alone now on the field except for the sub who had been sitting next to him on the bench.

"Hey, Andrews. You lucky son of a gun. You got your letter."

"Lucky." He tore loose the chin strap and threw his helmet hard to the ground. "Lucky? I held them, didn't I? They had four goddam tries and couldn't make it." Tears glistened fiercely in his eyes and blood trickled down the wrinkles around his mouth.

"Yeah. You held them. Two touchdowns too late. We lost, remember?" The eyes moved back and forth, questioning him, the voice dry, sarcastic.

"What do you mean, lost?" and after all the years he could still remember how his anger had closed his hands into fists. "I held the sons of bitches. Didn't you see that last play? Tried to come right over me . . ."

But now even his fellow sub was fading into the haze of early darkness, crunching up the cinder path toward where the chapel bells chimed the last late hours of afternoon. He reached down and picked up his helmet, then looked around him at the empty field. Three long years. His nose was beginning to hurt a little now. He snuffled, and felt the drying sweat chill his flesh to goose pimples. I guess we did, at that, he thought with a kind of surprise, and then suddenly depressed, his helmet dangling by the strap, he had made his way along the cleat-pocked path to the showers. . . .

And Emily. Emily DeMarco. A late Renaissance Madonna with full, melting eyes, oval-faced, soft-bodied, the sun of Naples still upon her in spite of the fact that she had been born in western Massachusetts. His last year at Harvard, a Thanksgiving dance, she a friend's blind date in a dress all pink and purple flowers, her black curls bouncing, her face flushed and glistening, bearing her clumsy innocence before her like a shield. Suddenly joyous so that she laughed with her whole body, then awkwardly apprehensive, then giggling again, tossing her hair and immediately pushing it flat, a street urchin peering through the shadowed gold mask of the Virgin.

Before he knew anything else about her, he knew that she was poor. It was as obvious as her perfume. Everything about her—the violent dress, the alertness of her eyes, the way she had of stopping, staring, then bursting into laughter which trailed off into a guarded kind of smile as though she had just remembered something, the large mannish watch she wore on her wrist—all of it bespoke a world as distant from Andrews's as the florid alleys of Naples. He watched her, fascinated, engrossed, as though trying to recall where he had seen her before and then all of a sudden remembering those lines engraved on the base of the Statue of Liberty which his father had read out to him solemnly one afternoon from the windswept deck of a ferry boat. *Give me your poor, your huddled masses*—something like that. He had stood there at the edge of the dance floor very straight, very grave, almost as though he held above his head the torch of hope, in some strange way needing her for all that she, or those she sprang from, had lost, or never had.

Some of it he learned that night on the train back to Wellesley —that she came from Pittsfield, that she was a scholarship student majoring in French with a minor in Mathematics (she didn't know why except that it seemed to make her parents more comfortable), that she adored the Romantic Poets but did her math last each night because she slept better that way, that her father had a small cheese, wine, salami and red onion grocery and was president of the Dante Society of Pittsfield (nine members, an emaciated plaster bust, a room above the store with two card tables, a radio, and stacks of Italian periodicals gathering dust in the corners), that her mother could scarcely speak English but had somehow, somewhere heard someone speak of Wellesley and then through the sheer weight of her incomprehension had bullied the bewildered high school principal into securing the application forms and finally had sold what few possessions she had of any value for the train tickets, the books, the clothes (the outrageous dress?) before collapsing at last into operatic tears at the thought of Emily going so far away from home. That she wanted to go to France and see for herself what kind of life it was that could distill such poetry from absinthe and chestnuts, cathedrals and cafes . . . And to get there—well, there was always Mathematics.

The rest, including Naples, about which she never spoke, he

learned on weekend trips to Pittsfield. Somehow they always caught the train on the run, and she would be chattering at him, giggling and making faces even as he pulled her along, and after they were settled in their seats, out of breath and laughing all at once when their eyes met, she would go on talking, touching him lightly with her hands, still very much a girl, while he half listened, looking up from his book, nodding, smiling now and again. And then suddenly, sometimes in the middle of a sentence, she would reach for his hand and lay her cheek against the train window and let her eyes follow the woods which disappeared behind them. And in this mood her face assumed a kind of wistful earnestness which made her seem sad and distant, like a tired child.

Emily's mother Andrews found simply overwhelming in the manner of some billowy Aïda. Her face was a trembling composite of rouge and mascara, and her frequent tears drove multicolored trails across the expanse of her cheeks. Inside her voluminous robes, dusty, clumsily cut, and yet with a certain ruined magnificence as though they belonged to some discarded theatrical wardrobe, her body moved like ball bearings in the interior of a wheel. Her hat trailed plumes, and she wore it always, wandering like some ancient recluse through town with her straw shopping bag, spending dreamy hours in the five and ten, standing majestically over the stove in the kitchen that was her stage, a poignant and solitary figure seeking blindly that chorus of voices around her which alone could restore her to life. Her only concession to the role of housewife was the apron she always wore inside, putting it on when she came into the house and going directly to the kitchen, and the long spoon with which like a baton she conducted her own endless soliloquies until her husband's caustic replies brought her to the kitchen door, spoon upraised, plumes shaking above her shoulders, eyes glistening with the tears that seemed ever to hover just above her cheeks, her whole body in motion in that doomed effort at communion, which always failed because no one was ever listening. Except Andrews, as far as he could tell, and he could not understand the rolling surge of her Italian. To him she was like an aged actress, a baroque creature who lived in a garish world from which she could not escape and which no one else could enter, a person upon whom he could scarcely look because their glances could never meet but merely collide, in some impossible way Emily's mother, to whom he listened without comprehension and without even really being sure that she saw him at all, as though in fact she might be blind, until the Christmas when he gave her a stove to replace the gas burner and then she had swept him into her arms, sobbing and repeating his name, "Ahn-droos, Ahn-droos," while the powder rose from her bosom in a cloud, until at last her husband had appeared at the kitchen door, his hand held high, his outraged voice almost drowned in the seas of her sobbing, repeating "Soma dignity, Momma, soma dignity."

It was in him rather than in the mother that Andrews found the source of Emily's long and oval face. But the soft gold patina of her skin was in the father a parchment stained from constant handling stretched tight across protruding knobs of cheeks and stuck close to the hollows of his skull. His eyes were pale and rapid behind small panes of glass encircled with what appeared to be strips of tin. Most of the time when Andrews tried to talk with him, he would stare straight before him angrily and then raise his newspaper, rattling it and saying "Mmmmmmmmmm, Mmmmmmmmm," in a gradual diminuendo. Then after a moment he would look over the top of the paper to say "Yes," clicking his teeth and looking somewhere over Andrews's shoulder. Behind the paper his lips moved silently as though he were in constant conversation with himself—arguing with some unseen and eternal adversary, making calculations, perhaps just reading to himself—Andrews could never quite make it out. When he and Emily came into the room, her father would be seated in the frayed Grand Rapids armchair, the radio tuned low at his ear, his Italian newspaper spread out on his knees, where he often kept it until someone spoke to him. He would interrupt his silent monologue to nod to them, and then perhaps continue some unfinished duet with his wife, both of them speaking at once, he lifting his hand before him in an imperial gesture and addressing himself as always to that invisible witness whom he seemed ever to invoke against the operatic tirades which rolled in upon him from the kitchen with the rich smells of her cooking.

And in this very gesture there seemed some perpetual anticipation of disaster, as though the great unreason of his wife could in the end undo him and by some unfathomable combination of foolishness and passion prevent his eventual return to Naples. For he had in fact come to the United States exactly for that reason, to be able to go back and live in the only place he knew and loved and which, like some fickle woman, would only accept him when he no longer needed her.

As for Emily, Andrews imagined that the old man had probably ceased to understand her from the time that she had learned English, and now with Wellesley and Harvard, and the sudden smell of wealth which Andrews bore into that rotting frame house like the richness of new leather or the heavy fragrance of the lilacs that bloomed in spring above the junk that littered the back yard, he seemed more worried than ever, muttering into his newspaper, spending his evenings upstairs in the smoky, explosive card games of the Dante Society, throwing up his hands at his wife in tragic gestures of despair while she supervised the pasta through her tears.

With his own parents there was neither despair, nor tears, nor gestures of any kind beyond the barely perceptible raising of his mother's eyebrows and the stiffness in the slight bow his father made when he took Emily's hand—a faint excess of politeness against which Andrews watched Emily flutter helplessly, laughing too much, blushingly silent, looking round her anxiously as though she expected her parents to appear at any moment—no doubt as servants. Her giggling bursts of talk, the eager lifting of her face, the impulsive way her hands went out to Andrews—all smothered in the vast gloom of the silent house. That they refused to take her seriously, that they treated her with something akin to the cool, detached condescension with which they had always, somewhat impatiently he had thought, dealt with him, bothered him less than the fact that she did not seem to understand. The result was an aggressive determination on his part to protect what touched him most about her—her poverty, her innocence, her childish simplicities—from the withering and complacent scorn of the world in which he had grown up, as though nothing less extravagant than a chivalric romance could shatter the snobbery by which he felt himself surrounded.

Thus there was a certain dogged quality to his devotion, however poetic it might have seemed to him. This too, he realized later, thinking back at how much time they had spent together during those years, wondering what they had talked about, amazed that all those hours had now been planed into such smooth oblivion. During the war they wrote to each other regularly, he from the infantry training camp in Alabama where he was stationed, she from Cambridge where she was now in graduate school, waiting with a kind of peasant patience for his return. In the late summer of 1918 she had visited him during a long weekend; there had been rumors of a transfer overseas and he had cabled her to come. They had walked the sun-drenched streets of the little Southern town while she told him all in a rush about her life that he knew so well already—the loneliness of Pittsfield and the two old people to whom she no longer seemed to belong, the transports and tribulations of the Poets, the afternoon his mother had asked her to tea (he remembered writing the letter, insisting), and how she had overturned her cup and got jam on her dress and finally fled, chilled right through to the bone. "She just doesn't like me, Andrews; she thinks I don't belong," while he shook his head, knowing all the same that it was true. Then that evening the ball, Emily all gold and white in a mist of muslin, he starched and creased in his new lieutenant's uniform. The night was awash in perfume, magnolias spread their limbs like lavish candelabra, and at the furthest corner of the balcony in a cloud of honeysuckle he told her that he had decided to marry her. She did not reply, and at the time he thought that it was because she took it for granted. Later he reflected that perhaps she had wanted to be asked, remembering something she had said to that effect. Yet he had been too absorbed in himself to notice, involved as he was in a series of tactical moves which he carried out with all the precision of a troop-leading exercise.

Later that night they tiptoed up the back stairs to her hotel room. He had wanted to be calm, even matter-of-fact—he was going overseas, they loved each other, what could marriage be other than a formal seal upon a union which must be found sacred in God's eyes, and how else could they say goodbye for who knew how long, if not forever—but he found himself seized by a violent trembling which he could not control. In his stomach and in his knees he felt a sudden weakness, and in his hands a nervous strength. She was sobbing before they went to bed, and cried out when he hurt her and then his trembling was gone and he held her in his arms like a broken bird and told her that he was sorry and that everything would be all right. The next morning he watched her from under his eyelids, pretending to be asleep while she pinned her hair, biting the hairpins so assuredly between her small teeth. There was something still and certain about her now, some part of her which he had not known and which now looked steadily out of her eyes in a way that left him half frightened, half guilty, awkward as a boy before her even when she sat beside him on the bed and told him that she was very happy. That weekend was a world of summer, her voice like birdsong in an orchard, his senses opening like desert flowers in the rain. And it was not until the train had borne her away, the flutter of her handkerchief fading from sight, that he had been able to regroup his emotions in their usual formation of close-order drill.

But he had not gone overseas after all. Years lost from his life; months and months of training for The Game—he was bitterly reminded of school and of his long years as a scrub. The Armistice had come, and when the officers talked it over he had suggested that the men be restricted to the camp in recognition of their general disappointment that the war had come to an end with them far from the trenches where Civilization had been defended, stuck here in Alabama with not even a service ribbon to show for all the years. The others had heard him out in silence, then gone ahead with plans for celebration. It surprised him that no one seemed to share his feelings and yet at the same time he was used to it. So he sat and smoked until the meeting broke up, then went back to his room.

Someone had put the letter on his pillow. He recognized her

handwriting, then saw the Special Delivery sticker on the envelope and wondered what was wrong.

MY DEAREST ANDREWS,

I think of you all the time and wonder how you are. Are you still going overseas? The papers say that the war is over. I am praying all the time that this is true because I don't want you to go away. We have a whole life ahead of us and *we have only lived one weekend.* I mean that, Andrews. Nothing really matters to me any more except when I am with you.

There is something else, my dearest. Now you must not be bothered or upset because I am not *absolutely* sure. But I am sure enough, I guess. Well, I think I am going to have a baby. *I am not upset, Andrews.* I don't know quite what to do yet, but I am *very happy.* Even if you have to go overseas and I have to have the baby alone, then I don't care as long as I know you love me. I have even thought that if anything should happen—maybe I shouldn't say it, Andrews, but at least I would have *something.* How could I think about living the rest of my life without you.

I am not *absolutely, absolutely sure,* but I *think* so. Just write and tell me that you are happy and then I will know that everything is the way it ought to be. I haven't said anything to my parents—they are *very, very Catholic,* Andrews, and they could not understand. If we could get married soon it would be the best, certainly for them. Even if I guess there really isn't any way to hide it. I just can't say about *your* mother and father. They won't be happy no matter *what* happens because they don't like me and that is the truth.

So really you must decide because of the war and everything. Whatever you think is best is all right with me. Because I am *very, very* happy, Andrews, happier than I've ever been except for our weekend. I'm not ashamed or frightened or anything like that—except glad because this makes it *all right* if you see what I mean. I mean having the baby and all. It makes it serious.

He put the letter down and lit a cigarette. That was it—serious. He listened to the drunken whoops of celebration beginning to echo down the hall, and smiled quietly to himself. Yes, it was right. For some reason it seemed like Christmas, and he thought suddenly of the Virgin Mary, and the Immaculate Conception, and Jesus born in the stable, and Joseph so poor, just a carpenter, and the story of it glowed for a moment in his mind, like the painted figures beneath the Christmas tree at Pittsfield, seen by candlelight. He saw them all with remarkable clarity, and when he thought again of Emily her face now was like that of the Virgin, painted on the wall of his mind like some Fra Angelico fresco.

They were married a month later in Pittsfield. Everything about her seemed a little larger, though no doubt it was only his imagination. She seemed frightened, and when she cried she looked like her mother, and this shook him some. But the rest was reassuring, or at least appropriate—the dark little church smelling of incense, silent except for the sobbing of Emily's mother and the furious sotto voce conversation of the father and his two fellow officials from the Dante Society, conspiratorial, really, since they were alone save for the priest and since the church wedding had been arranged, even if at arm's length, through certain Thayer contacts in Boston, and then the turkey and squash and succotash and cranberry sauce and Lacrima Christi all improbably served at the wedding supper, no doubt in an effort to span the distance between Massachusetts and Calabria. And for him more than anything else, his own swelling sense of nobility as he looked around again at the torn and dingy wallpaper with its stamped-out repetitions of shepherds and shepherdesses in some faded Arcadia, the framed Madonna like some member of the family, a photograph of Victor Emmanuel, and one sunset landscape vaguely resembling a Spanish omelette.

Later that night she said, "It wasn't right, was it?"

"What wasn't?" he asked sleepily.

"In the church. I won't go to church any more."

She was silent, and he thought she had gone back to sleep.

"It meant so much to them," she said after a while. "It was really for them, wasn't it? They have to have something they can remember."

"I've rescued you from all that," he said, turning over toward her and frowning because the words sounded like something he had read a long time ago.

But she lay perfectly still and there was no reply.

Well, that's behind me, he had said to himself, sliding back into sleep.

And five months later Amory was born. . . .

With the law he had never felt particularly comfortable. He had gone through the drudgery and done well—his fellow club members at law school had even given him the traditional silver cigarette case, inscribed with the names of those in the club of his own class, awarded each year to the highest-ranking man. Then came the New York firm, ostensibly impressed as much by his name as by his grades, where in the normal course of martinis and squash at the Harvard Club, and bridge with an ascending succession of couples carefully screened by Emily, he would have become a partner before many years had elapsed. But somehow the law was too much a domain of its own, too pre-eminently concerned with merely material arrangements, with trade and traffic, commerce and litigation. It worked the shallow waters well within the limits of visibility. It was king in that sordid realm where stone axes had once rendered decisions more summary if, in one way at least, more costly. It was intricately allied with that instinct for preservation which Andrews abhorred, and he was afraid of all imperceptibly drifting back to the dead seas of his youth. Partly, too, because Emily seemed so content. The laughter in her voice had quieted, her hair was pulled tight over her temples to a dark bun, her hands had become more careful, her body broader and heavier. She spent hours over Amory's clothes, dressing him in patent-leather shoes and tiny flannel suits with Eton collars, nor would she hear of cutting his hair, which hung in feathery curls around his face. Her address book grew black with names, and the silver bowl in the entrance hall was filled with calling cards, the mirror above it hidden by invitations to exhibitions, openings, charities, shows so that Andrews, bewildered, felt that termites were at work in the very foundation of his life. There was a calm, purposeful, almost ruthless intensity in the way she managed it all. He had protested once that none of these people were their friends, and when she replied that social life had nothing to do with friendship, he began to wonder if somehow he had not run aground. Surely somewhere there must be waters wild enough, a wilderness savage enough so that God's voice would roll like thunder over the cricket cries of men.

One day in Washington on business he had lunched with a friend at the Army-Navy Club. Retired service people mainly, stiff, trim, some crippled, all marked in one way or another by some indefinable quality that set them apart. Like monks, perhaps, or thieves, they seemed to live on the edges of society. Hangmen, rather. But stern old-fashioned men of duty, almost men of the cloth, in a way of which Andrews approved. The friend was a classmate who now worked in the Department of State.

"You admire them?" he said to Andrews, wrinkling his forehead over the menu. "Absurd. They exist because we fail. They're just a piece of political machinery. A particularly brutal and ugly piece. Nothing more." He looked at Andrews with irony over his glasses and hooked his thumbs into his vest. "Didn't all that mud last time around teach you anything? War is too serious, and all that. Not a brain in a carload."

"I'm not worried about their brains," he laughed. "I like their —well, their character, to use an old-fashioned word. The fact that they belong to something bigger. I'm tired of working for myself," he said suddenly.

The friend lifted his shoulders with a gesture of resignation. "All right. You want service. A sense of purpose, I suppose you'd call it. You want to do something for somebody else. I'm always suspicious of that, frankly; sounds too damn much like minding other people's business. But let it pass. You say you don't like what's happened to the country—prohibition and coonskin coats and Stutz Bearcats and flappers and Little Sicily and back to Normalcy, official hypocrisy and unofficial fleshpots. You still believe in the big words, after all the mud and guts. You should have been there, my friend. So what do you want? Stop the flood? Just get away from the stink? Go to Paris, for God's sake. Can you afford it? But that wouldn't do either, would it. There can't be many big words left over there."

"I'm not looking for big words," he said quietly. "I grew up on them. And there's nothing for me in Paris either, Ed. I mean it. Money? That's not my problem—there'll be more than enough someday. As for the rest of it . . . No, I don't like it. Do you? You're not down here for the cash."

"No," Ed said drily. "I'm not in it for the cash. But you can't stand hypocrisy, Andrews. You wouldn't have the stomach for it. Honesty is not our business."

Andrews lifted his hands in protest and started to reply.

"Wait a minute," Ed said, looking up from his soup, then leaning back in his chair. "Of course. A small job—that's what you want. Like settling the score for what's been done to this virgin country of ours, since you seem to believe that countries, and women too, probably, are better when they're virgin. The United States Indian Service, my boy. They'll underpay you, transfer you inconveniently from one choice spot to another, all those marvelous places we sold to our own colonial population, run all your idealism through the bureaucratic mill until the day comes when you'll begin to think that the Indians were created for the Service instead of the other way around. Thayer," Ed said solemnly, lifting his glass, "our class needs you. We've got a Class Poet, why not a Class Saint? And Emily—won't she love it out in the Dakotas or New Mexico or Oklahoma—wherever it is they've got the poor devils fenced in. Say—anybody in line for your job?"

He laughed and let it go and went back to New York that night. But somehow the conversation stuck with him. Through family friends he got in touch with the Commissioner, and the next time he was in Washington he called in at the Department. In less than a year he and Emily were living in Georgetown and he was working on legal aspects of the various Indian educational bills before Congress.

"Andrews was never really suited to the law—real law, anyway," Emily would say in that calm, final way of hers to her guests over bridge. "He's such an idealist. He just loves the Department."

And in his way he did, because from the very beginning he

could hear a distant music, faint at first as tom-toms, minor and plaintive as an Indian song, which gradually grew inside him like the beating of his blood and drowned his disappointment with the time-clock mentality and general cynicism he encountered, with the fact that it was still the law, dry, cautious, edging forward sideways like a crab. It was as though he heard the theme returning of some remembered life, played by different instruments now in a soft and savage key, strangely tragic, almost a dirge, but still his theme, noble, heroic, a cry of despairing love, which always sooner or later reduced the words of those around him to a kind of incantation, uniquely concerned with his own spiritual adventure, his own progression toward that terrible hill where one meets God at last face to face. Stations of the Cross—his childhood, school, marriage, the rest of it. And now some faintly felt intuition of a final trial—with Emily? with himself?—which shimmered in the distance like a dying star.

He had been in the Department just short of a year when, returning one day to his office from a particularly trying hearing, he had found a message from the Commissioner asking him to call as soon as possible. He phoned the Commissioner's secretary, then went up the dusty stairs and down the long hall to his office. Some technicality on the bill, he thought wearily, wondering which Congressman they would have to try to placate this time. But when he had crossed the anteroom and opened the door, the Commissioner's face told him that it was something else.

"How are you, Andrews." His greeting was warm but tired. He had a way of listening with half-closed eyes which suggested profound fatigue, yet his face was square and strong and tanned beneath bristling, short-cropped white hair. He indicated a chair, lit his pipe somewhat absently, then seemed to study Andrews through the smoke. "How's the bill going?"

"Still in committee. We're in good shape—it's just a matter of getting through the questions."

The Commissioner nodded. He didn't seem to be much interested in the bill right at the moment, Andrews reflected. Reports were strewn across his desk; his pen lay uncapped where he had put it down when Andrews had entered the room. Now he reached for the phone.

"No more calls today, Miss Evans, I'm out."

He replaced the phone, then leaned back in the chair as though trying to relax. "Well, Andrews, you've been here almost a year. How's it going?"

Andrews shifted his legs and reached for the cigarette case. "I don't know how it looks from where you sit, sir. I've spent most of my time on the bill—plugging the loopholes, mainly—translating a lot of good intentions into language a court can deal with. Other than that—well, I haven't been here all that long."

"Mmmm." The Commissioner was silent for a while, rubbing his thumb along the bowl of his pipe. "You know," he said pensively, "that bill's not going through. It won't get out of committee this session. You should be prepared for that."

Andrews half smiled, trying to read the Commissioner's face. "Something we've messed up? Webster and I have been through that thing so many times—I think I could recite it from one end to the other."

"Nothing like that. There are people on the Hill who don't want it passed. Not now, anyway. You've been looking at it from the strictly legal end, and quite properly. It's just that—well, law will take us only so far. Then," he shrugged and slumped forward, looking at Andrews with his head tilted sideways, "call it conflict of interest, if you will. One cliché is as good as another."

"Then we'll just have to stick with it," Andrews answered, wondering where this was leading. "One doesn't expect miracles, but the bill is sound. I'm sure of it. If not this year . . ." Then he stopped because it sounded foolish.

"Yes. Yes, next year, maybe, or the next. The natural process of erosion. We'll get it through."

"That's the main thing, isn't it?"

"Not entirely. It would be, except that there's so much else," and he pointed with his pipe at the reports which littered his desk. "The bill is siege warfare, after all. Time should take care of it.

Meantime, if we're losing all the little battles, and some of them not so little—frontier skirmishes, outposts overrun, breakouts from the reservations, killing, robbery, epidemics . . . I've seen them all over the last forty years, and in one way or another they go right on, even if under different names. Sometimes the law seems to move too slowly, like an army that just can't quite catch up to where the battle's being fought."

"I don't know exactly what you're getting at," he said uneasily, wanting to force the issue. "But I'm here to serve. I told you that the first time we talked."

"Yes," the Commissioner said slowly, "that you did." He was silent then for a while. "That bill. It will be a kind of legal, oh, little slam, anyway, for the man who brings it off."

Andrews shook his head. His mouth was dry. Suddenly, unaccountably, the kaleidoscope had frozen here in this drab, underfurnished government office, the desk before him littered with yellowing paper, the Commissioner biting his pipe, watching him intently. "I told you that, too. I suppose I'm the type who would have been in the army, or the church."

"Or a whaler?"

"That, too."

He nodded again, as though he had expected it, but there was no satisfaction in his face. "Careers are made here, not in the field. That's something you ought to know."

"They're made in New York, too. I left that when I came here."

"The family? You've been here less than a year."

Andrews held his hands before him, then let them drop again to his lap. "What is it you want me to do?"

The Commissioner looked at him a moment longer, then swung around in his chair and pointed to the map. "Grey Horse. Grey Horse, Oklahoma. Ever hear of it?"

"No."

"You've heard of the Chetopa."

"Oil, I believe," Andrews said uncertainly.

"Oil and a lot of other things that came in with it." He nodded toward the papers on his desk. "Some of the story is in there—most of it isn't. Oh, everything up to twenty years ago, perhaps—at least from the white man's point of view. But since then . . ." He filled his pipe slowly, tamped it with a long nail he carried in his pocket, then came around the desk and sat down beside Andrews. "There's no use going into history. You can get that from the files, or as much as you'll need. The Chetopa Agency is in Grey Horse, county seat of what used to be the old reservation. Our Agent there is a man named Blair Booth—been there since hell and gone—great fellow." He looked quickly at Andrews, cleared his throat, and then kept talking. "Married a girl by the name of Red Hawk—Mary Rose Red Hawk. He's had a rough time of it—come in for a lot of criticism—bad press—talk about it in Congress. I've stood by him—I've known him for so many years—Sewanee—law school at the University of Virginia —the finest kind of Southerner, if you follow me. Anyway . . ." His voice trailed off as though he had forgotten what he wanted to say, and the lines cut more deeply across the bones of his face. "It was three years ago that we got the first request from the Tribal Council. They wanted help—thought one of the prominent Chetopa families was being killed off one after another so that someone would end up with all the headrights. Brutal killings —poison, dynamite, shootings, the works. Of course, who knows? Anything is possible in that town. Too much money. Way too much money. Look, in 1916 there was a public auction of Chetopa lands. Twenty-five thousand acres. Brought in forty thousand dollars. Three years later an oil company brought in a gusher—there on the map, over on the eastern edge of the reservation. There's a town there now, or there was, at least, as of last week. Places bloom and die overnight in that part of the world. Named Whizbang. The main intersection is known as Shotgun Corner, so many people have been gunned down there. At any rate," and he made a sweeping motion with his hand as though he wanted to push the details away, "there was a second public auction three days after the strike. It was a damned gold rush—oil-company representatives, bankers, gamblers, speculators and promoters of every kind. I went out for that, just to help Booth keep the lid on. You never saw such madness in all your life. The tract that that gusher was on—one hundred and sixty acres, mind you—went for six hundred thousand dollars. Six months later bids were in for more than six million. The biggest single lease I know of went for close to two million—one hundred and sixty acres—plus a royalty of one eighth of the value of each barrel of oil produced. It reached the point where an average Chetopa family was taking in fifty, sixty thousand a year." He pushed himself back in the chair and looked hard at Andrews. "Stone-age people, boy. Not all that used to white people, and dealing more often than not with the very worst. Not to mention money. Their minds didn't run to money. Think on it a little—all that money. This used to be one of the camping grounds the Chetopa used when they made the big buffalo hunts—for further back than any of them can even calculate. They've been there for centuries. Now it's got three banks. It's got more lawyers than they probably need in the whole state. Every kind of crime you ever heard of, and some you haven't. Most people just sort of get trampled to death in the rush, I guess you'd say."

"But there must be some control somewhere. What's his name —Booth? How does he handle it?"

"Handles it damned well," the Commissioner replied quickly. "But the family with all the killings—that was when the Chetopa Tribal Council got in touch with me. The name was Red Hawk," and he stopped then to let the sound of it at least sink in.

Andrews raised his eyebrows, then drew in his breath with a low whistle. "Go on," he said, as though the Commissioner had stopped in order to find out if he really wanted to hear any more.

"Blair took it especially hard because he's married to Mary Rose. Mary Rose Red Hawk—or Booth, now—that's her name. That made Blair part of the family, if you will. Hell, he's been worried sick about the thing."

"Married into the tribe? Into that same family? With all the killings?" Andrews shook his head slowly in disbelief. "No wonder there's been—"

The Commissioner lifted his hand as though to stop him. "I backed him on it, all along the line. People talk—they always do.

But I'd trust Blair with anything. He wanted to marry her—that's his private business. Gentlemen don't read each other's mail."

"No, no," Andrews said quickly, "I didn't mean that. Just that it must have put him in a touchy position, that's all."

"More than touchy. Absolute hell. I haven't got a man in the place who could have done it. A man's got to be born to it, Andrews. That's something you would understand, I think."

He means feudal, Andrews thought. Nose as hard as armor. Not having to give a damn what people think or say. The luxury of being able to be careless. And for some reason he suddenly thought of Emily, how different she was, and how precise and careful, for whom giving was hard but receiving even harder. And yet she hadn't seemed that way in the beginning.

". . . his own wife's family. Five sisters, three brothers, I believe, a cousin or two, I don't remember exactly. An ambitious project, you'll admit. One other sister is married to a man named Carter. Rita Red Hawk. I mention her because she was something of a celebrity as a ballet dancer, New York, Europe. Yes, I thought you'd know her name. And she's living, a mark of distinction in that family. Two other sisters are dead, as well as two of the brothers and at least one cousin. The only one in the family with a child is Rita—I think I'm right in that. If everybody were wiped out except the child, all the headrights would go to her, or him, whatever it is. An income of well over two hundred thousand a year—in trust. That would mean a guardian—a locally appointed lawyer. Not much of a trick at that point. If it were Rita or Mary Rose who was left, it would be the same, except no guardian. The husband could control the money."

"You talk as though—well, I don't know, as if it were like the weather or something. My God," he said, smiling in spite of himself, "this isn't the Court of the Borgias or Elizabethan England. It's a hick town way off in nowhere. Whizbang! For God's sake."

"You would have to see it," the Commissioner said slowly, not smiling. "I think of that reservation like some medieval hill town, the whole place a fortification, built for protection against an enemy that was always there. Have you ever seen one of those little European towns—people huddled together like sheep in a fold, slits in the walls for windows, the place a regular beehive, built on the edge of a cliff, hacked out of rock—never mind. The Chetopa have no walls around them. They're plains dwellers. They lived in the open, fought there too—on foot at first, then after the Spaniards, on ponies. They'd die of suffocation in the kind of place I'm talking about."

"So they asked for help."

"They got it, too. We sent a team of investigators out there. Local officials not much help in a thing of this kind. Took almost two years, working undercover, every kind of difficulty. They got their man, though. Funny sort of a fellow. Famous in his way. Roper. Shoat Dalton."

"What happened to him?"

"He's dead."

"Hanging?"

"No, accidental. That was the coroner's report, anyway."

"In prison?"

"On the county road, gravel, straight as a die, western part of the reservation."

Andrews looked at him, puzzled. "I don't follow you."

The Commissioner pulled at the lines around his mouth, then relit his pipe. "He was acquitted. Jury was out for two and a half days. Let him go. As for the so-called accident, they claim he was drunk—car went off the road. Wife killed too, along with Dalton's nephew."

"She was a Red Hawk, too, I suppose."

The Commissioner shook his head. "Dalton's nephew, Orval Sikes by name, had married one of the Red Hawk girls, Nellie. She's still living."

"Maybe you had the wrong man."

The Commissioner stood up, stretched, then went around to the other side of the desk. "That's what a lot of people think. As for the jury . . ."

"How about you?"

"I like to think he was the right man, and that somebody wanted to get rid of him to keep him from getting even."

"Maybe he was the wrong man and somebody wanted to hush him up for good."

"That would make the jury right and us wrong," the Commissioner said. He leaned forward, his hands on the desk, his eyes down at the papers so that he seemed to be talking more to himself than to Andrews. "If he was the wrong man . . ."

"It would have to be someone who stood to get the money."

The Commissioner nodded. "There's another thing. The state peace officer on the case. He was shot a month ago in his own house. Someone had climbed up on the porch and cut the bedroom screen—got in that way. He had worked on a lot of other cases, and he had plenty of enemies. No need for me to invent one."

"But surely—all these things can't be connected. The place is savage, lawless. Does Booth walk around in a bulletproof vest or something? He ought to, from the sound of it."

The Commissioner pushed his fists down hard on the desk and Andrews saw the backs of his hands turn white. "Blair has never so much as been threatened," he said without looking up. "If Shoat Dalton was the wrong man—if he was framed and someone wanted to lower the boom on him because that jury was afraid to hang him, or knew better, one—then we're in real trouble."

He looked up then and Andrews saw him for the first time as an old man. The veins that rose at his temples made his head seem fragile; the skin beneath his eyes was dark, as though smudged with tears and ink. Only a moment ago he had seemed strong, and then Andrews realized that he had never really looked at him before. "You're the son of one of my oldest friends. What I'm saying to you now is because of that. They're already asking for an investigation, Andrews. That's why that bill won't go through this session. I've made a lot of enemies here, and the people I've fought for—the Chetopas and the rest of them—can't help, even if they wanted to. I'm too old for it, son—my whole life has gone into this. I couldn't stand an investigation. My God," he said suddenly, his face gone dark and his hands trembling, "think of the people I've protected, and covered up for—the lies." He closed his eyes then and shook his head. "So much that a man can never tell. But the tide always goes out, and leaves it all on the beach—the tar, the driftwood, the bones, the refuse, the debris of a lifetime . . ." and his voice trailed off.

"And if Booth . . .?" Andrews said tentatively in the hush.

"Yes," harsh and pained.

"You haven't told me—what you want. Of me, I mean."

The Commissioner had opened his eyes, but Andrews could see nothing but darkness in his face. "We've reached a dead end. I'm down to my last card. I want you to go there . . . I want to know what's happened . . . I want to clean it up . . . with a knife if that's what it takes." He was like a wounded man, cornered, fighting for his life, all pretenses gone. "I'm asking you because I believe I can trust you. Now do you understand?"

He had carried the papers home that night, and after dinner he told Emily as much as he could say. She took it well, he thought; restrained, but she was like that now. No complaints, at least. They had put the atlas on the floor and run their fingers over the page until they found it. "Way out there?" was all she said, quietly, as though it frightened her a little. Then she had put her hand up to his face, something she had not done for a long time, touching him softly as she once had touched him in the night. He had patted her shoulder gently, almost absently, and then they put the atlas away and he went upstairs and began to read the files. . . .

And finally at long last the town, as though he had been waiting for it all his life, and yet so all of a sudden now that it seemed that time had telescoped, and even as he heard still the dying sound of the Commissioner's words (*Grey Horse. Grey Horse, Oklahoma. Ever hear of it?*), there came the rhythmic slowing of the train, the conductor's peremptory cry rising and falling like an echo—"Grey Horse, Grey Horse"—the land no longer blurred and fleeting but a series of lantern slides, compositions of barns, cattle, slow swells of prairie, telephone poles leaning against the sky, a bridge, long sheds painted green and red, rust-colored railroad cars on the sidings, two spotted horses side by side, heads in opposite directions, houses scattered, then becoming ordered with yards, flower beds, elm trees, dogs and children and old ladies turned in porch swings to watch, more and more slowly, rocking in the roadbed so that people reaching for parcels clutched the backs of seats, lost hats, stumbled and staggered under the weight of suitcases being pulled down from the overhead racks. "Grey Horse." A last call from the end of the car. Then a prolonged, squealing slide, the clash of couplings, a lurching, grinding halt, and finally the panting of steam in clouds that rolled out from under the cars and fogged the windows.

"Is this where we're going, Daddy?"

"This is it, son."

"Careful with the hat box, Andrews—it doesn't fasten."

Pushing slowly through the crowded aisle to the platform, then down the steep steps to where the porter smiling in black and white had assembled their luggage.

"Much obliged, sir."

The train whistle sharp and urgent, the steam careening along the ground in a burst of wind, the sky full of bright blue light that made the sun seem cold, the station casting a triangle of shadow that lay like something solid upon the earth, and over it all a glittering brilliance of such clarity that they had to shield their eyes, looking across at the different groups of people who stared at the train with concentrated apprehension. Around them were the small cries of greeting, the fluster of embraces, hats clutched, the slow drawl of men's voices, murmurs of laughter, the silvery jingle of harness suddenly loud, then lost again in gusts of air against which people seemed to lean like trees.

Andrews felt the pressure of Amory's hand as his eyes, narrowed against the glare, swept across the high-crowned straw hats hard as helmets, the faces beneath them red and rough, the heavy-chested, small-thighed men in tight pants and high-heeled boots, and then off to the side a single small group of Indians, blankets pulled close around them, high soft hats on their heads, and behind them a Negro chauffeur leaning sleepily against a hearselike car.

"Mr. Thayer?"

His eyes moved back across the faces, then stopped. Two men, two women, looking at him. He took Emily's arm and stepped forward. The train behind them whistled, then abruptly crashed into motion, and he half turned as though he had forgotten something. People waved from the windows; beside him Amory waved back. The ground seemed to shake beneath his feet, and he looked suddenly for a sign just to be sure. It swung in the wind before the dull-red station, set down like a box beside the track. "Grey Horse." Then he looked at them again, the tall, lean man in whipcord, a beige cowman's hat shading a long and pointed face, a heavy-set, flushed man beside him with rumpled grey hair and a suit that seemed too big for him, the women dark, half-hidden by the men.

"Mr. Booth?" he answered, and then they were all laughing and shaking hands and Amory was being lifted high in the air by Booth to see the caboose as it rattled out of sight.

"A real pleasure, Mrs. Thayer. Meet my wife, Mary Rose. This is Mrs. Carter, her husband, Clay. Well, young fellow," and Booth rubbed his knuckles against Amory's scalp, then gathered up as many bags as he could hold.

Andrews, watching Booth with the suitcases, smiled uncomfortably in spite of himself and then quickly brought his fingers to his lips as though to hide the stiffness in his face. All of Booth's features were oversized. His face was whiskey-pink, his nose sprouting and veined at the edges of the nostrils, his forehead framed by thick grey hair that waved back along the tops of his ears. When he spoke his voice boomed as though it carried with it its own echo, and he brought his face close to Andrews's as though he were hard of hearing and might not catch the reply. He tugged repeatedly at his belt, running his thumbs back and forth inside his pants waist. And while he talked loudly and generally to everyone he was already urging them toward the car, directing the movement of the bags, making a joke with Amory, and then stooping to retrieve papers that fell suddenly from the bulging pockets of his coat.

"First trip West?"

Andrews turned with relief toward that quiet voice, blurred to a drawl that was neither Southern nor the nasal whine that he had heard further north. He nodded while Carter's eyes, concentrated around tiny points of yellow light, searched his face rapidly before assuming an expression of poised and guarded repose. A tall, slightly stooped man who walked with an easy slouch but in whose face Andrews seemed to sense something wild and restless as a wolf. Perhaps it was merely the alertness of his movements, or the short yellow hair that shone in the sun high along his cheekbones. Yet his hand rested gently on the boy's head, and he had taken off his hat and bent forward from the waist when he had spoken Emily's name.

"Came from New York City? Some trip, yes indeed. Let's see, that means you changed in Chicago. Right across town. The Santa Fe. Oh, I know it all right. Went through there quite a number of years ago. But I'm a Virginian, you see—a real one, not by way of Texas and Lord knows where else like Clay here. Oh, I get back to Washington now and then on business, but that's St. Louis, of course. Got everything? Where's your suitcase, boy? Hah! Look out. Thought he'd lost it. Leave it on the train, Amory? Now you get right up in front here with me and your mommy and Mr. Clay, son boy. Mr. Thayer, sir, you will have the pleasure of our ladies in the back seat. If you please."

Andrews had not really looked at her before. Mary Rose— somber, her black hair pulled very tight to the back of her head beneath a small woven straw hat, her eyes expressionless behind the rimless glasses she wore. He followed her into the car, settled himself and turned toward her slightly to make room for Carter's wife, then reached back across Rita to close the car door for her. His hand closed upon hers on the door handle, their eyes slid to a stop on one another, and then they both laughed.

"Sorry—I thought—"

"No, I only meant—"

And then they laughed again, bumping against each other now that the car had started, his shoulder hard against her arm, his leg feeling the softness of her thigh, her breath warm on his cheek. He could see no further into her eyes than the sunlight which sparkled on the surface; her skin was burnt umber along the fine bone of her jaw. He wondered suddenly if she dyed her hair, for it was black with undertones of blue, and from the widow's peak at her forehead it fell loosely back in full waves to her shoulders. Her eyes looked straight into his as she laughed, and then moved down to his mouth. She had not lifted her hand. He took his away at last, but he could still feel the pressure of her body through his coat.

"I hope I'm not crowding you," he said, turning to Mary Rose. She looked at him briefly and shook her head, and it seemed to him that he saw something both bewildered and terrified in those weak eyes before she turned back to the window and began to hum quietly to herself, her fingers beating a kind of rhythm where they lay in her lap. They're sisters, he said to himself, remembering. Rita's the dancer, and when he turned toward her again she was still smiling, her face bemused, a hint of a frown just above the bridge of her nose, her long fingers with their almond nails playing with the fur of her coat. He wrenched his eyes away from her, conscious that she was still looking at him, and stared fixedly out of the window. For a long moment he saw nothing, then there were trees bent inward just at the level of his eyes and the bumping rattle of a bridge beneath the car. He turned quickly to the back window, then glanced to the side again.

"That must be Rocky Ford," he said, "or what used to be called by that name. Isn't that Clear Creek down there? What do they call this street now?"

"By George, Thayer. You've been reading maps, sir." Booth strained around to look at him, then began pointing with his finger. "This is Main Street now, used to be the lane that led from the center of the Agency out to the ford. One of the camps was just off to the left there—between here and the creek. And further in there—"

"The freighters' camp? Wasn't that where it was?"

"Well, sir." Booth threw back his head and laughed and Andrews saw how the flesh of his neck trembled over his collar. "What do you think of that, Amory son? Your daddy now . . ."

She laughed too, beside him, shaking her head so that her hair fell like a wing across her face, and this time he saw her teeth, white and grooved like tiny columns. "How would you . . ." and her eyes wrinkled with wonder. "Why in the world . . ." and then she was no longer laughing, just smiling, suddenly quite still, looking for something in his face as though trying to remember where she had seen him before.

"It matters to me," he said, surprised that the words came to him so simply, and yet uncomfortably aware that there was something both pretentious and intimate in the way he spoke to her.

"The Agent's Office used to be down here before it was moved up on the Hill. I had to get up there where those buyers and sellers couldn't get at me so easy—isn't that right, Clay?"

"The town is growing," Clay said quietly. "We've got a good town here, Mr. Thayer. We've got the cattle business, the Chetopa payments, oil-field people do their buying here—when I come here twenty years ago it wasn't hardly anything. Now there's pavement everywhere, sidewalks, stores—we got three banks."

"Clay, you always talk like you built the place with a hammer and saw," Rita said loudly. "What do these people from the East care about how many banks we've got."

Booth cleared his throat and glanced over at Carter. Then he swung himself around toward Andrews again. "Back up on the other side is Cedarvale Hill. The road runs up that way to Kansas."

"I understand that they used to bring the payments in over that road. Had to get the money up at the railhead in Kansas and bring it down here by buggy or horseback, hidden half the time because of the outlaws . . ."

"Well, Mr. Thayer, you have just heard the first and last lecture from me on the subject of Grey Horse. Won't do in front of the ladies and this little fellow here to let you show me up, now will it, son. Mrs. Thayer, are you as much of an expert . . ."

Mary Rose still hummed, looking out the window on her side.

Andrews cleared his throat once in her direction, then gave it up.

"Take your hotel," Clay said evenly, as though no one else had spoken. "You'd have to go to Tulsa or Little Rock or Kansas City to beat it—and that's a long ride. Opera House down the street's been here for a while. Burnt down a few years back—had to build her over again."

"Oh, Clay, for heaven's sake," Rita protested, kicking the pointed tip of her shoe against the seat.

"I don't really know much about the town. I've read a lot about the Tribe . . ." and then his voice trailed off. It sounded strange somehow; a medieval historian insisting on talking to villagers in bastard Latin. He had seen from the train a hundred towns like this one—Main Street, frame houses, storefronts with men leaning in the shade, cars and signs and country people staring at the train. American towns, the way it was now. This one was the same. And the only Indians he had seen so far were in the little group at the station standing before their chauffeur-driven car, and now these two women on either side of him.

"Steadiest payroll in northern Oklahoma," Carter was saying as he turned slowly into the curb. "I think you'll like it," looking at Emily and the boy.

"Everybody out—State Hotel—I'll just scare up a bellhop or two." Booth squeezed his way out through the door, but the bellhop was already coming down the steps. "Mr. Carter's guests are here," and there was in the way he said it something that made Andrews look quickly in Booth's direction as though he had not understood. Mr. Carter's guests. What was that all about?

"All these bags. Careful of the hat box. Right on up to the suite. They know we're coming."

The lobby was large and dark, filled with a random arrangement of lumpy furniture, like a warehouse where people seldom came. Two long-horned steers stared glassily down from the walls, and Amory stood staring back until Emily seized him by the hand and pulled him along.

The manager came quickly across the polished floor, rubbing his hands, addressing himself to Carter just as everyone else seemed to do. "Yes, Mr. Carter, the room is in order. Everything as it should be. I've seen to it personally. Mr. Thayer, is it? Whatever you need, sir. Phone the desk anytime. Always happy to have Mr. Carter's guests with us."

"Now folks," Booth said, spreading his arms expansively,

"we've got a little wait before dinner. I imagine that you, ma'am," turning to Emily, "would like to freshen up a little. So you just go right on upstairs and get yourself settled and we'll have a drink or two down here and get ourselves warmed up some."

"Well," Emily began uncertainly, "it's awfully kind of you, really, but Amory—you know, the train ride was so long—"

"Now, Mrs. Thayer, the host has certain privileges, too, and certainly Southern hospitality . . . ladies . . . sleep ever so much better . . ." and they heard his voice booming behind them all the way down the hall until they had closed themselves into the silence of the suite which in its drabness seemed as sealed off from light and air as a tank in an aquarium.

Emily raised her eyebrows and tightened the corner of her mouth. "Let's hope we're not as jovial every day."

"It was nice of them to meet us at the train."

"Booth," she said, "and that poor sad Mary Rose of a wife."

"Mmmm."

"I suppose Carter's nice enough. What's her name—Rita. Something cheap about her." She was taking off her hat, holding the pins like knives between her teeth. "Do you think she's really his wife? I don't know—just a feeling, that's all. She was on the stage, you said," her voice tinged with something like accusation.

Andrews looked at her for a moment, then nodded vacantly. "A dancer. Ballet. You probably want to take a bath. I think I'll lie down for a little. Come on, Amory. Bring your book over on the bed and read for a while."

He took his shoes off and hung his coat and tie on the back of a chair and then lay down with his arm across his eyes. A whole world lay about him in pieces, strewn at his feet like the petals from a bouquet blown apart by the wind. He had seen it all so clearly in his mind—as it had been a half century ago. And now it seemed merely another little town, a white man's marketplace full of flyspecked store windows, streets laid down by T square upon a culture or at least a way of life dead, dead, forever gone . . . What's needed here is not a lawyer but a goddam archaeologist, he thought to himself grimly. What in God's name am I doing here in Grey Horse, Oklahoma—Clay Carter's guest in a fleabitten hotel in some town nobody ever heard of. Amory asked a question and he answered listlessly, remembering how eagerly he had planned the trip, even down to the last details of packing, finding out about the weather and the kind of clothes they would need, preparing himself as though for an expedition into the jungle, or the desert. And withal a sense of mission that he carried with him like a secret document and which he had hidden beneath a kind of casual negligence throughout the final visits at Christmas to Boston (where his parents had reserved their affection entirely for Amory, treating him like some missionary crank and Emily— well, the way they had always treated her, as though somehow she did not really exist), and to Pittsfield, where her mother listened in a state of tearful bewilderment, snuffling and moving heavily back and forth from the kitchen, while her father buried himself more deeply than ever behind the pages of his newspaper. Amory they had treated gingerly as though he might break, and he dealt with them in the slightly aloof way of children with unaccustomed servants, accepting in dignified silence the endless sweets produced from the kitchen.

Thus he had moved in a kind of dream through those last weeks of preparation, of farewell parties (with Emily looking so damned brave), and then the long train ride over the blue-green wall of mountains and down the forests and foothills to Chicago and beyond, level land, fields of furrows stretching to the horizon, cows, fences, water tanks, windmills, silos, railroad crossings, all seen through the thickness of the train window in a kind of unmoving permanency like the models and the toys that made up the world around Amory's electric train. Still part of the dream, still seen from behind glass, until that shuddering halt and the panting, steaming silence that seemed in some strange way alive, and suddenly a kind of nakedness, the window shattered, the dream blown away by the wind and no barrier left between him and Carter's searching eyes, the hoarse pressure of Booth's voice, Rita's open mouth quivering with laughter, Mary Rose lost in some spell the past had cast upon her. Maybe she was the one who could best understand, he thought, for upon her face there was a silence like a veil. And yet he was not really sure that he understood himself. It was simply that he could feel as surely as he felt the blood beating in his temples that something irrevocable had happened, that in a moment of illumination as though from a sudden blinding bolt of lightning they had looked at each other's faces and none of them would ever again be quite the same. It happens that way, he thought. A face you look upon that changes your life forever. And yet not so much their faces as their very lives, calling out for him just as he in some way whose source he could not fathom had always searched for them. Held there in the suspension of that moment beyond time as though drawn by the will of God as inexorably as the sea draws its rivers to it; a strange inevitability about it all, a pull as certain as that of gravity; neither whole without the other, he their deliverer, they his salvation.

"They're waiting, Andrews." Her voice was calm but insistent as she smoothed the powder flat along the sides of her nose, then shaped her hair with restless fingers.

He raised his arm and opened his eyes, blinking at the mottled ceiling above him.

Amory kicked his feet against the bed, sucking his forefinger, reading the dime Western which Andrews had bought for him at the station in Chicago in spite of Emily's objections.

"Why do you keep reading it over and over?" he asked softly, turning his head so that he could look at his son's profile, the small tilted nose, the slightly grained skin, the fine colorless hair where the cheekbone joined the ear.

Amory removed his finger and went on reading. "I don't understand it," he said. "I like it to be like that." He turned the page and put his finger back in his mouth.

"You're right," Andrews said, swinging his legs off the other side of the bed and getting to his feet. "Much better that way, reading the same ones all the time. That way you always know how it's going to be and that you're not going to be able to figure it out and that you can always start over again anytime you want. Like watching stars, maybe. Grey Horse ought to be a great place for that. Where's the flask, Emily?" and he put his hand on her shoulder, smiling at her image in the mirror.

She turned and looked at him as though she could not see his

eyes for the shadows. "Oh, Andrews, please. They've been waiting a long time as it is. Let's get it over with. If you—"

"Emily, my dear," he said with mock seriousness, unscrewing
the top and filling the small metal jigger. "They've been waiting
all their lives, believe me. What else can you do in a town like
this? There's no rush. Relax." He lifted the jigger. "Grey Horse.
A long way from anywhere, but we found it. Just like salmon
heading back upstream."

"Oh, do be serious, Andrews," Emily sighed, turning again to
the mirror. "I'm worn out, Amory's hungry—"

"I'm hungry," Amory said, to no one in particular.

"That's one thing you understand," Andrews laughed, lifting
him kicking from the bed onto his shoulder.

Later he wondered why it had come into his mind to say it.
He had, after all, known better. To warn them, to put them on
guard, was the last thing he had wanted to do. He had touched an
exposed nerve and now they would be wary of him. And yet
what did it matter really if they heard far in the distance but
coming ever closer the hound of heaven, closing in. The fear that
froze their faces, the way each of them had shrunk back into
watchful silence, meant that ghosts still walked among them. It
was as though he had unceremoniously placed before them on the
table a tiny shrunken doll-like head such as those that his great-
grandfather had brought back from some barbarous coast of
South America, the features preserved in hideous miniature perfection and known to them all as well as they knew the bone and
cartilage and flesh and hair of their own faces.

They had sat long over dinner, and he was restive from the
blurred days on the train. The food seemed to him tasteless—plate-
size sirloins overdone, cole slaw, hash-brown potatoes, lemon
meringue pie, all of it washed down with ice water. They were
served by a waitress dressed like a nurse and painted as though by
an undertaker. Everyone seemed to know each other; she patted
Amory's head and asked Emily ("dearie") if the trip hadn't been
too tiring. After they had been served, the restaurant owner,
short, bald, sweating, wrapped around in a soiled apron, came out
of the kitchen and sat down at the table for a while. No one

seemed to notice him—he listened, smoked a cigarette in silence, then disappeared again behind the swinging doors.

Booth went on talking, his face flushed and beaded around the mouth with perspiration. Something in their conversation that afternoon had turned his mind to the past, and he told one story after another of the early history of the town, of the Chetopa themselves, of their place in the struggle between the French and the Spanish in this part of the country, of their prowess as warriors, their habits, their language, their great chiefs, the legendary past, telling it all with sweeping gestures as he ate and laughed, leaning to look into one face or another as though he thought that no one quite understood. And for Booth it was not merely history, Andrews had reflected. Rather it was part of his life, for somehow he had managed to put down roots into this clay soil and to draw from it something he could live on in the way one lived on memories of childhood. It was there in the warmth of his telling, the way he made his points and then waited, looking from face to face, and then went on, beyond caring really whether anyone was listening because he relished so much the telling of it. And watching him Andrews was aware in a vaguely uncomfortable way that there was a kind of artifice about it, that it was something that Booth had constructed like a stage whereon he might play out his life. As though he really belonged here, Andrews thought wonderingly, looking across to where Mary Rose sat stoically—yes, that was the word for it—listening perhaps but making no response, her hands folded before her, her face without expression. And whenever Booth, flourishing his knife triumphantly over some point or other, would return to his sirloin, Carter would turn to Andrews and mention something about the town—the country club, say, or the golf course, which had just been put in ("oiled sand greens of course, but with those little round drags it works all right"), or the quarter-horse races—things which for the most part seemed a little remote from him but which were the right things to tell about, as though the town were after all something more than a graveyard or an archaeological dig. "I'd say that this bluestemmed glass here makes for as good grazing as you'll find in the United States—hell, there've been spreads here for better than fifty years—ranchers used to live up in what they called the States—Kansas, it was—leased acreage in the reservation. There's one or two old-timers still left from those days—some of our ranch families started out that way—town people came later, mostly." Measured, grave, courteous. Yet it was curious that he never mentioned the Chetopa when he spoke, any more than he looked at his wife, Rita. Just the town, as though it were a special creation of his own.

"Where did you live in Boston?"

Andrews glanced up quickly, but Rita was speaking to Emily. She was leaning forward a little on her elbows, her hands together in front of her face, holding a cigarette. He noticed again the faintly quizzical expression in her eyes, the way she held her head a little to one side. And yet there came and went a sudden flashing wildness in those eyes, a quick flaring of the nostrils when she breathed, which made him think of a high-strung, thoroughbred horse.

"I didn't live there." Emily was carefully cutting Amory's meat into tiny squares. "I was in school in Cambridge. Do you know Boston?" Her voice was poised, polite, cool.

"Hotels—the theater. Not far from the Common, I remember. I used to walk across the park in the morning—came back the same way at night. Not much more than that. Funny twisty streets. Wonderful seafood. Dirty brick, and everything looking like there ought to be fog, except there wasn't. At least not while I was there. Except once in the fall, along the river . . ."

Her voice fell, and Andrews turned as though she had spoken to him. "I understand you dance."

"Danced," and she laughed and threw her head back and her hand went up to catch the waves of hair and pull them from her face. "I didn't do anything else for thirteen years. Not any more." She looked again at Emily. "Then it's your husband who's from Boston."

"Yes. My husband's home is there."

"I can hear it in the way he talks. You don't seem to have his accent at all."

"Really."

Why can't she be civil, Andrews thought irritably. He had lost the thread of Carter's conversation; something about one of the big oil men starting a polo team, strings of ponies, special clothes—there had even been a team from South America, not much to look at on the ground but hell on a horse.

"A lot of damned foolishness."

"Well, now, Blair, I'm not so sure. If it's all right in the East, what's wrong with having it here?"

The dining room was almost empty now. The owner leaned behind the counter, picking his teeth, listening without apparent interest. Near the door sat a small man who had been there when they came in. Booth and Carter had greeted him, "Evening, Jack," then explained to Andrews that he was a very successful criminal lawyer, Jack Bird by name. "Defend just about anybody," Booth had said. "Sometimes he's with us, just as often he's not. Not much sentiment in Jack—probably should have been a major-league statistician, keeping the records and so on. There every night, reading through the stock quotations, making notes —God knows what he's worth."

In the far corner sat an Indian couple, swollen with fat, silent, motionless. They had been sitting like that throughout dinner. Once Mary Rose had excused herself and gone back to speak to them. No one seemed to notice her departure, and she said nothing when she returned to the table.

It was a long room, paneled in pale, varnished pine. Cluttered with similarly varnished chairs and tables, wagon-wheel chandeliers, a long counter with stools—the stylization of the West. For decoration there were brands burned into the panels, a calligraphic language of ownership. And above the paneling, large framed photographs of horses, of cattle, of landscape, of cattlemen, those to whom this land belonged. Andrews idly read the legends, then beneath a picture of two velvety beige horses, *Palominos Bred on Dalton Ranch, Chetopa County.*

"Dalton ranch," he said aloud, more to himself than to anyone else. "Would that be Shoat Dalton?"

"Where'd you ever hear of him?" Clay's question uncoiled quick as a striking snake.

He looked at their faces: Rita no longer smiling, her eyes wide and wondering; Mary Rose carved from walnut, without movement, as though she no longer breathed; Booth white-faced, his mouth half open; Carter staring at him with the intensity of a hunting hawk. Out of the corner of his eye he saw Emily, too, put her fork down and look at him.

"Shoat Dalton," he said again. "The rancher. I'm sorry—I know it must be painful for you. I read about it—the trial and all . . ." He reached for his cigarette case, his thoughts racing ahead of his words.

Then suddenly his mind was clear, as though he had sailed through a storm and out the other side and there were the stars again and he was back on course. That's all it took, he thought to himself. Just the mention of the name.

"It was your family, wasn't it?" he said abruptly, turning to Rita. "And he was acquitted."

"Shoat Dalton was a killer, whether they acquitted him or not," Carter said roughly. "They didn't have the guts to stand up to him. Afraid, all of them. So they let him off."

"But he died just the same," Andrews said, looking into those narrowed eyes where yellow bars of light burned like candle flames.

"Yeah, he died. Too much car, too much whiskey, too much gravel, too much Shoat. We don't need his kind around here."

"And Kirby?" Andrews continued relentlessly. "The peace officer? Another accident? You seem to have a high proportion of accidental deaths in this part of the world, Mr. Carter."

"No accident, Mr. Thayer. Kirby was gunned down by a man he helped put in the penitentiary. Everybody in Grey Horse knows it. The fellow's got a woman staked out here. He comes to see her pretty regular. Everybody knows that, too. Who's going to arrest him? That's why Kirby was killed."

"Who are these people, Andrews?" Emily's voice was hushed, hardly more than a whisper. "You didn't tell me any of this—"

"Mmmm," Andrews said. He tapped the cigarette slowly against the back of the case, then lit it. His fingers trembled; he felt a sudden sense of exaltation. They were afraid of him, of what he knew. Well, he had put down his bet; it was up to them to call or quit.

He looked again at Rita. Her eyes had not left his face. He colored a little and looked back at her unblinking. Something was slowly emerging into light from the depths of his mind.

"I remember now. You danced in Paris," he said, smiling at her. "We were in Switzerland that summer. I came up to Paris to see my parents. Your name—of course—it struck me at the time. I saw it somewhere . . ."

She answered as though they were alone in the room. "We stayed there for two months. Twice we were there. Clay was there, too. He came to get me in Paris. I had a great success there—they were very kind to me."

"You've never been back."

"It would break my heart to go back. I loved it too much."

"You're sleepy, aren't you, dear," Emily said, looking down into Amory's face. She put her lips against his hair, then smiled at him. He looked into her eyes, unsmiling.

"Don't you feel that way?" Rita said, turning to Emily.

"Paris is so many different things," Emily replied, looking up brightly. It was what she called her party face. "It would depend on the person, wouldn't it?"

He wanted to keep them separate in his mind, but they were both in his line of vision—Rita so dark that even her lips seemed bruised, her face smooth and high-boned, her mouth seeming always to tremble on the edge of laughter, and the laughter itself pouring from her as generous as rain. A face which to Andrews was almost painfully familiar for reasons he could in no way understand; a face one saw in a recurring dream that always faded away before wakefulness. The quick grace of her walk, the flutter of her hands . . . And Emily—pretty, soft-fleshed, square-jawed, controlled and determined as a New England schoolmistress in spite of, or perhaps because of, Naples and the Dante Society and the long road from Pittsfield to Boston. Unselfish in a peculiarly selfish kind of way, Andrews thought suddenly. Was that the difference, finally?

"A cigar before we break up?" Carter's face was composed again into a leathery facsimile of kindness and concern.

"I'll get them, Clay," Booth said quickly. He brought the boxes back, offered them around, then lit Carter's cigar before sitting down again.

"Thank you, Blair," Carter said easily, exhaling the smoke slowly and turning the cigar in his fingers. And there was something so comfortably patronizing in the way he spoke, in his very gestures, that Andrews had flushed with anger and abruptly pushed his chair back. Booth was older, and independent of Carter. He was the United States government in this forgotten town. What could he owe Carter? What was there between them?

And then he saw again as though it were a ghost the face of the Commissioner as he had seen it that day when they first had talked of all this—the hands white against the desk, the black smudges of fatigue beneath eyes that seemed tired of seeing. "Clean it up, Andrews—use the knife if you have to . . ."

Lights slid across the open window of the office like a hand moving before a projection lamp. Then a car door slammed shut and her heels as she ran were quick and staccato on the stairs.

⌨ ⌨
⌨

"THEY'VE GOT CLAY. You know that, don't you? Came right up on the porch—I was upstairs—I heard them." She stood there in the doorway, her head back so that he could see the curving swell of her throat, a wing of raven hair trailing loose across her face. "I could hear it all from the upstairs bedroom. Then he came and got a bag . . ."

"Did he say anything to you?"

"To tell Jack Bird."

"Have you?"

She nodded, holding her lower lip in her teeth.

"Don't stand there in the door, Rita. What else did he say?"

She took her hand from the door and pushed it through her hair. Then she walked toward the desk with her peculiar swaying grace. "He said something about you . . . and me. That you were after something . . . bigger was what he said." Beneath the lamp she was all black and bronze and gold. Her coat was draped carelessly around her shoulders, and she cradled her arms against her breast, waiting for him to answer.

"You don't believe that," he said carefully, watching her. "How much does he know?"

"No," she said quickly, her eyes widening, her bosom rising and falling more rapidly. "I don't believe him any more. You know that better than anyone."

"Look," he said abruptly, and then he stopped. Whatever he said to her would be wrong. The light in which she moved was always a little too lurid—that way she had of standing with her legs apart and her hands on her hips and her belly thrust forward —her laugh too loud, too coarse—everything about her both clumsily natural and studied, as though she were always aware of being watched, a double exposure with her slenderly elegant and sophisticated image superimposed upon the expressionless, dumb wondering animal she most deeply was. All of it had a way of making him uncomfortable, so that he was forever saying "But that's not what I meant." And yet they laughed and cried together, which was so much more important to him just now. "Let's don't talk about that."

"About what? I don't understand. Tell me what you mean."

"About you and me. It has nothing to do with us."

Her laughter was full of scorn. "What does it have to do with, Mr. Thayer?"

"Don't talk that way, Rita. Not now," and his voice rose, trembling. He hammered his fist suddenly against the desk. "Not until it's all over."

"We can't play games with each other. My whole life has been some kind of an act. I don't want it any more. That's finished."

There was a wild pride in her face that made the back of his neck tingle with fear. His fist unfolded and he clutched the edge of the desk to support himself. He could smell danger acrid as gunsmoke in the air; she had gone beyond where he could reach her, her eyes burning, the very way she stood inviting disaster. She seemed so wantonly triumphant, and it was terrifying to him precisely because triumph, what little experience he had of it, had always been for him a secret feeling which expressed itself by his face becoming increasingly hard and cold, his voice more cutting, his emotions more deeply buried than ever. And now she stood there like some tragic heroine, poised in her triumph at the very edge of doom.

"We've got to go slow—get that through your head once and for all."

"What is this all about?" she said softly, as though she no longer knew him. "You love me. Have you forgotten that already? You went down on your knees and cried—you were like a boy—all those things you said." She leaned across the desk and he could see the bone where her breasts parted and smell the mingled musk of whiskey and perfume.

He tightened his jaw and rubbed hard against the corner of his eye socket where the nerves flickered like lightning. Then he opened the desk drawer and took the folded foolscap and smoothed it out before him.

"Rita," he said deliberately. "I'm going to read this to you. You're going to listen to me. Shut up now and listen. You started this. This is what you told me. This is your voice you're going to hear now, Rita. I want you to say, 'Yes, it belongs to me, that is what I said.' You've got to stand behind me, Rita. The place is locked and we can't get out. Do you understand? You've got to stand behind me." And then he realized that he was whispering, and that the words that he had just spoken were the words that he always used about Cody. Stand behind me. *What in God's name am I asking her to do?*

"Time to lay down the hands is what you mean, isn't it? You've called him," and she came around the desk to where he stood and leaned against him so that when she spoke he could feel her breath upon his face. "Clay's the one who needs somebody behind him. He's all alone. I'm with you now."

Then he felt her arms around his neck and her open mouth searching his until her teeth were sharp against his tongue. Her stomach was hard against him, and he ran his hands roughly along the taut strength of her hips.

"Who's afraid now?" she murmured, her lips rubbing against his.

"Nobody's afraid," he said harshly, jerking his head to the side so that she drew back and looked at him, her eyes wide, direct, uncomplicated, savage.

"What is it, then?" Her lips were open against his throat and he could feel the tip of her tongue like the point of a knife. "You know I love you. I'll do anything you say. Just tell me. We're free now." Then she looked up at him again. "Are you worried about the money? You know I have money."

Pain pierced Andrews's temples and all the nerves in his body meshed in an iron effort at control. "This is about Booth, now, Rita. About Booth and Clay. About your family. All the things you told me," and for a moment he thought that he would either hit her or be sick with vertigo, looking down into the bottomless depths of her eyes.

"We've both been so alone," she moaned, and took the back of his neck in her hands, and then when her mouth found his, his nerves broke and he felt the tears wet and salty down to where their mouths clung.

"Come on," he said unsteadily, holding her gently, "we can't stand here like this."

The night stared in through the blind eye of the window until Rita, looking up to touch the tears on his face, reached back and found the chain of the overhead bulb and brought the darkness down around them. Then her teeth cut his lips and her fingers beneath his coat ran up and down his back like streaks of fire. For a long breathless moment they fought each other, and then he sank to the floor, his head pressed against her thighs, his arm pulled tight against the backs of her knees.

"I don't want to live without you," he sobbed, shaking his

head and turning his face into the soft silk of her dress. "I can't help it. It's all wrong but I can't help it. Oh God, what has happened to me. I just can't make it this way. Rita, I don't know . . ."

In his ears there was the roar of the sea and her voice seemed to come from a long way off. He held onto her desperately as though to keep from drowning. His body shook, and when he tried to speak the words fragmented into little cries of pain.

At last he was aware again of her fingers in his hair. The winds that had shaken him had blown themselves out, and what he heard now was the steady humming of his nerves. He was feverish, and the back of his head ached, and yet he felt strangely lucid as though he had gone without sleep for days on end, living on coffee and aspirin.

Finally he got up without looking at her and fumbled for the foolscap in the dark. Then he pushed it into his pocket and said harshly, as though his throat were full of blood, "There's no more time, Rita. I've got to talk to you now." He seized her by the shoulders and shook her. "Do you understand what I'm telling you? You've got to do what I say."

At the door he stopped her and turned her toward him again, searching for her face in the darkness, and then in a furious whisper he tried to rid himself of the weight that sank his soul. "You got us into this—now you've got to get us out."

It wasn't what he had meant to say, but as he sought her eyes in the dusk, she gave no sign of having heard him.

"Rita?"

There was no reply, and then terribly, she laughed.

"Come on," she whispered, digging her nails into his arm.

Twice he stopped on the stairs, lost in darkness, his eyes burning, the back of his neck needled with pain. Below him he could hear her breathing, then her urgent whispers, and finally her hand closed on his, guiding him blindly toward the door. Still something held him back, as though with one foot he were searching for the edge of a precipice, and then her hand, long-fingered, certain, pulled at him like a tide, and he followed her helplessly in a way that was beyond his willing. And there on the stairs he felt again more deeply than ever the eerie spell that lay upon him light as fog, impenetrable as a dream which he had known somewhere, sometime before, beyond the reach of memory.

At the door he lit a cigarette, then looked up through the trees to the brilliant, quivering silence of the stars. The night was redolent of wet grass, dust, honeysuckle, clear air; its coolness lay like dew upon his face. The hair at the back of his neck lifted a little and he shook himself, feeling his skin shudder ever so slightly. Then he followed the crunch of her shoes in the gravel until he could see the truck against the sky.

He lit a cigarette for her and put it in her mouth while she worked at the starter until the motor coughed and caught. Then as it idled her face turned toward him in the dusk, looking at him now as though she were no longer sure who he was.

"You know something?" she said, picking the tobacco from her lips with fingers that moved with the delicacy of pincers.

He shook his head, watching her profile cut through the soft blur of night as she bent to release the brake. The beam from the headlights swept across the chalky columns of the porch they had just left, grew gold and diffuse with slow-motion swirls of dust, then resumed an empty clarity as the truck moved through the alley.

"I want some drinking whiskey. I want a drink of whiskey like I haven't wanted one for a long time." She looked at him again, leaning toward him as though to find his eyes. "You put the son of a bitch in jail. You locked him up. Nobody ever did that to Clay before. We're going to drink to that."

"If you want to drink to that, you'll drink by yourself." He threw the words at her, then looked away.

"Don't get mean."

"Nobody's getting mean. I can't seem to make you understand—"

"Understand what?" The truck jarred to a halt, sliding a little on the gravel as the dust boiled up again through the lights. "We might as well straighten this out right here."

He looked at her hopelessly, then shook his head and rubbed

his hands hard against his knees. "Why can't you just once forget about us in all this? Why can't you wait until it's over, let me do what I have to do, help me by just leaving me alone, goddammit."

"That's what you said up there," and she motioned with her head toward the office. "You've got Clay in jail—now it's all different."

"No . . ."

"Don't talk to me like that. You'd like to forget all about it, wouldn't you? Tulsa, that day at the ranch, the nights whenever you had the guts—"

"Shut up, Rita."

"I told you don't talk to me—"

"Shut up." He seized her wrist and twisted it until he heard her catch her breath. Then nothing. Neither of them breathing, the motor shaking them gently as it idled, and then his hand relaxing its grip. "Rita. Rita. Why does it have to be this way?"

She pulled her hand away and shrank from him, seeming to grow smaller in the darkness until he saw only her eyes, cat's eyes luminous and glowing with some strange light that burned inside her.

"What is it you really want?" she said slowly. "What did you come here for? What is it you're after?"

He reached for her then, but she moved away from his hands. Then he clenched his fingers together and lowered his face, eyes closed, so that he seemed to be praying. "If you will just give me time. Don't make me say it now. Let me go through these next two days without saying it. Just two days—forget about what's happened between us. Forget about you and me in all this. Forget the things I said—all of them. Just two days."

"But that's why it happened. Isn't it."

It was not a question, and as her whisper fell to a hiss he sat in silence, something inside him broken, his hands opening and closing with the convulsive movement of a crushed snake. Between them the silence smoldered like a smothered fire until at last she started the truck forward again through shadows that lay deeper than night upon the road.

"I want some drinking whiskey," she said thickly. "All right, I'll drink alone. It won't be the first time. But there's one thing I can tell you, friend," and he winced as she ground the gears into low for the long descent into town. "There's no place left to hide. You're not fooling me and you can't fool yourself for very long. Just remember one thing—you better be careful what you want. Because you may get it. Maybe you haven't thought that far ahead."

The words no longer meant anything to him. It was simply sound, ugly, primitive, which sawed at his nerves like the scream of a dog run down in the road. He slumped in the seat, staring without recognition at the buildings which swam slowly through the light. He had been here for months, and he scarcely knew the place. Now it was no more than fragments of a ghostly landscape glimpsed briefly between cliffs of night.

She drove into the alley behind the drugstore and parked outside the cone of light that hung from the lone street lamp. She waited then, as though she expected him to say something, but his throat had closed upon a sob, and he did not move.

"All right," she said. The door closing behind her was a jangle of clashing tin, and then the light glanced from her hair and gleamed along the backs of her legs while the click of her heels carried her into silence.

Very slowly he brought his hands up to his face. He had to hold onto something. It seemed to him that he could feel time moving swiftly by him in the night, soft as wind, drawing him deeper into a dream he could not fathom. "She's got to sign— whatever else happens. I've got to make her sign and then go after Cody. Then Booth. All of it in Dickey's hands by Monday." He spoke between clenched teeth, his body chilled and trembling, and suddenly more than anything else he wanted to run without stopping all the way back to the small white house with the striped awnings and the cottonwood tree where Emily sat beside the bed of his sick son. "Oh God, what am I doing to them?" and the pain that rose from his chest pounded at his temples and burned again behind his eyelids. "Booth," he groaned, and then as though through a door that swung slowly open in a distant part of his mind he saw, dreamlike, far away and yet within his reach, an ethereal image of someone he had always wanted from before the time that he could remember, Rita in a smoky haze of flowers, virginal, her past destroyed, all the jungle of corruption that clung to her cleared and burned in a purifying holocaust. "She's got to wait—she's got to give me time," and then her image faded and he sat alone in the darkness, seeing the street light focus the night before his narrowed eyes.

He fumbled for a cigarette, then watched the smoke spread paler than light across the windshield. Not to turn loose—that was it, and he closed his hand into a fist and pounded it softly against his knee. Not to let the smell and feel and look of her shatter the carefully constructed scaffolding where the hangman waited. She had said them too, the very words that he had used with Cody. Or had he? . . . It seemed so long ago now, that talk with Cody in his office. How certain he must have appeared then. *There's no place left to hide.* So in control. *You're going to need help . . .* That was it. But there was no need to hide, damn it. *The thing is to remember. The Lord is my shepherd . . .* To tell it over and over like the beads of a rosary until it was all clear and strong and absolute again, so grooved into his mind by repetition that it could stand through centuries of disaster, like a hieroglyph on some Egyptian column half buried in the desert. Or perhaps . . . perhaps if he could just say once what it was that he wanted, name it just one time. *Be careful—you might get it.* She'd said something like that, too. *Maybe you haven't thought that far ahead.* But that wasn't it at all, because there was no space left with the past crowded up so tight against him. What he wanted lay back there somewhere. . . .

Then, of course, the letters. One every week, typed without carbons at night in the office. All through that lurid and violent spring into the stunned green silence of summer, June bugs battering the screen, his typewriter littered with tiny insects the color of new asparagus, crawling back toward the light that dropped them burning to the table. Letters he knew by heart, because they were part of him—his voice, his thoughts, a record

of his passage here, and more as well . . . the diary of a journey
that ever more obscurely turned in upon himself.

I HAVE BEEN DOING MY BEST *to keep you informed of my progress,
if one can call it that. So far I've gone very easy, sticking close to
the kind of routine jobs a Tribal Attorney would normally be
involved with. Not that anything is normal in Grey Horse, of
course. You know the place; you've seen it, anyway. I thought
I knew something about it before I came. One illusion less, at least.
No one would believe what goes on here. My time is pretty evenly
divided between the city jail, the hospital, the bank, the sheriff's
office, and the Agency. I get into my office when there's a breathing
spell. Violent crime is a commonplace. If I stayed here long enough,
I suppose I'd end up getting used to it the way doctors get used
to maimed and broken bodies. But I haven't been here long enough
yet for that.*

*Take the town's reaction to the Red Hawk killings. I've talked
to lots of different people about it by now. They don't mind talking
about it, the way they would talk about the weather, perhaps, but
nobody wants to go any further than that. I think they're relieved
to have the whole thing over and done with. Nobody has suggested
that the case ought to be reopened, and yet nobody ever comes
right out and says that Shoat was guilty. They say things like
"Old Shoat, yeah. He was a hell of a roper, Shoat was. Claim he
was mixed up in that there Red Hawk ruckus. Claim he was behind
it, some folks do. Oh, I don't know. Shoat was mean, but I never
figured him for that kind of mean. Killing mean, that is." They're
used to killing, and they were used to Shoat. So they laugh a little
and say how you never can tell about an Indian. It may be just
that I put them off. These people don't care much for outsiders,
especially Easterners, and more especially Easterners with the
federal government. They're friendly enough in the ordinary sort
of way, but it doesn't go much beyond that. You can see it in their
faces—mistrust certainly, maybe fear. Sometimes I think everybody is just plain scared to death.*

*Last week I took the opportunity to look up Nellie Sikes,
Orval's wife. Some chicanery over a car she had bought and paid
in part because that was the price quoted and then it was repos-
sessed. You know the trick. I could have called her in but I wanted
to talk to her alone, if possible, where she lives. She was Orval's*

wife, after all, and it is her family that was being systematically killed off. If anybody should have something to say, Nellie would be the one. Well, I went to see her. Tried to see her, that is. I never got past the gate. She's turned the place into a fortress. Walled in, with electrified barbed wire on the top. Floodlights on at night. Dogs inside, and an armed guard at the gate who wouldn't say a word, just took my message, delivered it, brought it back, no reply. I can tell you this much—Shoat Dalton may have been the man, but you'll have to prove it to Nellie Sikes. She's so terrified that she might as well be dead and have it over with.

. . . made a case for the prosecution. A good enough case, I think, as these things go. It set up all right on paper, when they talked it out among themselves. Then they brought it into court, and that's part of the story, too, because if they could have moved it to the district court, out of this incredible town, they might have won it all—and then Jack Bird (more on him later) started talking and by the time he was through there wasn't enough left to make it stick. Yet still enough to keep that jury (and I really ought to take it apart for you man by man, except once you start looking that deep, where does it take you) out for over fifty hours. But the prosecution's brief—you know the outlines of the case. They had four key witnesses to put on the stand—Stringer Burk, who was brought up from the state penitentiary at McAlester, his wife Mary Lee, whom Traynor and the other federal agents on the case had picked up in Shreveport, La., Dwayne Looney, also from the penitentiary, and finally Orval Sikes himself, old Shoat's nephew. That's quite a lot of testimony when you consider it—Burk an eyewitness to the killing of Ruth Pinto, Mary Lee corroborating the story right up to the point of the killing itself, Looney swearing that Dalton offered him money and a car to blow up the Gunn home in Choctaw, and Orval's signed statement implicating Shoat as the brains behind it all. They wanted Shoat more than anybody, and Orval next, and they were ready to make deals with the others to get the big boys. There were soft spots, of course; Burk stuck to his story that Orval killed Ruth Pinto, and Orval claimed the opposite. That gave Jack Bird room for maneuver, and he didn't need much. But more than that, it made Orval feel that he was being double-crossed, and that's why he turned around and disavowed the statement he had signed, saying that his signature had been

obtained under duress. If he had other reasons, I don't know them. Anyway, this was all Bird needed to build his defense. He charged torture and extortion by Traynor and his boys and accused the federal government of falling for a frame-up (he hinted at worse) in order to get the case off its books. He knew what he was doing— the very first decision with regard to venue had been rendered on that basis—local versus federal authority—in favor of local jurisdiction. From what I have heard about him, Jack Bird is not a man who has to be shown twice where the jugular vein is. I don't doubt that there was bungling—the case could have been better prepared and better argued. I think our people were overconfident —well, after all, they did have a case and some pretty strong testimony. Here is a piece, just a piece, of what Stringer Burk said on the stand:

"Well, Orval and me we picked up the girls and went on out to Cedar Canyon. We had plenty of whiskey. Orval said Shoat told him to leave whiskey around the place so it would kind of look like the rot gut poisoned her. Ruth, that is. There's an empty cabin out there. My wife Mary Lee Burk come with us. She was the one got Ruth to come. Told her there would be whiskey and fun and all. We sat in the car and drank and told jokes. I kept giving my wife these paper cups full of whiskey and she passed out. Shoat hadn't wanted her along anyway, but we had to get at Ruth some way or other. So Shoat told me to shut her up—fix it so she didn't know nothing, or he would do it himself. Soon as she had passed out me and Orval carried Ruth, kind of drug her like, into the cabin. We had already talked it over, about killing her and all. Orval was supposed to do that job. We set her on a chair and I held her up by the shoulders to where Orval could get his hands real good around her windpipe. He just kept on squeezing and I told him to go easy. I didn't see why he had to go and break her neck. Wasn't nobody paying us to do that. Shoat had said that he wanted the body found in a few days before it had started to fall apart so they would know who it was and it would look more or less like whiskey. Wasn't any need to leave her neck all messed up. I told Orval to ease off. Probably I should have stopped him. He wouldn't though. Orval's like that, I never did think he'd turn loose."

That's from the newspaper coverage of the trial, and there's a lot more like that, and worse. No wonder they thought they had the thing won. But they didn't figure on Jack Bird and around here that's a mistake you don't make twice. Worse, they didn't take the town into account, and that's a mistake they shouldn't have made even once. They thought it was like any other town—neat lawns and sprinklers and elm trees full of locusts in the summer, a country club and a dozen or more churches, square dancing, pie suppers, put your heart in America or get your ass out. Grey Horse has all that, but something more. You want to know what it is? I'm not sure I'd want to tell you even if I knew. I don't have that kind of mind. I don't even like to think about it. Maybe it's because of the Chetopa, the way they were once, and then all the money. But whatever it is you can smell it in the air, and it doesn't smell like oil. It smells like blood, if you'll forgive a flight of fancy. The whole place smells like a rendering factory. To me, anyway. I tell you that jury sat through days of the kind of thing I've just quoted—I don't imagine they took much more than a kind of professional interest in it. "More dead Chetopas. How did it happen this time? Strangling? Uh-huh. Dynamite? Say, that don't happen every day." Why would they turn them loose otherwise? You read the testimony and you'll say the same. Either that jury was convinced that Shoat and Orval were not the guilty parties, or they were all just so damned deeply involved in it in some way or other that they couldn't find it in their hearts to put the blame on any single individual among them. If I were sufficiently cynical, I'd say that at least you couldn't accuse them of hypocrisy. . . .

Of course they are nothing more than names to you. And I can't begin to do them justice. Shoat Dalton. He's been around here for a long time. Rancher. Married a Chetopa girl and got his start that way. Squaw man, they call them here. Apparently a roper of some fame. Traveled with rodeo shows, even got as far as Europe from what I can find out. Old Shoat standing up there on his hind legs right in front of that there King. That's how they say it here. Flamboyant, Old West, boots, black hat, guns, the whole outfit. Reputation of a killer. Always in self-defense, according to court records, and if you believe them. Small, and wiry, and tough—the last of the range riders. But it's been a long time since he rode any ranges. Free with his money. He was popular, all right. His funeral was one of the biggest they ever had around here, but what it means, I couldn't tell you. I mentioned his name to Blair and Carter

*the first night I was here—they have no use for him. A good
suspect, in short, which must have been the way Traynor felt about
him. The right kind of man to build your case around, or pin it on,
or frame up, depending on who you are and what you want. He'd
done everything a man could do except get caught. Including holding the premium on an insurance policy worth twenty-five thousand
dollars when Frank Red Hawk was shot to death in a pasture north
of here a few years back. Why didn't they ever pin that one on
him?*

*Then there's Orval. Orval Sikes, his nephew. Big where
Shoat was little, weak where Shoat was strong. Nobody ever talks
about him without mentioning Shoat at the same time. His own
role, before he turned around and denied everything he'd said, was
that of a go-between. That would just about describe it, I think.
He was Shoat's handy man. Looked after the ranch when Shoat
was traveling, did Shoat's dirty work for him when it came to
collecting debts or picking a fight for laughs. The kind of hearty,
heavy-drinking, big-bellied cowman you see in this town who'll
shake hands on a five-thousand-dollar loan and gun you down in a
barroom quarrel. A crazy mixture of generosity and meanness—
barbarism if you want to call it that. I don't pretend to understand
them, and they certainly don't understand me. But then they don't
interest me, either. If I knew them better, perhaps—but not Shoat,
or Orval either. Criminals dressed up like cowboys as far as I'm
concerned.*

*Now Jack Bird is something different. Remember I know Shoat
and Orval only from hearsay. Jack Bird I've seen several times,
talked with him casually once or twice. The thing that makes Bird
different is that he's shrewd, very shrewd indeed. You say you
never met him. He's the best-known criminal lawyer in this part
of the country. Southern, stocky, slow-moving, slow-talking, very
fast-thinking. Probably a remarkable poker player. Reputedly rich,
mostly from the market. Lives alone in the State Hotel, divides his
time between the hotel, his office, the bank, the hotel coffee shop,
and the courtroom. Not so very different from your Tribal Attorney, and why not. He's just holding the other end of the stick. And
yet in some way I can't yet explain, Bird strikes me as an outsider.
I haven't really talked with him in any serious way, but I will. At
any rate, he gave us bloody hell in the trial. His line was simple—
federal versus local authority, Shoat and Orval victims of a*

frame-up, hints of some kind of a cover-up by someone, for some-one. He never made it clear. He took Shoat and Orval into that trial like a couple of desperadoes and brought them out as the men who won the West. I don't mean that he's the Darrow type. Just comfortable, one of them, talking to that jury low and easy until you'd think they were sitting around a campfire somewhere. I imagine it that way from the one time I've seen him in action and from what people say about him. I don't know where he learned his law, or how much of it he knows, but given the tools he's got, he's a tough man to handle. The only part I just don't grasp at all is the distance he keeps. He's a lonely man. If he didn't work so hard I'd be tempted to believe that he just didn't give a damn. Well, maybe it's the money. He wouldn't be the only one. And then those prosecution witnesses were made to order for Jack. A whore, two inmates of the state penitentiary, a switched plea charging Traynor and the others with extorting a confession practically at gunpoint. If that jury wanted a way out, Jack was the man to show the way. That's the kind of thing he understands.

. . . work your way through all the records, the newspaper stories, the hearsay, the barroom gossip, lawyers' shop talk and all the rest, and you're convinced that however it went in court, there wasn't much doubt about Shoat and Orval being mixed up in the thing somewhere, even if the federal case got a couple of pieces upside down or backwards. You get to the end pretty well con-vinced, and then you run up against something that sends you back over the whole thing again. I mean the way they died, Shoat and Orval, alone, the two of them, in Shoat's Cadillac. On a road that had one curve in fifteen miles of driving. Flat. Straight. And they had to pick that curve to finish themselves off, after all the years of fighting, fists and guns, the rotten whiskey, pneumonia from nights in the rain, not to mention the probable incidence of vene-real disease and God knows what else. They were drunk, I suppose. At least there was whiskey in the car. And there was nothing or nobody on the road that anybody knows of, except the tracks of a car that had swerved alongside the Cadillac in a way that could have forced them off the road. Somebody must have seen them crack up because the car tracks were there, but nobody reported the crash. Not until late afternoon of the same day when a rancher driving back from town found the car on the other side of the

ditch, sitting on its top, glass and blood and whiskey and upholstery all over the place. Maybe it was an accident, but I'm not much of a believer in accidents. At any rate not with people like Shoat and Orval whose lives are so crowded that there just doesn't seem to be any room left over for chance. And then those car tracks swerving across the road so that you would swear that Shoat had been forced into the ditch. Driving fast, half drunk—he would have needed all his luck to get out alive, and he wasn't a man who hoarded his luck. And if it wasn't an accident . . . well, that makes Bird's case look pretty good. Because looking at it that way, you would have to say that when the frame-up didn't work, whoever was doing the framing would be more anxious than ever to get Shoat out of the picture. Which would also lead you to think a little more about who did the framing, and who was being covered up by the federal people, if what Jack said was true. Which, if you're strictly logical about it (which means letting logic be just as nasty as it has a tendency to be) leads all the way up to you, doesn't it? Through Booth, I mean, because who else would there be to cover? Except that Booth isn't that kind of man, and nobody has the slightest idea of who would have forced Shoat off that road or why, and everybody is damn well ready to let Shoat and Orval and all those Red Hawks stay quiet in their graves and be done with it. Unless a Congressman, or some of his constituents, who never have liked the way you kept them in a neutral corner when they had the Chetopa all set up for the kill . . .

You asked about Booth. All right. But what is there that I can tell you about the man that you don't know already. How is he looked upon in Grey Horse? His relationship to the people who run things here? The tribe? Where he fits into all this? Of course, if I could answer your questions we would be a lot closer to the truth about everything than we are at present. But let me concentrate on just one aspect of what we're faced with. Blair Booth and Carter. Especially Carter. Rancher, but much, much more. He seems to own a large part of this town. Whatever it is, he is, for good or for evil. Quite a man, Clay Carter. A kind of mountain peak in these flatlands, mainly hidden by clouds. Mysterious is not the word, but no one really seems to know *a great deal about him—where he came from, what he did before—that kind of thing. I'm trying to find out now. At this stage, everything helps. But Blair seems*

*almost obligated to him, treats him with a remarkable kind of—
well, deference, damn it. Of course they're married to sisters, both
Red Hawk girls. But Blair goes out of his way to be considerate
of him. As though he owed him something, to put it frankly; as
though he owed him a lot. It would be pretty close to the truth
to say that Carter runs Grey Horse. Now I don't mean the Agency
when I say that, because I have never considered Grey Horse and
the Agency to be the same thing. If Blair ran the Agency the way
Carter runs the town, then all right. But it just doesn't feel that
way. However, feeling isn't proof, and I don't have any proof,
other than the fact that even a casual inspection of the financial
records shows that a remarkable amount of Chetopa expenditure is
funneled through Carter. That could be accidental; Carter does
own half the town. Well, you'd have to see them together. The
sense of complicity between them. And especially given the difference in the men. Blair is a man of breeding, background, a certain
culture; Carter is a man who has come from nothing and it shows.
But that may tell us no more than something about the kind of
concessions a man of Booth's character has had to make in his long
years here. I wouldn't want to have to judge that, especially on the
basis of what little I know. And it certainly doesn't explain who
framed Dalton (if that's indeed what happened) and why whoever
did it would want it that way. We're looking for a very devious,
very sinister, and absolutely diabolical man, if that's what it is.
Somebody who could undertake this wholesale carnage, then find
a way to make Dalton hang for it. Booth isn't up to that. Is Carter?
Complicity. I don't know how else to put it. One last thing. There
is a story to the effect that Dalton tried to break Clay Carter years
ago. It started with a quarrel over stolen cattle. There was some
shooting. Shoat had his wrist broken by a man named Cody, some
sort of crazy gunfighter who hangs around Carter's ranch as a
kind of foreman. Just that, and no more. Except the man who told
it to me was letting me know that Shoat Dalton was a man powerful enough to have enemies on that scale, enemies powerful enough
to find ways of getting rid of him if it came to that. . . .*

*But I suppose what it all adds up to is that I've begun to think
that you can turn this thing upside down. Suppose—just suppose—
that Bird was right and that Shoat Dalton wasn't the man. That
leads us back to what Bird kept hinting at throughout the trial,*

some kind of federal frame-up. But that's out, for reasons I don't even need to enumerate. Logically, this leaves us with an individual, one or more, who in fact stood to gain from the progressive killing off of the Red Hawk family and who would be ready to cover himself by framing Shoat. I'm referring here to Blair and Carter. You know Blair better than I do, so I don't really need to go into that. I mean that Blair, whatever his faults, is not a man for murder. I think he's let things get out of hand here, has gone soft, in fact, so that there is corruption everywhere. Money is not properly accounted for, records are not kept up to date, mistakes, perhaps fraud, are glossed over, proper discipline within the Agency is not observed, not to mention certain special arrangements of a financial nature which I believe to exist between Blair and Carter. No, Commissioner, Blair Booth is not my kind of man, and in the long run I think you would do well to be rid of him before a major scandal develops. But that is quite a different thing from cold-bloodedly murdering his wife's family in order to amass a considerable fortune for himself. Then there's Carter. Frankly, Carter is a man from whom nothing would surprise me except to learn that he was generous, decent, upright, and moderately disinterested. I don't know how to explain it—something in the way men came together out here, a kind of horizontal organization of society where power is so nakedly a matter of guns and money, where the men who rule are people without the slightest pretensions to breeding or background. As though everything out here began yesterday, which in fact it did, I suppose. So much for the old eternal dream of casting off tradition and starting all over without the inherited taint and corruption of society. The result is men like Carter—self-made with all the brutal connotations of the term. That Carter would want the money and be ready to do anything to get it is self-evident. That he would be ready to frame Shoat in order to clear himself and get Shoat out of the way is also self-evident. But if you carry this thing one step further, you can imagine Shoat in on the deal, one of Carter's tools, persuaded by Carter to go along with the frame on the promise that he would be let off. I think Carter handles this town like a chess set, and that bribing juries or anything else in that line is for him routine. Then Shoat, having been pinned with the accusation and freed, would in Carter's eyes become expendable because he knew too much and because Shoat dead would carry the responsibility for the killings with him into his grave. All this is probably too elaborate. But there is a certain mystery about Carter, his origins, the way he's come to run this town, which makes me believe him capable of anything at all, no matter how treacherous, no matter how foul. And yet his wife is something else again, and this may be the place to drive the wedge. Rita Red Hawk. The coincidence is that I almost saw her dance in Paris years ago. I remember seeing her name on posters along the boulevards. It fascinated me at the time. She's an intelligent, civilized woman, who has experienced life at a level beyond anything Carter can imagine. That's part of the mystery, too. I mean how she ever got involved with a man like Carter. I want to get to know her better. If she would have confidence in me, talk . . .

. . . that we should just go along with the town and forget about it, let the dead stay buried, close the books, write it off, and hope nobody ever gets interested again. I feel that way when I'm tired of rummaging through the records and listening to the simpleminded drawl of some lawyer or rancher to whom I've been talking about the case, when I'm thoroughly fed up with this ignoble little conglomeration of people who have turned a beautiful and historic valley into a septic tank. And then I remember who the Chetopa were and measure them against the parasitic filth which has fastened itself upon them. No, there's no way to let the dead stay buried. Somehow we've got to cut and scrape and burn the malignancy out of this place if the Chetopa are ever going to walk erect again. And something else you must never forget—Jack Bird built his case on a federal cover-up and won it. Which leaves Booth on the spot, and don't think for a moment that there's not talk. When are the Congressmen from these parts going to start talking loud enough for the press to hear, and how long will it be before somebody lays Shoat Dalton's body in front of your door, because you wanted to cover Booth and thus yourself. I'm only trying to tell you where I think it could go. Let's have no illusions at all about it— there are many people here, most, in fact, who want an absolutely free hand to deal with the Indians any damn way they please. It's a free country, ain't it? And Grey Horse is a long, long way from anyplace, especially Washington. And frankly speaking, Booth just isn't the man to make anybody feel that Washington counts for a

hell of a lot around here. The point is simply this: there is some-
thing evil and monstrous going on which nobody has the
courage to face. There is something standing in the shadows, not
only of the Red Hawk case and Dalton's death but of the very
town itself. That's the man we have to get our hands on if we're
ever to stop the rot here. And if we don't . . . But we're not without
hope. There is someone who can help us. I've told you about her
before. It may seem to you that I'm playing with fire. You've
simply got to trust me from here on in. . . .

And yet so much that there had been no way to tell because it
was another life, some of it old, some new, all of it as seemingly
inevitable as the slow revolution of nights and days.

The house that Emily found, white, one-story, a roof with red
tiling, a small concrete porch in front supported by two columns.
Between the porch and the street, on a dying lawn where sprinklers whirred, two catalpa trees which produced long green pods
that curled and turned black in the withering light. Along the
driveway a cottonwood tree among whose drifting haze of
branches Amory climbed and nailed boards together to make a
kind of raft in that pale sea. Red roses climbed the sagging backyard fence, and hollyhocks hid the garbage cans at the edge of the
alley. In a corner was an elm where an oriole built its long brown
pocket of a nest, and a sandbox where lead soldiers lay face down,
and then a swing with green-and-white-striped cushions that
looked out upon Amory's miniature jungle in the neighboring
vacant lot. A small white garage upon whose roof mulberries
rotted; the shaded, screened-in back porch where Emily slept
through the breathless afternoons. Catbirds mewing in the empty
hours of eventless days; mockingbirds sardonic all night long.

As much a home as he could ever have in this desolation of
sun and wind and dust, until her face, slowly taking shape in the
dark room of his mind, superimposing itself ever more power-
fully, ended by bleaching into blankness these images of his life.
Days of blue and brass when they met in the windy streets and
she held her hair and fluttered her eyelashes against the light.
Saying hello, merely nodding, a movement of the hand in the

coffee shop amid the low voices of cattlemen becalmed by winter, drowsing, reminiscent. Her smile a flash of white on bronze, her mouth describing arcs of happiness and wonder, her lower lip caught suddenly in her teeth, then moving radiantly across her face, laughing at nothing. A grace too fluid for her body to translate, as quick, as elusive, as delicate, as awkward as some exotic animal. And yet, until her smile effaced them, the lines like inked grooves in the copper plate of her face, the dark hollows around her eyes, the yellow smudge of nicotine along her fingers. A face that was always on the wing, like a game bird in autumn.

And through the days that fell and disappeared like windblown leaves he came and went from the little house on the hill as though it were now merely some kind of boarding house where he kept his suitcase and took his meals—his thoughts remote, his mind fumbling endlessly with the pieces of a puzzle which he could not put together, her laughter warming him through the winter like a fire until finally days without her were the color of slate, days when no birds sang, when the wind haunted the empty streets like a ghost, and life ran dry.

Then at last a day in early spring when they had met by chance on the county road north of town. They rolled their windows down and reached across the emptiness and smiled as their hands touched. The bluestem grass was bent beneath the breeze, and meadowlarks whistled from the fence posts. Across the flawless bay of sky great flat-bottomed clouds sailed pompously.

"Wonderful," she said. "And you." Her hand was in her hair, holding it from her eyes, and her long full lips were curved like a bow upon her face. Her skin seemed darker now against a lemon-yellow blouse, yet everything about her was somehow so familiar that he might have known her forever.

"Yes."

"You've never seen the ranch. It's just down the road. Come on."

Then she was gone before he could answer and he laughed, turning around and driving fast after her through coils of dust until she turned off the road and bounced across the cattle guard and then stopped in a grove of blackjack trees. And almost immediately he was aware of it, tiny sounds that wove the fabric of a silence he could almost touch. Blackjack leaves rattled above him, and standing beside him she looked into his face as he stood listening, then quite simply took his hand in hers. They pushed through the bronze-green grass as though it were the sea, looking at each other, not wanting to talk. Larks jumped and flew before them, trailing their wings like broken fans. Butterflies hung suspended at their knees, and crows all in black flapped in slow motion across the clouds. The earth hummed, the wind whipped their hair, and the blaze of sun on grass burned to the horizon. He did not hear her when she spoke; all of his senses seemed concentrated in his eyes, seeing everything at once, as though motion continued but time had stopped, a sudden fusion of the rhythms of her body, the subtleties of her face, the undulation of earth and grass and cloud through which she moved. Then on through waves of grass until they stood beneath trees again on a high point of land and saw the two pale ribbons of road that stretched like softly penciled parallel lines across the prairie to the house. She moved her arm in a sweeping motion before her, telling him something, and he watched her, not looking where she pointed, until she stopped and looked at him, then closed her eyes and a tiny sound came from her throat. Then her eyes opened wide and her mouth bubbled with laughter and she turned from him, running now, both of them knee high in grass with birds and grasshoppers and butterflies exploding around them in the silent air until he caught her and held her in his arms. He stood clumsily upon the uneven ground, pressed against her body, her mouth open beneath his, and then he rubbed his face against her cheek until the skin stung where their tears ran together.

"You don't even know who I am," he said, in a voice he scarcely recognized.

"I don't care," she said, throwing her head back to look at him, sobbing and laughing all at once, until he pulled her face again against his shoulder and smelled the springtime in her hair.

"I've always known who you were," her mouth wet against his shirt. "I don't care."

A small, one-story white house with green-and-white-striped awnings, a cottonwood, two catalpas, and an elm, a driveway where Amory scraped roads in the gravel for his toy cars while Emily dug around the roses and watered the lawn and waited. He could feel her waiting and he stayed away, leaving before she was up and returning late. But no matter how late it was he would find her reading in the living room, dressed as though they might be going out, the powder caked pale as dust upon her face, somber shadows in the hollows of her eyes, rising to greet him at the door, then going to fix a drink for him and to refill her glass. And after he put his papers away he would go to his son's bedroom and stand above that small flushed face that was always hot to the touch, and then he would bend down and brush the silken hair away and kiss him in the little hollow where the cheekbone met the ear. Often he would stand there listening, frowning against the tears that burned his eyes, wondering what it was that pulled so painfully at his memory, until he heard Emily in the living room again. She would tell him about the roses, the tree house in the cottonwood, the walk that she and Amory had taken to the woods above the town, and in the silence he listened to the laughter of the mockingbird. Then she waited, and he avoided her eyes, and filled the silence by cursing the town, its people, the frenzied corruption, saying more than he felt, surprised himself at the ugly violence of his words. At such moments it seemed almost that he spoke to himself, using whatever lay at hand to disguise feelings that were beyond his comprehension, beyond his control. And at these moments it was as though she were someone whom he had once known but forgotten, as though some obscure purpose had been served once he had married her, as though now that Amory was there she was no longer needed. And so he waited, too, for a stray word, a clue, any sort of indication that would point the trail into those shadows where he knew they had to go; waiting, too, while some part of himself of which he had known nothing reached up from the darkness toward the light.

And then in the sudden space of a night and a day, no more than a moment, really (had he read of it somewhere, perhaps in that curious library of his childhood wherein it was told of saints and whales and harpooners of men's souls and those terrible moments of glory when God's glance came down like lightning, transfiguring him upon whom He looked), life rearranged itself around him as though by an accidental turn of a kaleidoscope, the fragments of his years instantaneously come together in a sudden pattern of such stunning clarity that he could scarcely breathe. A country club dance, the dew-drenched fairway gleaming ash-grey beyond the perimeter of light, the waters of the pool slapping softly at the side, streaked with the reflected rainbow of colored lights. Ice and laughter tinkled through the rustle of gowns, feet scraped against the music of saxophones, men perspired and looked for whiskey, pushing fingers beneath their collars, while the women sat in straight-backed chairs along the dance floor, talking about each other. Carter had asked Emily to dance, and Andrews moved through the crowd to the bar, wondering irritably when Rita would arrive. This was the night she gave ballet lessons to a group of girls in Indian Camp and she had said that she would be a little late. He looked at his watch, then half turned to get his drink, and found himself looking directly into the dour, tortoise-featured face of Jack Bird.

"Evening, Thayer."

There was a curiously haggard quality about Bird's face seen close up. His bloodshot eyes protruded, the corners of his mouth turned down, the surface of his skin was crossed by a series of arroyos that might have been cut by tears. Armored in bleakness, he stayed apart, drinking steadily, looking at the crowd without expression, raising his hand now and then to return a greeting.

"Good evening. Mind if I push in beside you? This bar's a little crowded."

"Come ahead," and he edged his bar stool further into the corner.

"Nice night."

Bird nodded, saying nothing.

"A little hot."

Bird looked at him. "Yeah. Say, tell me something. You went

to Harvard, didn't you? Somebody told me you were a Harvard lawyer."

"That's right. Why do you ask?"

"Oh, just that you're a lucky man, Mr. Thayer. That's all. I've known one or two Harvard lawyers in my time."

"Well, I don't know," Andrews laughed. "There aren't many Harvard lawyers around who know as much law as you do."

Bird pursed his lips, then sipped at his drink. His eyes might have been laughing; his face did not change. "What I mean to say, Thayer, is that people of that kind—your kind—have got the law what you might call bred right into them. It's part of something you grow up with. Law out here tends to be something a man has got to work out for himself—sort of home-grown, if you see what I mean. A lot of the time it's not even what you would call law, strictly speaking. We've got lots of lawyers around here, Thayer, but you may have noticed that we haven't got just a hell of a lot of law."

He offered Bird a cigarette, then lit his own. "You turned on quite a bit of law in that Dalton case, at any rate."

The wrinkles gathered around Bird's eyes as though the memory of it pained him. His face had changed, but his eyes were very still. "You interested in the Dalton case, Thayer?"

"Everybody was interested in the Dalton case. I've read the newspaper accounts, some of the court records. You put up a powerful defense."

"Well, that's what they paid me for," his voice suddenly weighted with something between sorrow and contempt.

"That couldn't have been an easy case for you."

Then he felt a tug at his sleeve, and when he turned he saw her eyes mocking him, her lips half-parted in a secret kind of smile.

"Come on," as though there were no one else to hear them, as though it wouldn't matter anyway.

He felt Jack's eyes upon him and he tried to warn her by the stiffness in his face. "Rita. Late as usual. Let me get you a drink. There's not an inch of space here."

She stood there just as she had come, holding her ballet slippers by the ribbons, her hair swept back so that the light slid along her cheekbones. She was flushed, and he wondered how much she had drunk in the car before coming in.

"One, and then we'll go," she whispered as he handed her the drink.

Then he turned back to Jack. "Looked to me like they had Shoat pretty much in a corner," smiling as casually as he could, wondering how much Jack had seen.

Bird lifted his eyebrows and spun the ice in his glass. "I suppose my kind of law is a good deal more like politics," he drawled. "I mean you got to know what kind of people you're talking to—what they're afraid of, maybe, who they vote for, what church they go to. What they want out of life."

"You mean you couldn't have talked over that Dalton jury with straight points of law."

"No," Bird said slowly. "That's not what I said. I said that sometimes it's worth more to you to know who you're talking to than to know your straight points of law. Even for a Harvard lawyer."

"Come on," she said again in a whisper he felt sure that Jack could hear. Her face seemed to have gone dark and she was breathing quickly and he could see the beads of perspiration now just where her nostrils flared.

He laughed and handed her another drink, moving so that his shoulder blocked her from Jack's view.

"At any rate you won your case. But one thing still puzzles me about the whole affair. I mean the way Dalton and his nephew were killed."

"You mean the way they died," Jack said quickly.

"All right. The way they died."

Bird was silent for a moment, then he looked down and flicked at his pants leg as though to brush away something that clung to him like lint. "I'll stick by what I said at the trial," he said impassively. "Shoat Dalton was framed." He seemed to look over Andrews's shoulder then, to see if Rita were listening. "Whoever framed him wanted him out of the way, one way or another. When the jury let him go, Shoat was a marked man. Nobody was paying me to be his bodyguard."

"Who around here would be big enough for that?" He had put his glass down and was looking directly into Bird's face as though searching in that map of the man's life for the road he had to find.

"We've got some pretty big men around here, Mr. Thayer. Surprised you haven't learned that already. I reckon you will, sooner or later." He stubbed his cigarette and turned to the bartender, holding out his empty glass.

"Aren't you through yet?" She dug her nails into his hand so that he winced and turned toward her.

"Have you gone out of your mind?"—indicating Bird with a movement of his head.

"I'll be in the parking lot." She put the glass in his hand. "One more for the road."

"You're drunk."

She took the glass he gave her and slipped through the crowd around the bar, her slim body half-turned as she held the glass behind her to protect it, her upswept hair bobbing above the slender curve of her neck.

He turned back to Bird, but Jack was now talking to someone else, and Andrews knew that whatever hope he had of learning something from Jack was gone, at least for tonight. He had no occasion to see Bird, and talking in an office was not the same thing. To have been so close, just to hear the way he talked and to look into his face . . . Why did she have to be so damned careless.

He set his jaw hard and pushed his way to the door which led to the parking lot. She was there in the shadows, looking at the pool, one arm across her breast, the slippers hanging at her side, and in her other hand the glass, which she held pensively to her lips.

"Goddammit, can't you ever wait for just a minute?"

She looked around as though he might be speaking to someone else.

"Couldn't you see that I was talking to Bird? And don't you think he could hear you?"

She turned then very slowly and faced him. "I don't care what Jack Bird knows, thinks, imagines, sees—he doesn't exist as far as I'm concerned, hear? And why should it matter so much? Are you ashamed of something, Mr. Thayer?"

"Rita, don't be stupid. We can't spread this thing all over town."

"Why not?"

"Give me that glass."

"You're afraid I'm drunk. It's all right when we're ten miles out of town, but let a nasty little man like Jack Bird—"

"Give me that drink, Rita—"

The glass burst around them like fragments of a shattered star. He looked down at the concrete and saw the jagged stain where the whiskey had spilled.

"You don't want anybody to know. You want to hide it in a corner. You want me to shut up and stay out of sight and live off the crumbs. And then you tell me you were talking to Jack Bird." Her voice caught in her throat and when he reached for her she hammered at him with her wrists.

"It's important to me," he said to her under his breath, "whether it matters to you or not. My God, don't ruin everything this way. Stop, Rita. Stop it," and he saw her teeth and her tears in the olive light as she swung the slippers at his face. Then he hit her.

She did not move for a moment, her head still back where she had jerked away from him, one hand still raised, the nails curved inward like a claw.

He had drawn his hand back and pressed it to his mouth, swallowing hard as though he would be sick, and then slowly, almost abstractedly, she knelt and pulled the slippers on, and when she stood erect again her face was bloodless, blank, perfectly composed save for the tears that fell silently from her cheeks. Then her arms moved lightly above her head, and she floated across the lawn toward the pool, her hands swaying ever so slightly like flowers in the wind.

He watched her, disbelieving, powerless to move until she was in the water, the slow wet stain modeling the dress to her body, and suddenly she seemed to crumple and fall so that she lay for a moment like a lily upon the surface of the water while the reflection of the colored lights rippled across the darkness of her hair.

Then he was running, calling her name, struggling through the water until he had her in his arms. Her hair clung close to her skull, and her arms trailed in the pool like broken stems as he waded back through the shallow water, holding her cradled against him, hearing suddenly the absence of sound and looking then to where they stood in the moonlight, watching him.

"Bring her in here." The voice was hard and peremptory. It was Carter, making way for him through the crowd, indicating a couch in a small room just off the dance floor.

Emily stood at the door, her fingers touching her temple, her mouth partly open, her eyes upon him sightlessly. He stopped a moment before her, then pushed on past and knelt to lay Rita on the couch, the water running from her hair like tears.

Clay rubbed her lips with whiskey, then moved the bottle back and forth beneath her nose until she opened her eyes wide, then narrowed them again.

She mumbled something: "Why . . . wait . . . too long," words he could scarcely hear.

Then she closed her eyes and he rose, looking around him at the faces that stared at her. He left the room, looking for Emily, feeling as though he had abruptly awakened from a nightmare, and then at the far end of the dance floor he saw a door close behind the flutter of her dress. He walked quickly after her, his arm before him as though he would reach out and catch her, and then as he went by the bar he stopped. Jack Bird was still sitting there, holding out a glass.

He took it neat, and then looked down at his wet clothes, the shoes which sloshed when he moved, the water forming in little pools there on the floor of the bar.

"Your wife went out through there," Bird said, looking down into his glass. "I'd go easy if I were you."

"Meaning what?" he said thickly.

"Nothing," Bird said. "Nothing at all." Then he got down from the bar stool and walked slowly toward the crowd that still stood in silence, staring at Rita Carter.

Emily was in the car, and she looked away from him when he began to explain.

"Tell me some other time," she said, her voice small and distant. "I don't want to hear about it now. I don't want to hear anything you've got to say just now . . ."

When he arrived at his office the next day it was already mid-morning. She was sitting there, her face swollen, the color of a bruised peach.

"My God, Rita," he said, closing the door softly behind him.

"Your secretary let me in. Clay wants to kill me."

"Your face," he said, his voice scarcely more than a whisper. "What did he do to you?"

"I don't mean that," and she clipped her words as though it hurt her to move her mouth.

He lit a cigarette for her, unable to stop the trembling of his hand, sick with shame and desire and overwhelming weakness when he looked at her.

"What did you come out here for, anyway?"

"Rita, don't talk that way. Why? Why did you do that last night?"

"Either you want to know or you don't. If you're afraid to listen, say so and I'll go."

He put his hands on her shoulders. "Don't talk that way to me. There's no need for it. You know how I feel. Didn't I show it last night?"

She stood up then and moved against him and put her head on his shoulder, and he touched her face where the skin was blue and broken.

"I'm afraid." She lifted her face to him. "Do I have to tell you why? Don't you know by now? He wants to kill me." Her arms were tight around him and her mouth was against his neck, blurring her words. "I thought you were different. The day I saw you get off that train I knew somehow that God had sent me someone

—that you had come here for me. I've lived with it all these years—couldn't even tell the priest. I'm trying to save my life. Can't you understand?"

"Maybe I understand." He was afraid to say more, seeing the wildness in her eyes, knowing the madness that could sweep across her like a prairie fire. He wanted so terribly to hear it all, and yet now he was suddenly afraid of where it might lead. He felt that he was on the verge of finding what he had been searching for, waiting for all these months, and yet why should it come so easy? Clay Carter's wife walking into his office in the Agency Building on a June morning with the fans creaking in the heat and the powder on his secretary's face already beginning to look like a contour map and the occasional distant explosion of Blair Booth's laughter from his office at the far end of the hall. A morning like a hundred others with the sun like a copper shield nailed to the sky and the shadows running thin toward noon and the sounds of the typewriters and the adding machines and the filing cabinets becoming tiny and differentiated and fixed like flies in amber. The kind of morning when Booth would amble down the hall, his face florid and massive above the floppy white linen of his suit and the hard collar that cut his neck like a vise, trailing cigar smoke that lingered like an oil slick on a becalmed sea, washing some early suppliant to the door on a wave of good fellowship, followed by the heavy padding of his feet back up the hall to Andrews's office.

"Can you imagine the proposition the bastard put to me?" he would say, mopping his face, his heavy grey hair glistening with brilliantine. "Twenty per cent on cost for every Chetopa buried through his funeral parlor," or again, wearily, after going through the morning mail: "More bullshit from Washington. Can't you find some legal trick to take them off our backs on these things? Look, I'm the Resident Agent here, you're the Tribal Attorney, this is Grey Horse, Oklahoma; we're an outpost in enemy territory, surrounded," roaring, sweeping his hand toward the town, "not a goddam mission school in the middle of some poor-ass desert reservation."

But not Clay Carter's wife, here in the office, talking about murder.

"Was it about Booth?" she asked suddenly, not looking at him now but turned toward the door so that he saw her profile stamped against the blackness of the wall. "Is that why they sent you? Were they worried about him—back there?" tossing her hair and then looking at him again. "You haven't forgotten that Mary Rose is my sister," and her words seemed to echo in the silence of the room.

He stood studying her, not moving. He had to get her out of here, now. Right now. If anyone should hear them . . .

"You have a right to come here and see me on business," he said coldly, "though today was not particularly well chosen. You are not to come here for anything else," slowly, spacing the words, emphasizing them one by one. "If you are here on business, you have stayed long enough. There is no need for me to tell you anything about small towns."

And even before he had finished she was pushing herself free of him, moving toward the door with an easy grace made insolent by fury. Then she turned and smiled stiffly, her eyes reckless and scornful. "You're not any different. Last night I got the crazy idea you were a man. Today you turn out to be a nasty little boy scout. I should have known from the way Booth and Clay salted you down that first day that you wouldn't cause any trouble. Well, good hunting, Mr. Thayer. There may be a concession or two still left. A man with your legal training should be able to work out some kind of a deal. Help yourself."

He winced as the door slammed, then went to the window and watched the pickup leave the Agency lot. It was a risk he had to take; one more at this stage wouldn't matter. With her, anger came on like rain in summer and blew itself out just as fast. He could call her at the end of the day; she would probably be waiting for him. But suppose she weren't telling the truth. She had it in for Carter, for last night and many other nights. She wanted to hurt him, perhaps destroy him if she could. Yet it could be that she had something real to hurt him with. Six months of trails that led nowhere, of clues that wouldn't match, with corruption and guilt hanging heavy as smoke in the air and yet no trace of fire. And now, right in the middle of a June morning . . . She asked about Booth, he said to himself. Carter's the gunman, but it's Booth's show. He could have wept with joy.

So the pieces had rushed together to form an entirely new pattern, as though a magnetic pole had moved and changed its orbit of attraction. And then came weeks of meeting alone, hiding, finding excuses, waiting for each other in the lonely places of a world suddenly reduced to just the two of them—the pickup parked on a deserted road, the golf course after dark beneath a night sky powdery with stars, a First Street hotel room in Tulsa with cries and coughing down the hall. And always her voices, all of them, sad and sweet, cajoling, wistful, blunt with anger, doomed. All of them, as though she hadn't talked for years, while he smoked, and listened. . . .

CLAY IS A MAN YOU COULD LIVE WITH ALL YOUR LIFE *and not know any better at the end than when you started. When he's quiet that way it's like he's thinking, but I'll bet he hasn't had two consecutive thoughts ever, except for I want this and I want that. Really. I mean days, weeks can go by without his giving you anything but the time of day. All wrapped up in himself. Clay's got two moods—one is grey, the other one black. Sure it's impressive. I was impressed, wasn't I? No, I suppose it wasn't that either. It was the way he simply walked into my life—just took me over, sort of. I don't know, really. It was Paris, after all. He seemed so tall and tanned and dignified—he's handsome in his way, you know, and it showed up even better over there, all those little Frenchmen so smooth and talking a mile a minute. He made me remember so many things—all of this life here when I was a girl. Of course, you know, when you see it like that from way off . . . Paris was grey and rainy. I remembered the sun. I kept thinking about my own people. I'd been away so long, you know. And then something else. I had a feeling like I didn't belong anyplace and I wanted to because I was tired of trains and buses and boats and suitcases and restaurants and all the different hotels and my God yes, the dancers, too. Too many emotions running around loose. And the men, if you could call them that . . . I think I must have felt that with Clay I would, well, sort of be somebody definite and have a place. Come from someplace, you know? Maybe I just wanted to come home and there was Clay with that Southwestern drawl of*

*his and plenty of money. That counted too, of course. He made
things so easy for me. He was crazy about me. You know, when a
man comes that far and nothing is too much trouble and he obviously just worships the ground you walk on . . . What I didn't see
was the other side—the cruelty—the loneliness—that way he has
of keeping to himself. Clay is the loneliest man I ever met. But
really—and I mean lonely. The only person who ever seemed to be
close to him at all was that crazy Cody. Oh, he and Booth get along
all right, but that's a story in itself. Sure he knows everybody—he
gets along just fine, or maybe the way to put it is that everybody
gets along with him. So lonely it would make me cry if I really
cared. That's why I married him, too. I loved that side of him, I
admit it, and the mystery about him, too, because I was dumb
enough to think that I could change all that. The only thing that
changed was that now there were two of us lonely instead of one.
The mystery? Oh, where he came from, what kind of people he
had, how he lived before he came to Grey Horse. I don't know how
to put it, exactly, except that with him you always have a feeling
like things are planned out, like nothing happens by chance.
There's always something special about a person like that. And
once I got to know him, I was sure that there was something
hidden back there somewhere. Like maybe he was one of those
babies that start off life in a basket on the steps of a church
and didn't want to say so, or maybe had been in jail for a while.
Who knows? I wouldn't put anything past Clay. Why he came
to Paris, all that way? Well, after all. I shouldn't have to tell
you. All the reasons were there—I was famous, young, beautiful,
even had money—yes, I know, it's right out of the ladies' magazines. But there it was. No, there was more. There had to be.
Something I couldn't name. Sometimes I think I understand it a
little, but I can't explain it. Would it make any sense to you at all
if I said that he wanted me in a chapel, like the Virgin Mary? And
yet at the same time, I swear it, he wants to kill me. Because he's
afraid of me. He's afraid I'll break out, run off, two-time him. He
wants me in a blanket and braids, like Mary Rose, silent, submis-
sive. And he and I just a little bit above and beyond it all, like we
were a king and a queen. I'm telling you, Clay is a strange man.
Of all the family, Mary Rose was the only one he ever liked.
Frank—he's dead now, like Ruth and Jewel—he was a drunk and
a panhandler. I think Clay would have paid him a salary just to*

stay out of town. And poor Ruth—dope and liquor and no-good men. Jewel was all right—all she and J.B. cared about was church. I don't know why anybody would want to kill them. Any of them, for that matter. People talk about the money because Nellie was married to Orval Sikes and he and Shoat got a little bit richer every time one of us died. I don't know. Clay hated all of them because they spoiled something that he had worked all his life to have. Shoat was all the things in this town that Clay will never be. Generous to a fault, great with a rope in his hands, fancy tooled boots right up to his knees, that black hat he always wore. Kids used to follow Shoat around in the street. Full of stories. Always in trouble. Shoat was everything that's wrong with people and some of what's right, and if there was any failing he lacked, then his nephew Orval more than made it up. But he had his troubles written all over his face. Not all closed up like Clay. Maybe they did it, Shoat and Orval. Maybe they were planning to kill me. I never thought so, anyway. And I guess Nellie didn't either, judging by that fort she's built for herself. Now Booth—he's a glad-hander. I don't think he'd like the feel of a gun. He's not the kind of a man I like, but he's popular with the Tribe. Partly because of Mary Rose, I guess. And then he takes a lot of trouble. He's got some crooked deal with Clay. Most of the Chetopa business goes through him one way or another. I suppose Booth gets a kickback—there's got to be something in it for him—and Clay takes the profit. But Clay goes out of his way to be fair—like he wants to take care of these people, but always on his own terms. Like he was doing it for himself, if you see what I mean. He's the kind of man would rather see you dead than falling below his idea of what you ought to be— and then he'd expect you to thank him for pulling the trigger. Of course I mean it. Just that—he's waiting to kill me. I can't explain why, but I know. I know like I know how I feel about you. There are things you can't explain. You're not that kind of man. You wouldn't know what it means to be that way. Ruthless, cold, all brain—Clay's a poker player. He could play twenty-four hours a day. I think he bought the Smoke House just to have a place to play cards in. Clay wouldn't want to play on somebody else's home ground if he could help it. The trouble with him is he lives like he's in a poker game. Listen. Not long after we were married. He said he wanted to show me where his mother was buried. Up to then he hadn't said word one about his family. I never even thought of him that way, family and all. That's what I mean about him being so lonely. Just like that: "We'll be leaving early in the morning. I want to show you where my mother is buried. Down south of Oklahoma City. Be gone about ten days." So we drove down. It's different there—not mountains, of course, but good-sized hills with pine trees. It was spring and very fresh—flowers all over the place. There was this little town—a wide spot in the road. We drove on through and then he said, "That's the town." "What town?" I asked him, but he was watching both sides of the road looking for a cutoff. It took him a while but he found it—I don't know, as usual he wasn't saying anything. Clay never explains, you know. Either he thinks you're too dumb to understand, or he figures that you can't help but be thinking what he's thinking, or he just doesn't give a damn. So I sat there wondering what it was all about while he watched the road, leaning out the window so he wouldn't miss anything. I didn't see any tracks but we turned off anyway, and there was some kind of a trail all right through the pines and after a while we came to this clearing. I didn't see anything at first. Clay got out of the car and walked around, just looking. I stayed in the car. I was mad. He acted like he had forgotten I was along. And I didn't really want to walk in all those weeds—I wasn't dressed for it, heels, stockings, you know. But he had stopped, just standing there looking at the ground, and finally he turned around and waved for me to come. Well, it was his mother. What could I do? When I caught up with him I could see that it was the foundations of a house, all overgrown the way they are after everything has been burned or carried off. I asked him what had happened. "The house burned. She was in it. Never got out." That's all he said. Then down at the bottom of the clearing I saw a farmhouse, kind of silvery-grey the way the board gets after a few years in the weather. The shingles all curled from the rain, the whole thing leaning together like a card house. There were four dirty little kids on the porch, standing in a straight line like toy soldiers or something. And then this pitiful woman, pregnant, kind of pushing at her hair, all of them standing there wide-eyed like they were scared to death. I waited while Clay went down and talked with her and then we waited some more for her husband to come. He was a dirt farmer, slow-talking, wondering why we were there. All of a sudden Clay asked me to go back to the car and wait. I was hot and tired of standing, so I went. I waited while they talked. The farmer

squatted down on his heels and worked at the dust with a stick.
The mother and kids stood there on the porch like they were nailed
to the boards. It was hot and I took my jacket off and they went
on talking. Then Clay took his wallet from his hip pocket and I
could see him counting out the money. They shook hands and Clay
came on back to the car. "It's all right—they'll pack up this afternoon." Something like that. Pack up? I never know what he's talking about. I remember how he looked at me, sort of half laughing
in that way he has where there isn't anything to hear. He had
bought them out. "They'll be off the place by sundown." I hadn't
liked it much before we got there. From that point on I simply
hated it. Seeing them going off that way, piled in the back of the
wagon with all they had, which wasn't much. I waved, and one of
the children waved back. Clay never looked up. He had spent the
afternoon going over every inch of that property, like he had lost
a diamond ring or whatever. Well, looks like there is something
he cares about after all was what I was thinking. But I couldn't
like it, no matter what. Next was the stonecutter. We located one
finally, and Clay found what he wanted—a long rectangular piece
of polished black marble, plain, no inscription. It seemed just a
little too plain to me, being black and all, all right for Clay's grave,
maybe, but for a woman . . . well, it was his mother, not mine.
They found a helper and the three of them set it in place in the
middle of the old foundations. Then Clay cleared out the foundations, weeds and all, and we had to drive all the way back to
Oklahoma City again and find a landscape gardener and pick out
shrubs and trees and flowers and then back again to plant, clear,
clean up . . . We were down there a week. Running from one
place to another. I've never seen Clay like that before or since. He
couldn't think or talk about anything else. I tried to get him to talk
about his family, but that was no good either. Just said he didn't
remember any of it too well, but had always wanted to mark her
grave. Said it made him feel like a tumbleweed when he hadn't put
any marker down. So he didn't remember it, but he knew the place
like the back of his hand. I could see that easy enough. Something
about it didn't add up. Then, just like that, we drove on back to
Grey Horse. That's what I mean about ruthless. The way he bought
that dirt farmer up—and I mean they were miserable—the crazy
concentration to the point—well, he certainly didn't have any time
for me. I'm afraid of him. I think he wants to kill me before I can

get away. He took such pleasure buying that gravestone, landscaping all around. That's what he'd do for me and then he wouldn't have to worry any more. I'm even afraid to talk to you this way. It's like he can hear me, no matter how far away I am. And he knows. He's got to know. I just keep wondering what he's waiting for—one mistake, some excuse. Don't smile. I know him. I know what he would do. That night at the country club. After we got back. I didn't tell you about it—it makes me sick just to think of it. I was so ashamed for you to see me like that. O God you don't know how I hate that man. I knew how mad he was and I was glad. I wanted to hurt him. I wanted to break through that armor he wears all the time. I wanted to make him howl. But you see what it took. I could have drowned. Of course it was because of you. I only meant . . . he hates to see me drink. He's afraid of me when I drink. He's jealous—crazy jealous. He didn't say anything on the way to the ranch. I went upstairs to my room while he put the car away. Everything was real still. I heard him come up the stairs and go in his room. I was sure he was in there drinking, and that's something you don't catch Clay doing very often. He stays away from whiskey like it was poison. You know I think he's afraid of it, like he's afraid of anything or anyone that might get behind that mask of his. Then he came into my room and I knew he had been drinking. This was the other mood, black, black as the ace of spades. I came out of the bathroom to see what he wanted. I was still putting cream on my face, I remember, and that made me mad that he would barge in that way. He had a belt in his hand. He called me a whore and then he started whipping me with that belt. I had my hands up to my face and I kept them there, but I wouldn't run and that made him wild. He grabbed my wrists and pulled my hands away so that I was looking at him and then he started slapping me, hard and slow, back and forth across my face. I thought my head would just plain break open like a pumpkin or something. Then he stopped and held me by the throat. I could hardly get my breath. He kept saying over and over, like he was drunk, "I won't let you change. No matter what I have to do I won't let you change." And then something I knew he meant. "I'll kill you before I let you tear it all down again." I could barely understand him. I'd never seen him like that. He went over to the door and put his fist right through it. Then he grabbed me by the wrist again and made me come in his room. His room is funny—like a little museum, or one of those tombs that Egyptian kings fixed up for themselves. At that time he kept a Mexican saddle in there on a sawhorse. "You know why I keep it? Because I rode into this town on that saddle. To make me remember. Now you tell me why I should go on remembering. You cheap whore." I may not remember the other part exactly, but I remember what he called me. Then he picked up the saddle and threw it right through the window. Glass all over the place—the noise was terrible. You'll wake her up, I said to him. I remember I could hardly talk, my mouth was all swollen and bleeding. My daughter always sleeps in the next room, at the ranch and in town both. Adjoining doors—one of his crazy ideas. He said he wanted it that way so he could be sure and get her out if there was ever a fire. "She'll never wake up," and then I did truly think that he was just gone, he looked at me so strange. "O God don't let her wake up." He was howling like a wolf and I was cold all the way down my back, and yet I have to admit that it did me a lot of good to see him that way. Then all of a sudden I saw Cody at the door to the room. My first thought was that I was cut and bloody and my nightgown was torn and I wanted to get away from where he could look at me. You know him, don't you? You've seen him, anyway. Cody scares me. I think he could kill somebody just for the fun of it. Without any reason, I mean. Clay would have a reason, at least. That funny white hair. Like some kind of overgrown idiot. I never understood how he and Clay ever got together in the first place and why Clay kept him around. Friends, even. I don't know. But there he was. "You've been drinking, Mr. Carter." Could you believe it? Me standing there all black and blue and bloody, the window all over the floor, and Cody says something like that. Clay just hollered at him, "Get the hell out," something like that. He called him a name I hadn't heard before— Buddy?—something. I can't remember it now. But Cody was real quiet and he came on in the room. I don't know whether he saw me or not. He was watching Clay, talking to him, saying, "You oughtn't to drink like that, you haven't done that in a long time," and he kept circling around, getting ready to jump him. I could tell by the way he carried his hands. I hadn't ever really noticed just how big his hands were before that. I wanted to scream, I must have tried to, and then Clay took a cut at him with the belt and Cody ducked and rushed him. They stood there straining at each other for a minute, then I turned my face away. It was so *awful, seeing them there like that. For some reason they seemed like a couple of brothers, which made it that much worse. Why anybody should ever take that pair for brothers, the Lord only knows. I heard them fall, and after a minute a sound like an ax on a hollow tree, and I could hear breathing and after a minute I looked around and Cody was pulling Clay up onto the bed. Clay's face was full of blood and this time I knew the scream was going to make it and just then Cody reached up and put his hand over my mouth. He told me to go on back to my room. His face was all pink under that kind of rabbity hair he has. I wanted to get away from that awful hand before I threw up. "He'll be all right. Whiskey just don't agree with your husband. If I was you I'd just forget the whole thing." Like you could forget it, just like that— ever. Anyway Clay never said a word about it, just like it never happened. Just like a nightmare, and sometimes I really do wonder if it ever really happened at all . . .*

Don't you understand now what your coming here meant to me? Don't you think I can see what your life is like? Don't I know somebody who's dying of loneliness when I see him? Both of us. When I saw you getting off that train. The first time you looked at me in the car. I knew that you would know, too. You, too? Like a face you've been dreaming about ever since you were a child. But I can't—not when he's walking the streets free the way he is now. He wouldn't let me leave him. He says so, like I told you. He'd kill me first. Wherever I went, he'd find me, him or Cody or whoever it was. That's why Clay has to be put away where he can't hurt people any more. He's like some kind of wild animal—look at the way everybody in town is scared of him. Nobody ever says a word, no matter what happens. They're all cowards. You've been here long enough to see that—this town smells like a garbage heap. You could cut the stink with a knife, and nobody even holds his nose. Andrews, let's get out together. Send them back East. Something. Anything. I have money. You're so cold about it. I don't under- stand. All this about keeping the two things apart. That just doesn't mean anything to me. I've told you already. Clay has got to be put away where he can't get at us. I know a killer when I see one. How do I know what he's done up to now? You expect me to prove it or something? Nothing would surprise me. No, I mean it. And what does Booth matter, anyway. Booth isn't anything without Clay. Take Clay out of it and this whole town blows away like dust.

Good riddance. What are any of them without Clay, when you get right down to it? All I need is a suitcase—I think there's a train from Tulsa to El Paso. Anyhow, Mexico's not so far. Look, I did it once, didn't I? No, I don't want to hear you say you love me unless you'll take me away. I don't care any more about how you feel. I want to know what you're going to do. I want to know if you've got the guts . . .

Who'll talk to you as long as Clay is free? Of course I know things, lots of things. Plenty of people know lots of things in Grey Horse. And what about Booth? Wouldn't he be glad to get it off his conscience, if he has one left? My God, even Cody. Clay has had us all locked up for years—nobody to talk to, afraid to talk even if somebody came along. The whole place paralyzed. That's the way it's been—that's the way it is now. Somebody has to make the first move. Yes, like I told you. I heard him talking with Booth about J.B. and Jewel—what Booth ought to say to the press, whether the Council would call for an investigation, what Booth ought to report to Washington—and then all the dynamite in the garage just two weeks before it happened. Sure he keeps oil-field equipment out there, but I never saw so much dynamite in my life. With Cody, too, when Frank was found dead. They had some kind of argument about it. It started on Frank and ended up on money. They got pretty loud, Clay saying something about how Cody wasn't going to make any more money off dead Indians and Cody saying that it looked more like Clay was the big man in that business. Just what I'm telling you. I may not remember it exactly, but it was something pretty close to that. He always wanted to know all the details, what people were saying, who found the bodies. Oh, it was more than curiosity. It was morbid, you might say. It made me sick. It was a kind of hunger, to hear about it, to talk about it. Didn't you know? He was the one who found Ruth. Out hunting one day. Brought her back here in the car. Came into my room, standing there trying to talk, just making sounds like a baby. I thought he was having a stroke or something. He was sick in the bathroom and I got him to lie down and then he told me. I had to call the police. He said he hadn't known—maybe she was still alive. Like maybe his conscience had got the better of him, and then just backed up and overflowed. Well, what do you think? Were Shoat and Orval up to that kind of killing? Maybe they were. Maybe anybody is. They're my family, Andrews. I think he wants

*them all dead—all but me and Mary Rose, maybe. For money?
Why should he need the money? No. So he can put me in a chapel.
Like a shrine. No, I mean it. He hated them, Frank a drunk, Ruth
just a whore if you want a plain word. Because they spoiled the
picture. The way it is now, if he doesn't kill me I'll end up killing
myself. Why should I say it if I don't mean it? I can't stand it this
way any longer. Seeing you like this, hiding all the time, never
knowing what he's found out or when he might go crazy again.
We have a chance now, you and I. Either we take it or I don't want
to go on. Do you understand? For what? More of his madness? No.
You can get rid of him. You are in a position to do what every man
in this town would like to do, and doesn't have the guts. You can
knock that little tin god back down in the dust. But nobody will
move while he's on the street. I know this place. I grew up here.
I know how they are. And you'll never get Booth unless you get
Clay first . . .*

*Of course I'll help you. I'll do anything you want. Don't you
believe me? Don't you understand? I want to get as far away from
here as possible. I'll go wherever you ask me—I'll leave her behind
if it has to be that way, except it would kill me to do that. What
would Clay do to her? But you're what matters to me. I want your
kind of life. I want to be with you. What I'm trying to say is this—
there were always parties after the theater. Civilized people, not
this kind of trash. That was the world I wanted. I was always looking for you—I kept trying to meet you—I knew what you would
be like if you ever came along. This is our only chance. You know
it just the way I know it. If it wasn't that way, then why did you
take me from the pool? Everybody watching. You didn't even think,
I know. That's what I mean. But don't lie to yourself about it. Why
did it happen, then? Tell me that. Why is any of this happening?
You know how much I hate him. I'll do anything to get rid of him.
But I have to be sure. You have to make me sure. That it's me you
want, that's what I mean. That you're doing it for me. I don't care
about the other reasons. I don't want to hear them. I want you to do
it for me, to offer it to me, to bring it to me on your knees, me, just
as I am, not in a chapel and not on a poster like some martyred
angel in pink satin and ruffles. But don't ask me to put the thing
together for you—don't ask me that. Listen. I've looked at their
bodies, shot, strangled, blown to pieces. I've had all I can take.
Don't make me look at them again. Oh God don't make me talk*

*about it any more. I love you—can't you hear me? Isn't that what
counts? Don't you know what it means? Yes, I believe you, of
course I do, but how long do we have to wait? Because time is
running out. I'll wait, you know that, but don't make me wait too
long. As long as I know you're doing it for me. No—don't talk that
way. Don't try to make it something else. We're in it together now.
You know what Clay will do if he ever finds out—we can't hide
this way much longer—he'll get us both. All right. All right, then.
Say it any way you want. But I know why you're doing it, and I
love you for it. I'll always love you for it—no one else ever had the
courage . . .*

Seeds of snow from the cottonwood drifted down upon the
driveway where toy cars glistened in the sun. The lawn turned
yellow; the earth around the roses dried to crumbling clods.
Along the elm's rough bark Amory found the desiccated shells of
locusts like tiny armored vehicles, and lined them up in battle
formation behind the cracks in the porch. The house had a red
tile roof that gaped like a wound in the flawless flesh of the sky.
Quite sensible in such heat, as Emily had put it.

"You're so thin," he had said to her one day, suddenly surprised at the shadows in the hollows of her face.

"Yes," she replied. "You, too. You don't sleep enough, you
know. Andrews," she said then, looking at him earnestly. "What
has happened in this town can never be undone or set right. Not
by you. Not by anyone."

"It's not that." He hadn't wanted to talk about it. What was
there to say, after all?

"What is it, then?"

"I made a promise. I said I'd do my best."

"What is it you really want?"

"I'm very tired," he answered. "Give me just a little time.
Things will work out." It all sounded so hopeless.

"How long, Andrews?"

"Why do you ask me that? You know what all this means to
me."

"How long? Amory scarcely sees you any more. You're almost a stranger to us. You're never here. Do you realize what this kind of life is like for us?"

"Emily—it means so very much. I can't stop now to sort it out. There isn't time. I've got to keep going, that's all I know. I've got to go all the way . . ."

Through the long nights of summer the mockingbird sang until dawn. He knew that because he was so often awake. And early each morning he said a hushed goodbye to Amory while Emily slept, his face sometimes full of sudden tears as he bent and clutched the yielding body to him, hiding from those eyes that were so wide, so clear, so grey beneath the silken hair.

"I'll bring you a little car," he whispered.

While behind him the days vanished one by one.

So that he was awake the night she phoned, almost as though he had been expecting it. And yet it wasn't until Emily rose sleepily on one elbow that he got out of bed.

"I'll get it," he said, slipping on his bathrobe, and when he picked up the receiver her voice overwhelmed him in the silence.

"Andrews. Oh damn you why won't you ever listen. It's Jimmy. Clay hasn't been here all night. I phoned Mary Rose to tell her. Booth's gone too. Jimmy's dead. Someone phoned. Oh my God I can't stand it any more. Just said, 'That kid brother of yours is out there in Cedar Canyon—dead.' I don't know who called. He hung up. I've got to get out there."

"Have you called the sheriff?"

"Nobody but you and Mary Rose."

"I'll call him, then. Wait there. I'll be over to get you in a minute."

"I told you. What does it take to get you to believe me? Now will you do something? Now will you get me out of here before it's too late?"

"I can't explain now," he said to Emily as she watched him dress. "It's the Red Hawk case again. The younger brother this time. I hate this place so much. I'd love to see them all burn in hell. Rotten trash—all of them." He touched his lips to her forehead, then left the house on the run.

It had taken them half an hour to reach Cedar Canyon, and she had cried all the way, leaning against the car door, her handkerchief wadded into a tiny white ball in her hand.

"You see?" she kept saying. "Do you see now? Shoat and Orval are dead. And now Jimmy. Why won't they leave us alone, or kill us all now and get it over with."

"Don't talk that way, Rita."

"No, you don't like to hear it, do you? You don't like to think that maybe it wouldn't have happened if you had had the guts—"

"Shut up, Rita."

"No, I won't shut up. Not any more. I did it your way—we kept apart—you worked on it, finding out about Clay's past, going over it all again. What do you expect him to do, turn himself in to the sheriff?"

"But we've got him now. Nobody will believe any longer that Shoat was the man."

"Who believed it before? Your people in Washington? So you wouldn't have to think about Booth?"

"We had to wait, Rita."

"And Jimmy had to pay the price. Oh, Andrews, you fool. Why did I ever believe in you? He was just a kid. You should have seen him play football. I can't believe it. I saw him downtown just yesterday. Three brothers, two sisters—gone. Just me and Mary Rose and Nellie. Who's next? It's all so horrible."

"Whoever killed them will pay," he said to her lamely, putting his hand on her knee.

"I can't take it any more." Her voice was low and broken. "I've got to get out of here now—with or without you. I'm finished. You've got to decide now."

They swung off the county road and followed the grooves of dust that wound through the scrub oaks. The lights from the sheriff's car had been visible from the road, and now as they drove into a small clearing Andrews saw the sheriff leaning against the fender of his car, his headlights bracketed upon the other car which sat there empty and alone like an unused stage prop.

"I'll stay here," she said. "You talk to him. Do whatever has to be done."

"He may ask you to identify the . . ." Then he held her hand very tight.

"Mr. Thayer, is it? You've brought along Mrs. Carter? Sorry about this, Mrs. Carter."

He walked to the other car with the sheriff.

"Gun on the floorboards. Shot from real close up. Whiskey all over the place. Looks like he pulled the trigger on himself."

"I can't believe that," he said sharply. And then for a moment all the anger left him and he had to seize the car door to keep from falling. Jimmy was slumped behind the steering wheel, his mouth hanging open, his face strangely lopsided. A thin crust of blood followed the line of his neck down into his shirt, where the stain was dark as wine. He might have been dead drunk, except for the powder blast that blackened the side of his face around the bullet hole.

"Does she have to see this?"

"Not if you will identify him."

"It's Jimmy all right. This was where Ruth got it—not far from here."

"Not far. Further on down the road some. This looks different to me, though. Just the one set of car tracks—the gun and all. I'd say suicide."

"Don't start covering up already, sheriff," he said quickly. "Nobody's made any accusations yet. This boy's name is Red Hawk, don't forget that."

"Take it easy, Thayer."

Then they heard the sound of footsteps on the road, and the sheriff's flashlight picked them out of darkness before they had stepped into the light from the cars.

"What the hell goes on?" It was Carter, stopping to look briefly at Rita huddled behind her handkerchief and then coming on toward them with Booth following a step behind. "What is it, sheriff? We saw your lights from the road."

"That's what we're here to find out, Clay." Andrews had moved around so that the light was full on his face, and he took a step forward so that Clay would have to look directly at him. "Rita got the news by phone—a voice she didn't recognize. You weren't there. She called Mary Rose but Blair was gone, too. She asked me to bring her out here. She's very upset, as you might imagine. She wanted me to come along."

He looked at the two of them, their bodies bulking against the light, their shadows stretched across the road to where Jimmy lay dead. Booth's shaggy head hung low like that of a bull whom a picador has lanced; Carter was as alert as a coyote smelling blood.

"Come along for what, Thayer?"

For the first time Andrews heard something menacing in his voice, something flat and hard, the voice of a man who could slap a woman until she bled.

"For Jimmy. He's in the car over there. Take a look for yourself."

Carter turned and looked at Booth, then went over to the car and bent down so that he could see in the window.

"Don't you want to see, Blair? Or have you seen enough already?"

Booth raised his head slowly, ponderously, and looked at Andrews for a moment without speaking. Then he half turned, gesturing toward the car.

"What is all this, Andrews? The way you're talking, the look on your face . . ." and he shook his head. "No, I don't want to see. I've seen it before."

Clay walked halfway over to where Rita sat, then turned back toward them as though in a daze. "Jimmy?" he said confusedly, as though trying to remember something. "Your kid brother?" He rubbed his hand across his mouth and then looked again at Booth. "Now what in the hell did he go and do that for?" he said softly.

"Do what, Clay?" Andrews felt like a fighter, moving with him along the ropes, waiting for the opening.

"Why, get himself killed like that."

His lips tightened with disgust. "The sheriff here has already made up his mind. He can tell you." Then he took Booth by the arm. "Come along," he said, looking into those bloodshot and strangely stricken eyes. "You've got to see. After all . . ."

"Yes. Yes, I suppose so."

Andrews could feel the soft flesh trembling beneath his hand as he led him to the car. Then Booth mumbled something indistinct and hid his face in his hands.

"I want to see you first thing in the morning, Blair."

Booth was crying, and Andrews wanted to shake him.

"It's so late. Mary Rose—it'll hit her awful hard. I don't know when—"

"I'll be in your office at nine. The sooner we talk, the better."

He walked back to his car and opened the door for Rita. "Now that your husband's here . . ."

She got out without looking at him and stood swaying there in the night as though she wished that the darkness could hide her forever. . . .

Booth had heard him out the next morning in the silent heat of the office, snuffling over a cigar, getting up to pour himself a whiskey and then another. He moved in his swivel chair like some wounded animal, making grunting noises in his throat, until Andrews had finished. Then for a long time he said nothing, relighting his cigar, sloshing the whiskey in his glass.

"Son," he said finally, "are you awfully goddam sure you know what you're doing? Do you really want to get into all this?"

Andrews looked at him contemptuously. "What does what I want have to do with it?"

Booth brushed away the cigar smoke that clung in a wreath around his face and then looked at Andrews with eyes that were swollen with fatigue, with pain, with sorrow. He waited for a moment as though listening to a voice Andrews could not hear.

"You've laid it out pretty straight this morning. Among a lot of other things, you've hinted more than a little about the fact that I wasn't home last night, nor Clay either. Well, you're right. We have no alibi, even if we needed one. We weren't where anyone could see us, or hear us either, on purpose. We were parked on the side of the Cedar Canyon road, and Clay was talking to me about his wife—and you."

Andrews flushed and reached for a cigarette. "I wouldn't have thought you capable of that, Blair."

"Of what, just exactly?"

"Of that kind of insinuation. Don't think you can scare me off like that."

"No," Booth said. "No. I'm trying to understand, that's all. You know, the fact is that I didn't follow too well all of what you've been saying to me this morning. I'm not even sure I could remember any of it after you walk out of this office. It might sound all right in law school, Andrews. Not here. You talked to me this morning. Clay talked to me last night. Sometime in be-tween a poor Indian kid got himself drowned in whiskey. Shoat Dalton didn't have to do it this time. Jimmy didn't need any help other than the man who sold him the bottle. If I were you, son, I'd let it ride. You've got another problem on your hands. What you and Rita do is your business, but I know her maybe a little bit better than you do."

"None of that matters to me at all. I'm going after him, Blair. I'm going just as far as I have to go to get him. Now, as soon as I can get the sheriff in motion." He waited, but Booth did not reply. "I wanted you to know," he said, just above a whisper. "I wanted you to approve."

Booth got up from his chair and pointed his cigar at him, taking aim as though he had a pistol in his hand. "You goddam little prig, you. You go after Clay and I'll have your ass busted out of here so fast—"

"You're not scaring anybody, Blair." He remembered that he had had a strange feeling of magnanimity toward him, a curious blend of pity and kindness. "I'll have to go over your head, that's all. I'll give you twenty-four hours to figure out where you stand. That is," and he got up then, "if there's anyplace left for you to stand . . ."

She moved like a shadow through the circle of light, and when she opened the door and looked at him it seemed to him that he had never seen her before. "It's all right," she said. "I've got it," and she tapped the bottle with her fingernail. "I know where we'll go. Nobody will ever look for us there."

Something in him was trying to cry out, and he struggled against the dream, but it was too late. There was nothing left but pain, pressing inside his chest, beating at his temples, throbbing at the back of his neck. Putting it together like that, remembering it all, what did any of it mean? And suppose that there was no meaning at all, just the blind unwinding of the film of his life. But that was madness . . .

"I don't want to go there," he said hopelessly.

"Yes, you do," she whispered. "I know what you want— better than you do." And then he felt her hair fall upon his face like strands of burning wire.

*   *
*

"REMEMBER THE DAY we first came here?" They were parked in the grove of blackjack trees, just off the county road. "Remember?" She brushed the hair from her face and filled the paper cup again with whiskey. When she looked at him her eyes were charcoal blurs in the bronze of her face. She seemed to laugh. She held the cup before her face and made a mocking little bow. "To the day you first kissed me—right here—on Clay Carter's ranch. You made me wait a long time."

He looked away from her, out of the window toward the emptiness of night where twisted trees reached up toward heaven as though in grief or terror. "I have too much to remember as it is," he said softly. "I need two clear days without any remembering at all. Without past or future, either one. Just doing what I have to do now, tonight, tomorrow, until Monday morning."

"So it's like that—you won't even remember. You can't let go even for a minute."

He shook his head. "I remember that three hours ago I had

Cody in my office. We're too close to the ranch road. Suppose he should come along."

"Cody." She seemed to spit his name. "You have no feelings. You're always talking about love, about how much you love me. You don't know what the word means."

"Do you? I've told you we have to wait."

"For what? We've been waiting for something ever since I met you."

"Until I've finished with this town. With Clay, and Blair, and Cody—"

"And with me, too, I suppose."

"Don't make me say things I don't want to say. You know how much a part of it you are." He reached for her hand, but found only the bottle instead. "I've got to go through with it now. We've gone too far. There's no way back. You should know that."

She put the paper cup to her lips and drank, and he could hear her catch her breath.

"Rita, can't I make you understand? That this is not the time . . ."

Her hair had fallen forward across her face again so that he could no longer see her eyes. She did not answer.

"He was in my office," he said after a while. "Only hours ago. I think I scared him. I wanted to scare him enough to shake him loose from Clay."

"You're wasting your time." The words were slurred, as if she could not move her tongue. "He's too stupid to be scared."

"We need him on our side," he said doggedly. "Rita," and then he waited until she looked at him again. "Without you, and Cody, and Blair, there's no case. Clay will beat us both. We'll be finished. You've got to realize that."

"Cody," she said again, her mouth twisted with scorn. "That two-bit Buffalo Bill. I wouldn't ask him for the time of day. If it's him you're depending on—" and she slopped some whiskey into the cup. "I'm going to finish this bottle. Then I'm going to drive over to the ranch and get the money. I know where he keeps it. I can pack in twenty minutes. We can be in Tulsa by midnight, on our way to El Paso. We can be in Mexico before Clay's out on bail. Then let him burn in hell."

"Who are you thinking about, Rita? Is it Clay, or us?"

She moved closer, as though she could no longer see him in the darkness, and then her eyes closed with the effort. "Oh God, Andrews, isn't that what I've been asking you for the last three months? What do you want, anyway? All I ever wanted was to have you, to get as far away from here as we can get. I've got money—we won't have to worry. We haven't done anything wrong."

She was filling the cup again, and crying, and she pulled away from him when he tried to wipe away the tears. "No, I don't want you to do that. I want to know where we're going. And if you're not coming, then get out of my way—I'm going alone."

"Don't say it unless you mean it."

"Why shouldn't I mean it," she said, and the words were a series of sobs. "You believed me when I told you he was a killer. You believed me enough to put him behind bars where he can't get at us." She turned and stared at him then as though through a haze. "What's it all for, then? Why are you doing it? He'll kill you. Don't you believe what I'm telling you? If he knew—he'd just as soon kill you as look at you." She swayed a little, and her hair moved like a curtain in the wind. Then she drank, and coughed, and laughed, as though she were suddenly alone, wiping her lips with her fingers, then tapping the bottle lightly against the cold silk of her knee. "Why are you asking me about Clay? Are you jealous, Mr. Thayer? Well, you don't have to be. He never wanted me. I was just a piece in that crazy puzzle he's been trying to put together all his life."

"That's his cross to bear," he said coldly. "One of a great many. Can't you forget it? Won't you for God's sake read what I've written here and sign it, Rita, so that I can go after Cody? Won't you listen to me while there's still time?" He could hear her broken breathing, a kind of whispering to herself. "Look. It's all here. With this—"

She pushed the paper away, glaring at him. "Ever since he killed her. You know so much about it all. Which one of them?

Did you put that in your paper? Did anybody ever tell you that?"

"Who are you talking about? I've put down everything you told me about Ruth and Jewel . . ."

"No. They're all afraid. Of Clay, of each other." The cup fell from her hand and she leaned against the steering wheel, looking for it in the darkness. "They're the ones who brought the syphilis, don't forget that. Not us. Like he wanted to pay God back or something. Nobody will ever be clean again. Burned. That's something to ask Cody about." She tilted the bottle against her lips and he could hear the gurgle of the whiskey.

"Stop it, woman. What's the matter with you? Just when luck is with us—"

"With me? Didn't you ever see a woman drunk before, Mr. Thayer? How about your little Sunday-school teacher. A few drinks might help her where it counts."

"Leave her out of this," he said quickly. "If you're not going to listen to me then we might as well go on back to town."

"Listen to you?" she said, shaking her head at him. "What else have I been doing?" And then she was crying again, shaking all over, holding the bottle with both hands. "I can't stand it any more. You've got to take me away. You promised. Let them all rot. Please, please, please . . ."

He lit a cigarette, trying to control the trembling of his hand, and when he spoke his voice was high and harsh. "I'm going to tell you once more. We're not going anyplace. Not now. Not until it's finished. Clay is back there in jail, but I don't give a damn about him. I came here to get Booth. He's guilty, and I've got to get him. Clay's part of it and you're part of it, and without Clay there won't be anything and without you none of it would matter any more. But my job is Booth. Clay belongs to these people here," he said contemptuously. "He's one of them. They'll have to look after him. As for you and me—I've told you a thousand times. Right now I want Booth, Rita. Rita!" he repeated sharply, because she was not looking at him but staring straight ahead, cuddling the bottle in her lap like a child, as though she saw someone coming toward her through the night.

"You're talking shit," she said, not even looking at him, and he winced at the ugliness of it. "You want Clay out of the way as much as I do. You told me you loved me." It was like a line of verse which she had memorized and could never forget.

"Why do you talk like that?" he asked hopelessly.

"You made love to me." It was the voice of a child, reciting a litany. "You went down on the ground in front of me and cried."

"You know how I feel about you. You don't have to say these things."

"No. That's just it. I don't. Not any more. What did I ever mean to you? Clay wanted to set me up in a chapel. What did you want—your own private whorehouse? How long has it been since you slept with the Sunday-school teacher? Or are you sleeping with both of us? What are you telling her, Mr. Thayer?"

"No. No, for God's sake. That won't get us anywhere." He closed his eyes and put the back of his hand hard against his mouth to stop the pain that pressed against his throat. Nothing. Nothing. All of it strung together like beads on a string he couldn't tie. His hands opened and closed and his voice was hoarse, hardly above a whisper. "The paper. Listen, just for a minute. You've got to sign this paper. First you, then Cody." He stopped then, because she was starting to laugh, a low menacing laugh that ended in a strangled moan.

"You fool," she said. "You coward. Never meant any of it. Crying—beating your hands on the ground. All for me." She drank again from the bottle, choking and wiping at her mouth, and then she spoke to him in an urgent whisper. "Look, there's money at the house. Plenty. Clay always keeps it. I know where. Money. Mine anyway. The train . . . El Paso . . . wouldn't he howl." And then there was merely the sound of her breathing, like some animal in the dark. "I remember, whether you do or not—all of it. Could laugh you right out of town. I want you. Saw you getting off that train. Lost. You, too. Both of us. Last, last, last chance. No more. Just the jail, and El Paso . . ."

She fell against him and her hands reached for him and he felt spilled whiskey cold on his leg.

"What it was all about," and he heard her giggling with a kind of childish cunning. "Wish he could see me—old Clay—naked—right in front of him."

Suddenly he hated the smell of her, her hands pulling at him, her incoherence. He shoved her hard against the steering wheel. "Have you lost your mind?" Then he slapped her twice, shouting at her now, waving the paper before her face. "You've got to sign—it's only what you told me—oh, you fool—stop it—stop."

She snatched at it, fought him for it, laughing and crying all at once. Then the bottle rolled against his foot and she pushed at him to reach it, forcing her way down to the floorboards until he caught her by the hair and dragged her head back so that her eyes bulged wildly from her face. Then from somewhere light broke against his temple like an exploded moon and he heard glass falling like hail and through a blur of blood his hands made a necklace around her throat and he was beating her head against the dashboard, sobbing, calling her name, wanting her to listen. And when at last, as though from a long distance, he heard his own voice speaking through the silence, he stopped and looked at her, her head hanging from his hands like a dead flower. And then his eyes lifted to the window and looked upon a grotesque montage of nostrils, tongues, wild staring eyes, ears and jawbones, the climax of some fearful dream whose very terror now jolted him into sweating wakefulness. The truck seemed to lift and shake beneath him, and the eyes rolled wildly white against the glass, and it seemed that he was looking into the very depths of hell. Then in a great surge of fright he kicked the door open and leapt running from the truck. The earth was lost in darkness, and the trees clawed at his face, and the breath rushed from his open mouth so that he could not cry aloud. Then something massive struck him high on the back so that he stumbled, and as he tried to raise his head, it struck again. He tried to reach around to the back of his neck, and then the earth tilted violently and he lay headlong with the taste of dirt on his tongue. He tried to breathe. Salt air was what he needed. There was a ship out there in the rain, and sunlight like a ruined column fallen across the sea. The darkness was closing in, and it was late . . .

2

HE WAS SITTING THERE IN THE DINING ROOM WHEN THE front doorbell rang. Never had liked that bell. No reason why a man couldn't knock if he wanted to see you, or call through the screen when it was warm enough to keep the house open. Little Mex came in through the swing door that led to the kitchen, wiping his hands on a dish towel, smelling like hot peppers and chili powder and beans, whatever it was that he was throwing together out back.

"Want me to see who it is, Mr. Carter?"

"I don't see why they have to ring that damn bell. If it's for her she's upstairs sick. She don't want to see anybody."

Wearing those sandals that had sweated all black from his feet. What the hell was it he called them? A long Mexican name full of wa-wa. Like those ratty little dogs. That hole in the wall of a cafe down in the whorehouse part of Mexico City. Christ, didn't it smell good. Chile, tamales, hot as hell, all of it. Hired him on the spot, carried him right the hell back to Grey Horse, never had a better cook. The whole damned family—well, for greasers you couldn't beat them. If you liked it hot.

"Sheriff."

"What the hell does he want. I already voted for him once."

That mahogany table hit Little Mex right about his belly button, and his legs were the longest part of him. But little or not, he was good at keeping his mouth shut when he didn't know something, which was just about all the time. Must have been half Chink or something.

"O.K. Set another plate."

) 127 (

"More than one."

"Then goddammit, set out as many plates as you need. But get your ass in the saddle."

His chair squeaked like leather when he pushed it back, and the soft reflection of light off silver and glass and mahogany moved with him into the living room. Too goddam Frenchified with those spindly-legged chairs and a hundred-year-old piano and wall hangings and paintings and God knows what-all. Took three vans to get the stuff hauled out here. Well, you got to pay for what you get. Rita was that way. So to hell with it. He could still sit in the dining room or upstairs with his saddle and all. Nobody ever sat in the living room anyway. Nobody ever came but Blair and Mary Rose now and then. In the summer they sat on the porch and in the winter they'd just as like as not go sit in the kitchen. Roust Little Mex out of there and get up close to the stove. What the hell. Anyway the ranch was where he hung his hat.

"Boys, you're right on time for dinner. Glad for the company. Come on into the dining room. Cook's fixing your plates."

The sheriff didn't look right. As a matter of fact he looked like a preacher. He held his hat there in front of his belt buckle and looked about as sad as a preacher with a collection plate.

"Reckon not, Clay. Much obliged."

He waited, but none of them said anything. They all three of them looked like preachers. Like somebody was dead or something.

"Well, what can I do for you then. You ain't interested in grub—what's your business?"

"Business is we got to take you in, Clay."

Everything kind of slowed up then and he looked into their faces real good. He stooped down so he could get a better look. They had guns on, too, all three of them. Then he took a deep breath. Well all right, Old Man. You finally made up Your mind, or maybe just got around to it, one. So be it.

"You sure you got the right name on that warrant? You wouldn't want to do something dumb, would you, sheriff?"

"Clay, I'm doing what they tell me to do. You ought to know

that. I got to take you in for murder. You can read it if you want
to."

He had a little trouble with his stomach for just a minute, and
then he was all right. "I don't reckon I need to. Now Little Mex is
going to bring you boys something to drink on while I fix myself
a bag. I guess you wouldn't mind me taking my razor and so forth
along. No more than five minutes."

It wasn't like thinking, then. It was like something he'd done
so many times he could do it in his sleep. Like throwing and
branding a calf, or moving up on a covey of quail and letting go
when they flushed. Things he didn't have to think about. Something he'd waited for so damned many years . . . He'd always
known just exactly what he'd do.

So he pulled the Gladstone from under the bed and wiped the
dust off it and put in socks and shorts and a straight razor and a
toothbrush. Then he got his flask from the bureau drawer and
slipped it into the side pocket of the bag, and on top of the shorts
he laid the last two numbers of *True Western Stories*. Then a half
dozen lead pencils and a Big Chief Tablet and a hand pencil
sharpener. He thought for a minute—after all you couldn't plan
ahead for everything—and then he took his Bible from the night
table beside his bed. He closed the Gladstone, then opened it
again. Still room enough for a bottle. He would be sitting up until
late and that flask wouldn't last past midnight.

He slipped the locks into place and then looked around, waiting to see if he had forgotten anything. The shiny brass bed from
Paris (he hadn't told her that, how he had always wanted one ever
since that two-week cross-country drunk and when he finally
woke up he was in a New Orleans cat house tied hand and foot in
a brass bed so shiny it made his eyes hurt), the leather chest from
Mexico down at the foot, the engraved rifles and powder horns
and muskets on the wall, the sweat-stained saddle mounted on a
sawhorse in the corner. Right black, rawhide, worn down to the
iron on the horn. Mean-looking. Cut and torn where he threw it
through the window that night out at the ranch. Damn her hide.
The standing lamp made from the horns of a Texas steer. The
cut-glass decanter of whiskey—somebody gave it to him for his

wedding, Blair, yes, that would be him—brown as tobacco juice. The room kind of empty-like and real still except for the shadows from that big old weeping willow that reached right up to the second story.

Then he took his hat and closed the door carefully behind him and went on down the hall to her room. He pulled the door against the frame and pressed on the handle while he turned. But when it opened she was looking at him, laying there on the bed, the curtains drawn so it was half dark, her arm stretched across her forehead. He looked around for the whiskey, but she had probably hidden it when she heard the door. The bed was covered with women's magazines and brown papers from a box of chocolates. Next to her on the table there was the usual collection of medicine bottles. Ever get hard up she could open a drugstore with all that junk she kept around.

"Headache?"

"Mmmm." She leaned up on one elbow, looking at the bag in his hand. "Going someplace?"

"Somebody wants to see me down at the jail. Couldn't be that lawyer friend of yours, or could it? Sheriff drove all the way up here just to give me a ride."

"You don't need your bag for that. Be serious, what's it all about?"

She was friendly that way—always that little edge to her voice. Either she was sick or she wasn't, one. All this laying around in bed. She had moved a little closer to the lamp and now he could make her out a little better, crow-colored hair hanging loose around her face that was shaped more or less like a tulip on that long pretty neck of hers, her legs pulled up under her in a way that made him think of a cat. Or maybe a jaguar, whatever they called it.

"You're the one that ought to get serious. What the hell do you want from me I haven't given you? You want my head served up to you on a plate of grapes, or what?"

She didn't say anything for a while, just looked mean and kind of half sick like she'd taken a drink of extra-green whiskey.

"Get out."

Her voice always got soft when she looked like that.

"Get out of my room, Clay. I made one mistake marrying you. I don't need to make another one listening to whatever it is you have to say. Besides, you've said it all so many times I don't think even you know what it means any more."

"You know what, little lady? He's after something a lot bigger and a whole lot more important to him than you'll ever be."

"Like you were, Clay? Who did you marry when you married me? The Blessed Virgin or somebody? What were you after, anyway? Absolution?"

"How come you only talk Catholic when you're hopped up, Rita? You ever think about that?" Then he put his hat back on. "I reckon you can reach me in jail if you need anything. Let Jack know I'm there if it don't strain you any."

On down the hall he stopped in front of Rona's door and put his hand on the knob. She would be eating now with the governess. Why the hell upset her? Then he shrugged his shoulders and went on down the stairs.

They were still waiting there on the porch where he had left them.

"You boys get your drinks?"

"Might sorry about this, Clay." The sheriff looked sorry, too, or scared, or mad, or something. "I guess we ought to get a move on."

Even at the jail he was the only one who seemed easy about it all. They printed him and took his picture and the jailer cussed and fussed and shouted to beat hell at some drunk they'd just locked up who was singing some kind of gospel stuff down the hall. Well, he could afford to be easy. You didn't wait for eighteen years for lightning to strike and then not be relieved when it finally came. He was even cheerful, in a mean sort of a way. At least he wouldn't be waiting any longer for them to come.

He opened the bag and poured himself a shot of whiskey from the flask, then settled down on the cell cot with his legs drawn up to make a kind of support for the tablet. He sat that way for quite a while, remembering it, thinking on back, looking out through the cell window to where the Agency Building was slowly fading into night all except for one window full of light, turning the pencil in his hand and then finally opening the tablet to begin:

LORD I KNOW THAT YOU MARK THE SPARROW'S FALL. *If it was only to tell it to You again then there wouldn't be no reason to put it down. But I am putting it down this way so that You will know I know it too. Or anyways to show You how much I know and how much I don't know if that makes any difference. Or maybe I'm putting it down for the girl, or the boy maybe if there ever is a boy. If I'm lucky enough to have him is what I mean. Or maybe just because there ought to be a record—put it in the bank, probably. Somebody someday might want to read it, if anybody besides You cares. I maybe was bluffing everybody else but I never figured for a minute that I was beating You. I been waiting for You for a long time. So think of it kind of like a confession, or even a prayer, if you will. Or like laying down a hand. Lord, these are all the cards I got. So all right. Let's begin.*

Like how come I got mixed up with her in the first place. Anna Poteau. South of Pauls Valley. Game-legged when I met her. Not able to get out of bed without help by the time she died three years after. But back of that even. I come up from West Texas to find the home place sort of, if you could call it that. I don't even know why I ever thought of it that way. A windy sort of a town with a couple hundred pop., man, mule, and beast thrown in. One street, mud one day, iron the next, a grocery store full of cans and barrels and harness, hitching timbers in front of what few buildings there were, all of it smelling somewhere between horse shit and raw gut whiskey and pig farmers on Saturday and coal oil and all them mountain pines. Especially the pine trees when the wind was right, or maybe when there wasn't any wind at all. Anyways, I rode in on a March day that was warm in the middle and kind of frosty around the edges. It was empty-like—you might have thought a tornado had blowed through there and sucked all the people right out through the windows. It sure was empty, I remember that. I had been on the road for quite a spell by then, bumming my way north, hiring out by the day, you name it I'll do it, stringing fence, winning a quarter horse race here and there because I was skinny and could ride like hell. Gone from home because I didn't like what my Dad had married after Mom was dead, and she didn't like me no better. But those sod-busters yonder didn't need much in the way of fence and they sure wasn't looking for races. Pig farmer stuff and like that. And I had gone about as far as I wanted to with nothing between ass and ears except wind. And then I knew the place, more or less, or maybe I should say I remembered it. Anyway I had been heading for it, half thinking about it, kind of taking a bead on it if you will. I hadn't thought too much about why. I sat my horse at the end of the street and something about it smelled like home. What I mean is that it smelled like being a kid, there or somewhere like it. I'm not putting down just what it was, but it must have smelt lucky. And it was for a fact, if a man could call it luck. We picked our way down the street, mud that day, as far as the grocery. I tied up and went in and said right off who I was and where I was from. Somebody spit at the stove so it sounded like eggs in hot grease. I said I was hungry and could work. Nobody lifted a finger. Course I had been through it all before—whoever it would be there who had some work he needed done would figure he could get it just a little bit cheaper if I was just a little bit hungrier. Nobody was in any kind of a hurry. Tomorrow would do fine. And a quarter cheaper. Quarters had got to where they looked pretty big to me. So I went on back out in the wind and walked my horse to the edge of town and took his saddle off and rubbed him some and hobbled him in high grass. Then I made me a good fire and lay down with the saddle and horse blanket. That blanket. I wish I still had it. It always smelled good and stayed warm for a long time. Funny how it's things like that a fellow remembers longest in this life—like it was all just hot and cold or hungry and full. Weather. What kind of a day it was. How long it had been since you ate.

It was dark after a while and I got up close to the fire and worked at a newspaper I had picked up in Fort Worth and carried for reading matter. Somebody along the line put me onto reading, bless her soul wherever she lays. Well, hungry it was better asleep than awake. Those days I slept good. I had probably been awake for about an hour the next morning and had watered my horse and washed up myself when the wagon went by. Not much of a wagon. A bunch of planks held together by baling wire. One old horse, head down, a long ways away from a curry comb or brush. Up in the seat what had to be a woman or a kid, too little for a man, wrapped in a blanket against the cold. Well it wasn't real cold, just

*early morning sharp with a wind rolling the tops of the grass and
the pine smell pretty clear and a couple of stars fading out. Then
I could tell it was a woman—a touch stiff with the reins. The wagon
was close and I called out to her Howdy the way anyone would in
my part of the country. Her head come up out of that blanket so
I could see her face, flat and a little darker than a dead pine. Indian.
She looked at me like to find out what I wanted, then pulled the
blanket around her face again. Well, I started whistling and said
to hell with it. People always said they never talked anyway. You
couldn't prove it by me and anyhow it was a nice morning. I had
business on my mind and nothing on my stomach. I wanted eats,
as quick as I could find a way to put my hands on some. There was
a blacksmith shop and stable on the far side of town. I had seen it
coming in the day before. I rode on past the store where the wagon
was hitched out front. Buying her sugar and flour, I figured. Even
the goddam Indians had enough to eat on. But the horse looked in
none too good shape, head down around his knees, his hide moving
a little under the flies. The blacksmith was out front when I got
to the stable. He looked at my horse first, then at me. Horse looks a
little windy, he said to me. I told him the horse hadn't been eating
regular. I told him I could clean stables, saying it slow and not
pushing it. I told him I was ever bit as windy as my horse. Now
that little devil wasn't no A-rab stallion but he had been looked
after. Blacksmith could see that easy enough. He told me he had a
day's work. To me it felt more like he had made a deal with my
horse. Well, by sundown I had a half a dollar in my pocket and
a whole lot of beans and bread under my belt. It wasn't what you
would rightly call a homecoming, but then I hadn't expected a
whole hell of a lot, either. It would give me a push on up the road
toward the Chetopa Reservation and the cattle country where I was
heading. They had told me it was the best grazing land there was.
I knew a lot of West Texas stock was driven up there for fattening
on the way to Kansas City. And it would be good to see short grass
country, looking off thirty miles to where land and sky run together
and still water and shade and not just a cactus farm with a skinny
bunch of half wild Mexican steers as fast as quarter horses. That's
what I had left behind me and I couldn't really say what it was
otherwise that had brought me here and kept me rolling North. Or
what gave me that feeling of home.*

Somewhere around here my mother was buried from the time

Dad had tried to make a go of it in the Territory. That was a good enough reason. But nobody seemed to remember the name. Maybe all the others who'd been there, just like my folks, had just kept moving on. Well, I had paid my respects after a fashion. It was like a cut that had stayed open and now might have a chance to heal. And there was damn sure nothing here to hold me except a kind of sadness if you will. The way a man feels when he's lost something he wanted a whole lot to hang onto. But there wasn't nothing left anyway, not even a grave marker or at least I couldn't find it, and the quicker I got my ass on up to where there was cattle and maybe money the better off for me. That was the way I thought about it then. But still that wouldn't be tomorrow. That half a dollar felt good and heavy, but it wouldn't carry me that far. What I mean is I still had a long way to go, and it turned out to be a hell of a lot further than I figured.

The street was pretty near empty when I rode back past the store. There are those things you remember real good. I got maybe a half dozen of them in my life. You can even smell the day like. Remember the weather. I remember a black and tan hound that worked his way down the line of stores with that funny kind of sideways run they have and there was some dust in the air, spinning kind of. That old saddle was talking a little and there was a hawk up there turning around like he'd been hung from a string. I guess I was tired and if it was like a lot of other days I've had I probably shivered some when the sweat dried. I can kind of see me back there in that little street, bent over under my hat, letting the horse do the thinking, and then his neck come up and his pace changed and another horse sounded off not far down the road. I looked up and saw the wagon where it was pulled off on the side not far from where I had slept the night before. She had guessed right. I had figured on sleeping there again tonight before pushing on in the morning. There was something about sleeping two nights running in the same place which seemed kind of good right then, even if it was just high grass and red clay and those straight up and down pines still smelling a little warm from the sun. You might say that that way it would be a little more like I had been home. I eased on past the wagon to the trees where I'd built the fire the night before. I got down from the saddle and was loosening the cinch when I heard her calling. I straightened up and looked at her over the horse's back. She asked me if I was the one who was there

*this morning and did I want work. I came out from behind the
horse so I could see her better but the sun was setting back of that
wagon and it was just like she was right in the big middle of a
bonfire. I closed my eyes a little but I couldn't see much more than
a kind of streak of black which would be horse and wagon. I told
her I was and I did, and then she told me to follow her on home.
I nodded my head, wondering what kind of a deal I had made.
Probably I should say here that with women I was always a little
on my guard, maybe on account of growing up without any mother
and feeling a little ashamed about it. I didn't know how to handle
them and still don't probably. I only knew them as school teachers
or like the Mexican girl I spent a night with in San Antonio. Or
like Dad's second wife who was young enough to be my sister and
wanted me the hell out of there, so it was all mixed up. I wondered
what she had in mind for me to do. Well it was work and a chance
for me to fatten up a little and rest my horse. I needed the money.
And I even figured that maybe I could still find somebody who
remembered. I had it bad just to look at her gravestone if there was
one. Even just once would be something.*

*So I followed behind the wagon for what must have been four
or five miles. No talking, just the sound of my saddle and the rattle
of that wagon across the ruts and once in a while the horses blowing a little. The house was up on a little rise cleared not too long
before with quite a few pine stumps around. I figured she hadn't
done much of the heavy work, and watching her get down so awkward and stiff from the wagon, favoring that one leg, I wondered
who had cut those trees. She pointed to the stuff to carry in and
I waited until she had limped up to the door and then I shouldered
the sacks and brought them to the porch. By the time I was ready
to bring it all in she had lit a coal oil lamp. She was Indian all
right. She had put the blanket down and I could see that long hair
black and rough like a horse. Bunk house at back she told me.
Breakfast here. She talked like she'd been drinking, but that was
because she hadn't ever learned English any too good. But she
always got across what she had on her mind. She gave me a lamp
and I carried it along leading my horse until I found what she had
called the bunk house. It was a shed a couple of hundred yards
from the main building. Over to the right I could see a part finished
barn. Smell it better than see it, I should say. Anyway I got my
horse and hers fed and watered and then went looking for my bed.*

I had been sleeping on the ground for longer than I liked to think about. There wasn't nothing extra in that shed, just a bunk and a wash pan and one old chair and a piece of cracked mirror on the wall. It had been pretty well cleared out by whoever had used it before me, if anyone had. All except for the hat. I can see it still, hanging on a nail at the foot of the bunk, sweat marks showing around the brim and a whole lot too big for me. It was a man's hat, and it started me thinking all over again about who had put this place together.

He stopped then and poured himself a drink. He needed to catch his breath. It all came back faster than he could make his hand move so that it was a race just to keep up with it, like a kid hurrying to get something out that he had memorized. The muscle on the side of his hand hurt and he rubbed it, and pared the pencil down to a fine point with the sharpener. Then he drew two blunt brackets like fencing in the middle of the page.

I AM STICKING THIS IN HERE *because You may think I'm crazy or something to remember it all like this. I don't know just what to compare it to, but it's maybe like remembering your mother's face, or your first woman, or if you ever got shot bad and lived over what it felt like. It's still just as clear and sharp as that. More so if anything. Burned right into me like a brand. My life kind of shaped up around it like hide healing over the sore. I've just thought about it so much, don't You see, gone over it so many times to remember every little old detail. Not a bit of it is made up, not even when I put down what we said. You have to hear it like that, like it was spoke. I don't know how to do that any other way except put it down like real talk.*

He took a pull from the flask and then went on writing, not as fast as before, rubbing at his hand now and then, but steady.

BUT THE HAT. *She explained that to me one day later on, if explain isn't too strong a word. By that time I had more or less settled in. I liked it too because it was steady and because as the days went by it began to feel in a way like I was working for myself. Not all the way, no. It was still her place. But setting there in the middle of those mountain pines it had that smell like home. I don't know what else rightly to call it. Put something back together that had been all jimmied up, you might say. And by the time I had finished pulling the stumps and clearing another section for planting corn and stuff and finishing off the barn and adding on some to take care of the extra cow I had talked her into buying, I just couldn't help having the feeling that I was building a place of my own. I'd always had somebody on my back before. Now it was like I wanted to. Course I didn't really think that way, which is to say I didn't feel sore like it really should belong to me, title or anything. It was just kind of a feeling, working steady through that summer, sweating over that holding until I knew every inch of that place like the back of my hand. Plus, I was eating all my meals now at the house and sitting around on the porch of an evening or sometimes working through a catalogue longside the stove there in the kitchen. She wasn't what you'd call a talker, and there wasn't ever a whole lot to say anyway. It was more like she was a housekeeper, cooking, taking care of the chickens, keeping to herself and letting me run the place the way I thought best. The only hitch was that she paid me, ever month like a clock, and whenever she handed it out I wondered about the hat and where the money came from. Then one day sometime around the middle of that first winter I noticed that the hat was gone. That night at supper I asked her about it. She didn't want to talk about it at first, but I kind of leaned on her some. By now I had put too much into the place not to want to know. She had one of those faces like they have. Nothing for you to see in it and if you do see something it's only what they've gone and put there to throw you off the scent. But this was different, and when she finally told me she looked more or less like she was staring right down the throat of a diamondbacked rattler.*

What I finally pieced together was that the hat had belonged to a Missouri man who had done his business out of the Ozark country some east of Joplin. His business the best I could figure was holding up banks and trains and killing when he had to. How she took up with him she didn't get around to, and she said just about as little as I'd let her, looking at me like she thought I was going to kick hell out of her any minute or that maybe somebody was standing just outside that door. He had been able to hide out pretty good in the Ozarks for quite a time but they finally tracked him to where he had holed up, somewhere not far from Pinesville.

That may not be the name but it's close enough. He shot his way out and headed south on a fast horse with her riding behind and a U.S. mail bag full of money across his lap. That plus the pistols he carried and the rifle in the saddle holster was what they had when they hit the Kiamichi country. Seemed like he liked it right off because it was far enough from Missouri and because it was low mountain country, the kind of country he felt like was home. He figured he could lay up here quite awhile without being bothered. And then the other reason was that she had been shot in the leg when they had broken out up there and he had dug the lead out O.K. but kind of messy if you will and it needed a doctor. Horse medicine or whatever. So they came in from the north side late in the afternoon, spring. Came on around the town and picked up the road on the far side, following it until he saw the little rise in the pines where I would run across his hat a year later. They started with a lean-to and that summer he cleared enough timber for the house and a piece of the barn, enough to get them through the winter. She never left the place at all and he went into town just as little as he could whenever he had to pick up beans or flour or a side of bacon.

Then it would seem that one night he got out his guns and sat in the kitchen and cleaned and oiled them. He told her what to pack in his saddle bags and when they went to bed he said he would be gone for a few days, doing a little business. He never told her more than that. The next morning just after sunup she watched him ride away and that was the last she ever saw of him. No word, no news of any kind. Just like he was dropped down a well. And sure as hell figuring on coming back because he had left the money in the mail bag. Later that night we went out to the barn and she showed me with the lamp where she had hid it under the slope of the roof. So that explained the money and the hat and quite a few other things too. Like why the place had that kind of squatters' look about it, built none too good by people who were none too sure about staying, nothing really finished off or built to last even if he had gone to the trouble to put down a foundation, and why nobody in town ever called her by name and looked funny at me when I come into the store for staples or a plug or what have you. It made a whole lot of sense, if you will, but I still hadn't licked the problem of that hat. What I had begun to get around though was me and her. When she had told me all that she was going to

*tell, I hadn't said anything for quite a while. I didn't like it because
she looked like she was going to cry. Then I said to her that there
wasn't much reason for her to try and hide that hat or keep it
around cause I had tried it on that first night and it didn't fit.
Something along that line. She knew it was all right then. She
smiled, but still like she was going to cry. I moved my stuff into
the house that night, what there was of it.*

*We still didn't say just a hell of a lot to each other but it had
all changed or anyways I had. Like I said I never had figured
women before for anything but school teachers or whores except if
you will my mother who was different because she was dead and
way off like a saint or so. Take it as you will, wasn't any one of
the three my idea of what a man would call a good time, anyhow
not on a steady basis. Now I was finding out about something else,
just plain woman, straighter in some ways than a man, tougher
pound for pound, steadier on the trigger when you found the right
one. I was picking this up from her, watching her gimp around the
house, feeding the chickens, drawing and hauling water back and
forth from the spring, washing and cooking and all the things big
and little I never saw. She looked after me and didn't talk about it
and never whined. It was enough to make me feel like doing things
for her some. Not any big thing, all right, but putting up shelves
around the stove so she wouldn't have to walk so much, getting her
a mail order rocking chair so she could rest now and then. Damn
little, sure, but it was good just wanting to do it for somebody or
to have somebody to do it for. I would have to say we liked each
other O.K. which is worth a whole lot more than I could know
about at the time.*

*So it went along pretty good, the place a little more easy to
live in and putting out better as the months went by. We bought
pigs and added on more corn and I had taken a pretty long step
down the road toward being a pig farmer. But I still had a couple
of things on my mind, what you might call just being plain hungry
for horses and cattle and empty space, something I reckon I was
born with, and the other about what would happen if that Missouri
man came back. I was always figuring out which way he might be
likely to jump since I knew damn well he had not taken off for good
and left that sack of money behind just for the hell of it. No, he
had to be in jail or dead, one, and I would have given considerable
to know which one it was. The place had been bought in her name*

which had been protection for him and could now be the same for me. But suppose he should come back some day when I was off somewhere, figure out what happened, and maybe kill her. Hell, if he was anything he was that kind of man. It was then I begun to think about having her make a will, deeding the property to me in case of death. That he would take it bad you could count on. The question was how bad. And where would Anna put her money if he got her between a rock and a hard place. And even if she stood with me, then what. I had put a hell of a lot of back and elbow into the place. Looked at that way it belonged every bit as much to me if not more than to him. I just didn't cotton to the idea of him walking back in some day and moving me out like a hired hand. Then more. There were the stories in town. The jokes got pretty raw before I caught on. There was one big redheaded sod-buster in particular who liked to lay it on kind of thick whenever I showed up at the store, talking out of the side of his mouth about how much did stud horses bring these days and some people having a natural taste for dark meat and on like that. The day he called me Stud I asked him out to the road. Inside of ten minutes he had beat me down to my knees. The next week it was the same except it took him about twice as long and he was just barely standing on two feet at the end. The next week it was me barely standing, but standing. I whipped his ass good. There wasn't any more of it when I was around after that. But that didn't mean it had stopped. And it would start up again bigger than ever the day somebody rough enough came along to keep me on my knees or worse. Then too, like You know, it was where my mother was buried. I hadn't found her grave even if I had finally run onto some old folks who kind of remembered her. Just the same, she was still around here someplace. It made a difference. There was something about it didn't seem right. I hadn't come here to make her ashamed of me, even if there was hardly anybody to remember. And then something else, a feeling I had then and still get ever once in a while real strong, like nothing in Your heaven or earth don't happen by accident and that all of this was taking me up to a fork in the road where I'd have to go one way or the other. But I don't guess there's any reason why I should be telling You about that. So finally one night I come out with it, not saying anything about the fights or the jokes people were telling but just that it seemed to make more sense that way. I knew she was a good deal older than me but it never seemed to make much difference. I liked being home, having my own place, and she didn't bother me any. That may not seem reason enough for getting married. Anyway it wasn't in a church. And there are worse reasons I can tell You from what I have learned since. When I put it to her that way she got that scared look on her face at first and then it went away. She didn't say anything. That was good enough for me. It took talking a little rougher than I had counted on and a little more money than I had wanted to turn loose of before I could convince the preacher that he was doing the Lord's will, but he finally saw it Your way and mine too. So I had nailed it down. Everything but the cattle, and who was to say we couldn't sell out and head north one day if we felt like it. I even wrote out a kind of a will. The preacher got to me again on that one since he was a lawyer to boot. Which she signed and the hired help witnessed deeding the place to me in case anything happened to her. Not just because I thought once in a while about that Missouri man but because whatever that lead had done to her leg unless it was just a bad kind of rheumatism was spreading. It kind of went to her back. It got to where she couldn't hardly get out of bed unless I helped her and even then she had to spend an awful lot of time in that rocker. It just got to the place where she couldn't make it up at all unless there was somebody around to give her a hand.

So that was where the hired help came in. He was a kid. Well, maybe not really a kid either, not so much under my age at the time but he seemed a whole lot younger to me. I ran across him one day in town when I went in to get some shoeing done on my horse. He was hanging around the blacksmith shop, looking kind of lonesome and a long way from his last meal, not all that different from the way I had been a couple of years before. The only difference was that he didn't seem to be working but more like he had just picked out the stable as a nice place to take it easy in. That, and then he was dressed peculiar, like what we later called drugstore cowboys or what you see in the circus if you will. He had on a kind of buckskin outfit and boots with a high shine and not much marked up and a belt made of little round pieces of silver about the size of dollars, beaded on rawhide thongs and pulled in tight around his waist. Tanner, he said his name was. Bubba Tanner. He wasn't exactly ugly, just dumb-looking. Big in the shoulders and husky. Frowned like he never could quite make out what you said. Not much on talk either, but that could mean a *lot of different things. With a couple of hours to kill while the blacksmith was working on my horse, I had time enough to make up my mind that he might be just about what I was looking for. His teeth were all yellow and he had one of the sharpest Adam's apples I ever saw. Well, it wasn't so easy to find—a man to do housework, clean out the chicken house, maybe even take a shot at cooking. Pick up the slack for Anna is what I'm getting at. But there was something about that outfit he wore made me think he might just bite. Or maybe he just looked hungry, one. So I put it up to him in a general kind of way. Then when he brought his horse around from the back of the stable where he'd tied him, I knew I had my man. That was surely one of the damnedest horses I ever did see, big like some kind of an elephant and older than dirt. The only thing missing between him and that horse was the plow, and as for riding it was pretty plain that his idea of that was just to hang the hell on. I don't suppose that ever mattered too much to him. His idea of a cowman was how he looked, not what he did. Taken from that angle nobody could complain.*

So I set Tanner up in the bunk house and he got busy on the chores. He did them all right enough, except that it was plain as his Adam's apple that he hadn't left that farm in Nebraska for anything as mud fence plain as that spread of ours. From what little he said about it I got the idea that he had been heading for Texas or wherever it was he called West. But he was like me that way and eating regular started to seem pretty good to him after he hadn't for a while. It was O.K. with him to do what couldn't have been so darn different from what he had done up home except now he had a cowboy suit to do it in. The little money I paid him had gone into a sixgun and shells. Evenings I would hear him out back, practicing. I don't know that I was entirely easy about that gun. He had a kind of dumb, hard meanness about him that bothered me some. Take the way he'd kill a chicken, not something you just did so you clean it and cook it and so on but like he got a kick out of it, wringing their necks so hard that their bodies would fly clear across the barnyard and then flop all over the place, bleeding. I didn't like the way he stood there, holding onto the head, laughing at that flapping mess. He put a little too much into it and got too much fun out of it to suit me.

Well, we went along like that through the summer. I had run through three by that time. When September came I figured I would try to get Anna up to Oklahoma City just as soon as we got the corn in so she could see a doctor. Early one morning I told Tanner to follow me down to the cornfield as soon as he had emptied the stove. Then I went on down to the far side of the field and started picking. That field was about a mile from the house and it was some little while before Tanner got there. But that didn't bother me any. He knew his way around a cornfield a hell of a lot better than I did. By noon he would have caught me and left me behind. After an hour or so the sun was coming down full blast. I stopped to take a breather, pushed my hat back, and looked up the row to see how far along Tanner was. Then my eyes just kept on going, seeing that smoke way up over the trees and fanning out just a touch in the wind. All I could think of was why wasn't there any noise? Just smoke, a little darker than the sky, or come to think of it maybe it was lighter, standing up there like one of them there California redwoods. Hey, I hollered at Tanner. You see that? Yeah. That's all he said. Slow and kind of confused, the way he always talked. But I was already running as hard as I could, kicking my way through those damned corn rows and him pounding along behind me. By the time I had cleared the cornfield I could see it was the house like I was afraid of. Now there was noise and plenty of it. I could hear that fire just chomping its way through that house and then Oh My God I could hear Anna screaming short and high, one after another, like she couldn't get her breath. That house was like a nest of snakes with flames shooting all over it like tongues fast as greased lightning with that smoke all thick and ugly and rolling over slow. I got as close as I could, holding my hands in front of my face and there was such a hell of a racket, dogs barking, her screaming in a way that made me feel that the skin was being stripped right off me like you'd skin a rabbit and then that high neighing of the horses that made me look at the barn. There were trailers of smoke around the roof and flames kind of licking up around the edges. Lord, everywhere I looked there was fire and my head was ready to bust with all that screaming. By now I didn't know which was Anna and which was the horses. Then, looking at the barn roof, I remember the mail bag. Every bit of money we had was in it. My mind was moving full tilt now like a jumper coming up to a fence and I thought looking at Tanner real fast there where he had come up beside me Man there is no time now to explain. Get Anna I yelled at him. Get her the hell out.

*I'll go in the barn and cut the stock loose. I swear to You Lord
I don't know even to this day why I said or even thought of it that
way. He had been looking after her. That must have been part of it.
And then the money, there was no time to tell him about it, and
three years of work and all I had to my name was right on the
edge of going up in smoke. But he didn't budge and I stared hard
into his face and it was just like the way he watched those headless
chickens spouting blood all over the yard. She's your woman was
all he said, frowning like he always did and kind of scared-looking
too but not moving. I don't guess it was very long but I felt like I
stood there staring at him for about half of my natural life. Then
those screams broke in on me again, Anna, horses, oh my God I
can hear it still. How many times have I jumped out of bed at
night, still hearing it, still trying to figure out what to do. Tanner
you son of a bitch get her the devil out of that house. I hollered at
him just as loud as I could and then ran like a bat out of hell for
the barn. I scrambled my way up to the loft and got the bag and
then beat my way back through the smoke and got the horses out.
By that time I could hardly see, coughing and crying and trying
to rub my eyes and to hold on tight to that bag all at the same
time. Then all of a sudden there was just nothing. One big silence.
It was like I had gone deaf or something. No screams. Nothing.
I watched just standing there in a daze. That fire like one great big
bonfire and the house a little old black box inside it, smoke still
rolling up heavy and dark. I couldn't hear it because I was trying
so hard to remember something. A smell. While I had been fighting with those horses. The smell of coal oil. I looked around quick
and there he was, Tanner, leaning against the fence I had built
myself, a piece of grass in his mouth, still looking scared or just
witless, one, but not straining hisself to do one goddam thing.
Then all of a sudden the smoke I had swallowed seemed to back up
on me and I was down on my hands and knees, sick as a dog. And
when I had heaved until I thought I was going to turn inside out
and the sickness kind of passed on away I just lay there, crying and
scratching my fingers in the dirt, still sick in a way I didn't know
how to get any medicine for. I kept hearing her, those screams, like
echoes now in some big old quiet canyon someplace and I said right
there, out loud, over and over, Anna there just wasn't time, hear,
and then I would look up like I thought to see her limping on across
the yard to bring me a cup of water or something, real quiet and*

kind of beat down a little, the way she was. I meant to save you.
Believe me. It was everything we had, don't you see? I told that
fool son of a bitch. He was the one. Well, I cried it out after a
while. Then I lifted up my head and looked around, wondering
where the bastard was. Oh I hated his guts. I wanted to kill him.
I don't mind telling You that. I wanted my hands around his
stupid neck. I called his name, loud and then louder yet. Then I
got up and started looking for him and I couldn't help feeling
afraid when he didn't answer, like maybe he'd gone to town to
call everybody out in the road and tell it, out loud right there in
the sun in the middle of the road, just like that. By that time I was
running, hollering out his name. Finally I ran all the way back to
the cornfield. He was down in the corner in the shade where we
had left the jug. He was nursing it and when he took it down from
his mouth I could see the whiskey running down his chin. Taking
his ease if you will. He didn't look scared any more. You know
something, Tanner? I tried to make my voice mean but I couldn't
stop trembling. I smelled something I didn't like there in the barn,
boy. Smelled just like coal oil. Like I was daring him to answer.
He had a flat way of talking through his nose. Funny he said back
at me. I kind of figured I smelled it too. He grinned at me
then, showing me those yellow teeth of his, and dropped his eyes a
little. I guess that's all there is left. I looked down to where he was
looking then and I saw the sack. I still had it in my hand. And
when I looked back up at him I felt like I was seeing my shadow,
something I could never shake loose from again no matter how
hard I tried, no matter how far I ran, like we could neither one of
us do without the other ever again.

He sat there with his arm aching all the way up to the shoulder.

"Well," he said aloud, and then he laid the pencil down. He ruffled through the tablet, looking at the soft grey penciled words. A piece of his life that big, right here in what took up just a little better than a Big Chief Tablet.

"Yes," he said then, his voice harsh and cracked, turning around and blinking rapidly as he heard the cell door grate open.

"What the hell is all this about?"

It was Bird, Arkansas accent, bug eyes, mouth tight as a coin purse, gritty as West Texas dust and just about as friendly. For a criminal lawyer he had all it took.

He put the tablet down and took the top off the flask. "I don't have to testify against myself, do I, Jack?"

"Testify, hell. I'm your lawyer."

"Since when?"

"I found a message from your wife. She tried to call me at the hotel. I just got in from Choctaw."

"Well, you saw the warrant."

"I just wondered if you had."

"Now, Jack, don't talk so much business. You look tired. A little whiskey for what ails you."

"I want to get the bail set and you the hell out of here. Here's to you."

"Now that's what I had on my mind. You see," and he rolled the whiskey around until it burned his tongue, "I'm just not so sure I want any bail. What I mean to say is, I figure I'll stay put. Till it's all over, that is."

"You scared of somebody, or what?"

"Nobody you'd know. Well, what the hell. When you get right down to it, what other way is there of knowing whether a man's guilty or innocent. I reckon I'd like to get it settled."

Bird wet his cigar down and then took his time lighting it. "What do you mean, get it settled, Clay? That sort of business is between you and your Maker. All the law can do," and then he pointed out the window, "is just patch things up for the here and now, one day to the next."

"That's all I'm asking the law to do, Jack. I'm taking care of the Lord my own way. But what happens out there will give me an idea of what He's got on his mind."

Bird nodded, not saying anything, smoking his cigar, sitting on a three-legged stool that the jailer had brought in for him. "Well," he said after a while. "I guess we ought to do some talking. There are some things you ought to tell me. But I'm just not real sure that you're making a hell of a lot of sense tonight."

"Oh, I'm making sense all right, Jack. I've been sitting in here for what—damn near five hours—and I'm making more sense tonight than I've made in a long, long time. My mind is clear, clear as spring water. Now what do you want me to tell you?"

"Look, Clay. Somebody wants to pin the Red Hawk murders on you. Now if a man wanted to make a case, wanted to tie you and Booth together on this thing—well goddammit, you heard me at Shoat's trial. I start off with the premise you're not guilty. But don't horse around with me. I've been through this once with Shoat already—"

"Not guilty of what, Jack?"

Bird turned the cigar in his mouth, just looking. "You got something more you want to tell me?" he said finally.

"Brother, I've got a lot more. I've got a hell of a lot more. Now you get yourself as comfortable as you can because you're going to have to hear me out tonight, Jack. I've got a whole lifetime to tell you about, and not very long to do it in. And then I'm done. I'm putting it in your hands for out there, and in His—up there—for the rest. Because I'm standing. Ain't nobody going to shake me loose from here until all the cards are down. Now listen."

Jack had heard some of it before, not like this, not the weather and the scenery and the way they talked, not in Clay's soft drawl with him sitting here on the cot like some English king carved on a tomb, but he had heard it. In one form or another he had heard something like it about the lives of half the men he knew here. Sit in the coffee shop long enough, or the lobby of the hotel, or the Smoke House, a man could learn all he ever needed or wanted to know, and more. Too much, for a fact. About Grey Horse, Oklahoma, anyway. But there always came a time when there wasn't anything to do but listen, sit there the way he was sitting now, sipping his whiskey, watching Clay turn the pages of the tablet, wondering what it was all about. He's one of the old breed all right, Jack thought as he lit another cigar. A real hardshell Puritan underneath it all—writing his own Testament, building his own Church, naming his own Saints, putting it all in from the Garden of Eden to the fiery furnace. Original sin to boot. The whole goddam country's nothing but preachers and lawyers, and more often than not a mixture of the two. And here we sit, me trying to get him out of jail, him trying to get a final settlement out of the Lord. He always was a modest son of a bitch.

The voice went on, stilted, singsong, a little distant like a phonograph record. Down the corridor somebody sang out of tune; keys rattled and a tin cup banged against bars. The jailer came once to the door of the cell, stood there listening for a moment, then went away. From the street below he heard a man calling insistently, "Hey, Red. They got you in there, boy? Hey. You up there, son boy?"

Jack listened impassively, watching the cigar turn from leaf brown to silver ash. And behind the voice he could see it as though it were a silent movie, the figures moving somehow disjointedly through the grainy, flickering blur of light and shadow. Horse and rider leaning against the wind, a wagon bed shaking above the slow revolution of the great spoked wheels, a silent face framed by a blanket, the house like a box in the clearing, the ragged edges of corn stalks and pine tops, then smoke, the walls caving in, the wild-eyed horses rearing and pawing the air, two men staring through the silence, one with a jug, the other with a mail pouch . . .

"You see?" It wasn't really a question. Clay had laid the tablet beside him, tapped it on the top a couple of times, then pushed his fingers into his shirt pocket in search of a cigarette.

He thinks he's proved something to me, Jack said to himself, studying Clay's face for something he could not find. He really believes he's told me something big. "When did you say that was?"

"Nineteen-ought-eight," Clay answered, frowning. "Now what the hell does that have to do with it?"

Jack shrugged his shoulders. "An awful lot has happened since then, Clay." He chewed his cigar and wondered how much Clay had had to drink before he got there. "So she died in the fire."

"Oh, for God's sake, Bird." Clay swung his long legs off the bunk and strode to the window. "What do you think my life's been about?"

"You asking me? All right. I think it's been about women and cattle and money and having things your own way—running the show—all in reverse order, of course." He took the cigar from his mouth and jabbed it at Carter. "I'll tell you about when I was a boy one of these days. I was a pretty damn good bush-league catcher, too. I've got two kids in Dallas—but not tonight, Clay. You've got a charge pinned on you that could stick. My business is to beat it however I can. If it's a lawyer you want."

He stopped because Carter had turned away from the window and was staring at him, his face hard, set. "Look, Jack," he said softly. "Get something through that Arkansas razorback head of yours once and for all. I'm not trying to beat any charge. To hell with your charge. Don't you think I could buy my way out if that's what it was all about? I don't want to hear that kind of talk, Jack."

"Clay, I'm your lawyer, not your priest."

"Don't talk Catholic to me. Nobody's looking for any priest. And don't go getting fancy, either. We're not in one of your damned courtrooms. I'm trying to make you understand." Then he began to pace slowly, methodically, seven steps from the window to the door, seven steps back, his hands behind him, his eyes lifted reflectively to the ceiling. "Take Booth, now. You mentioned Booth, the fact that him and me are brother-in-laws." He stopped for a moment and looked toward Jack. "Well, don't you see how it all hangs together," he cried suddenly, his face flushed. Then he bent down, seeking Jack's eyes. "I *made* Booth, Jack. I picked up a handful of dust—two handfuls in his case—blew on it, and there he was. He's always been mine, get it? No, I didn't buy him. It wasn't like that. You might say I helped him some in the beginning and it just got to be a habit on both sides. All right? Ahhh," he said disgustedly. Then he drained the flask and held out his hand for a cigar. "What's your word for it—corruption? Or don't they put that word in the lawbooks," and his mouth opened downward in that soundless laugh of his.

"We don't really need to waste good time on definitions when it comes to Booth, do we now, Clay?" Jack said, taking out his watch.

"Put it back in your pocket. It's my time. I've bought it. You listen. Booth." He was pacing again, seven steps each way.

"I figured you'd come to him sooner or later."

"Shut up, Jack. You've got a dirty mind. I remember him when he came, you know? Mr. Blair Booth. From Virginia. Real South, Jack, not like Arkansas, or Texas either for that matter. A Southern gentleman every inch of the way. He was a man I could like. I knew it the first time I laid eyes on him. Old Blair. You know how we got started?" He leaned against the top bunk, gesturing with his cigar, half smiling, looking at Jack the way he might have looked at someone he hadn't seen in years. "Out at the stomp dances one night. I used to go quite a bit. Still do now and then. He hadn't been here long at the time. It was June, and he come out there where they was dancing. Blair was in better shape then than he is now—harder around the belly. Tall, fine-looking fellow. I always likened him to some Confederate general or other —right out of Dixie. Now there's a real lawyer for you. Virginia and all. So he's setting there. Important, you know. Dignified-like. Blair knows how to carry himself. So this drunk fullblood comes in there looking around for a seat and damned if he don't go up and sit right back of Blair. Sitting up there with a jug, talking to everybody. Pretty soon he leans down and says something to Blair. I could see one or two people right around him start to laugh. Then he passes the jug. Blair sitting there like an old-line cavalry officer, not moving. Well, it was old Frank Red Hawk, God rest his soul, drunk as a skunk. Everybody kind of holding their breath, figuring Frank to puke all over him or fall in his lap, one. But what could Blair do? Dignified and all. So I climbed down from where I was sitting and walked around the stands until I was in back of Frank. He was up there on the top row— well, you know, there isn't any kind of a back rail or anything. I climbed up those cross timbers like a goat and got my arms around Frank and just pulled him right out of there, ass over teakettle. Whomp. I heard him hit the ground behind me, then I got down and hustled him out of there. Well, somebody must have saw me, cause the next time I ran into Blair in the coffee shop, he made some joke about it. That's how we got to know each other."

"Yeah. So you started out with the Red Hawk family, and now it looks like you're going to finish with them, too."

"Man in his position, he kind of naturally needed advice. So many people trying to get at him, for this or that. For crooked deals you'd have to go a long way to beat Grey Horse, which will not exactly come as news to you since you have got what a man might call a ringside seat. Blair trusted me, Jack. If the business came my way, it's because Blair knew I played it straight."

"I figure you made something out of it, too," Jack said drily.

"I don't like that kind of talk, Jack," Carter said, raising his voice. "Man, it wasn't like that. Oh, I know. Don't think I don't know what people say. But I'm here to tell you that we looked after those Chetopa. From the day they were born right through to the preacher at the grave."

"Ten per cent? Twenty?"

He was pacing again, stopping at the window, then the door, then back again. "Any other night I'd kick your teeth in for that. Look at the difference. I hit this town drunk on a rainy night with nothing on me but my clothes and a worn-out Mexican saddle and a bag of money somebody else stole. Running. Blair came here like he was George Washington or somebody. Right out in the open, nothing to hide. I don't mind telling you that if it hadn't been for Blair . . . What the hell was I doing? But you don't see people like that. Everybody's just naturally a bum as far as you're concerned. You wouldn't even give a preacher a break."

"Preachers especially."

"O.K. So Blair comes along. This town wasn't up to him. He's been busting his ass for years trying to look after these people. When he married Mary Rose everybody accused him of wanting the money. Then all the trouble . . . What's he ever done, just tell me that. He's too good for this trash. All right, maybe he does drink a little too much. Who the hell wouldn't, job he's got. What's he suppose to do, go into the Smoke House with an ax and bust every bottle in sight? I call him a goddam saint. Then this other son of a bitch shows up."

"I've heard Booth called lots of names, but I never even heard a preacher call him a saint. I can see where this thing would hit you pretty hard, but—"

"Minute he got off the train. There's your Episcopalian preacher for you. Smart-assing around, talking to everybody about Shoat Dalton. Hell, he hadn't been here two hours before he was shooting his mouth off about the killings, right in front of Mary Rose and Rita. You know, a regular creeping Jesus. Then damned if he don't start nosing around my wife. Well, you were at the club. You saw him. Now will you tell me what the hell for? Go to bed with her? That kind of a son of a bitch don't sleep with a woman but twice a year—on his birthday and the Fourth of July. Maybe New Year's if he's feeling extra horny. No. Not him. He's looking for something. I knew it right away. So did Blair. And goddammit if Blair didn't start to sweat. But why? Thayer isn't big enough to carry his boots." Then he stopped, and for the first time he looked at Jack as though he wanted some kind of an answer. "Jack, he wouldn't be so stupid as to kill them off."

"I wouldn't be surprised if he isn't thinking the same thing about you." Jack yawned and shook his head. "This isn't getting us anyplace."

"Look. The night Jimmy was killed. Blair was out at the ranch. I had asked him to come out, told him I was going to run Thayer out of town if he didn't stay away from Rita. Blair took up for him, said I was just being jealous, that Thayer was too straight for that kind of stuff. We drank a lot and he argued with me. Well, I listened. What the hell. There's not many people I listen to, but Blair's one of them. Blair's the kind of man you've got to respect whether he's got any money or not. But he was so damned nervous. I said to him, 'What's wrong, man? This isn't your fault. You didn't pick him out. You didn't ask for him.' Then he said, 'That's the whole trouble,' something like that. He'd been drinking too much. Then we spotted the lights and went over to see what was up and there was Jimmy. Dead. Thayer, too, and Rita with him, naturally. God knows where they'd been before. Well, you'd have thought that old Blair had seen a ghost. I tried to joke him out of it. So we were both a little richer, so liquor got to Jimmy before syphilis rotted him out. Jimmy put that pistol to himself, so what the hell was eating Blair? Something's eating him. Something's been eating him ever since that Eastern bastard got here."

"Clay," Jack said slowly. "I'm going to tell you something you're not going to like. Thayer's not anybody to fool with. He's dangerous. He believes in something that goes beyond what he can get his fingers on. I wonder how much you know about that kind of man. And if you've got something you're trying to hide from him, you'd better let me help. He's pure. He's clean. Man like that will watch you die and never feel a thing except good."

"What the hell does he believe in?" Clay said scornfully. "No, Jack. He wants something. Rita? You can't make me believe that. She's way too much woman for him. Me? I never did anything to him. Except just the way I am, Jack. Like he hates me for just the kind of man I am. The way I can't take him. But why? Does he believe he can prove I killed—he can't prove anything."

"He thinks he can. Anyway he's got you flat-ass in jail. And nobody can say that you're guilty of resisting arrest. I never saw a man more at home in a cell. And all that crap in that notebook— what's that for?"

But Carter was pacing again, rubbing at his lip with the knuckle of his forefinger. "What does he want her for? And what's she been telling him? Or maybe it's Blair. What the hell did he come out here for? Maybe it's Blair, at that. Maybe it's his hide he's after."

"How much of this do you know?" Jack said impatiently, stubbing his cigar. "This business about Rita. Have you written it all down in a tablet somewhere? What the hell am I doing here? You want me to draw a will, or get your bail set? Make up your mind, damn you."

"There doesn't need to be any bail," he said stubbornly. "I got no place to go. I took off once and got as far as Grey Horse. This is the end of the line. Know?" he said, turning and looking at Jack as though he had just heard him. "How much do I know? You bastard you," and he sat down abruptly on the cot. "I never told anybody. About Rita, I mean. I don't even know that it matters

that much, except that Thayer is in it now, and there's got to be
an answer somewhere. You tell me, Jack." Then he put his hands
out in front of him, big and blunt and square, and began counting
off the incidents in her life, slowly now because this was something he had still not learned to live with. "She was twelve when
she went to California the first time. Visiting family out there in
Los Angeles. Mary Rose told me about it later—showed me pictures. Even then Rita was long-legged, hair falling down her back
straight as a mane. That stubborn look on her face, already wanting more than this little cow town could give her. Well, it was
one of those things that just walks up and hits you in the face—
she told me the story herself. How she went to a theater one
afternoon to see some woman with a Russian name dance. Well, it
hit her about the way it might hit some bushy-headed kid around
here to watch Shoat handle a rope, or more like it, see Walter
Johnson pitch. She couldn't get enough of it. Started keeping a
scrapbook. Still got it up at the house. Crazy over dancing. I don't
mean tap stuff—the real thing—sort of Frenchified you would
have to say. Well, I left Texas because I wanted to see real grass
and fat cattle—part of it, anyway. She caught sight of something
that summer she wanted—oranges or palm trees or water, or just
being up there on that stage with all the lights on her. God knows
we got sunshine enough here."

"It's being able to look around you and see something," Jack
said. "Instead of looking off for thirty miles at nothing. Hell, I
know that from Arkansas. As for the other, well, I guess I know
something about that, too. I played ball for a living for damned
near ten years."

"Whatever it was, she made up her mind to go back, however
she could, once she saw that her folks were bound and determined
to keep her in Grey Horse. She was in the mission school out
west of town at the time, just going home on the weekends. It
took her six months of stealing what was left in her old man's
billfold when he was sleeping it off of a Sunday before she was
able to get enough money for the ticket. One Monday she told her
folks she was going to stay at school the next weekend, and that
Friday she told the Sisters she was going home like she always did.

Then she hustled on down to the station and caught the bus to Tulsa. Next morning she was on the train, heading west for L.A. And then the dancing started for keeps. I guess I must have heard about her first from Mary Rose. They used to invite me over to their place every Saturday night for supper. Blair was always open-handed that way. Most of the time she didn't eat with us but ever once in a while when Blair would have to go down to the ice house or somebody would call or something, she'd come in from the back room. You know I looked up to Blair for that. I mean about Mary Rose. Now I couldn't tell you why he married her in the first place. He treated her real good is what I'm trying to say. He married her and he looked after her and he didn't give a shit about all the talk. You've got to admit it. Blair's big that way. Big-hearted and open-handed—give you the shirt off his back. Generous to a fault. 'Well, how goes it, Mary Rose,' I'd say, something like that. You know, you can't talk to them just the same way. She liked me, too, the way Blair did. Maybe she knew I'd been married with an Indian woman. That would count, don't you think? Depending on what she'd heard, of course. Anyway, sometimes she'd tell me about her little sister—oh, but she was proud of her—how she was studying this dance business and so on. Sometimes I thought Rita was all Mary Rose really cared about other than Blair, not having any kids of her own. Well, I never gave it much thought until two or three years later. There was a picture of her in the paper, up on her toes, hands over her head, just as straight as a die. Perfect was the only word for it. There was a story—local Chetopa girl international success— something on that order. But the picture hit me—and not the way you might think, Jack," he said, holding his hands up in front of him as though Jack had covered him with a gun. "Not like that. I'll tell you what it was, dammit. She just looked all combed and curried if you will, like the kind of horse you might see in Louisville for the Derby. You know what came to my mind when I studied that picture? Beautiful. That word came right into mind and I knew I hadn't ever had any idea of what it meant because judging by this picture I just hadn't ever seen a beautiful woman before. That night I went over to Blair's and surprised the hell out of him by asking Mary Rose to come sit with us on the porch. A lot of what I'm telling you she told me that night. Maybe she had already told it and I just didn't have any hook to hang it on. Now I wanted to know all she could tell me. I felt like there was a move I ought to make and I didn't rightly know how to start."

He took the bottle from the Gladstone and measured out two drinks and then went on telling it and Jack listened, smoking, sipping the whiskey, thinking that he might as well ride it out because Carter would not be likely to do this again. He's that kind of a man, Jack said to himself—never says anything at all and then once or twice in a lifetime he gives you twenty-five years in a single night. Funny he picked me, but then who the hell else would it be, unless Cody. But then maybe talking to Cody's too much like talking to himself. Something's stuck in his craw—he'll tell me if I can just last him out.

And through the telling he imagined that grave watchful face under the porch light, looking at the pictures and clippings which Mary Rose proudly brought to him, then suddenly hearing the silence and looking up at Booth's astonished face and saying almost surely either "Some kid sister, Blair," while laughing that soundless laugh of his, or "Honor to the family—mean it, Blair, honor to the family." His two public moods, Jack thought. Slyly sentimental or solemnly sentimental, but sentimental however you slice it. It was good ground to stake out—made the other fellow either a little uncomfortable or a little too comfortable and both were good. But let him use it on somebody who doesn't know him like I do. I'm tired of the bastard. I don't want to carry his cross for him tonight or any other night and I don't want to watch him sweating with it, either.

But he went on listening as he always did, nodding behind the cigar smoke as though what he heard was merely confirmation of what he had known for a very long time, not just about Clay but about the very way life worked. How Clay had taken the train to New York City without really any idea of what he meant to do when he got there, but knowing she was there and that he had to see her.

"I only had a light suitcase with me. Left the place in Cody's hands and headed out for New York. Just like that. Got into the big station there, coming on in from Chicago, went upstairs and bought me a hotel room. Fancy clerk in striped pants. Didn't tell him I owned me a hotel myself, just gave him a twenty and told him what I wanted. That's how I got the ticket. First time I ever saw her dance. I had to look for her some—she was kind of in the back, and all those girls looked alike for the first few minutes. Then she put her hands up over her head and I spotted her and it was just like in the picture. I could have picked her out then if they'd put a thousand of them up there. I never did figure out the story of it—princes and such, dairymaids was what the program was getting at, but no cows of course, and people running through the woods and sword fights and the girl dying in the end, sad-like. People clapped every now and then but I couldn't see why especially. It was all kind of pearl-and-rosy-colored—men, too, with plenty of muscle but not looking too strong, in tights like what you'd see in a carnival, and then a whole flock of girls, thin to beat hell and prancing around like they was walking on eggs. Jack, I want to tell you she was pretty. She was more than pretty. She was beautiful if you want to say it that way, and why not." He stared up out of the darkness and there was youth and purity, legs that moved with effortless perfection, all silken and silvery in the soft light, and then he had closed his eyes so that he was all alone with the violins and wept a little, not knowing whether it was because of something lost or something found or just because of all the sweet, sad music, saying God You have made me travel a long, long way. And when the lights went up again he felt that he had come into a new world, and that she had led him there. At intermission he pushed his way through a blue haze of cigarette smoke and tuxedos and pearl-draped bare shoulders, looking for a program. "I found her name in it all right. Rita Red Hawk. Born in Grey Horse, Indian Territory, 1897, and then that picture again, her arms up over her head, her face looking down to one side, well, like a goddam rose before it opens up," he said a little hopelessly, as though knowing that no words he could find could ever conjure up that enchanted world for a man whose appreciation of legs outside of a bed would be pretty much confined to a shortstop who could go deep to his right and still make the play at first. "Anyway, I stuck the program in my hip pocket, went back and got my bag, checked out, went on downstairs to where the trains were and caught the first one out for home."

"Move over," Jack said. "It's my turn to walk for a while." When he came up off the stool he felt as though he had just finished catching a double-header. "So you came back home. You spent the better part of a week on the train for one night in New York City where you saw a half hour's worth of dancing girls—what the hell is all this about men in tights, anyway—"

"Let it go, Jack." Clay was up on the cot again, sitting with his legs pulled up against his chest, looking straight ahead at the grey wall. "I didn't see her again for two years. Mary Rose would show me the clippings and the photographs and the post cards and once in a while a letter. She was getting to be kind of a star, you might say. They made a big to-do over the fact that she was Indian and all—especially across the water—France and so on. Well, she was a very big dancer, Jack, that's all. I read it in the programs she would send. Hell, they're all athletes before they get drowned in rotgut."

"Yeah," Jack said. "Like all niggers can sing. Come on, Clay, if she was all that good—"

"I was waiting for that. Why did she come back is what you mean," Clay said softly. "Well, you son of a bitch, she loved me. You're just going to have to swallow that, friend. I was able to give her something nobody else could," and he waved his hand to a ghostly crowd of listeners, as though he had forgotten that he had a real one for a change. "I was ready to hang the moon for that girl—anything she wanted. I went after her, all the way to Paris, France. I had waited for a long time, don't you see. Worked, built it all up. I wanted her to have it. She knew it, too. She knew I was putting everything I had right at her feet. Men? Up to here in midgets. Every kind of count and lord, most of them with not much more than a mustache and fancy English. I had to kick my way through the lot of them the way you'd kick your way through a pack of hounds that had run a deer to ground. Them boys had plenty of class," he mused, laughing a little as though to himself. "I had a hell of a lot more money. Besides," and his voice turned harsh, "she was what I needed and she liked that. All women do, Jack. What the hell was it for her by that time but a bunch of scrapbooks. I knew who she really was and that's what mattered to me."

"Well, it makes a nice clean story," Jack said, looking at Clay with his head cocked a little to one side the way he'd look at a dumb pitcher who had missed a sign. If you played the percentages, he thought to himself, it would have to figure—Rita Red Hawk risen pure as a flame from the darkness where Anna Poteau's ashes were as restless as the Oklahoma wind. "But I haven't figured out yet what you're trying to say. If this is your way of telling me that you never killed anybody then you've wasted your breath and your money both. If you're working your way around to explaining how you and Blair were carrying out more of your missionary work on behalf of the natives by killing off a couple of drunk troublemakers which like all your other philanthropic enterprises ends up by putting another roll in your pockets—then I'm not buying. Sorry, Clay—souls aren't my long suit. As for your wife—first you tell me she's two-timing you with that kid lawyer and then you say she turned down half the titles of Europe to be Mrs. Clay Carter. No. I want to know what I'm being asked to do before I look at the pictures on the money. To tell you the truth, if it was anybody but you I'd say you were stalling."

"Jack," Clay said bitterly. "Jack Bird, you Arkansas son of a bitch. You haven't understood one goddam word."

They both turned toward the cell door then, listening. The jailer's voice had risen to a pitch of defeated self-importance and footsteps grew louder in the hall. Then Cody stood there in front of them while the jailer fussed helplessly behind him. "All I asked to know was what he wanted." The jailer addressed himself to Clay as though he owed him an explanation.

"It's all right," Clay said, waving him off. "He's not going to hurt anybody."

I wouldn't bet on that, Jack was thinking, watching the way Cody stood there at the cell door, his knuckles yellow where he gripped the bars, his eyes big and staring as though he were walking in his sleep, something haggard and desperate in the drawn tightness of his face. To Jack he looked a whole lot more like he was in the cell than outside it.

"Well," Carter said sharply.

Cody held onto the bars as though he were afraid of falling. His stained mustache trailed down over bare, discolored teeth, and his goatee seemed no more part of him than his hat, ready to fall off at any moment.

"Undone," Jack said under his breath. "He's come unstrung. Like some damned clown who can't find his way back to the circus."

"Well, what the hell is it?" Carter had swung his legs off the side of the bunk and was staring angrily at Cody. In the silence Cody's breath came in short, swift pants and he looked at Carter like a winded hound. Then through the shadow cast diagonally across his face by the brim of his hat his eyes rolled whitely in the direction of Jack, settling again in a stare fixed on Carter's face.

"All right," Jack said, "but make it quick." He didn't like it, the dumb fear on Cody's face, the furtive closeness between the two men. He had never had any use for Cody, about whom there was always an air of something staged, as though he had taken the wrong turn in a Western movie and ended up sitting with the crowd.

Jack let himself out the cell door and went on down the hall to the toilet at the end, then cadged a cigarette from the jailer and stood outside in the night, smoking and wondering what it all added up to. There can't be any good in it, he reflected, so the question is—just how bad is it? Yet Carter hadn't been faking with all that talk—he wasn't that kind of smart. Those stories had to lead somewhere, the kind of a meandering trail a man makes with his life. No, Clay was carrying something around his neck, had been ever since that woman burned to death damned near twenty years ago. The words all had a special meaning for him— trial, murder, judgment. And it wasn't acquittal he wanted, but absolution. "I told the son of a bitch I wasn't a priest."

He flicked the cigarette into the darkness and walked slowly around to the Court House steps. The lights of the town spread out beneath him, flickering like a valley full of fireflies in the night. One place was like another now. For the moment at least this was, if not his town, then the place where he hung his hat. The Court House, the hotel, the post office, the coffee shop, his office. Pick them up and set them down anyplace else, what difference would it make. Loneliness made every place the same, about as much like home as a hotel room. And how was a man supposed to go on living when his heart had gone dead. It was late. He'd be tired in the morning. He had meant to write the kids tonight. Like those papers he used to write at the barber college that called itself a law school. More like that than letters. Well, it was getting on toward the World Series and he wanted to write the boy about that. The girl was different. How the hell was a man supposed to know what to write to his daughter about. When he only got to see her once a year. And they never answered his letters any more, anyway. Just a few pictures that he had pretty well thumbed to death . . .

He shivered a little, then went back to the desk where the jailor dozed. He waited awhile, trying to pick up voices over the ticking of the big alarm clock, then went back down the corridor to the cell. The first thing he saw was Cody standing directly under the naked bulb, his hair pale and thin as cornsilk, his hands holding his hat before his chest, his body twisted and bent forward as though he were about to kneel. Then against the far wall, beneath the window, he saw Carter fallen to his knees, head down, arms outstretched, his hands gripping the bars and his back laboring as though he were trying to pull the wall in on top of him. Time seemed to have ebbed from the bleak grey cube, leaving Cody and Carter fixed in ancient attitudes of grief. Cody's eyes were closed, his face gone white, and the cell lived only in the hoarse sound of Carter's breathing, the straining of his body against the cold iron of the bars.

"What is it, Clay?" Jack asked quickly. "What's happened, man?"

Nobody moved, and then Carter groaned and pushed his forehead against the wall. "Give me five minutes, Jack. Leave me be—just a few minutes." His voice barely made it above a whisper.

Jack looked hard at Cody, but nothing moved in those dead eyes. "All right, Clay. Five minutes. But get hold of yourself. None of this will help."

Well, what the hell else do you say, he asked himself bitterly as he shook another cigarette loose from the pack on the jailer's desk and stepped back out into darkness. He took three quick drags and then sat down on the steps. He hadn't much liked it before—now he didn't like it worth a damn. Just the message telling him to go see Clay Carter in jail. That was enough of a shock to last him through one night. Ghosts up and walking again after he had thought they were buried for good when Shoat and Orval were planted six feet under. On the way to the Court House in his car he had tried to put together what little he had to go on. Hell, anybody who wanted to could hear plenty of talk, and hadn't he himself based his case on the claim that Shoat had been framed? But goddammit all, that was for the jury. The way that green kid Thayer had leaned on him at the club that night. But Carter wouldn't need it, wouldn't have a reason, unless there was just something twisted in the man, some fault that had to play itself out whatever the cost. Cody, maybe. And then in the cell, that strange air of satisfaction, those stories so like a confession. Had Carter been leading him on, unable to say it himself, waiting for Jack to stumble over the bodies in the dark? And now the two of them in there, Carter down like a poleaxed steer, Cody still petrified by whatever it was that had happened. Well, he's got to tell me now, Jack muttered grimly, taking a last deep drag. Then as he got to his feet, Cody came out through the screen door. His head jerked around when he saw Jack, his mouth opened as though he would speak, then he jammed his hat down hard on his head and was gone, the sound of his boots fading after Jack had lost him in the dark.

"You ought to be in a sideshow somewhere," Jack said, loud enough for him to hear, and then made his way back past the snoring jailer to the cell.

Carter was sitting on the stool, holding a tin cup full of

whiskey in one hand and the bottle by the neck in the other. The flesh on his face seemed to have drawn in, leaving his eyes hollow and staring, dulling the sharpness of his features so that he looked a good deal more like a beagle than a fox. His scalp was freckled beneath damp wisps of carroty hair and the sweat stood out on his forehead as though he had been wrestling.

"Bad news?" Jack said, taking the cup gently from Clay's hand.

With nothing to hold on to, Carter's hand began to shake. "Bad news," he repeated, just getting the words out.

"Cody always looks like bad news to me," Jack said, handing the cup back to Clay and wiping his mouth. "What was it he had on his mind?"

"You call him Cody, too?" Carter swung his head up and seemed to be searching for Jack through a fog of alcohol fumes. "His name ain't Cody," he said roughly, looking back down at the floor. "He made that name up, or borrowed it I guess you'd have to say. His name is Tanner—Bubba Tanner. He gave himself that name when we came here. Dresses like Cody, rides the same kind of horse, cuts his mustache the same way, goatee—didn't you ever notice?"

"William F. Cody was never more than a name to me," Jack said. "Buffalo Bill. I always said he belonged in a circus."

"Well, he was a hell of a lot more than that for Tanner," Clay said, his mouth twisting into something like a smile. "I know that son of a bitch real well. Better than I'll ever know anybody else. Jack, I know him like he was me—that good. He thinks he *is* Cody," and then he threw his head back and laughed in a way that was half croak, half sob. "Like we was chained together for the rest of our lives, you hear? Waiting there all day in the clearing till even the wind had died down and the ashes didn't move any more. They might as well have put the handcuffs on us right then. From that day on, I swear, when one of us moved the other one was on his feet. Like the two sides of the moon, Jack, the light and the dark." He drained off what was left of the whiskey, then banged the cup on the concrete floor. Then he lurched across the cell and seized the door, rattling it wildly until the jailer appeared.

"Key's in the door if you need anything, Clay," the jailer said sleepily, looking back and forth from Carter to Jack.

"Cards," Carter roared, "and something the hell to play on."

"I guess I'd heard that before," Jack said, biting the end off another cigar. "I never knew for a fact what was behind it. I'm not so goddam sure that I do now, if you want to know the truth of it." Lighting the cigar, he said to himself that Clay would have to give him something to hit sooner or later. Wait him out until dawn, then the hell with him.

The night thinned out as they played until the sky on the grill of the window was the color of the cigar ash at their feet. Stud, draw, blackjack, pitch, red dog, Jack lost at all of them, studying Carter's broken face. Shuffling, Clay would stop a moment and say, "You know something, Jack. I don't quite get you. You act like maybe you believe I really killed somebody. Do you believe that, Jack?" His body swayed on the stool and his mouth hung open around the cigar. "I'm not a killer," he said softly. "I never had the guts for it. What I wrote down there in the tablet—that's God's truth, Jack. Tanner's what you want when it's time for blood or fire. Ashes," and he laughed that silent, agonized laugh of his. "Leaving them all scattered out behind me like a string of campfires on the way to hell. Card?"

Jack drew a ten and turned his cards up. "Busted," he said, and put his hands on the cards that Carter had started to pick up. "What about that carnival freak, Clay? What did he come here to tell you? He knocked the shit out of you with something. You better tell me now, if you mean to tell me at all."

"Tanner?" Clay said loudly, slurring the name. "Just a dumb kid off a Nebraska pig farm looking for a cowboy suit and a sixshooter and some Indians to kill. Buckskins and Justin boots and trick guns," and he wiped his mouth disgustedly.

"He's a cowman, like the others. What did he—"

"Cowman, hell. I wouldn't let him near my cattle. He adds up the feed bills, works out shipments—anything to do with numbers. Money, Jack. Like a sod buster with a lead pencil, toting it up."

"How much per Indian does this pigsticker earn, Clay?"

Carter narrowed his eyes. "You're a mean little bastard, Jack. You're not big enough for any of this . . ."

"For a cell in the Grey Horse jail? For a sentimental drunk who stalls me all night with hard-luck stories about working his way to the top? For a line of shit a yard wide about fancy dancers and—"

Carter rose straight up, hurling the table away from between them. "Call her name just once, you foul-mouthed, bush-league—"

"Shut up, Clay. Put that bottle down."

Jack saw him stop with his arms still in the air, the bottle high above his head, and then he heard it too, the long-drawn-out banshee wail of the fire siren, hovering over the town like a pall of smoke. Clay waited, motionless, through the curve of sound that swooped low and rose again. Then he flung the bottle with all his strength against the wall. Jack closed his eyes and ducked away from the splintering glass, and when he looked up again, Carter had fallen to his knees before the window. On his face was that same tragic mask that passed with him for laughter, except that now there were tears running down the lines of his jaw. He rocked back and forth against the hard shiny heels of his boots, saying over and over again in a whiskey-hoarsened voice, "Praise be to God, Thy will be done."

Jack watched him, his face meditative, bleak, skeptical, too skeptical, as though he needed it for protection. "Like being on the wrong end of a no-hitter," he said sourly. It didn't sound good, even to him, but there was nobody else to hear.

3

HE STOPPED THERE IN FRONT OF THE BANK, UNDER THE clock, looking down at the toes of his boots which gleamed like silver dollars. Too late. Boys done gone home, maybe, or over to the pool room. Could use a shine.

"I need a goddam shine," he said aloud.

Then down the street was the barber pole lit up like a stick of peppermint candy. What the hell. Of course. Ferg was still open because tomorrow was a holiday and everybody was still in town.

"I don't need any of his help, that's for sure."

He squared himself and walked along the street that was empty except for the dark. And for one or two people who stared at him. Kids and such.

"I'd like to face him down right here in the street, full day, everybody the hell out of sight. He hasn't got nothing on Clay. He can't have nothing on him. He sure the hell can't have nothing on me."

The light was just right on the plate-glass window of Woolworth's and he stopped again and looked at himself. Tall, real tall, lean and mean.

"Draw," he said softly, and his hand jerked along his thigh. "Put your money where your mouth is, friend. You're talking just a little too goddam big."

He straightened his hat and wet his fingers, then ran them over his eyebrows and goatee and then his hand stopped and his mouth fell open while he tried to get his breath.

"Clay won't let you get away with it," and he stood there

trying to think, trying to remember, so he could tell it straight and careful if he had to.

"Look what the wind blew in." Ferg was scraping the lather off somebody's face. The air was warm and sweet and sharp, like the smell of Lucky Tiger. "Rest yourself, Cody. I'll be done in a minute."

"I need a goddam shine."

"Mose'll shine you. Wake up, Mose. You got business, man."

He climbed up on the leather throne and set his boots hard on the iron feet.

"Don't look to me like I can do much for you, Mist Cody. Ain't no boots in town got a better shine than what you got. Lessen I put on some varnish or paint or something."

"Lay on, son boy, lay on. You can tell more about a man from his boots than anything else he's got."

"Don't argue with Cody, Mose." Ferg's flat boxer's face shone sweaty in the light. "These here Indian killers are trouble. You may be a lot of things, Mose, but you sure as hell ain't no gunfighter."

Mose laughed and whistled a little, spreading the wax with his fingers as though he had a spatula in his hand. "Whoo-ee. You done said right, Mist Ferg. You don't catch me foolin with no gunfighter."

"I didn't hear you too good, Ferg." Cody stroked the pale bars of his mustache along his lips. "Man talk about Indian killers to me, he better speak up."

"Why Cody, I reckon you're the expert on that." Ferg wiped the razor on his apron, then stropped it hard on the length of leather that hung from the chair. "Ain't nobody else in Grey Horse can match you when it comes to Indians."

Cody half closed his eyes, watching Ferg's face, trying to figure him out. "You're talking about the way it used to be," he said after a while. "Well, there wasn't never any good Indian but a dead one. Did you ever see one could work? Or handle whiskey? I never figured them to be all that different from buffalo, when you get right down to it. Had to be cleaned out, all of them, make room for the Americans." He kept waiting for Ferg's face to change, but Ferg just went on shaving, scraping away like he was cleaning the hair off a hide. "I guess I killed my share." *Around him the pines surged fitfully in the wind that swept ever downward from the great rocky peaks of the Sierra. The tall walls of the canyon went straight upward, like a structure built by human hands, like some great cathedral hailing the glory of the Creator, to the heavens. And from the sky the full round moon shone down, though every now and then a sullen cloud passed over and hid the light of the vestal orb as if the dark-hued courier of the sky, sailing upon the bosom of the air, was jealous of the silver sheen. Cody, the man upon whose strength and judgment the whole wagon train depended—whose life from boyhood had been but one spotless record of standing up to evil and villainy—trembled, standing in that mountain canyon, at a sound the pure night air had brought to his ears. A sound not quite close enough to Nature's voices for he who had spent his life on the wilderness trail. With every sense on the watch, he stood like a statue against the sky. His hand clutched the handle of a revolver in his belt. Two sixshooters were buckled to his waist, and the blade of a broad, keen-edged bowie knife thrust through his belt, gleamed silver in the moonlight. Out there somewhere in the darkness skulked a dusky band who hungered to lay their heathen hands upon him, for who else stood between them and those women and children who dreamt all unawares through the hostile night? You're going to have to do some tall thinking about who your friends are before this is over. You're going to have to figure out whose side you're on.* "Well, who the hell's side were you on, Ferg?" he said angrily. "Answer me that. It wasn't just so awful goddam long ago that a man would be proud. Kids call him by name and all." He licked his lips and looked around the room as though it were full of people listening. "You act like you're calling me a name or something. Ain't nobody I ever heard of made a name for himself by *saving* Indians, did they?"

Ferg rubbed his hands briskly across the head and face of the man who lay dozing in the chair. Then he looked up and grinned over teeth that sprouted unevenly like grains of corn.

"That never gave me no trouble, Cody; I always knew which side I was on. Hell, we were in the same business, them Indians and me. But a man couldn't rightly make a living, cutting hair their way—trouble was the customer never came along but only oncet. Now haul your ass over here. You're up. Old Mose'll go right through to bone if he works on those boots any longer . . ."

Being in the barber's chair meant that for a while a man knew what was going to happen and could cut loose and drift, all the way back to a day in North Platte when the Wild West Show rolled in on flatcars and everybody was saying his name. Colonel Cody, Colonel William F. Cody, which sounded like a made-up name because his real name was Buffalo Bill and my God Almighty what didn't he have in that tent that stood up there blowing in the sun like some kind of an A-rab palace. You say horses, he had horses. Indians out of that army what had laid George Custer in the dust. Cavalry from countries that weren't even in the geography books. Trick shots and bareback riders and flags and whips and a military band. After a while he had slipped down from his seat and out from under the tent and run behind a tree where he could throw up and then he sneaked back in again and it was still there, Buffalo Bill in the dead center of the ring on a thin-legged white horse that sure didn't look like it had been near any plow, sitting there like he did in the pictures, buckskin and boots and pearl-handled Colts, with a mustache and a little bit of a beard and a big white hat, just making them all hop to. Well, it beat anything, all that music and the horses a-wheeling and the hooves pounding away like tom-toms and right at the end a flag about the size of the sky and *The Star-Spangled Banner*. He felt like he hadn't hardly taken more than one breath and held it and then let it out, and there he was with damn near everybody gone, still sitting there in overalls and workboots and his hand sweating where he held onto the nickel that was left over.

The sun came in from the far end of the tent where it was open and there was dust in the air like a cloud of gnats and he went down to the ring where the ground had been torn up by a thousand hooves. He couldn't help himself because he had to know, and then he looked and said it right out loud.

"Them cow ponies don't even shit like what we got out to the farm."

He ran then like somebody might have heard him and he kept on running most of the way back home. Back to the low little house on that treeless rise, the barn behind, the fields and the fences, the windmill, all of it blunt and solid like it had been hacked out of the earth and propped up against the sky. He came into the kitchen, breathing hard. Nobody looked up.

"I've still got a nickel," he said, like he was ashamed of it, and he laid it on the table.

"Don't bother that there red hen when you clean out the chicken house. She's settin'."

He looked at them and it was like he couldn't see their faces because he was already crying, even before he had the bucket and was outside and on his way to the barn.

He cried in his dreams all night and when he woke up his face was still wet and he knew it was on account of it was all over and he couldn't even say goodbye. He rolled up the few clothes he had and tied a piece of twine around the dime novels he hid under his mattress and then he went on down to the barn through the cold blue dark of early morning.

"It was a cold stormy night when after kissing his mother's pale cheeks for the last time on this earth, the Kid rode out into the darkness."

"I can't make out what the hell you're saying," Ferg said. "Them towels too hot, or what?"

"I never could figure it out. Now you take Buffalo Bill. As fine a looking gentleman as you would ever want to see, walking or riding. But you talk about your Indian killers . . . And how was a kid my age to know any better? Hell, he wore white gloves and a white hat, rode a white horse—by God, I even believe his boots were white. Now the truth of it was that out on that prairie you couldn't hardly move without kicking up a cloud of flies that damn near hid the sun. Sounded like a hailstorm or something. All that blood and bone and guts—buffaloes, Indians, grouse, and antelope—I mean to tell you. Hundreds of thousands gone. Clean as a hound's tooth. Where was the West in all that? How was a kid like me suppose to find it?"

He had looked for it clear across Nebraska and Kansas, and he was still looking when he crossed the Arkansas River and rode into Indian Territory, working his way south and west through that lonely land of puckered-faced farmers who all looked at his horse and then at him like they wondered whereabouts he had stolen it. Hiring out by the day or the week, then traveling on until he was too tired or hungry or lonesome to push it any further. Generally he left the towns alone, crossing them, when he had to, by night, except for Ogallala and Caldwell and Ellsworth and Dodge City, cow towns full of saloons and women in satin and runty little bowlegged cowpunchers who talked Texican and rode through town shooting out the gas lamps or fought each other like dogs in the dirt in front of the bars. He figured he could shoot a man if he had to, but what could you do with that kind of woman? He tied up his horse and hauled the saddle over to where there was shade and leaned up against it so that he could think some. Laying there in his buckskins and the honest to God Navaho Indian Silver Belt that he had saved up for and bought out of the catalogue, he would undo the twine and read a little.

TALL AND SHAPED LIKE A KIOWA, *he might have been mistaken for a warrior of that wily nation, but he was not.*

He was a white man, but the climate of many Indian lands had tanned his face; he was the best trailer, the grandest fighter, the greatest scout that ever crossed the Mississippi. A keener eye was not to be found in the Indian lands of America; a deadlier rifle never rested upon a saddle.

He was a plainsman in every sense of the word, yet unlike any other of his class. In person he was about six feet one in height, straight as the straightest of the warriors whose implacable foe he was; broad shoulders, well-formed chest and limbs, and a face strikingly handsome. Add to this figure a costume blending the immaculate neatness of the dandy with the extravagant taste and style of the frontiersman, and you have Wild Bill, then as now the most famous scout on the plains.

But not here in this muddy collection of cattle pens and sporting houses where he listened to the hum of horseflies until he fell asleep, dreaming further on, further on . . .

Most of the way across Indian Territory, which was lonelier than anyplace because there wasn't even much in the way of farming and he lived on what he could steal until that day in the blacksmith's shop. Clay Carter his name was. Something over six feet tall, reddish-complexion with quick blue eyes. Some of that cowpuncher look in his clothes, but taller, straighter, something in his face that made you believe him. Hell on a horse along with it. From Texas, it turned out, and he talked like it. Half Southern-like, slow, not like a dirt farmer either but like a man who didn't only have to do his talking with his tongue. He wasn't even wearing a gun, but he had frontiersman written all over that big tanned face of his. So this was the way it happened, more pine trees than prairie, the blacksmith banging a shoe into shape, Carter standing there tall against the sun. West.

"I would have followed him to hell."

"Take off the towels or speak up, one," Ferg said.

"Maybe that's what I did, come to think of it."

"Go on back to sleep, old man. You've been working at the whiskey again . . ."

That ride into Grey Horse, everything gone but what they could carry. Which was mainly the mail sack full of money that Clay had snaked out from the barn, running out of there crying and coughing and holding the sack away from him like it was too hot to hang onto. Anna left for dead back there in the ashes, except when Clay would wake up in the night hollering her name like she was right there in front of him, and he would have to feed him some more whiskey like he was a baby you couldn't wean. Dead drunk for a month—the frontiersman, the scout. Riding into Grey Horse like coming back from hell. Sitting there in the hotel room, having their meals brought up, getting him women and whiskey and explaining to the desk clerk when people complained about all the screaming at night, and Clay throwing it in his face until he damned near believed it himself.

YOU ALWAYS MEANT TO KILL HER. *I knew there was something wrong with you the day I watched you kill your first chicken. You would have liked to wring her neck, wouldn't you. Out in the back where she would have flopped around for a while. Well, you got to hear her squawk, anyway. You didn't miss that part. You knew there had to be money somewhere and you figured that one day I'd be taking off, leaving you high and dry with a skinny little pig farm and a crippled Indian squaw and not a dime between you and winter. So you beat me to it, no doubt with the idea that I would be glad to split the money as your price for keeping your mouth shut. Because you hated her, and you hated looking after her, and you wanted to kill yourself an Indian. Didn't you know I would smell the coal oil, you clumsy bastard? And then you had me all wrong, didn't you. You thought I'd go in there after her. You thought I was some kind of hero or something. Wearing a white hat, sitting on a white horse that probably never did even have to raise its tail, it was that pure. And heroes are dumb enough to go and get themselves dead for somebody else. Leaving you with the money, because you figured I would go for that first. Don't you think I see that? Don't you know I'll kill you someday? You turn your back on me once, you Sears and Roebuck cowboy. Just once. How could I go in there when you didn't even know where the money was? That's how I know it was you. Tanner, I'll see your soul in hell no matter how long it takes, man. Sitting there with that jug, drinking. You don't like it when I've got a girl in here with me, do you. You don't like those silly clothes they wear. You don't like the way they smell. You waiting for Calamity Jane or somebody? Carries a gun and wears pants, smokes cigars maybe? Go out and get laid, Cody. Find your own women and your own whiskey or else go down in the lobby and read those goddam dime novels of yours and stay the hell off my back.*

And what about the coal oil, anyways. The place always smelled of coal oil. He had filled the lamps that morning and he had built up the fire to singe the chickens. Christ, the way they jumped all over the place when the head came off in your hand. Maybe that's what a man's heart would do if you tore it out of him while he was still living. Hadn't the Indians done that when they captured somebody, or maybe it was with buffaloes? And then he had taken the coals out of the stove; except that was what he could never remember. He had been in a hurry because he wanted to sip from the jug a little and read a few pages before heading down to the cornfield. Suppose he hadn't dumped those coals. Or suppose she had knocked the lamp over, trying to get up by herself. Or Clay. There would have been time for Clay to slip back there while he was down at the spring taking a couple of belts to get him through the morning. Clay was so damned worked up over it all, and since when had he cared so much about that gimpy Indian. Probably somebody's whore anyway. They were all whores. Clay hadn't never talked to anybody wasn't a whore, lessen it was his mother. Man only had one mother. So who was to say, and where was the proof, unless it was that nosey lawyer? Was that what he was talking about, or was this something Clay had cooked up, to do what he'd always said he'd do, to finish the job? All that way in the rain, Clay drunk, shouting and crying like a revival preacher, riding into Grey Horse like two ghosts out of a drunken dream, back out of hell to the way it was in North Platte that day so many years ago, buckskins and blanks, Indians that got up off the ground when the show was over, *Old Glory* and *Stars and Stripes Forever*, no more bones and blood and guts and that pile of ashes that smelled like chicken feathers burning, except that now there were Indians dead again, their heads blowed half off, dynamited, poisoned, however many ways a man could think of to kill, and people talking again about Indian killers and nobody clapping and sure as hell no *Star-Spangled Banner*. Plus Clay in jail where they could put a bottle in his mouth and make him talk all night long.

He sat up straight then in the barber chair and lifted the towels away from his face and looked at Ferg who stood there open-mouthed, the razor suspended in air like maybe he thought he was John P. Sousa or somebody.

"You talking about Indian killers and such, Ferg," he said.

"Now I know you are not a reading man. I want to quote you something that a very great American said one day along those lines. Remember these words. They're fit to be carved in stone where a man is put to rest. 'Let a man kill a few desperadoes, in the discharge of duty, and to save his own life, or the lives of others, and before long he is branded as a man-killer, a name that no one who has a true heart cares to hear; but like the official executioner, a true son of the West must stand ready to take life when the occasion demands it.' Wild Bill Hickok, gentlemen. That's where I take my stand."

And all of this a man could almost live with until the hot towels came off for good and his face was dusted with powder and he looked himself over in the mirror and handed out a little change all around. Then out on the street again with the wind cold as rubbing alcohol against his skin, wondering what in the hell it was all about, whether Clay had finally decided to put a match to him and leave him for dead, whether it was the money, or Anna, or the Red Hawk business, or something else he'd never even thought about. He stood there by the barber pole, squinting down at his boots that glowed in the dark like fool's gold.

"I need a goddam drink," he said aloud, his hand moving restlessly along the buckskin at his hip where there ought to be a Colt, and then he cut catty-cornered across the silent street to the Smoke House.

"Nobody ever gave the Kid a chancet. Come West like that, lost his mother, mining towns and all. Man don't have but one mother, don't forget it. Killing. Yes. Twenty-one notches, the books say. Twenty-one hired gunfighters, outlaws, trash . . . all of them for rent for a few pieces of silver. And whose side was he on, anyway? The rich? He never had a dime when he died. Just his clothes, and a pair of matched Colts. Gunned down in his sleep by that Judas Garrett. Money? Wouldn't mean nothing to a boy like that. He was more on the order of what you might call John the Baptist out in the goddam desert, looking for one clear stream that wasn't all muddied up with blood and bones and such. And he couldn't find it—it just wasn't like that. They didn't ride any white stallions where he was, and it got to him so that he just damn well set out to make it that way. I kind of figure him as always dressed in white, right down to his boots. One little old sawed-off Kid with a couple of equalizers. But good. Too good, too bighearted for what people can put up with. So they gunned him down in his sleep."

His foot slipped off the rail and he caught himself with his elbow against the bar. The saddlemaker stood next to him, his neck rolled over his collar like a twist of hide, his tooled belt holding in his belly so that he looked like a buffalo bull on its hind legs. In the back of the room the faces of the cardplayers were blurred with smoke.

"Hit me again," he said to the bartender.

"Never knew you to take to whiskey, Cody," the saddlemaker said, sliding his glass back and forth through the wet ring on the bar.

"I guess my money's about as good as anybody else's in here."

"Ain't nobody in here worried about your money," the bartender said, shifting his toothpick. "You might say we were just naturally bighearted, like the Kid. Huh, Cass?"

"Shit," the saddlemaker said, and laughed down into his glass.

The whiskey was hot in his stomach and he closed his teeth hard and held onto the bar, partly just to stay steady, partly to stop his hand from trembling.

"Well, you tell me then. I say he had some kind of a picture of things that he wanted so much to make it come true that he was ready to kill. I say he was on the side of the little fellow, and the big ranchers had it in for him. How come people love him like they do, then, if it ain't like that? How come they helped him escape and hid him out and wouldn't turn him in?"

"I'll tell you, Cody." Cass turned his head slowly and the light slid across the glasses that rested in the folds of his face. "He was the one was a hired killer, a little two-bit gunfighter like what the woods are full of. Around here even, used to be. Meet one, you've met them all. I've made saddles for them—all want the same kind.

Mexican, with enough silver to break a horse's back. I wouldn't trade you one good horse for every gunfighter ever shot somebody down from behind."

"You ain't talking about the Kid." He had trouble getting the words out and he could feel the sweat running inside his hat.

"Shit yes, I'm talking about the Kid. Who you think I'm talking about? Whoever they hired to kill them Red Hawks? I don't reckon he cared nothing about money either, did he. Anyway, he never got any of it, whoever he was."

"Shoat Dalton killed them Red Hawk Indians, Cass. Shoat and Orval."

"Some people say so. Some don't. They let him off, didn't they? And then he just kind of accidentally turned over out in the big middle of nowhere."

Somebody shuffled a deck of cards, and the bartender cleared his throat. He picked up the money, then rubbed his rag along the bar. "Old Clay's married to one of them Indian girls, ain't he, Cody?"

He took the bottle and poured himself a drink and then held his breath while it washed its way down his throat like a lit match. He pushed his handkerchief up under the sweat band of his hat and then wiped his mouth hard, like maybe he could get the words out better that way. Somebody had asked him something, and he stood there like he was waiting too, listening for his own answer. When it came it was like he had never heard it before.

"She's done dead, Clay's wife."

"Yeah?" Cass said, looking at the bartender now. "Since when?"

"They got Clay up there in jail." He waited, but there wasn't any more. Then he moved his jaw with his hand, just a little, like maybe it was broken.

"Yeah?" Cass said again. "Then how come you ain't in there with him? Huh?" And then he laughed, shaking his head. "Cody, I swear to God. Tell us one of them stories about old Wild Bill. One of them Buffalo Bill stories about how they won the Civil War together."

His face felt the way it did after he had been in a fight, and he knew there was something he had to say. He was breathing hard now, and the sweat was rolling down through his sideburns. "I am running this game and I want no talk from you, sir." Like his mouth just opened and those were all the words he had. Like that.

"Hah. You're a card, Cody, goddam you." Then the saddle-maker brought his face up close, so close that Cody could see the dirt in the pits of his nose and the crisscrossed lines in the purple flesh behind the glasses. His eyes grew larger and when he spoke he sounded like a preacher, the way the oil ran through his voice, so long ago. "I say, Mr. Hickok, how many white men have you killed to your certain knowledge?"

The blood rushed in his ears and he shut his eyes, but when he opened them the glasses were still there, the eyes all red white and blue. He tried to keep his mouth closed, but the words were already there.

"I suppose I have killed considerably over a hundred."

Then slowly, the words he knew by heart, in the same way the kids at school used to ask why do you stay so long in the outhouse. "What made you kill all those men? Did you kill them without cause or provocation?" Cass's breath smelled like sour mash, and up close his face was all shiny with sweat and oil.

Then like he had passed out or something he heard himself saying the words, like drops of water, always with the same sound. "No, by heaven, I never killed one man without good cause."

Laughter blew like the wind in an empty house, and he felt the sound of it shake the bar.

"No, by heaven," Cass's voice repeated like a voice Cody knew but could not remember. "Set 'em up, goddammit, a drink all around. To Hickok and the Kid and Buffalo Bill Cody."

"No." The sound was so loud that it seemed to exist outside him, like another person. "Shut up, every goddam one of you." And in the sleet of broken glass he looked down and saw the top half of the bottle in his hand, sawtoothed as the mouth of a jack-o'-lantern. There was nothing but his breathing, his feet grinding the glass, nothing moving but smoke, the faces lifted, silent, hands holding cards, glasses half raised.

"I said shut the hell up," he cried into the silence, and then what he felt on his face was no longer sweat. "He's up there in that jail. He could buy and sell every one of you sons of bitches. She's dead and I'm telling it to you once and for all. But that's done been finished, and by the time we rode the hell out of there, wasn't nothing but weeds anyhow, and who's going to pick up the first rock. And besides, there isn't any proof," and he could feel them watching him like a jury as he backed away, step by step, holding the jagged bottle in front of him like he was covering them with a Colt, reaching behind him with his free hand for the door.

He was all the way back to where he had parked the pickup before he remembered the broken bottle in his hand. He looked over his shoulder, then laid it against the curb in the shadows. Then he sat down on the running board to catch his breath, wiping his hand across his mouth as though he could rub away the effects of the whiskey. "Women, tobacco, cards, corn whiskey," he said, trying to see into the darkness beyond the light that fell from the street lamp. "This ain't no time to start." He listened for footsteps, but there was nobody following him. The clean, rubbing-alcohol chill was gone from his face, and now he was hot and out of breath. "What the hell did I say in there, anyway? How come old Cass was asking me all those questions? That's all anybody's done all day, just ask questions. I ain't no goddam Moses."

He stood up and rubbed his hands hard on his hips, then opened the truck door and reached in under the seat. His Colt was there and his belt and as he buckled it on he knew he couldn't help it. He wanted to hurt somebody, and there wasn't any way around it. The whiskey fumed in his stomach and his fingers tightened the way they would around a chicken's neck.

"Drink. Guns. Well, who the hell's fault is it? We rode away from all that, didn't we? Weeds grew up so fast a man couldn't even hardly see them foundations any longer. Huh?"

His voice was loud and he looked around him at the darkness, waiting for an answer, swaying a little, one hand at his hip and the other clutching the door handle.

"Don't lean too hard, friend. I don't bluff that easy. If you got something to say, say it. But if you got Clay in jail, how come I'm standing here like I am? You want me to cut and run? Well," and then he pulled his shoulders back and let both hands hang easy at his hips, belt high, his fingers stretched wide. "You get this straight. Ain't no cheap gunfighter gonna run me out of here."

He held his breath, listening, and then he climbed carefully into the truck. But with the motor turning over and the wheel shaking in his hands, he felt the pain spreading in his chest like it did when he was lonesome, and he wanted to cry again.

"No, Jesus," he whispered softly. "That's all behind me now. I want to stay where I am. Let me be, God, let me be."

He tried to smile, and leaned out to look at the sky. The best thing was to go on back to the bunk house, the little one-room place he kept for himself, with his guns and his scrapbooks and his dime novels. And maybe the moon would break through later and he could shoot at tin cans. Maybe one of the boys would throw a few for him, if everbody wasn't in town tonight.

Beyond the lights of town the night closed in around him and he drove alone in the darkness, the dashboard lit up softly so that he could still see the faint gleam of his boots. That made him feel a little better, that and the pull of the Colt at his hip. He tried a couple of songs then, but he couldn't keep his mind on the words because he was trying so hard to remember, as though part of him still stood back there in the Smoke House, facing those hard eyes, waiting for someone to tell him what the charge was.

"That ain't too much to ask, is it?" He was sweating again, remembering the bottle. "I busted it on the bar. Did I hurt anybody? Pray God I didn't hurt anybody, Tanner, what the hell do you want? Who asked you to come back, anyhow. Go on back where you belong, man."

Clay would know what he meant. But Clay was in jail.

I'll be waiting for you. You're going to need me, Cody. A lot more than you ever needed Carter. You're going to need help, brother, all the help you can get.

Then the truck was bucking under him like a bronco and he realized that his eyes were shut and when he opened them he could see the fence running fast across his windshield. He hit the brakes hard and pulled sharply at the steering wheel and then as the truck slid he cut the motor. He was braced against a shock that never came, as though he had run headlong into a wall of dust which now boiled up dense and yellow, shutting out the sky.

He climbed out cursing and began looking for the flat, and then he saw he had bumped across the ruts, slid halfway off the shoulder, and then run up onto the road again. He kicked one of the rear tires and mopped his forehead and then something stopped him where he stood. Some movement in the night which he felt, as though a bird had brushed his face, something which he could not yet see in the darkness which crowded in upon the pale drift of dusty light before the car. He reached in through the window and switched his headlights off, waiting for his eyes to pick it up. And then as the night took shape, he realized that he was not far from the cattle guard that separated the county road from the road that branched off to the ranch. And what he saw at first was the darkness itself moving, like water, and then he began to make out the shapes of cattle, plodding single-file along the fence, following somebody, going somewhere. And not frightened or bunched up along the wire the way they would be in a storm but steady, blind, heads down, for all the world like they were going to water or to feed. But this wasn't the time or the place for feed, and water was a long way off. So there was something not right about it, and he rubbed his hand hard along his jaw, figuring that whatever else there was he had on his mind, he had better have a look-see.

He walked unevenly for a quarter of a mile or so along the road until he came to the cattle guard and then he squatted and sat on his heels, moving his finger in the dust, watching the cattle going by him toward a small stand of trees not far off the ranch road. He could see better now, but he was working more on what he could feel. Something, or someone, was drawing them on a beeline up to those trees. He studied it awhile, remembering the wheel tracks that he had seen before in under the same scrub oaks. That would be it, those two or three head that they missed now and then, pretty regular lately at that. Some of the boys had figured that the rustlers came up at night in a truck, got ahold of the cattle by putting out feed, and then loaded what they could into the back and took off. It wasn't no big deal but it was steady. Man keep at it long enough, he could make out all right.

He brushed the dust from his boots and stood up, pulling his hat tight on his head and loosening the Colt in the holster. Slow and easy, taking his time, he worked his way across the guard and along the road. Then he stopped again because he could see it now, a solid block of black in under the trees. That son of a bitch is a feed truck, he thought, straining to make it out in the darkness. Pretty near like what we use. He could see the cattle milling around it, their heads lifted and rubbing against the sides. He slipped his gun and started to move closer, and then he heard something like a groan that set his teeth together hard, and then the far door banged open and somebody had jumped out and was already running clear of the trees by the time he could set himself.

"Hold it. You, hold it there," but his arm had moved like a whip and he felt the shock right up to his shoulder and then he heard his gun. He heard it three times, and then he stopped, and the sound died away like thunder rolling off after a storm. Still rumbling way off in the distance, his own voice, the shots, something falling in the brush, and then he had to get close behind a tree while the cattle rushed by him. Then that too was washed over by the silence, and there was only the trembling he still felt in his feet after the sound was gone, and the black outline of the truck high like a hearse against the night which was almost as black but not as hard, and maybe somewhere out in the brush somebody stretched out on the rocky ground. All beneath a sky where now from a long way off the moon was trying to push on through the clouds.

He waited behind the tree, doing his best to hang onto his breath, watching the truck. If you thought about it even a little it just didn't make sense, because there would have to be two of them for handling the steers and all. It was a pickup truck, all right. He could see it better now. Just like what they used for hauling feed around the place. Smart. Real smart. So one down and one to go. Maybe. If I got him and he had a partner.

So he waited and chewed on a piece of grass and thought about it for a little. It would figure that the other one would probably be in the truck bed from where he could put out the feed. They must have spotted him and the one up front had decided to run for it. Unless it was just a decoy and somebody was coming around his back right now so they would have him trapped in the middle of nowhere. He reloaded his gun, and then he cleared his throat.

"You might as well come on out of there, friend," he shouted, scared a little at the way his voice carried in the empty night. "I got your pardner—make it easy on yourself."

He wanted some kind of sound—anything, and if it wasn't a voice then at least the creak of springs. He wouldn't miss it. It was that kind of a night where even the click of a hammer being cocked would carry as far as he was from the truck. And all of a sudden, in a way that made the backs of his knees grow cold and sweaty, he wanted something to shoot at again.

He dug his feet in and took a deep breath and then lumbered forward low and hard, ducking through the trees until he was even with the front of the truck and then cutting back and coming in quick under the front fender. He held up for a moment, waiting for some kind of sound to direction on, and then he crawled forward as fast as he could on his knees and elbows and jerked open the door on the driver's side. Something moved heavily in the darkness then and he felt his throat close and the sweat spring through his body like a million points of fire. He fell away from the door, firing blindly, shouting above the roar of the revolver a name that he could only hear when the silence surrounded him again like a great loneliness. *Tanner* was what he heard, though the sound was gone. And looking down at the hand that still held the revolver, eager, poised, cold for the kill, it seemed to him that it belonged to somebody else.

Something black and shapeless had fallen from the truck and he could see it now sprawled forward where it made a pool of deeper black against the chassis.

I got them both, he thought, trying to swallow. That should be it.

He lay trembling in the grass, waiting again for some sound, but he was alone in the silence.

"Well, I can't wait here all night," he whispered. "I've got to chance it."

He shifted his weight, getting slowly to his feet in a half crouch, and then moved around the front of the truck to the other side. His legs hurt now and he wanted another drink. *I say, Mr. Hickok, how many white men have you killed to your certain knowledge?*

"There isn't any proof," he said aloud, and then he looked at the gun in his hand as though it did not belong to him before moving cautiously on around the truck until he felt sure that there was no one else. "But suppose they're alive? I ought to get a doctor. My God, what's it going to look like? What in Jesus's name is happening?"

Then more than anything else he wanted to run hell-bent back to his own truck and drive on into the ranch. Let somebody else find them tomorrow. For a brief moment of hope he looked around to see if anyone was watching, and then the weight of it settled on his shoulders. He slipped the gun into its holster and walked wearily, almost carelessly, up to the body that lay half out of the truck and stirred it with his boot. Limp as a half-empty sack of feed.

"Mister," he said softly, and pushed again, and suddenly there was something wrong in the shape of the head. Hair. Hanging down like grass. And then he knew it was a woman. He looked quickly at the truck as though he might recognize something and then he knelt and put his hand into a mass of wet and clotted hair.

"Oh Sweet Jesus," he moaned, and turned the head in his hand, knowing in some sad and terrible way whose face his eyes would find beneath the matted blood. Then his breath caught in his throat and he backed away, stumbling, his own face fallen to pieces in his hands, every hair on his head afire, and then his stomach seemed to cave in and he was down on his knees vomiting and praying all at the same time. Later, he couldn't tell how long, his ribs aching and his teeth chattering as though it were the dead of winter, he crawled back to where she lay and tried to strike a match. He broke three before he could get one lit, repeating to himself with a kind of sob, the tears burning his cheeks, "It's her. It's her all right. Sweet Jesus, what are you doing to me?"

Then he gathered her awkwardly in his arms, her head flopping brokenly against his leg, and when he had laid her out by the front of the truck he switched on the lights so that he could know. Her head lay back and to one side so that her neck seemed to be broken. Blood like an inkblot on her white blouse covered a bullet hole in her shoulder. Maybe the others had gone wide. And yet the hair, and the blood on his hands, and he was afraid to look . . . I couldn't have killed her, he thought desperately, his body running hot and cold with hope and terror, looking at the marks on her throat. Somebody beat me to it. Somebody wrung her neck. Then he remembered the other one who had run away, but it was too late now to be afraid.

"You've gone this far, Tanner," he said hopelessly. "You got to go the rest of the way."

He pulled his gun again and started walking, quartering the way he did when he was looking for dead quail. Back and forth he went, kicking his way through the brush, until finally he hit something solid with his boot and then drew back from it as though it were alive. His hand shook and he wanted to shoot so bad he could taste it, warm and salty like blood on his tongue, but somehow he hung on until it was past. Then he turned the body over with his foot and lit another match. He held it until it burned his fingers and still he didn't believe it. Then he lit another one, and this time he believed it. And once again he stooped and gathered the body in his arms, not sobbing now or shaking but just plain crying, and not for them but for himself. He moved into the light and it was Thayer all right—that fine-boned face with the narrow, high-bridged nose and the smooth skin, cut and dirty now on one side where he had fallen.

"Always acted like he was different from anybody else. Now he ends up like the rest of us," and he shook his head, finding with his fingers where the slug had gone in at the back of the neck.

He laid them out side by side and then crouched beside them, rocking back and forth on his heels, looking at them, unable to think, waiting for a sign that wouldn't come. Once he started to draw his gun, as though there were only one thing left to do, and then he pushed it slowly back. He felt tired all over and suddenly very old. His body ached no matter how he moved. The worst was that there wasn't any sense to it—Clay in jail, Thayer trying to tough-talk him, himself jumping his tracks in the Smoke House, and now Thayer and Rita dead, one of them and maybe both killed by his own hand.

"No," he said grimly. "Wasn't nobody but Tanner could shoot like that. God, sir, You took Your own sweet time about it, but now You sure as hell lowered the boom but good."

Then he drew the Colt and laid the barrel against his cheek, just to have something cold in the middle of all that fire, and as his senses came back he began to smell again, gunpowder first, then the whiskey. He knelt down and sniffed at the bodies, then opened the door. The broken glass glittered in the shaky light of the match, and there was something wet on the floorboards— whiskey or blood or both. And whatever it was, one thing was for sure. It was no damn good.

On the way back to town he wondered if he should have left the lights burning, like maybe that way they wouldn't be so lonesome or so dead. But then again, what if somebody was to find them like that, stretched out in the light, all by themselves in the dust.

"Not yet. We got to be ready when that comes, and we're a

hell of a long way from ready. I've done found them once and I've got to find them again."

He was thinking of those wet floorboards and how that handful of hair had stuck to his fingers and how their faces were so different now. Not like they were asleep, either. Just nothing, and Thayer staring straight up with those stony eyes he couldn't close. And then he pushed the truck just as fast as it would go, floorboarded her all the way, like whatever it was that had been chasing him all these years was just about to catch up with him at last.

"I never killed her," he repeated stubbornly as he jolted along the county road toward town. "I never killed her, hear? And you know it, too. You know whose fault it was, you mean son of a bitch."

He rolled into town through soft darkness that was turning hard where the wind had picked up cold. The street lights ran together behind him as he came on through the night along Main. At the turning before the Smoke House he swung left and shifted hard into second for the long hill leading to the Court House and the jail.

Suppose he's not there, he thought suddenly. Suppose the son of a bitch was lying. Where does that leave me? But it was not a question he could answer, and anyway he was already there with one car parked in front, and he knew whose it was.

"Bird's here already. That don't help any."

He looked quickly at his hands and tried to smooth out his clothes, and then suddenly remembering, he slipped off the gunbelt and stuck the Colt under the seat.

"Straighten up," he said in an angry whisper. "Great God-a-mighty, blood on my hands and liquor on my breath."

Then he hitched at his shoulders and walked through the jail door like he had reserved the best room they had.

"I figured you'd be along one of these days." The jailer looked half asleep, setting out the cards for a hand of solitaire.

"You got Carter in here?"

"Now what the hell else would bring you all the way up here to talk to me?"

If he ever needed any, he needed it now. Dignity. It was like trying to hold his pants up without a belt, but he stood his ground. "I want to see him."

"He's with his lawyer."

"Lawyer? I don't give a damn if he's with sweet Jesus Christ." His voice felt strained and he could hear how high it was and his hand went to his side where the gun had been. For a moment he felt as if he had looked into a mirror and seen someone he didn't recognize at all . . . *a figure that would have fixed attention anywhere . . . a certain unstudied carelessness in the wearing of his costume that gave a picturesque effect . . . buckskin breeches fringed on the sides . . . a red necktie . . . almost a sombrero . . . clear blue and deeply set, his hair short, wavy, golden in tint . . . mustache was long and tawny in color . . . complexion was florid . . . sun always burned his skin ruthlessly . . .*

"I said I want to see him," and then he started down the corridor, looking into the cells on either side.

When he found them he stopped as though a slug had hit him in the chest, and he took hold of the cell bars to keep himself from falling. It was Clay all right enough, there on the bunk, his legs pulled up against his chest, his head half-turned toward the door, his face kind of frozen over the way it got when somebody beat him at something, which meant that some of it anyway was true, if it mattered any more. Bird stood in the middle of the cell, facing the door, looking kind of tired and dumb the way Bird always looked. So he held on tight to the bars, waiting for something to happen, feeling that whatever strength had brought him this far had just about run out. My God, and he felt like praying, how much more are You going to make me go through?

But Clay was looking past him, over his shoulder, and then he heard the jailer at his back, making noises like a sparrow in the gutter. He tried to speak then but his throat tightened, and somewhere behind his eyes there was pain and he pulled at the bars as though he were trying to break his way through.

Then he saw Clay speaking—"He's not going to hurt anybody," like he believed it. And then he realized that Clay was looking at him now.

"What the hell is it?" Short, the way Clay always spoke to him in front of other people.

He stared back, twisting his head a little and pushing his jaw forward, saying so that nobody could hear it but himself, "Look, Clay. You ain't talking to Cody now. You're talking to Tanner, remember? We got a long road back there behind us." Then he flicked his eyes at Bird, standing there short, squat, fish-faced, just a little too lawyer-smart for comfort.

"All right," Bird said, like it hurt him to say it. "But make it quick."

He moved aside to let Bird pass, waiting until there was nothing in the corridor but shadows the color of the walls, and then went in himself.

Clay still sat on the top of the bunk, but now his face had changed. His eyes had gone narrow and his brows were up, a coyote sniffing the wind.

"You better get down off there, Clay. I got some things to tell you, buddy." His face felt tight and it jerked a little when he talked, like maybe a nerve had worked its way loose somewhere. When he saw where Clay's eyes were he looked down and saw his hands doubled into fists and then he realized that he was standing there like he was ready to throw a punch.

"What's eating you, Tanner?" Clay said softly. "You drunk or something? I never figured you for a drinking man."

"You recognize whiskey when you smell it, don't you, Clay. You know what it smells like when somebody's dead? Try to remember, huh? Just a little." He smiled, but his teeth stayed closed. He put his hands out in front of him and twisted and then pulled them apart like he did when he wrung those soft necks, real feathery all over. "You never liked that, did you, Clay." Then he turned to the wall and slammed his fist against it. "I never killed her," low, so that he could barely hear himself.

"Killed who?"

"Don't give me that shit." His voice rose and trembled, and his breath came and went quickly while he stood there and stared at the wall before he swung his eyes slowly around to Clay.

"Keep your voice down, Tanner. You're bellowing like a stuck hog."

"What did you tell Thayer, anyway?"

"This is my show, boy. Don't you worry that lopsided head of yours—"

"I ought to break your goddam neck. I should have broke it twenty years ago. You get this through your head once and for all. I didn't kill her, hear? Don't you ever, now or later, try to tell me or anybody else different."

Carter sat there watching him, quiet, too quiet, the way he would study a man's face over a poker hand. "Don't push me, Tanner. You know better than to do that. Now you better start all over if you got something you want to say."

"I'll say it all right. Three hundred miles horseback, most of it in the rain, you drunk as a skunk and crying your head off, counting the goddam money every night out of that United States Government Mail Pouch. You wouldn't turn loose of it either, staggering around hollering her name until I hoped you'd fall in the fire. Well, all your praying didn't help much. We covered three hundred miles before we stopped for good. Remember? But there isn't anyplace far enough away. She's dead, Clay. Don't you hear me?" he shouted suddenly, before he could stop himself.

"I hear you, man," like his mouth was full of dust, and fingering in his shirt pocket for a cigarette. "But you haven't said anything yet."

"You never had any right to ask me, Clay," and all of a sudden he wanted to cry again, trying hopelessly to say something for which he had never found words.

"There wasn't time," Carter said hoarsely, jumping down from the bunk and seizing him by the shoulders. "Shut up before—"

"There was time enough for the money, wasn't there, Clay? Wasn't there—"

"I told you to shut your mouth, you clod-hopping plow jockey."

"Clay," he said then, slow. "You go straight to hell, hear. You were ready to dump me—told the whole thing to Thayer, didn't you? Well, it's on your soul, you Texas bastard. She's dead and don't you try to stick me with it."

"Tanner," Carter said slowly, raising that long, red face until it was right in front of his eyes. "Tell me something, boy. What does Thayer have to do with this? What are you trying to tell me? Is he after you, too? Who in the hell are you talking about?"

He stared hard back at Clay and then broke away and walked over to look out of the small barred window. There was too much in his mind and he couldn't make it come out the way he wanted to. *No, by heaven! I never killed one man without good cause.*

"Thayer called me into his office this afternoon. Told me I was in trouble on account of you. Tried to scare me. Let me hear the sheriff tell him you were in jail. That was—well, it seems like a long time ago. It was late this afternoon." His voice was flat as though there were no emotion left to carry what he had to say. And he was much too tired to say it, but he went on anyway because there was no place left to go. "He ain't after anybody now, Clay. He's dead. Laying out there in the dust. Dead as he can be."

Clay looked at him, careful, like maybe he figured there was a gun somewhere. Then he let his cigarette drop to the floor and stepped on it real slow. "Dead, is he?"

"Yeah. Real dead. He couldn't be any deader."

"You talk like you know quite a bit about it."

"Now there's two of us that knows."

"Yeah?" Carter worked at the corner of his mouth with his thumb, not a flicker in his eyes, holding himself loose and easy like he might want to move in a hurry. "How would that be?"

"He talked like he had something on me. Like maybe you had told him—whatever it was you wanted him to hear." And then he heard his voice raising again. "How would I know, goddammit. I know what you thought—probably still think, for that matter. You said it to me so many times in the middle of all that rain and whiskey I figured you must have talked yourself into it. Counting your money, pushing that pistol in my face—"

"You done said that once."

"I haven't said a damned thing, yet."

Carter just kept on staring, his face in the bare light all smooth and wrinkled at the same time, like he'd been burned.

"Thayer talking like he did made me remember a lot of things I thought I'd forgotten. Not for keeps, of course—you wouldn't have let me forget for good, would you. But you know, the way I used to be with a gun. You haven't forgotten that, have you, Clay?" and he took a step closer to where Carter stood balancing himself like a fighter.

"Watch yourself, Tanner." Carter didn't move. "You're not making a hell of a lot of sense, boy."

It was that mean way of talking Clay had, but this time he wasn't going to play.

"Tanner. He's the one." He frowned at Clay, half smiling at the same time, as though he had just remembered. "Fresh out of Nebraska, long gone for Texas, looking for an Indian to kill. Hah!" The laugh caught in his throat and his fists trembled at his sides.

Then he felt the sting from a long way off, like rubbing alcohol on his face in the wind. Carter had hit him twice with his open hand, fast and cold. He moved his hands up but it was too late, and he let them drop. His eyes burned so that he could hardly see, and now he wanted to say it.

"All right. You asked me. I'm gonna tell you. I was in the Smoke House. I don't know what happened. I took a drink, then two or three more. Cass was in there shooting off his big mouth. There was some trouble," and he shook his head, concentrating, looking down at the floor. "I got out of there and went on back to where I'd parked the pickup and started out to the place. Somewhere in there I must have put on my gun. Parts of it are kind of hazy. I remember I damned near ran in the ditch—had to pull up just before I got to the cattle guard. That's when I saw the cattle." He looked back up at Carter now, beginning to feel it in his stomach again, remembering how it was, his voice gradually slowing like a run-down victrola. "They was all bunched up and moving, and it didn't look right," his breath coming faster as the words slowed and searched, "so I went along with them until I could see where they was headed. That little clump of trees just off to the right after you turn off the county road—there was a truck in there. Stock had come up to feed."

"All right," Carter said, not looking at him now because he had pushed on past and was holding onto the bars of the window, swaying back and forth. "Keep talking."

"It looked more or less like the truck we use for hauling feed. Well, it was dark, you see, and I couldn't make it out any too good. But the boys had been talking about how we were losing stock, couple of head at a time, and figured, you know, with a truck, at night . . ."

"Yeah?"

"So I walked up on it real quiet. The cattle was making noise and I slid in behind them and then before I was even set somebody busted out of that truck and took off across the pasture."

"Lord, I should have known better. White hair, that cowboy outfit, that goddam elephant for a horse. White, goddammit, not grey, white. Like some kind of freaking albino."

Who the hell ever gave me a choice, was what he thought, but there wasn't time to say it. "Like I said, somewhere in there I had buckled on my gun. I want you to know I could hardly see the son of a bitch, it was that black. Well, I could hear him in the brush, and kind of felt him in the dark, and then I couldn't hear him any more."

"What you're trying to say is that you shot him."

"Clay, I couldn't even see him."

"You're talking about Thayer. And now he's dead. You put the gun on him. That's what you're trying to tell me."

He couldn't answer, standing there panting like a hound, feeling all of a sudden like he wanted to laugh.

"You got anything else to say?"

He remembered then, and listened as he told it as though he, too, were hearing it for the first time. "There were two of them in the truck," disjointed, like he was talking in his sleep.

"Shut up," Carter shouted. "I've heard enough."

"Wait a minute. I didn't know what to do, see. Figured whoever was in there must have the drop on me. Only chance I had was to get the jump. So I go up alongside the truck and open the side door." It wasn't a sob, but it was close to it. "Something fell out." He bent over and crossed his arms hard on his chest, trying to keep his body from shaking, trying not to show it. "I never killed her, Clay."

"You already told me that." Carter's head had fallen forward and his body seemed to hang from his outstretched arms.

"No. No, I haven't told you yet. Scared? I couldn't even breathe. I shot her three times. Well, at her. She was—"

"Her? You better watch your mouth, Tanner. Talk sense or shut up, one," but his voice was thin and full of holes, the strength all drained away.

"Rita. That is, Mrs. Carter. Goddammit, Clay, your wife."

Then the breath seemed to go right out of Carter's body so that he slumped all the way to his knees, his arms still stretched above him, hanging onto the bars, his back trembling under his soft silk shirt, the soles of his boots dark and shiny.

There wasn't anything to do then but just stand there, turning his hat in his hands, leaning a little in Clay's direction like maybe he ought to hold out his hand and say goodbye.

And then behind him he heard that Arkansas drawl again, and he held his hat still, trying to catch up with the words and hoping at the same time they would go on past him.

But Carter was already answering, " . . . alone—just a few minutes," his body strung up there against the wall, his voice coming from someplace that seemed like it was way out of reach. He waited then until the steps had died away.

"Clay," thinking, reach him or not I got to say it, "like I told you, Clay, I never killed her. Her throat was all blue—her neck . . ."

Carter groaned, then reached across and pulled the bag to him and fumbled around in it until he got hold of the bottle. "I wish to hell you had. Here," and still Clay did not look up until he had taken the paper cup and thrown his head back, his throat pumping like a piston. Then he pushed himself straight, his head down like a beaten bull. He pointed his finger and jabbed it back and forth like a copperhead in action. "Look. I've heard all about you I'm ever going to need to hear. Now cut the shit and tell me what happened. Fast."

The only trouble was there wasn't any fast way to tell it. But the whiskey went down easier now, and he licked his lips and drank again and then ran his eyes back and forth over the cell floor.

"Well, there was whiskey, see. All over the floorboards. And broken glass. I pulled her on out of there—it was your truck, all right—her head flopped over on one side," and he jerked his head sideways, "like that. Busted, looked like. Throat all black and blue."

"Why? For God's sake, why?"

"Then I laid them out in front of the headlights where I could see. She had a bullet through her shoulder—mine, I reckon. Him I hit good twice, back and head. I guess I killed him at that, Clay." And it surprised him some when he said it, like maybe he was listening to somebody else. And then he remembered the bloody hair, and wondered . . .

Carter looked at him for a long time, the cup hanging loose from his hand, his body still swaying just a little, his face like some kind of a statue in rock. "You know what I thought? I thought you meant Anna." Then he closed his eyes and shook his head, like he wanted to get it straight. "I don't know why. Right up to the time you called her name . . ." Then he opened his eyes again, very wide, still all stirred up like a muddy pond so that there wasn't hardly any way even to look at him, let alone answer what he said. "I don't want anybody to find them like they are, Tanner. Thayer has me in here on a murder charge. Red Hawk. One of them—all of them. It don't make any difference. People find him and Rita dead on the place—see what I mean? Dead like that, anyway, with bullet holes and such." He waited, then poured some more whiskey in the cup. "There'll be more federal men around here than you can shake a stick at. We don't need that, Tanner. Neither one of us."

He tried his best to stare back, wanting to see what Clay was getting at, wondering how much more he was going to have to do this night. The back of his neck throbbed, and he couldn't get the sticky feeling off his hands, and Carter had that look on his face like a hawk sitting on top of a rabbit.

"No, Bubba, we don't need that at all." Then Clay hoisted himself up on the bunk again and leaned his head back against the wall. "Funny how after all that's happened you and me were both thinking about it again tonight. You know something? I can still hear her screaming. In the dreams it's always mixed up with the horses. If you didn't kill her, Bubba," and he just sat there looking at the smoke, "then who the hell did?"

"Her neck was broke—you can see where the hands came together . . ."

"Remember?" so low he had to strain to hear. "By sundown it was just grey ashes. Ready to blow away in the first high wind that came along." Then he sat up straight on the bunk. "Burn them, Tanner." His voice was like a saw on pipe. "Haul your ass out to where that truck's parked. Get them over to the ranch house. How you do it is up to you, but don't leave tracks. Park the truck in front of the house—leave her pocketbook on the seat, and his coat, maybe—something. That's for you to figure out. Carry them both upstairs to the big bed—my bed, goddammit, Tanner, do like I say. And then give the place a good going-over with kerosene. Coal oil—you know what it smells like. And when it's burning real good, you find yourself a telephone somewhere. When that siren starts to blow, I'll know we're in the clear."

"And Rona. What about—"

"You know she's not at the ranch. She's at the main house. I left her there this afternoon. Quit dragging your feet."

"I got to have me a story, Clay." He kind of hated to say it, but there it was. It always ended like this, Carter making him do what he wanted the way he'd prod a steer down the chute. He hated him for it, and yet he couldn't meet those eyes.

"O.K. Go to the hotel from here. Check in. Leave the pickup a ways off. Crawl down the fire escape, get your business done, come on back. That's story enough."

Like a hawk, all right, watching him there on the bunk, but damned if he wasn't like the rabbit, too. "So we burn the place down. What will be left? There ought to be something . . ."

"Teeth. A belt buckle, maybe. Buttons. What's left in the truck. One hair in the gravy, Tanner—that's all it takes. Who's going to put Clay Carter in the penitentiary for the sake of a dead Washington lawyer who burned himself to death in my wife's bed?"

"There'll be lots won't believe it, Clay." How many fires did a man have to set in his life?

"And there'll be plenty more than happy to. Anybody round here owe Thayer anything?"

I almost had him broke, and now his wife's laying out there dead and his mind's just as clear and mean as ever. "How about his wife? Suppose she wants to push it a little?"

"Let her push. How much of all this will she want to know? We'll just lift the rock up a little tiny bit, see," and he smiled. "She won't push after that."

"The ranch?"

He was smiling, for a fact, but it had no more laugh in it than the grin of a dead man. "We started with a fire, Tanner. Remember? You was just telling me about it. Now we're going to end with one."

"No more cattle?"

"Didn't you ever feel like throwing anything away? Just for the hell of it? Man, can't you understand?"

"I never had just a whole hell of a lot to throw. What you mean is that you're rid of all of us now. That's it. You're clean. Ain't nobody you need any more."

Carter nodded. "Put it this way, Tanner. Last time I wanted you to save a woman you wouldn't do it. You and I have been a two-man chain gang ever since. Now I'm asking you to take a sledge hammer and bust the chains off both of us." Then he raised his voice so that it was hard and high, like when he gave orders around the place. "Burn them, Bubba, both of them. Just a little bit of ash—the wind will do the rest."

He sloshed the whiskey in his cup and ran his tongue over his teeth where they tasted bad. "Clay," he said after a while. "Like I say I haven't got a hell of a lot to throw away except a name. Probably you won't understand what I'm going to say. Probably I don't get it any too damn well myself. But I'm going to say it anyway. Look. I want to set me up a curio shop. Cody's Curios. I'd like to burn Tanner in that fire, too."

Carter laughed without making any noise, and what looked like pain made his mouth close tight around his teeth. "The fire insurance on that house will buy you all the curio shop you can handle. Me," and he laughed again, draining the whiskey that was left in his cup, "I'm going to build me a goddam chapel for the mission school. Name it Red Hawk, after Rita. Huh?"

He got up and wiped his mouth with his wrist. "You always were a heartless bastard, Clay. Don't look like anything can change that."

"Get rolling—Cody," harsh and hopeless, and now all of a sudden his eyes were hard and shiny as silver dollars. "Get the shit out of here—gunfighter . . ."

He passed Bird at the door and kept going, lifting his knees high, walking mechanically toward the truck as though he were following a map. "Be at the hotel if you need me," was what he tried to say, but it came out more like he was clearing his throat, watching as careful as he could everything he did in spite of a heaviness in his shoulders that seemed to turn his bones to stone.

He parked the truck two blocks behind the hotel, then walked without a sound down that street that he did not even see, his eyes still watching those two bodies where they lay in the drifting dust.

"You want a room, you say?" The clerk acted surprised, although judging by his face it was hard to figure that anything could surprise him any more.

"Sleeping in town tonight," he answered.

"Haven't seen you around here in a coon's age."

"Used to have a little room at the back. First floor. Real quiet."

"Put you in there if you want."

"Much obliged." He put the money and five dollars extra on the desk. "You got a pint you could sell me?"

It was just one movement—money in his pocket and the pint on the desk. "Going to bed with a bottle tonight, Cody?"

"Good thing about a bottle is that it don't look any different the next morning from what it did the night before. Don't want to be bothered, hear?"

He walked on past the boy asleep at the elevator and climbed the stairs, trying not to hurry. Same wallpaper. Same smells. Good thing I didn't have to register. I would have written Tanner sure as hell.

He closed the door behind him and slipped the lock and then looked quickly around to make sure that he was alone. Iron bed, night table with an upside-down water pitcher, Gideon Bible, dirty lace, grey paint. He listened for a moment and then tiptoed through the small tile bathroom. As he raised the window, pressing it hard to cut down the rattle, the paint flaked away in his hand like rust. The fire escape lay black as a brand against the sky. He held the pint tight against him and scrambled through the window and down the few steps to the ground. Then he followed the alley for a couple of blocks before cutting over to where he had parked the truck. Once inside, he opened the pint and took a long pull and then headed her out of town, trailing dust.

And driving back through the night to where they lay waiting for him, he figured that this was maybe the way a man felt when he had decided to kill himself. There was nothing left to think about except that, and making sure of each step along the way, like closing all the pasture gates behind you so that there was no way out. A man would be so lonely that there wouldn't even be nobody left to tell it to. "That would be some lonely," he said aloud.

And the sign posts in his memory that pointed to the turnings in his life: Buffalo Bill with his hat on his heart when they played *The Star-Spangled Banner*; trying to get the horse moving that black-and-red dawn when he quit the farm; then Carter and the day Anna burned, scared as hell and laughing all at the same time, thinking that it had felt like the first time he ever saw a woman take her clothes off right down to bare ass, one of them carnival sideshows, so goddam scared it made him sick so that he couldn't even get his breath; then all the way to the cattle country with Carter drunk and crazy and hanging onto that government bag of stolen money—all of that and so much more, so long gone and yet so close, like ghosts that wouldn't give it up. Kind of like nothing that you ever did was ever really over.

And yet somehow it seemed that maybe tonight would be the end, and maybe that was it—like it was only over when you died, and tonight Tanner's time had come.

"I'm going to lay me down in that fire, too," talking to himself as the pickup bounced from rut to rut. "Then I can stop running. I been running all my life, trying to get someplace I never knew where it was and so it was Texas; trying to get away from somebody, God knows who or what or when he was, man or beast, father, grandfather, maybe Clay, who knows? And as for the why of it . . ."

It was not until he felt the cattle guard rolling beneath him that he could believe it again. He jammed the brakes hard and switched the ignition off. Nothing but the pumping of a well somewhere in the night. It might have been his own heart he heard. Then he got out and walked through the trees to the other truck. The bodies were still there, darker than the ground, like piles of dirt where somebody had dug a grave.

He stood there for a while, his hands in his pockets, wondering what he should do, and then he turned and went back to the pickup. It was still a good three miles on to the ranch house, through a heavy stand of scrub oak and across the valley into a second ridge of trees.

"Somebody could be there," he muttered, flicking off the lights again. "With any luck they'll all be in town. But I've drawn all I can draw."

A half a mile from the ranch house he stopped again and went the rest of the way on foot until he was close enough to see that there were no lights burning. Then he got the pickup and drove it down to the bunk house. Nobody around. All of them in town looking for whiskey that tasted better and women that were different. "Lord, just this once, let them have all they want. I promise You You'll come out ahead."

On the way down to the barn he stopped again to take a pull at the bottle, swallowing hard to keep it down as the white lightning ate its way through his throat. For a moment the harshness of it cleared his head and he looked around to find out where he was and then something like a hand took hold of him and he went on through the darkness like a man asleep.

When he opened the barn door the smell of horses and hay was so sweet and warm that he stood in the entrance without moving, like maybe if he didn't turn around the night behind him might just get up and go away. He waited, and heard the stamp of a restless horse, but nothing went away. The night was still there, and the dead, and another fire to set.

He went down to the last stall and saddled the mare and then rode back through the darkness. The moon was a blur against the black of night; the silence rang in his ears like telephone wires on a country road. Beneath him the horse stumbled once across the ruts and then trotted steadily on as though the world had not changed. Rocked in the saddle, he slumped forward a little, dozed for what seemed no longer than the gradual and weighted fall of his eyelids, and was suddenly and violently awakened by the horse shying and rearing back, then standing still, chewing the bit, skin shuddering across its body like water in the wind. He narrowed his eyes against the darkness and saw the truck, still blacker than the night even with the moon.

She smells them, he said to himself, and she don't like it a damn bit better than I do. Then he got down, stiff and tired from a day already much too long and a night that was far from over and walked the mare in a wide circle behind the truck, talking low, rubbing the long bone of the nose.

When she had calmed some he hitched her to a tree and went back to where they lay. Trees seemed to leap at him when he switched on the light, and he set his jaw and knelt to look at them again through the shadows that blurred their faces. It was Rita all right, her face dark as a plum, swollen as though with blood. Thayer might just have been asleep, his face smooth as bone china except for the dirty crusts of blood along his jaw.

"What in the hell ever made you come out here for, anyway?" he said angrily, and then he got under the body, cursing, and brought it up on his shoulder. When he had laid it in the bed of the truck he went back and picked up Rita and carried her in his arms to where he had laid Thayer. She seemed too light, as easy to carry as a child, and the soft silken feel of her leg against his hand made him hurry to lay her down beside Thayer and to pull the dress as close around her as he could get it.

Then for a quarter of an hour he fought the mare before he gave up. "Goddammit, I don't smell anything," he finally shouted in exasperation, hitting her hard on the side of the mouth, but she scrambled frantically away from the tailgate so that he almost lost the reins. Before he got her hitched he had had to move both bodies into the front seat.

"All right," he said, knotting the reins tight. "Shut up, damn it. You don't have to do nothing but trot along here behind. I more or less figured on having to do it alone, but there's some shit I don't have to take."

He turned his head and spat into the dust, trying to get himself in check. Mainly he just wanted to kick hell out of something or somebody—anything would do.

He had set the bodies on the front seat like dolls but now Rita had fallen forward against the windshield, her head twisted awkwardly away from her body, her hair like the broken wing of a dead bird, her mouth half open against the glass. Thayer was slumped against the far door like a sleeper trying to get comfortable.

Seeing them like that he groaned and felt the nerves bunch around the corner of his eye and the blood push heavily at his temple. Then he opened the door and climbed in under the wheel and when he switched the lights to bright the trees jumped up a little closer like maybe they had St. Vitus dance. And he thought suddenly of the Tulsa road and the way his lights would wash the night back from the trees, and then the signs lettered on the trunks, or even bigger on the rocks, or like a terrible shout all across the side of a hill: WHERE WILL YOU SPEND ETERNITY?

"You never gave me just a whole lot of choice," he said aloud, and then he had to push Rita back against the seat because with the throbbing of the engine her body had begun to slump toward him, her open mouth pushing blindly along the glass like the mouth of a fish in a bowl. Like a half-empty sack of feed, he thought again, his throat closing a little at the smell of whiskey that hung about her like the smell of somebody being sick. Whiskey and something else, like the powder smell that hangs in the air after a gunfight and someone is down with his hands at his guts and a man wants a drink to take the taste out of his mouth.

He bumped along slow so that the mare could follow, and the hair prickled hot and cold on the back of his neck, and the saliva ran in his mouth like he was going to start vomiting again. He stopped the truck and tried to roll a cigarette and suddenly his hands felt too tired to go through the motions. The tobacco leaked and sifted onto his pants, and he gave it up. One thing— just one little thing for himself, and he couldn't make it. When he didn't smoke a hundred cigarettes a year, much less women or cards. And why did it always have to be him? "I'd a hell of a lot rather be in jail, and Clay out here getting rid of his own wife. How many women do I got to burn for him before he's through?"

It was just so damn lonesome—two dead people squeezed into the front seat with him and a riderless horse behind. And not any of them wanted to be here.

"Who the hell ever gave Carter the right to run everbody's life like that?"

Then he pulled his hat down to one side so he wouldn't have to look at her face that was the color of dried blood, and started up again, straining his eyes ahead of him along the road, humming and mumbling and croaking his way through what verses he knew of *Rock of Ages* and *Nearer My God to Thee* and then just the tune of *Onward Christian Soldiers* because he couldn't remember exactly how it went. Rag-bag scraps from a thousand Sunday mornings, freezing his ass off in a pale-pine Lutheran church—lonesomest place he ever saw, even to the light, because there was so much of it, and all of it so empty. He shivered a little, feeling winter in his bones, wondering what had happened to them all—the family, his own people he had run off from. In winter you had to cut through the ground with an ax, grass scattering all over like somebody dropped a bottle, before you could get far enough down to make sure that the coffin didn't nose its way up like some kind of a mole in the springtime when rain hung up there like a loom for weaving between heaven and earth and the ground dissolved leaving grass like hunks of hair. Well, no trouble like that this time. A fire was clean, at least; ate right down to the bone and beyond until the marrow ran out like gravy in the ashes.

"Get off me, hear?" he said loudly, hitting into Rita's body with his shoulder until she collapsed like a broken doll across Thayer, whose half-opened eyes stared sightlessly at the moon.

By the time he reached the ranch he was more mad than anything else. He cut the motor and let the silence roll back into place. The only light was the faintest film of moon which gave the pillared and porticoed house the look of something seen dimly in a dusty mirror. So far so good, he thought, glad to get his feet on the ground again. Back of the truck the mare stood motionless, looking at him sidewise, one hind foot cocked like the hammer of a pistol.

"Now that's enough, dammit. I've had all the meanness I need without getting kicked all to hell and gone by you."

After he had dried her down and carefully put the saddle and blanket where they had been before, he went back to the pickup, figuring that whatever tracks he had left would be covered in the confusion of the fire and the return of the hands from town. Then he stood there studying the house for a while, his face thrust up toward the moon as though he were praying, his eyes half-closed with the effort to burn through the weariness and fear that fogged his mind. He rubbed his hand across his face and shifted the hat on his head. The silence still throbbed around him, soft as the beating of his heart, save that now it was more like time itself going by, running out like sand, quiet, cold as snow piling up on a tombstone. That was the hell of it; there was never any way for a man just to stand still. Beating like blood, running like the tide so that soon there would be no place to hide. He pulled the heavy watch from his pocket and turned it until it caught what light the night held, then thrust it back in his pants, hitched hard at his belt, and turned to those faces that stared with idiot blankness at something beyond his sight.

Later he wondered what kind of madness of the brain or heart it was that drove him blindly through to the bitter ash end of it all. For now he worked feverishly as though following a plan his mind had long ago and lovingly worked out. One by one, staggering in his haste, he carried the bodies through the great lifeless living room and up the carpeted staircase to Carter's bedroom. There he lay them side by side, decently, hands folded before them, arranged as though for a photograph of death. Thayer was in his shirt sleeves, his body small and strangely weightless now, one side of his face scraped raw, his eyes like the belly of a fish beneath the half-closed lids. He had tried to close them with pennies, but they kept sliding off.

"Let the little son of a bitch watch if he wants," and he put the pennies back in his pocket. But his own eyes he kept away from Rita, having felt again the clotted stiffness of her hair as he took her head in his hands and straightened it above her body as though he meant to glue it back on.

Thayer's coat he had left on the front seat of the truck along with his wallet and Rita's pocketbook. After he had laid out the bodies, smoothing the clothes, arranging the hair, he went back and scrubbed the blood from the floorboards. Then he poured what was left from the pint over the seat and floor until the other smell, blood or death or whatever it was, was almost gone. When he had finished he straightened up, holding his back, sweating a little, still uneasy in his stomach, his hands still sticky in a way he couldn't get used to. This is the way they would find it— the truck parked in front of the sidewalk leading up to the ranch-house door, Thayer's coat with his papers and money and Rita's pocketbook, enough whiskey in the air to convince anybody that they had been drinking together and got maybe drunk enough to set the house on fire with a dropped kerosene lamp or a cigar that went on burning while the bed cooled off. It wasn't exactly what you'd call proof but then, like Clay said, who the hell owed Thayer anything. As a case it ought to have just enough in it to close the closet door again. Nobody had ever wanted to look in there anyway. Bird could handle that part of it, all right.

The kerosene was in the barn and he was not satisfied until he had sloshed two water cans' full around the bedroom, down the stairs, all over the living room and the porch, and around the foundations. He put the cans back in the barn and started looking for a wad of paper he could roll into a ball and toss like a torch into the house. Then he remembered the sheaf of papers that had fallen to the ground when he lifted Thayer from the truck. He took them out of his pocket, lit a match, and read the first few lines.

I, RITA CARTER, WIFE OF CLAY CARTER, *do hereby swear that Clay Carter, acting in league with Blair Booth and William Cody, did knowingly and deliberately plan and carry out the systematic murder of the Red Hawk family . . .*

He whistled long and low, raising his eyebrows, and looked quickly through the rest of the text. "Won't hurt a damn bit to hang on to this. Might even be worth a curio shop someday, who knows."

Then he stuffed it back in his pocket and went into the house again, looking for something he could use as kindling. The rooms were big, as full of furniture as a warehouse. It was like a house that had been put together somewhere in a factory, like a doll house maybe, and then carted out here in one piece, furniture and all. Kind of like the furniture had been nailed in place, set up like one of J.C. Penney's windows—FOR DISPLAY PURPOSES ONLY. Flowered curtains and a flowered rug and paintings of mountains and sunsets against flowered wallpaper and immitation-walnut

Grand Rapids furniture covered with flowered upholstery. Just rooms you passed through on your way to the kitchen, or the bedroom, or the privy, which was where at last he found the Sears Roebuck catalogue. He carried it out front and lit it and when it was burning hard he tossed it up on the porch and while it was still skidding the kerosene caught and a spray of blue flame splashed up across the porch.

He watched it while the flames went from blue to yellow to orange and then he ran down to the bunk house where he had left the pickup. He drove back to the house and stopped alongside Carter's truck and sat there with the motor running, watching the flames climb through the windows.

"Threw it away like it was nothing. Just like he could walk out of one life and into another one without leaving anything more behind him than a little bit of ash off his cigar. Well, brother, you didn't get away from me last time, and you sure ain't going to leave me out of the deal this time either."

He reached under the seat and found the Colt and gunbelt, and then he walked up as close as he could get to the house before the heat made him turn halfway back toward the darkness. After he had emptied the pistol and the belt of bullets, he hurled it all into the flames that snapped and surged toward the roof. Then he backed off to where he could face the fire again and took off his hat and began to sing, loud and big, the way he sometimes heard people sing at funerals, standing there stiffly with his hand over his heart and his face raised just a little as though somewhere up there, in all the light, Old Glory popped in the wind.

"As I walked out on the streets of Laredo
As I walked out in Laredo one day
I spied a dear cowboy wrapped up in white linen
Wrapped up in white linen as cold as the clay.

I see by your outfit that you are a cowboy
These words he did say as I boldly stepped by
Come sit down beside me and hear my sad story
I am shot in the breast and I know I must die.

It was once in the saddle I used to go dashing
It was once in the saddle I used to go gay
First to the dram house and then to the card house
Got shot in the breast and I am dying today.

Oh beat the drum slowly and play the fife lowly
Play the dead march as you carry me along
Take me to the green valley there lay the sod o'er me
For I'm a young cowboy and I know I've done wrong.

Get six jolly cowboys to carry my coffin
Get six pretty maidens to bear up my pall
Put bunches of roses all over my coffin
Put roses to deaden the sods as they fall.

Then swing your rope slowly and rattle your spurs lowly
And give a wild whoop as you carry me along
And in the grave throw me and roll the sod o'er me
For I'm a young cowboy and I know I've done wrong.

Go bring me a cup a cup of cold water
To cool my parched lips the cowboy then said
Before I returned his soul had departed
And gone to the round-up—the cowboy was dead.

We beat the drum slowly and played the fife lowly
And bitterly wept as we bore him along
For we all loved our comrade so brave young and handsome
We all loved our comrade although he'd done wrong."

He sang all the verses he knew, his voice growing stronger as he went along, his boot beating time against the earth. By the time he had finished, the house flamed on the prairie like a great chandelier, and from every window the fire forked its way toward heaven. He pulled his hat low on his head and then said as loud as he could above the windy roar, "Tanner, depending on where you spend eternity, you just might want to have that old Colt along."

Then he climbed back into the pickup and gave her hell all the way back to Grey Horse. The road was empty, and so far his luck, if he could call it that, still held. He half circled the west edge of town until he got to the hill which led to the Carter house, the main house like Clay always called it, and then at the top he pulled the truck in under the trees and walked to the little office Clay had out back. He let himself in as quiet as he could and gave the operator the number.

"Fire station? I just come into town from the west side. There's one hell of a fire out there on the Carter place. You get your water tanks out there quick enough, you may be able to save Carter's bacon."

The voice at the other end was still talking when he hung up. He sat there trying to roll a cigarette, waiting, not moving until he heard the siren wail above the town like a dog in the night when somebody was cashing it in. He closed his eyes, suddenly too tired to care about the cigarette, and somehow just getting back to the hotel seemed the toughest thing he'd had to do all night. One way or another he made it, parking the truck where he had left it earlier and working his way back up to his room along the fire escape. He sat down on the edge of the bed, took off his boots one by one, flung his coat over a chair, and fell across the bed with the feeling that if he never woke up again it would be too soon.

But something held him up just this side of sleep like a hooked fish half out of water, until he remembered. Then he pushed himself up with a groan and fumbled through his coat pockets until he found the papers. He put them under the pillow and slid his hand in on top of them just to be on the safe side, and then he waited again, listening, until after a while the words came to him like a song his mother used to sing when night came down so many years ago:

I WAS TWENTY-EIGHT YEARS OLD *when I killed the first white man, and if ever a man deserved killing he did. He was a gambler and a counterfeiter, and I was then in a hotel in Leavenworth City, and seeing some loose characters around, I ordered a room, and as I had some money about me, I thought I would retire to it. I had*

*lain some thirty minutes on the bed when I heard men at my door.
I pulled out my revolver and bowie knife, and held them ready, but
half concealed, and pretended to be asleep. The door was opened,
and five men entered the room. They whispered together, and one
said, "Let us kill the son of a ——; I'll bet he has got money."
I kept perfectly still until just as the knife touched my breast; I
sprang aside and buried mine in his heart, and then used my revolver on the others right and left. One was killed, and another was
wounded; and then, gentlemen, I dashed through the room and
rushed to the fort, where I procured a lot of soldiers, and returning
to the hotel, captured the whole gang of them, fifteen in all.*

Then he dug his head into the pillow and pulled his legs up
tight against his belly, his eyes turned away from the first faint
flush of dawn that glowed in the sky like a distant fire.

4

THE LIGHT OF AFTERNOON IS LIGHT SEEN UNDER WATER.
Pale blue with dusty flecks of gold. In the ripples of the
sheets there are shadowed rivulets where afternoon flows toward
dusk. Shears snick among the roses. Later they will turn the
sprinkler on (who waters the flowers now?) and through the
screen she will see a tiny rainbow. The sprinkler squeaks as it
turns, like the passing of time.

She turns her head on the pillow so that her cheek is against
her hair. She brings her hand to her face and feels the heat of her
breath against her wrist. The pitcher is of crystal, eight facets,
clear as water except where there are tiny bubbles in the glass, or
maybe in the water. The drinking glass is upside down on a white
linen doily edged with blue and yellow stitching. Beside the glass
is a vial of pills.

Gently she moves her eyes, then her legs, to see if the pain
moves with them, and on the bed the latticework of sun and
shadow sways. She waits behind her eyelids for the red to turn to
gold, then looks again at the bedroom, a beach strewn with driftwood from the past. The antique walnut rocker, mounted on
springs, covered in faded green needlepoint; the deal dresser with
the mirror which tilts forward so that it seems to contain a contour map of hills, valleys, rivers to the sea, which she recognizes
as the reflection of the bed; the resinous cedar chest where the
linens are stored; the door to the adjoining bathroom, cream-
colored with an undercoat of blue showing through and a chipped
porcelain door handle shaped like a tear; a print of a nineteenth-
century whaler, flags stiff in the breeze, waves like green scallop

shells, a black cat in the rigging; photographs which she cannot see but which she knows by heart—sitting with her father in a rowboat on some northern lake where pines are displayed like spearheads upon a sky gone pale with summer; walking with her mother on the boardwalk at Atlantic City, both in round silken hats and ankle-length dresses and shoes that are wrinkled like gloves; Andrews's mother and father laughing on some golf course; then photographs which she can see and cannot look upon: Andrews in his lieutenant's uniform, his face grim in the sun; the two of them in front of the house, she in her wedding dress trying to laugh, Andrews in a cutaway, trying to smile . . .

Sun smells like dust, rain like honeysuckle. And somewhere, roses. (Who waters the roses now?) When the ice wagon stops at the curb there are children's voices and bare feet slap at the sidewalk. Harness jingles, hooves stomp, and the icepick makes a hollow plugging sound when the ice begins to separate. Sometimes the sprinkler smells like roses in the rain, or honeysuckle. Sometimes like grass. In the corners of the room shadows hang head down like bats. The sun is the color of the window shades whose dangling plaited handles twist and tap against the glass. The curtains are the color of light, or shadow, or water. They flow like water through the stillness, tossed like spray by the wind. Perhaps it will rain. The catbird sings in the catalpa tree.

When she turns her head her hair smells of lilac. The sun and shadow have moved like pieces on a chessboard; the sheets are heavy; light weighs so much . . . Now she no longer hears the wind in her ears, and light has ebbed, leaving a delicate lacework of shadow, fragile as her eyelashes opening upon the evening. Their mouths move but she cannot hear them because her eyes are open. They press upon her like the light, fingers burn her forehead, eyes search for her, Cora, Dr. Cooper; did she say their names? Faces coming up through the water, wavering, blurred. She sees them better with her eyes closed, their faces black against the red. Hears them now, a low murmur of words as though from another room.

"Every three hours . . . sleep . . . overtired . . . rest . . . cool towels . . . fruit juice if she asks . . . only for a few minutes, one at a time . . . kept right on going until she just broke down . . . don't need no more trouble than what we got here, little ole boy keep acting like his daddy's coming back . . . sleep . . . course I stays here Miss Emily like a daughter to me just went all to pieces right at the funeral little ole boy crying that way like to turn me inside out . . . every three hours, one."

Whose funeral? They said they wanted to bury Blair out on the Red Hawk ranch, some kind of Chetopa ceremony. Dead, poor Blair, all sweaty and gallant in that Southern way of his. Andrews didn't think so. Oh My God I said it to you and you wouldn't listen. We put you in the cemetery because no place else seemed right. Under a cedar tree, an old cedar bent from the wind. Poplars, too. They might make you think of birches. I hadn't thought of that, but they have leaves that twirl and shine like little tin cut-outs in the sun. The gravedigger told Amory that there was always wind and that the leaves were like flowers for everybody. Well Amory talks to people like that, you know. Or listens, anyway. Yes, yes, it was your funeral, of course. And we buried you there on a little bit of hill where the cedar grows and there was Cora yes dressed up in a dress somebody had given her probably after somebody else's funeral brave my heavens the trouble she's looked in the face Amory does love her so bless her black soul Dr. Cooper Father Stafford who read. Well not many of us. Amory and me. The gravedigger. Your father came from Boston. Mother. And oh yes Jack Bird. I don't know why he was there. I never knew he was a friend of yours. He's been nice to me. I don't know why. I wore that navy-blue dress with the little white pill box and veil. You were the one who picked it out, remember? That shop in Georgetown? Before, you see, I said to Jack right out—I never talked that way you know that but right out—Mr. Bird I am going to ask you one thing. There has got to be a funeral. I didn't know how to say it and then it just came into my mind and I came out with it. Ashes to ashes, dust to dust, just like the Bible. You had the goodness of heart to come up here and tell me while everybody else was looking for a place to hide, was what I said. Now I must ask you to see Father Stafford, the Episcopal minister. Because I will have to tell Amory, and he must have this to remember. He is going to see his father buried, and this town will know that there was a funeral, and Amory will have that to remember always. Because I don't know whether I told you or not, but we are staying here with you. Maybe we can't put up a statue to you, anyway not yet, but we are going to stay here where you are and be with you. And Amory. He didn't cry at all until, well, right at the end. I bent down and those little eyes got as wide as the sky and I told him Don't ever forget your daddy died a hero and don't ever let anybody tell you different because I wanted him to know, like I know, so deep that nobody can ever come along and take it away from him. He didn't say anything except to ask me if the handles on the coffin were like what they made silver bullets out of he read that somewhere and then he started to cry and I don't know then the sky got all dark and started to churn like it does when tornadoes come and I—I just don't remember, somehow . . . Her neck is being lifted, something bitter burns her tongue, then she lies back in the lilac of her hair. Her eyes will not open. The hands go away. She tries to open her mouth because there is more . . . *Because Jack Bird was the one who called. That was it. I remember that far back. You know I scarcely knew him. He called—it must have been early. Cora was still asleep—was she sleeping here that night? Anyway, I made coffee. He came, and he told me. Oh God I'm so afraid. I can't see, Andrews. I don't hear them when they talk to me. I want to be brave. I want to be cruel. Gone. Gone. And then I see you packing your suitcase. You have your back to me and you think I am asleep and you are packing to go. Why did you want to go? What did I do wrong? I call to you and you look back over your shoulder, and then you turn around, and your shirt and hands are all bloody and you shake your head. You look so grim, Andrews. I don't like that word but I'm always saying it and that's what it is. It's been so long since you smiled. Maybe for Amory* . . . It smells wet, like rain on honeysuckle, and the water is rising in the room. She holds her breath, wanting to stay, afraid of the waves that rock her, down, down into darkness. The wind rises in the evening and the waves suck at the shore and the sand gives way beneath her feet . . .

The liquid is in her throat and she swallows and then she smells the lilac. Her eyes open very slowly upon shades of grey. The mirror tilted forward is silver, containing the ashes of light. The sprinkler no longer turns, and the catbird is still. The catbird sings in the afternoon, the mockingbird at night. But it is not yet night. Night is steep and vast as mountains. These are the foothills of night, smoky, dreaming in mist. Everything is in its place, held in a hazed hush, the cedar chest, the antique rocker, the deal dresser with the photographs, the crystal pitcher, the bathroom door. The whaler has sailed into shadow, the sheets dark modelings in marble. The curtains hang weightlessly, and beyond the pale lines of the window the roses wait for the moon. Is there dew on the lawn? Have the cushions been brought in? But it is not yet night, merely the long suspended moment between daylight and dark. Voices fading behind the distant slam of screen doors. Boys on bicycles talking beneath the street lamps. She lifts her hand. Grey. Worn as bone. Polished by the sea, the grain showing through, nude.

Then on the waters of evening something pale floats toward her. Her hands know better than her eyes. She touches the hair, then moves her fingers through the heat of the roots, tracing her fingers through the silk to the silken skin of the neck. Hair the color of mourning, skin the color of old gold. Why are his eyes so wintry, so full of grey clouds, when the rest of him belongs in a grove of olives? Her mouth moves, and planes of shadow shift, forming again around his face, very small, very grave, saying words she does not need to hear. "Amory." The other words do not matter. She raises her hand again to his hair. "Amory." *In the elm the ringing of locusts beat like a pulse in the dying day. She lifted the damp rag gently from the boy's brow, soaked it again in the icy water, squeezed it dry and then lay it flat on the small, fevered forehead. He half opened his eyes, mumbled a name indistinctly, then seemed to sleep again. She pushed his hair back, feeling the dampness at the roots, moving her fingers along its softness to the smooth skin at the edge of the hairline. Hair so black, polished ebony, and his body the color of—she thought of herself as being olive although she had never known exactly what it meant. I never wanted to know what it meant, because what it meant was different, not white, not rose, not tan . . . Gold is a lovely color, like old buildings in Rome. Her colors, all but the eyes. They were set wide apart like hers, but their hue was the grey of an Atlantic sky swollen with snow. She remembered reading somewhere that the eyes were the window of the soul. If that were true . . . And yet his body was so full of sunlight. Mediterranean was the word she liked to use, if only to herself.*

She sighed wistfully, lightly touching his hair again, seeing in that small face set like a cameo against the pillow man and baby both, a blurred composite of family faces in which there was both past and future. And yet she wanted nothing so much as for him to remain just what he was at this moment, a boy whose long hair she had never wanted to cut at all so that she had cried the day he came back from the barber's longheaded and angular with all the softness gone, a boy who still in his roundness bore the traces of her body's shaping force. Most important, he was entirely hers, not with baby helplessness nor with the alien, resisting way of men but wholly, simply hers, the tides of his body moving as surely with hers as though they both ebbed and flowed from the same heart.

Amory stirred again. His cheeks were hot against her fingertips. She closed her eyes and saw the hospital phone number flashing across the troubled darkness of her mind like the beam from a lighthouse, danger and safety all at once. Then she looked hard before her at the faded English hunting scene on the wallpaper. No, Andrews wouldn't like it. He always said that you had enough trouble just having nature against you, but when you threw a doctor in too, then what chance did a person have. She closed her eyes again and the tears burned against her eyelids. It wasn't fun anymore. Once, maybe only in the beginning, English gentry on the wallpaper of a house like this in a town called Grey Horse, Oklahoma . . . Once they had said little things back and forth that had seemed gay, or at least made them smile. But nothing was fun any more. Oh God why doesn't he come, and she twisted her hands together in her lap, then brought the crumpled ball of a handkerchief to her mouth. Why couldn't he ever be here when she needed him. And even if things were different now, it was for Amory, after all. He was gone so much these days, and even when he was home he was abstracted, distant, so alone somehow, so out of reach.

She blew her nose and tried to stop the tears, but the pain spread upward from her neck, leaping like fire around her temples. She pressed her fingers hard against her teeth, half whispering the words through the sobs that filled her throat Oh God I'm so afraid why did he marry me if all he ever meant to do was to try and get away. Why didn't he leave me be I never asked him for anything ever just affection not even love tenderness the way people are with each other not so much not even the big things just the little things everyday his hand or a way of looking so I know that I'm alive.

She wiped her eyes and straightened the sheets and then she went on tiptoe to the bathroom. Above the medicine chest were three mirrors that she could angle so that her face was visible in all the ways that he would see her. She brought her face up very close, touching herself like a blind person, seeing her red and swollen eyes, the mole at the point of her cheekbone, the net of lines around her mouth that she liked to hope were from laughter, the blue-black smears of fatigue drawn like mascara beneath the sockets of her eyes. She touched her hair, moving her hand around to the tight bun in the back. Hard, clean, reasonable lines, a proposition in geometry. That was the way he had seemed to want it—no waves, nothing floating free, nothing left unsolved. The tears hung momentarily from her eyelashes and then dropped slowly, one by one, as she arched her arms above her head and unpinned her hair. Loose and sinuous, the heavy mass fell and hung to her waist, glowing in the wan light as she turned it with the brush. For a moment she seemed to recognize the face. Amory before his hair was cut. The way I was . . . so many years . . . when . . . is it all over, gone, forever? She switched the light off and slipped quickly out of the thin blouse. Then she pulled her hair forward across her shoulders until it lay upon her bosom and then she laced her hands with its blackness and pressed them hard against her breasts.

Then with her eyes closed, the heat of her hands on her breasts like the pressure of a lover's caress, she talked with him, saying the things she could never say, perhaps would never have a chance to say. All that I ever really wanted was you. You must have known it all along. Surely you know it still. You knew from the beginning what I came from. You said you didn't care, and I loved you for it, or thought so, but now I realize that you did care—no, not like that, but in another way. And not about me, but the way it was, like you wanted me that way and not any other, as though your life were a kind of house, all separate rooms, each to be furnished differently, this one native colonial, that one first-generation immigrant, a third Spanish colonial or Western in some way or other, and all of them necessary to your sense of your own history, or destiny, or whatever name you call it by. And always for you, because this isn't the way I wanted it to be. I've made myself this way for you. Because you seemed to want it or need it that way. Don't you ever just need me, without the furnishings? I can't be naked in front of you any more, or wear perfume, or even comb my hair where you can see. Maybe it's because I'm afraid you'll laugh, or that you just won't see me at all. And yet I know that you love me. What other reason could there be? People don't go through what we went through because they don't love each other. Do they? Because if you can believe that, then nothing makes any sense, and everything is out of control in a way that scares me half to death. That's the type of thing I just won't believe. Even if you tell me you don't love me, I won't believe you. Because as long as we're alone, the way we used to be, everything is all right. It's when the outside world interferes—other people—the way it is here. You've changed so much since we've been here. Oh you were always cold and a little afraid of me but you would have gotten over that. You always had the idea that you were too passionate and that you had to keep yourself in check, but these things aren't true. I know you, Andrews, so much better than you know yourself. What hurts so much is that you know I'm right and yet you won't listen. I'm not your mother. You don't have to resist me. I knew I could change you once I had you to myself. But coming here—oh, even before.

And now you have let her come into our life, as though you deliberately had to push yourself to the very limit. I know these things happen, but I would have thought we were above them. All I know is that I've got to get you out of here before something dreadful happens. You belong to me, and I won't let them take you away—not your parents, or this woman, or this blind brooding over things that are past and done with. Why do you still think about such things? Who cares about all those preachers and whaling captains, the farm full of colonial junk and books nobody's looked at for centuries, and now what you call the old encampment. It's always something. Sometimes I think I'll go out of my mind, trying to make you wake up, trying to make you face reality. I'm like Cassandra, Andrews, doomed to tell the truth which nobody will believe. But there's one thing you have to understand, or at least admit, whether you understand it or not. Sometimes I'm not even sure that I understand it, but in some strange way I've lived my whole life for you, from the time I was a child. I was brought up on the dream of marrying you, if you want to put it that way. I've got no place to go back to. You took me away from what I had, and now you've got to stay with me.

Her hands trembled as she switched the light on again, and then she quickly pulled and pinned her hair back into place, still crying but ashamed now of letting herself go this way. And suddenly as she studied herself in the mirror she felt that she was looking at the face of someone she no longer knew. She had created it but it didn't belong to her. It belonged rather to him, and to their life here. What was left that was hers when even her face had been twisted into something that was foreign to her?

She moved to the window and stared at the vacant lot beside their house. It had been burned off in the middle of summer, even the hollyhocks which she had planted along that side of the fence. Danger to adjacent properties—that was the phrase the fire department had used. Now it was charred black stubble with here and there a glint of sun where someone had tossed a tin can or a bottle in the weeds. A place so dry and dangerous it had to be reduced to cinder, burned right down to ashes that blew and stuck to the screens when the wind lifted. The whole town was that way. Desolate, without any life that counted, deadly. And what did it matter finally what happened to any of the people here. Quarantine them, let them carry on their savagery without infecting the rest of mankind.

In the silence the mockingbird was singing from the elm in the backyard. Tonight those songs which could seem so ironic and gay were merely the repeated mouthings of an idiot. Somewhere a streetlight went on in a tiny explosion of silence, blinding the night around it, drawing the careening bats like carrion birds. Down in the valley a freight train whistled, then moved with a reverberating crash as though a massive skeleton had been rolled over by the wind. The sounds of death in a land gone dead, burnt out, bone-covered, put to the fire.

Then she turned and went swiftly to the boy's bed and knelt beside him, seizing him in her arms and pressing him to her. "You're all I've got left that's really truly mine," she whispered passionately. "Nothing, nobody else. I won't let them touch you, no matter what else they do. Amory?"

"Emily?"

The voice seemed to travel toward her from an infinite distance, so that she heard the sound before she knew what it meant. She heard it again, and then as though time were moving backward she heard the crunch of tires on the gravel of the driveway. "Andrews?" She lowered the boy to the bed and smoothed her dress and walked quickly through the twilit rooms to the front screen. But why? There was no one there. Andrews was not there. Andrews was . . . Perhaps that had been in another place, at another time. Besides, they begin shoveling the dirt back in even before you leave the graveside.

The shadows move and form his face again. He is seated in the antique rocker, leaning toward her as though in answer to her voice. She cannot hear her own voice, nor does he ever speak her name. Her eyes swim up through depths of grey to a face the color of morning glories, obscured by a hat with a mauve plume. The face seems to be made of two parts hastily stuck together so that one half is out of line with the other. Soft and furry and smelling vaguely sweet, like a powder puff. Eyes lopsided and elephant-small in their wrinkled skin. One hand is on his shoulder, the other extended majestically toward the bed. The arched mouth still open, as though the last notes of the aria still lingered there, plumes and powder and yards of evanescent silk all watery in the mists of evening. She hears the language in which her childhood lies cradled, and inside her open conduits of pain for all the years gone and forgotten, the love dammed like a stream that, unable to find the sea, swells into a lake of tears. She is alive in both their faces, and feels herself again in their eyes, painfully, so that some sound which she can hear makes her lips move. Then Cora is there, the black seamed angry face absorbing the shadows, the yellow palm at her neck, lifting her head, then the glass, the bitterness flowing in her throat, a puff of lilac as she falls back into her hair. Her hand moves more slowly than her eyes, and she cannot hold them, those faces, black, gold, purple, consumed by fire when at last her eyes close again, still calling without sound, something still flowing out of her into them, currents of feeling without sound, swirling more swiftly, dragging her into darkness while her hands grip the sides of the bed as though it were a foundering raft . . . *How could I know it wasn't you when it was you I needed so desperately. I suppose I knew, really. After all, Blair's voice is something you don't forget. I wasn't listening, mainly. I had been sitting by Amory's bed, thinking about—it's so hard to remember, you see. I was blue, I remember that. Sad, sort of, and worried and nervous. Blair had called to me through the screen door, standing there in that rumpled white linen suit with the big straw hat and the brown-and-white shoes. It's just that I can't think of him without remembering all the rest. Blair in summer is a pair of brown-and-white shoes and a cigar and a glass of whiskey and a crumpled-up white linen suit with ashes on the lapels and everything looking about four sizes too big for him though goodness know he's big enough. Plus a straw hat which would make anybody else look like a farmer and on him looks like a panama. Because all the same, Blair has something elegant about him. Had, I should say, but I just can't, somehow. Oh God, Andrews, what has it all been for? If only you could find some way to let me know. But whatever happens, I've got to tell you so that you will know, so that everything is clear on my side at least, and then we can go on, the three of us, just like it never happened. Just like you were still with us, the main thing in our lives, the way it always was. It will stay that way for us, Andrews, for Amory and me, because Amory must not grow up without his father. And if it's all a jumble in my head—well, you see, even before we had left you there, this man, this hairy man in his undershirt was already shoveling the dirt—I mean you could hear the clods hitting the coffin lid and I was talking to Amory, yes, I was down on my knees so that I could look into his eyes, and that noise, it must have frightened him because his face just fell apart like something you hit with a hammer and then the sky all of a sudden was black, greenish black the way it gets when a tornado is coming. I thought that cedar tree was falling on me . . . So my mind isn't clear, except what I have to do. And then I couldn't bear the thought of your not knowing, because I realize what Amory was to you, and your hopes, and whatever else I was, at least I was that, am that I should say, Amory's mother after all.*

But it was your funeral. Poor Blair. Somewhere I got the idea that he was going to be buried out west of town, the way the Chetopas do. Was it Father Stafford who told me that? I know you'll probably think it was just another one of his drunken stunts. But then I always liked him better than you did. I thought his Southern manners were nice—at least he made me feel like a woman which is more than I can say for anyone else around here. He was so nice that night, and at the same time so awfully sad, or maybe desperate is a better word. He must have gone right home and shot himself. I could tell when I saw him standing there at the screen door, just the way he slumped and his head hung down and the smile didn't quite make it across his face and I said Blair? like it was a question, like I knew there was something wrong and he ought to tell me. He just kept looking at me. Maybe he thought I had something more to say. Then he smiled, all the way this time if you don't count the eyes, and asked if he could see you. I told him you weren't here, but that I was expecting you. Then I invited him in and he said he wouldn't mind sitting for a while in the garden if I didn't object to receiving gentlemen friends when

my husband wasn't there. You know how he would have said that
ordinarily, with that big laugh of his which made you laugh
whether what he said was funny or not. He didn't laugh, and I
wondered what was wrong. And I was afraid to ask because I
didn't want him to tell me. What other reason could he have for
coming besides you? I told him Amory was sick and that seemed
to bother him and he said something I didn't quite catch about
the climate being bad for all of us, and then he sat down in the
swing under the elm tree and just stared off into space, like he'd
forgotten what he'd come for or that I was even there. I went
back and looked at Amory again, and then I fixed him a drink.
With a glass in his hand he was more like the old Blair, compli-
menting me on the roses, telling me about the flowers and the
lawns where he grew up in Virginia. But laughing in a way that
made me wonder how much he'd had to drink before he came.
I've never been able to tell whether people are drunk or not. I
don't think I've ever been drunk. Whiskey makes me sick, I don't
know why. Anyway, sitting there all red and perspiring and fanning himself with his hat and his eyes bloodshot and he didn't
even look like he'd properly shaved himself—it wasn't right, that's
all, and I wanted him to go on about his business and leave me be
so that I could look after Amory and wait for you to come home.
I guess he saw I wasn't listening because then he did a funny
thing. He put the glass down and reached over and took my hand.
Just like I'd known him for years or something. I came here to
ask for your help. Just like that. That's how he started. It was like
a dream that when it starts, almost before, you know it's going to
be bad. I don't know what I said, just Oh Blair, something like
that. To make him think I thought he was just kidding, anything
to keep him from going on. I mean it, he said then, begging
almost, and I knew it was true and that I couldn't help him and
that most of all I just didn't want to hear it. Blair, I can't think of
anyone in this town who could be of less help to you. Really. But
there wasn't any use in trying to talk him out of it, and he didn't
even smile. His face was so sad, like he wanted to put his head in
my lap and cry, and I kept praying that you would come home,
anything just so I wouldn't have to hear it. It's about Andrews of

course. *I knew that was what he was going to say even before he said it, the way you can smell rain in the air before it comes, and then I had that strange feeling that I had lived it all before, or dreamed it, something, so that it's like seeing a movie for the second time and you know what's going to happen even though you can't remember the lines. And Clay. I shook my head at him then but there wasn't any way to stop him. And Rita. That was already too much, as far as I was concerned. Do we have to discuss all this, Blair? Isn't this something between you and Andrews? I didn't want to hear it, Andrews, do you understand? How could anybody else speak of these things without knowing how our lives had been, all the little things that nobody else can know and that are the most important, after all. Nobody had invited him into our life like that, so clumsy and vulgar and lacking any real refinement. That may not be fair, to say it that way. Blair does have manners and he's been used to money, you can see that, but bringing up that woman's name . . . Andrews won't listen to me. I was hoping I could get you to listen, and then talk to him before it's too late. I answered something silly, like I don't know what you mean by that, the kind of thing that just comes out by itself, like we were reading lines for a high school play. Nothing I said seemed to be connected with what I felt, and at the same time every word was taking me further along a road I didn't want to follow. I was waiting for you, and Amory was sick with I don't know what, and the last thing I cared about just then was Clay Carter and that wife of his. But there I was, sitting there in that lawn chair, watching Blair fix himself another drink, listening to him tell it. Your husband has got something on his mind about Clay and me. He's tracking me, Emily. The way you track an escaped convict through the woods with a bloodhound. His breath was coming a little short and he spilled the whiskey so that it ran down his chin and his eyes were just terrible. Andrews seems to think that Clay and I have made some pact with the devil to kill off the Red Hawk family, God knows what. You've got to listen to me before it's too late. Those words again—too late. Every time he said them my blood ran cold. Did I ever tell you that I'd had a premonition about something terrible happening, ever since we came to this awful little town? From the moment we got off the train, those Indian women without any expression on their faces, the men so still and yet somehow looking so violent, half-hidden in their blankets and big hats, the way the Negro chauffeurs lay asleep in the cars, waiting—for what? Everybody just waiting around for the train to come in? And against all that silence, Carter and Blair, like a song-and-dance team—there was something almost hysterical about it. It was all I could do to keep from bursting out in tears. I wanted to stay right there at the station and catch the next train out, to anywhere, it didn't matter. The stillness, everybody standing around without saying anything. It was like a funeral, Andrews, like we'd come to bury somebody. When you think of it like that, I guess we had. Anyway, I had no choice. I had to hear him out. A long, rambling, incoherent story that I couldn't understand very well. All about Clay and the town and everything that had happened over no telling how many years. I wonder if he ever told the story to anyone before. I mean he was so intense about it all—you'd think it had all happened yesterday instead of fifteen years ago or more. In the poorhouse or the City Home where they keep the old people you expect to hear that kind of talk, but Blair . . . How he had come here, how he had met Clay, all that they had done to help the Tribe, even if it wasn't always according to the book. To hear him talk you'd think they were a pair of saints. And then the Red Hawk business all over again, and how Clay had helped him get Shoat Dalton. There's one thing I want you to believe, he kept saying, swinging his hand down as though it were an ax to emphasize the point. Shoat Dalton was guilty, no matter what Jack Bird was able to get people to believe. Well, all right, I felt like saying, Shoat Dalton was guilty, and what then? I mean going on about it so, I've never understood why any of you keep after it the way you do. It's all in the past and they're all of them dead and what good does it do to keep mulling it over. But try to tell that to Blair. To listen to him, you would have to say that it was Divine Providence interceding when Shoat turned over in that car. Mortal justice had failed, so God stepped in to set things right. Then, still according to Blair, everything was just fine until you ap-*

*peared. What did he come for, Emily? Why? A man of An-
drews's background and ability doesn't get sent to Grey Horse on
a Tribal Attorney's job. Did the Commissioner take a hand in it
personally? Do they want my scalp, or what? Has somebody
accused me of murder? Not that he really expected me to answer
any of those questions, or even wanted me to. He sounded like he
was pleading a case, talking to a jury, speaking over my head to
somebody somewhere who could help him. Andrews isn't that
type—he won't let himself be used as a stalking horse. I never did
understand that expression and so that didn't make any more sense
to me than the rest. What could I say to him? Blair, I just don't
care. Whatever happens in this little town is something that has
nothing to do with me, however important it may seem to you. I
mean the perspiration was just pouring off him, sitting there
mopping at his face, freshening up his drink as he calls it, squinting his eyes at me like he was trying to see me across about a mile
of prairie.*

*Then he started in on Rita, all that Clay had done for her and
how ungrateful she was. I turned my face away from him as
soon as he mentioned her name, so don't think I was encouraging
him. There just wasn't any way to stop him. How Clay was just
wild about her, Texas-stubborn was the way Blair said it, the way
he could be about land or a horse or just somebody else's saddle, if
he wanted it real bad. Said Clay talked him and Mary Rose into
going to Paris. We're going to bring that Red Hawk girl back
home where she belongs. Well, that sounds like Clay all right. But
Paris. You know how I've always felt about French things, the
language, the literature, the elegance, the formality of everything.
Paris has been a kind of dream of mine ever since I was a girl.
Even before I started school my mother got me a book of beginning French—Les Aventures de Madame Souris—and started
teaching me. Heavens knows she would have done better to work
on my Italian, but then she always looked down on Italians. Anyway she said so. Well, the Romantic Poets, cathedrals in provincial towns, the Tuileries in autumn when all the trees are like a
pen-and-ink drawing, precise little parks where the children are
immaculate, painters and writers and sidewalk cafes, all those*

marvelous vistas—just the best of everything. It sounds silly, I know, but it was so much more real to me than Pittsfield. Rita—all right, she was a dancer of sorts, although I have my doubts about that too. But Clay Carter in Paris, with Blair and Mary Rose . . . I just can't tell you. Can't you just see him stalking around Paris, handmade boots, tailored whipcord trousers, a white Stetson hat, that face like old cracked leather and his yellow hair spiky as a dog's, lounging around waiting for somebody to tell him what to look at. I'm surprised he didn't take that idiot Cody along. That would have made it perfect. Clay Carter had no right to be in Paris, Andrews. Reaching for his bankroll whenever he didn't understand, using beautiful things that meant nothing to him as just a way of getting what he wanted, as oblivious to the history and traditions and true grandeur of that grey old city as some condottiere who had come to conquer it and to hell with the rest. What could he possibly care about what anyone before him had done, about a sense of the past as something living, to be cherished, unless he could use it in some way to be turned into money to buy whatever it was a man like that would want. He makes his own rules and lets you worry about whether you'll play or not. Classless, belonging to nothing, believing in nothing he can't buy one day and sell the next—I loathe him, Andrews. Whatever you've done to him won't be half what he deserves. And then Blair has the nerve to say Give him a chance Emily. Maybe he saw it in my face, some gesture I made without even knowing it. Maybe that's what the whole thing was about. Give him a chance. That's what he wanted me to tell you, I suppose. Nobody needs to give him a chance, Blair. He takes whatever he wants, and God pity the person who gets in his way. I guess it surprised him when I said it like that. He stopped, anyway, and went through his pockets, looking for a cigar. Finally he reached down in the grass and picked up the stub of one he'd let drop a few minutes earlier. I never saw Blair do that before, but he was beyond caring. I've never seen a man in such a state. Like he was in a death cell, with a half hour to go before they strapped him in the electric chair, still trying to prove his innocence. He loosened his tie and wiped his neck underneath his collar and chewed at the cigar stub while he talked. Nothing could have surprised me at that point.

So then he started in on Rita again. All the things Clay bought for her in Paris; clothes, furniture, jewels, and the house he built for her here. Nothing too good for her, nothing he couldn't find a way to buy if it was for sale. Blair was hinting at something, something he wanted to tell me and just couldn't find the words for, or just didn't care. Lord knows what it could be, because what he did tell me . . . Well, I guess it was meant for you. That very quickly, just as it had happened before, the place got too small for her. First whiskey, then dope, then other men, Clay taking it God knows why. That's what Blair seemed to have on his mind, why Clay kept on treating her like a porcelain princess, but he never got it out. Shoat Dalton's nephew was one of them, for whatever that's worth. Then some Armenian lingerie salesman from Tulsa—I didn't even want to listen. Mean and wild and she wants out of here. That's the way he put it. She'll use anybody or anything, including your husband, Emily. And if he's listening to her and believing whatever it is she's telling him . . . on and on like that.

But by this time I'd had about enough, even if it wasn't good manners to show it. None of this makes any sense to me, I told him, cold and short, just like that. Andrews wouldn't listen to that sort of woman for a moment, unless he had a special reason for doing so. She's common, cheap, vulgar—completely out of his class. If he's seeing her, it's not because he wants to. And if she's telling him things, Blair, then he's the one to judge whether or not it's true. Now I suggest . . . I got about that far before he broke in on me. He wasn't going to be put off that easily. And now I'll tell you exactly what he said. I can't forget it. Before any of it happened, before you called, anything, and the minute he said it I wanted to scream, because God be my witness, Andrews, I had known right from the beginning what was going to happen. All of a sudden he seemed to stop dead still as though the blood had frozen in his veins. He held the handkerchief there under his chin, and in the other hand the cigar hung down to the ground. Just the

*two of us sitting there face to face, not a breath of wind in the
elm tree, just the faintest feather of smoke drifting up from that
stub of a cigar. I had to strain to hear him, his voice had gone so
quiet. In that great hulk of a body only his eyes seemed still alive,
and all the life that was left in him burned there so intensely that I
could scarcely bear to look at him. Emily, now you listen to me.
Andrews is heading for terrible trouble. If we're lucky, you may
be able to stop him. I can't. I've tried, and he won't listen. He's
like a steer in the chute, walking head down toward the butcher
with the sledge hammer. Emily, he will bring disaster down on all
of us unless he's willing to listen. Maybe you can make him
understand, if it's not too late already. It's not the way he thinks it
is. I'm talking about life and death, Emily. Out here life is cheap,
and death is fast and easy.*

    *Then I stopped him because I'd heard more than I wanted or
needed to hear and I felt like the whole thing was getting out of
hand and I had to stop it, put the brake on, before we all of us just
went over the edge. I don't know how I got up the courage to say
it, but I did. It's none of my business, Blair, but now you're
making it my business so I'm going to tell you what I think. How
would it look to you? The way Shoat Dalton was killed, and now
you say that his nephew and Rita Carter . . . The whole family,
one after another, and all that money, and just the kind of man
Clay Carter is and then you come here and try to make me
believe he's some kind of Abraham Lincoln or other. What's happened in this town, Blair? Why is everyone so scared? You all
hate us because we're not afraid, because we've got nothing to
hide and we don't have to drink ourselves to sleep every night.
Who else would stand up to it all if Andrews didn't? One man
strong enough to tell the truth, and all of you run for cover. It's
so insane—as though anybody anywhere else could care the
slightest—it's like some kind of awful plague in some little medieval village. And you, Blair. What about you all these years . . .*

    *That was when you called. Just then. I don't know what else I
would have said. And then when I heard your voice, I had an
awful feeling that there wasn't anything more to say, that you
were someplace ahead of me in time and that it was too late for*

*me ever to catch up. I came down the back steps and into the
yard and he was sitting there with his face in his hands. He didn't
look up until I spoke to him, and then his face was so flushed, so
full of suffering, that I couldn't help feeling sorry for him. That
was Andrews, Blair. I told him you were here. He said that Clay
Carter was in jail and that you'd know what was happening. Jail.
Clay Carter, Blair. Is that what you've been trying to tell me? Is
that what you came here to say?*

*His mouth moved and then he turned his eyes away and
seemed to look at what was left of the whiskey for I don't know
how long. Then when he looked back at me, whatever fire it was
that had been burning in that face had gone dead. A face that size
when it's red—well, you get used to it. But when it's white . . .
He smiled an awful smile, absolutely scary, because all white like
that he seemed all bones and teeth, like a skull. Let me say good
night to Amory before I leave, will you? That was all the answer
he had to give me. I'd like to see Amory one last time before I go.
It does me good to see the boy. Twenty, thirty years from now,
what will he think of it all, how can he possibly put together how
it was, us, this place, everything that's happened, when it's all just
dust and ashes. Take care of him, Emily. You're lucky to have
somebody who might remember, who might even understand, at
least a little. Amory. Amory . . .* Cora wears a starched white cap,
and her hair twists around it like steel wool. Cora leads them,
Amory and her mother, going somewhere on a journey, waiting
for the train. She sees their backs, Amory's face in shadowy profile, Cora white and stiff, the gently swaying plume of her mother's hat. She reaches for them but her hand is too heavy. The door
creaks, opening a fan of light which brushes like the slow wings
of a suspended butterfly the deal dresser, the rocker, the cedar
chest, the crystal pitcher, the drapery of the sheets. She must hold
them, for she has not yet said their names, told them, found their
eyes . . . But carved by light they are eternal now, the forms of
her feelings, all time sculptured in them. Her hand drops, the
names fall from her lips, and the fan closes upon the room, folding
the light into its creases . . . *Amory was awake when we came in
the room. I was afraid that Blair would overexcite him, talking*

big the way he always does, but no, not at all, so gentle you wouldn't know it was the same man. He sat down on the bed and adjusted the little night lamp and then made shadow figures on the wall, elephants, pigs, giraffes, all sorts of dogs, birds, with all the squeals and grunts and barks and whistles—a lion that mewed, a donkey that talked like a Chetopa speaking English. You know. Amory loved it, of course. And I sat there in the dark like a goose and cried without even knowing why. And then he left. I don't think he knew I had been crying. I hope not. I couldn't have told him why. If I had to say, it would have to be because of what Blair must have been once upon a time, back at Sewanee, say, when it was all so different. When we said good night he was like some worn-out clown, still trying to get a laugh. He was gallant in his way, Andrews, in spite of all the rest. It was Mary Rose who called me. What was it I did wrong, Andrews? Something I said or didn't say? Why is it always that way? He must have gone right home and shot himself.

Dawn is a different kind of silver, rose somewhere. All night long the mockingbird sings, making the silence more perfect. Now there are sparrows, and the air moves among the languid curtains so that the plaited handles of the shades tap against the frames. Just as night dissolves into dew, so dawn dissolves into a fine ashen powder which coats with the slightest patina of silver the misted mirror wherein lies the disarray of sheets, the needlework frayed where the tacks have pinched, the schooner fastened to the scalloped waves, the screens which smudge the morning like a fingerprint. The bed empty, her mind empty and at rest, lulled like a small boat with sails furled riding at anchor in a southern port. The winds gone, leaving her becalmed in the still waters of death. Gone forever. Gone while it was still dawn, before the day could take root, and climb, and blossom into night. . . . *Before I ever really knew you, what it was you had lost, the kind of life you had built around your own particular kind of loneliness. Not knowing those things, which could have told me what you could never say, I tried to be what I thought you*

*wanted me to be. It was a little like the blind learning to read—
the sense of touch, that's what I had to use. And maybe the very
fact that I had to try was what was wrong. Of course I was
grateful to you in a way. I think I loved you, if that means that
you made my life seem important to me in a way it never had
before, gave me a sense of direction that seemed to be mine rather
than someone else's. I wanted you to love me, more than I ever
wanted anything. And if trying to be always what you wanted
means love, then I loved you. The trouble was just that—I was
always the one who had to change. I never asked enough of you, I
guess. I knew what I wanted, anyway, and that's more than I can
say for you. To tell you the truth, I never really understood why
you wanted to marry me, except that of course you needed me
for that strange world you were always working on in your mind.
I never knew anyone who lived so much in a world that was so
entirely private. I used to ask myself if you really loved me. I was
a necessary part of that strange, underseas world of yours, I knew
that from the beginning. But that's not the same thing. I need
you. I love you. Can you hear the difference? How can I tell you?
I tried. I really did. You must have known that. What did I do
wrong? In Cambridge I was somber for you, cut my curls and
made my hair into a kind of cap. Wore plain clothes. Looked
down on everyone except your friends. Went on weekends with
you to see my parents, not yours. Did you ever think how humili-
ating that was for me? I wanted to get away from them, and I
hated myself for it because I owed them everything. You were
what my parents came to this country for, and they were something special to you that I could never understand. So everybody
got something but me. Nobody ever seemed to wonder what I
wanted. And of course it was you, to have all for myself, anybody could see that, except that you would never let me get very
close—either your friends or my family or something serious—
sketches of colonial architecture, walks at Walden Pond, the
symphony on Friday afternoons. We could have gone on Saturday, money was no problem for you, but that was your way. Just
that once, when I visited you in Alabama, and even then it was all
so planned and organized. I don't know why, it's just that there*

*was always something disappointing about everything we did.
Even when we got married. You were the one who insisted that it
be in Pittsfield. I would have preferred Alabama, Paris, Mexico
City, Cambridge—as far away as possible. Why did you want to
keep me there? Life could have been so easy, Andrews. But you
wouldn't let it. I could never understand that about you, why
living pleasantly and normally had to be something—well, sinful
almost. Why couldn't we ever be like other people? Sometimes
you seemed to think that we were superior, and then sometimes it
was that we were too lucky, and we had to pay the price. Was it
too much to ask, just to be like everybody else? To me that was
something I'd dreamed of and worked for all my life. Maybe
your name and your family was something you wanted to forget
—all right, but we didn't have to end up as missionaries just for
that. And did it ever occur to you that I had things I wanted to
forget? I hated every day of my childhood. I wonder if you can
begin to imagine what that means. Living on the wrong side of
the tracks, parents who scarcely spoke English, dressed like a doll
in my mother's worn-out dresses, Mass every Sunday in a Protes-
tant town, Mother and Daddy skimping on meals and everything
else so that I could have piano lessons, ballroom dancing, even
horseback riding, none of which meant a thing to me. It was like
living in a factory with me on the production line, being assembled. I don't know what they were raising me for, or even where
they got the idea. Maybe that's what listening to grand opera all
your life does for you. And then college, a scholarship girl among
the rich, all of them with names like yours and that stuck-up way
of talking through their noses so that for a while I thought that
what I spoke wasn't even English. Funny, homemade clothes.
Afraid to go horseback riding, or dancing, to play the piano, even
to leave my room. So I did very well in French Poetry and by
some absolute miracle met you at the one dance I ever got up the
courage to go to.*

*Well, after that, perhaps you can understand why I always
thought we were pretty lucky, you and I. But you never seemed
to think so. Was it more you wanted, or less? I never really
understood. Wanted it, needed it, something. I could feel you*

going away, looking for it, almost from the beginning or at least as soon as Amory was born. Like you didn't need me any more, whatever it was that you had needed me for at the start, to go on looking for whatever it was you needed now. Did you find it, Andrews? I hope so, because it must have meant an awful lot to you. Anyway, whatever it was, it's taken you away and you're gone for good, and we're alone now, on our own with a long lonesome road out ahead of us.

Andrews, I'm so afraid. Maybe I wouldn't say these things if I weren't so afraid. From the time I was a girl I was always scared of being alone, of growing old by myself, and now Amory and I—this town. The things you are afraid of are what happen to you. This town, Andrews. Pitiless. Not a soul to turn to. Everything I wanted to get away from all my life, but worse. Not just common vulgarity, but brutality as well. They'll try to drag us in the mud before it's over, just because we're the kind of people we are, and they are—well, Cora's word is trash. White trash. I'm sure they'll even find a way to turn your death into something ugly and vicious. But you see, there's just no place else for us to go. We have to stay, whatever they say, however hard Clay Carter and his friends make it for us. I can't go to my parents, and I certainly won't go to yours. So I'm going to get a job, stay in this house, bring up Amory the way you would have wanted it. They'll have to pay for what they've done to us, Andrews; if there's any decency or justice in this world, someday they'll have to pay. Nobody's going to hide and nobody's going to forget. Just the fact that we are here, seeing them every day, carrying on your name, will take care of that. I want an eye for an eye and a tooth for a tooth. I want them to know how much I hate them, to grit their teeth every time they see me. I swear to you that I will be as bleak and hard as any Grecian queen, and that will be our monument to you. Something they'll have to look on every day and then curse the man who brought it on them. Because it was the town that killed you, as surely as though they had all gathered, white and Indian both, men, women, and children, into the encampment on the Agency grounds, and cooked meat and danced the ritual dances and chanted for your blood until Clay

Carter brought you among them and nailed you to the cross in full view of every living soul. Nobody there to say no. No one to say if it can happen to him I may be next. And now the town must pay for every drop of your blood if I have to stay here for a thousand years. And if anything should happen to me, there is Amory. He won't forget, you can be sure of that. Thank God he is old enough already so that you will stay in his memory, so that he won't have to depend on a few photographs and the little people can tell him. But more than just the way you looked and acted, he must remember why and how you died. I've told him, you see, and I'll go on telling him, so that together he and I can tend the flame . . .

It was the very day when I learned about what had happened. There were so many things to think of—arranging for the funeral, letting the family know, all kinds of grotesque little details that you just can't imagine until you've lived through it. Cora was doing her best to keep Amory out of the way, but of course he noticed all the coming and going. He kept asking for you and I kept putting him off, but I knew I had to tell him that day, before he learned some other way. Children have a strange sense of such things—it's almost as though they learn by breathing so that they know, whether you tell them or not. Somebody from the Agency brought the car back and parked it in the driveway—I suppose Jack Bird did that, along with so many other things, why I'll never know—and that afternoon after Amory had had his rest, I put him in the car and drove up the Cedarvale Road to that bend by the park where you can stop and see the town laid out down below. His fever was down, and there just wasn't time for him to be sick, what with all the other things that needed doing. He was quiet in the car. Once he asked me how come it wasn't dad who brought the car home, and I just put my hand on his knee and didn't answer, and he didn't say any more. Then we parked and he turned and looked down at the town and said that's the Agency building down there. That's where dad has his office, isn't it. Why doesn't he come home, and he looked at me then in a way that made me feel sure that somehow he must know. I took his hand and squeezed it tight and said Amory, now I have some-

thing I have to tell you. You see, your father will not be coming home anymore. He's gone away, forever and ever. I felt myself already slipping into a kind of fairy-tale way of telling it, and I didn't want that, not for any of us, but then you can't just say these things straight out to a child and what other language do you use. Why did he go away? He frowned at me, almost as though he were angry, and those eyes of his—how could I answer. His mouth was trembling, and then I had to think about myself, hanging on, not going to pieces, because if I did he would always remember that and not you. I fought it as hard as I could and thought my God whatever words there are use them say it anyway you can just say it so that he will stop asking. Then I thought that maybe I should have told him in the backyard where he would at least be home rather than here on the county road with the trees all grey and covered with dust and the grass burnt out by the sun and a grasshopper that had gotten into the car and kept flying up against the windshield, so that while I told him, Amory very carefully and patiently tried to catch the grasshopper, not looking at me any more, not even seeming to be listening. We will miss him terribly, but we must act the way he would expect us to. Particularly you, because you will be a man, and he loved you very much. And then we have our memories of him, and that way we can keep him with us, even though he has gone to heaven and we won't ever see him again. Maybe I didn't say it exactly like that, but more or less. I could hardly bear to sit there like that, seeing him so serious about that grasshopper and wanting to just grab him and cry my heart out, so I just kept on talking to keep from doing something foolish. And to make sure right from the beginning that he knew, once and for all. Your daddy was a hero, Amory, like the knights in your storybooks who kill dragons or the sheriffs who kill bad people so that there can be law and order. There are never many good men at one time in the world, that is part of our trial, and they are the ones who must be courageous and stand and fight against evil, no matter how difficult things may be. Like King Arthur, and George Washington, and Buffalo Bill—I think he was a sheriff. Anyway you've read about all of them. And our lord Jesus Christ. You are lucky to have had a hero for a father, Amory. Now we shall stay here and look after his grave . . . I hadn't meant to say that, but he looked at me quickly, and I knew I had to tell him about the funeral anyway. Tomorrow we will go to bury your daddy and you must be a brave boy and try not to cry. Is daddy already in heaven? I told him yes. I said that now we had a lot of things to do to get ready for tomorrow and that he must help me. Daddy won't be there when we get back, he said then, like he hadn't heard me. Your father will not be coming home any more, I said to him, squeezing his little hand as tight as I could. He's gone away, forever and ever. He didn't have any expression on his face except for a slight frown that made two lines just above his nose, the way he looks when he's reading, and yet I know there were tears in his eyes, even though he wasn't crying. Then he held his hand up to show me the brown spot on his finger. That's the tobacco juice the grasshopper spits. I nodded, waiting, because I could tell he had something else he wanted to say. Finally he leaned over and put his head on my shoulder. I want to go home now. I want to climb up in my tree house. I left my storybooks up there. I don't want anything to happen to them. It might rain or something.

It was as though someone had put an hourglass by her bed and thus set time in motion again. Degrees of light and shadow recovered their precision, and at appointed moments she washed, sat up and ate her broth and crackers, took her pills herself, looked at the pictures in the magazines because she had no heart for the newspapers, and listened to them talk. And though the fire behind her eyes was gone, and the drowning in darkness, and the inability to speak without a sudden and uncontrollable flow of tears, still she could not find her way back to them. Something had gone dead at the center now that Andrews was in his grave. And one by one their faces came and went, her mother lurid and indomitable in the heat, Mr. Thayer severely immaculate in seersucker, clipped mustache, and panama, the doctor knowing as a cat, taking her pulse and saying nothing, the smiling harried clergyman who talked her regularly into despair at the end of the afternoons,

Cora scolding and scornful, marching Amory in and out on schedule, and then Jack Bird, for no reason whatsoever that she could see except that he had been the one who told her, at least as much as she would let him tell her at the time. And then suddenly she realized that if he kept coming, hardly knowing her, a stranger to the house, it could only be because he had something more to say.

He was sitting there in the rocker, smoking his cigarette, his eyes bulging and his mouth pursed, looking somewhat sheepish like a boy who has been kept in after school and is waiting to be dismissed.

"Well," he said, "you're feeling better all right. You haven't focused on me that long since you took sick."

"I haven't really been sick," she said slowly. "Just tired. Something just gave out."

"I reckon there was reason enough for that. Person been through what you've been through's got a right to be tired. You just go on and rest now. I stopped in to say hello to that boy and see how you were doing. No reason to wear yourself out on my account."

His voice was hard and flat but gentle, too. It had patience in it. She had never noticed before how ugly he was. Maybe that accounted for it. He must have had things happen to him, too. She held out her hand, surprised herself at the sudden stir of feeling.

"I should have thanked you before. You've been so kind. I hardly knew you."

"Well, somebody had to help out. Man can't just stand around. I don't know."

"I mean the funeral—I suppose you realize why I wanted it. I'm sorry—I don't even know if you have a family."

He stubbed his cigarette, and she saw the lines in his face deepen as he half turned away. "As a matter of fact I have two kids. A good deal older than that little fellow of yours—what do you call him?—Amory. That's a real nice name. Don't hear that name out here much. Don't think I ever heard it before. More like in England, kind of. Now that we're talking about him, I was thinking of slipping around here some evening when he was in the way and taking him out to one of them Legion ball games. He's old enough," and then he left the words hanging in the air, as though he hadn't really meant to put it just that way.

"Why did you come that morning? Why did you think you had to tell me?"

"Well, like I say," and then he stopped again, and took his glasses off and rubbed them on his tie.

"No," she said quietly. "It wasn't just because somebody had to help out, Mr. Bird. There must have been something that you didn't tell me that morning. There wasn't much I wanted to hear just then. If there's anything else—I think you better tell me now. I want to get it over with."

On the lawn the sprinkler was turning and the room smelled of wet honeysuckle. He seemed uncomfortable there in the fragile rocker, too big for it, everything about him so very plain, so totally undistinguished, sitting there in a shapeless cotton suit with which he wore both belt and clip-on suspenders, one leg crossed upon the other so that she could see above the tan perforated shoe the top of a rolled white sock. And all of this curiously reassuring because he was so very common, and she did not know him, and he had been there when the trouble came, and finally because in the shadowy stillness of her lassitude she still felt beyond the reach of pain.

"Well," he said, lighting another cigarette. "I'm not so sure about that. I've thought about it quite a bit since it happened. Man gets into deep water pretty quick on these things." He turned and looked out through the screen toward the vacant lot. "I didn't hardly know your husband, Mrs. Thayer. I wouldn't even say that I liked him. What's more, he wasn't out here to do me any good." He looked at her and tightened his teeth as though he felt a sudden pain and then went on. "But I'm going to tell you what you're going to be hearing one of these days. When the case against Clay Carter is dropped, and it will be, that will be the reason, whatever legal technicalities we have to go through. I'm Carter's lawyer, Mrs. Thayer. I haven't got any business talking to you at all, but a man's got to draw the line somewhere. You shouldn't have to read it in the papers. You and the boy alone against the whole town. Mrs. Thayer, ma'am, do yourself a big favor and go on back to where you came from. There's nothing out here for you. Whatever it was that brought you all this way is over and done with now. Take my advice, forget it, pack up and buy your ticket and go just as soon as you can."

She lay very still, looking straight ahead of her at the little whaling schooner with the black cat in the rigging, becalmed forever in its silent sea.

"Are you threatening me, Mr. Bird?"

"Threatening you? No ma'am, I'm warning you. There's a difference."

"I wonder. Well, Mr. Bird, I'm listening."

"You just tell me if you want me to stop."

She lifted her hand, then let it fall, and closed her eyes.

"Well, where to begin. The day it all happened I come on back to the hotel around suppertime. I'd been in Choctaw all day on a case and I didn't even bother to go by my office. When I stopped to get my key, the clerk handed me a message. It was from Rita Carter—she'd been calling around town trying to get me. The message said I should go by my office as soon as I got in—she'd left word for me there. Obviously some kind of trouble she didn't want that desk man to get his big nose into. I went upstairs and washed and gave myself ten free minutes with a drink, then I went over to my office. My secretary had taken the message and put it in an envelope and propped it up on her typewriter where I couldn't miss it. It wasn't very long—just that Clay was in jail and wanted to see me as soon as I got in. Now in this town, Mrs. Thayer, people like Clay Carter don't go to jail every day. I guess it's the same everyplace. It takes one hell of a lot of pushing and shoving to get a man like Clay in there and then your trouble's just begun. Try to keep him there. It didn't make sense. I locked up and went downstairs and got a newspaper and then went over to the coffee shop and went over the box scores of the ball games. I needed to clear my head a little, get my mind around this thing, figure it out some. And by the time I had worked out how many games back St. Louis was and who was giving them trouble in the lineup, it was pretty clear that there wasn't anybody in this man's town who would be ready to take on Clay Carter except me, if I had to, and your husband. And since it sure as hell wasn't me, it didn't leave much choice. And if it was your husband that meant Indian business, and Indian business had to be Red Hawk, unless there was something which I didn't know about. And Red Hawk could only mean Shoat Dalton, and that's where I came in. Poor old Shoat. When you think of all the scrapes he'd been in, and all the trouble he'd got out of, and then to turn himself over in a car like that. Makes you wonder. God rest his soul, if he had one. Course I knew your husband was interested in the case. He spent quite a bit of his time on it, as a matter of fact. I guess you know all about that. Talking to people, going over the court records—he even mentioned it to me one night. Well, from a legal point of view it was interesting enough, especially if you were on the short end of the stick. The government had worked pretty hard at it, and when old Shoat got off I guess it hurt. But your husband surely knew his law, what with Harvard and all, anyway a far sight better than these cotton-pickers out here. It was all there in the book for him to read. So how come he was going after Clay Carter for something that had been wrapped up and put away and forgotten as far as this town was concerned? And just because they hadn't been able to pin it all on Shoat, that wasn't any reason for putting the noose on Clay. Damn near any one of those federal witnesses would have made a better choice. Anyway, I turned it ever way but loose and then figured I had better get on up to the jail and get it out of Clay, going on the assumption that if a man is put in jail he must have some idea of what he's in there for.

"So I got in my car and went up to the Court House. Clay was there all right. I don't think I really believed it before I saw it with my own eyes. He was pacing up and down that little cell— you know how tall he is—like a caged tiger. 'Man,' I said to him. 'What in the world have you gone and done? What have they got you in the lockup for? What's the charge?' He made me sit down and then he told me. Murder. I wasn't buying. I said, 'Who did you kill, Cody?' But he wasn't in any mood for joking.

'County attorney got out a warrant for my arrest—that Red Hawk business all over again.' Well, it had gone through my mind, but it had gone right on out again. 'Clay, I just can't hardly believe that.' 'Can't you,' he said. 'Then you go down and borrow the jailer's phone and call the sheriff. See what he says.' So I got the sheriff, at home of course, and sure enough, that's the way it was.

"I don't know whether you can really appreciate it, Mrs. Thayer. Clay Carter comes about as close to being a leading citizen as we got. There isn't much of anything around here he doesn't have his brand on it, one way or another. Chetopa County delegate to the last Democratic Party convention. Owns more and better grazing land than anybody in the county, and that covers a lot of acres. The King Ranch is bigger, maybe one or two other Texas outfits, but most of that's just cactus farm. I doubt that there's a stockraiser in the country better known than Clay. And there he is in the county jail with a tin cup and a straw mattress and roaches all over the place, right next to a drunk who's hollering his head off. And why? Because he's supposed to have killed off his wife's family so he could get at her money, him who could buy and sell more Chetopa Indians than most people ever seen.

" 'Sheriff says that's the way the warrant reads. I made him read it out aloud. He read it to me. Clay, what in the world is this all about?' I had to ask him like that because I may be a criminal lawyer, but I ain't no lawyer for criminals. There's a difference. I defended Shoat Dalton because I thought somebody was framing him. I believed then he was innocent, I do now, and I guess I proved it to the satisfaction of the court. But Clay Carter had to convince me before I would make it my business to convince anybody else.

"So we sat ourselves down, him on the bunk, me on the stool, and we talked. I mean we went at it. I was the prosecuting attorney, and I threw him every question in the book. Later on Cody came in to visit with him—Cody was staying in town at the hotel that night, you know him, big fellow with a goatee sort of beard with a kind of Buffalo Bill outfit you might call it, foreman out at Carter's place—and I took a breather. Then after Cody left

I went at it again until I had convinced myself to a T that Clay Carter was as innocent as a man could be. He didn't kill any of those Red Hawk people. We went through the killings one by one—there wasn't any question about it. He didn't have any more to do with that business than I did, and Lord knows I knew the case inside and out.

" 'All right,' I says to him. 'There's no question in my mind. Not about that, anyway. The question is, who put you in here, and why? Somebody tried to frame Shoat. Looks to me like somebody's trying to frame you this time.'

"Now Mrs. Thayer, I'm afraid I can't help getting just a little bit personal here. If you feel like you want me to stop, you just say so."

She said nothing. A kind of horror was spreading within her, something malignant composed of fear and shame, something that must surely end in a sob or a scream.

"So we talked about it that way, and I told him that your husband Andrews Thayer had taken a pretty keen interest in the Red Hawk case ever since he got to Grey Horse. I could tell that that had hit him from the way he looked at me. 'That isn't the only thing he's taken an interest in,' he says after a while. 'Meaning what?' I asked him. 'Meaning my wife, Rita.'

"Well, there I have to admit that he threw me one that broke like he'd rubbed a hole in the cover. I wasn't ready for it. Naturally I had been there that night at the country club, him pulling her out of the pool and all, but I hadn't thought much about it. In a little town you just got to ride along with some of that. Then Clay told me that he'd been so worried about it that he'd talked it over with Blair Booth. The long and the short of it is, Mrs. Thayer, that the thing had gone pretty far, right to the point where Blair had a talk with your husband about it."

"Mr. Bird, some of these things I know. Some of it is the kind of thing you hear when a person is no longer around to defend himself. If it's town gossip you feel you ought to tell me, don't bother." *Jack Bird? Yes. Wanted to see her? About Andrews? Trouble? Well, best if they talked about it together. Perhaps he could come up? Yes, he knew where she lived. Ten minutes. She made coffee and waited, and as she waited she felt herself becoming hard and shining as a lance. She remembered Blair's letter, and shook her head. No. Blair hadn't understood. Blair was weak and corrupt and he had let people take advantage of him. Andrews was the only one who had the courage to stand up to Carter. Blair was wrong, and the dead must stay dead. She would destroy the letter. No one could tell her anything about Andrews. Together they could triumph over the town, bring it to its knees, burn out the rottenness, restore some kind of justice. As for Mr. Jack Bird—but what could he want to see her about. And then she leaned against the icebox to keep from falling, because she knew it had gone wrong, something was deeply wrong, and she could only wait. I'll never believe them, she said aloud, standing there with the coffee pot in her hand. Lies, nothing but lies. Then she went into the living room and there was Jack Bird coming up the walk with that funny bowlegged kind of gait he had. And then—it was so hard to remember because of the pain. He drank his coffee, sitting sideways on the divan like a man who always drinks his coffee at the counter. Then: Well, Mrs. Thayer, I'm afraid I've got some bad news for you. There was a fire out at the Carter ranch last night. From what they found in the ashes this morning—well, I'm afraid . . . Got his coat out in the car. Yes, ma'am, seems absolutely sure it was him. Well, just ashes, I guess you'd have to say. There may have been other people there. You say you want to see? Well, there just isn't rightly anything to see. There doesn't seem to be anybody around at the Agency. Yes, they told me. Mighty sad, for a fact. It's a bad time for everybody, looks like. And Clay Carter, since it was his place— well, he figured you ought to know. So he asked me. Well, I don't know what to say to that. If it's the way you want it . . .*

He drove her there to the gutted shell of the house whose chimney still stood two stories high like the mast of a wrecked ship. A few cowboys stood around sucking grass stems; the sun was low and already hot and one bird, hawk or buzzard, wheeled the flawless sky. The wind was up, rattling the blackjack leaves, stirring the ashes. Nobody said anything. One of the men took off his hat, then came over and handed something to Jack Bird.

Found that there when she cooled down a touch. It was a black-ened silver cigarette case. She took it and pressed it to her bosom and then lowered her face and let the tears come . . . She had asked him if he would mind their just being silent on the way out, and now they rode back in silence, too. He stopped the car in front of the house and she turned to him, keeping her voice as hard and steady as she could: Mr. Bird, I am going to ask you one thing. There has got to be a funeral. Ashes to ashes, dust to dust. You had the goodness of heart to come up here and tell me while everybody else was looking for a place to hide. Now I must ask you to see Father Stafford, the Episcopal minister. Because I will have to tell Amory, and he must have this to remember. He is going to see his father buried, and this town will know that there was a funeral, and Amory will have that to remember, always.

"Well, it's kind of a ball of yarn, Mrs. Thayer. You want one thread, you kind of got to pull the whole thing apart, if you see what I mean. Anyway, we sat there talking the best part of the night, trying to figure it out, wondering what your husband really had in mind, if he was the one back of it, putting Clay in jail. Who else could it be, because this was Indian business and it sure wasn't old Blair going to put a gun at Clay's head. Still it was hard to believe Thayer really thought Clay had done all that killing. Unless somebody he would listen to had put it in his mind. Well, Clay has enemies, like everybody else around here. Shoat's people didn't like him any, which would mean Nellie. Thayer might have talked with her. I could name a few others. And then Clay's wife. I guess everybody knows that. Well, we went on like that. It must have been pretty near dawn, and then we heard that siren go. Neither of us paid any attention to it, of course. Just another fire someplace. But you hear that siren pretty good sitting there in the jailhouse. Anyway, I figured we'd done enough for one night. I had established to my own satisfaction that Clay was innocent of the charges, and I had managed to settle him down some and give him back his confidence and pride in himself which had been pretty well shook up. You can imagine that the thing had hit him like a ton of brick. Jail? Clay Carter? He was down but good when I first went into that cell, but by the time I went out he was as sure as I was that it was all just one great big mistake on somebody's part. He wasn't worried about himself any longer. I think he was mainly worried about his wife, and who was behind it. And he was mad because however you sliced it, his name wasn't going to come out any too good, and there of course he was thinking about his daughter. So I promised to have him out of there on bail just as quick as I could get to a working judge, and got in my car and drove on down to the coffee shop for an early cup of coffee. Usually I go over the box scores while I'm having my coffee but this time it was too early for the papers. So I sat there and looked it over one more time, trying to figure what kind of a hand your husband was holding that would make him willing to go for the pot that way. Finally I decided I would do better to sleep on it, and went on over to the hotel and got into bed. I couldn't have been asleep very long before the telephone woke me up and I got the news. I got dressed and hustled on up to the jailhouse and by the time I got there Cody had come, too. He'd been out to the ranch and back by this time, and he was the one who had to tell Clay. Clay was stretched out there on the bunk like a poleaxed steer. Ranch house burned to the ground. Truck parked out in front with your husband's coat in it. Other stuff they found so that they knew that whoever else was in that house, your husband was one. Like maybe he'd gone in there to ransack the place or something, whatever it was he was looking for. There wasn't anything for it but to get Clay drunk enough so he would sleep. So Cody and I sat there feeding him drinks until finally he just plain passed out. But he had already made me promise to tell you what had happened. He was just sick over it, like he was to blame or something. I think he would have wanted to tell you himself, if he hadn't been in jail like that. But of course that wasn't the worst."

She lay there with her eyes closed and her body rigid under the casual disarray of sheets. The match scratched sharply twice, three times, and there was a tiny tearing sound as it caught fire and then she smelled the faint acrid odor of cigarette smoke billowing through the scent of lilac. Whatever it was he was about to say, she wouldn't feel it, and she closed her hands so that her

nails dug into her palms. The worst had passed for her; surely
there were no darker nights than those that she had somehow
managed to survive.

"Cody walked out to the parking lot with me. Now Cody's a
fellow it takes a while to like, and even then you're not too sure.
Little strange in his ways, Cody is. Well, he was white as a ghost,
had been ever since he came back from the ranch. 'Any more to
that story than what you told Clay?' I asked him. 'There may be,'
he said. 'Like what?' 'Like maybe his wife,' so that I couldn't
hardly hear him. 'Looks like maybe she was in there, too. Trying
to locate her now, sheriff and so on. Looks to me like she just
burned right on up with that fellow Thayer.' They had found
some things—pocketbook and so on. But there wasn't enough to
go on yet, and nobody could be for absolutely sure. That's why I
didn't say anything that morning when I came. And after, well,
with you sick and all . . ."

"And now you're telling me that Rita Carter was in that house
with Andrews." Her eyes were hot with tears that burned her
cheeks like shame.

"Clay Carter lost his wife in that fire. What I'm telling you,
Mrs. Thayer, is what people are going to say. There was whiskey
in that truck. You could smell it against the wind. People are
going to say that your husband and Mrs. Carter—that as soon as
Clay was in jail, they went out to the ranch, had too much to
drink, dropped a kerosene lamp or got careless with their cigarettes, whatever . . . In a town like Grey Horse, it won't leave
much of a case against Clay. I figured that being sick like you
were, nobody would have told you, and you have a right to know
how it will be. The town's made up its mind, Mrs. Thayer. That's
why I said before, if I were you I'd get me a ticket and—"

"You go back and tell Clay Carter I don't scare that easily."
And now her voice was part of the pain so that it seemed to her
that it was her body itself that spoke. "Tell him he can't go on
pushing people around forever. As for the town—we'll see. Somebody's got to pay for what happened. Now, Mr. Bird, what
you've told me makes quite a story. Very persuasive for a jury of
your fellow citizens. I don't believe a word of it. What Rita

Carter was doing in that house doesn't interest me. Somebody killed Andrews before that fire ever started. Maybe the same person who killed Shoat Dalton. Nobody can ever make me believe otherwise. Well, they'll have to come after me next. Because I'm not leaving, do you hear. We're going to stay. My husband is buried in Grey Horse and I won't leave him here alone."

His eyebrows were arched up above his glasses, and he held the cigarette at his lips, looking at her through the smoke. Then slowly he got up and took his hat from the dresser. "Mrs. Thayer, ma'am, if you don't mind my saying so, you've got it all wrong. Clay would kill me if he knew I'd come to talk to you. I thought maybe I could make you see how it was. I'm sorry."

At the door he stopped, then turned to look at her again. "That boy of yours—I brought him a little something."

She followed his hand into the bulging pocket of his coat, then watched him lay the baseball very carefully on the dresser. The door closed behind him, and there was nothing left save the broken stubs of his cigarettes in the ash tray by her bed. And then she wept, moaning, no longer caring who heard, because whatever little that was left to her had been taken away, that too, right down to the marrow of memory. "Andrews," she cried aloud, and then she turned her face to the wall.

She woke in the very dead of night. The curtains shuddered at the windows and across the bed lay an ashen blade of moonlight. She had been dreaming, what was it, Amory trapped in the house and the house was on fire and she knew that she could get out but she could not find him and yet she saw his face looking at her, his eyes wide and clear and two lines creasing his forehead just above the bridge of his nose. So sad, so terribly sad. A longing so deep, so ancient, and now so keen . . .

She rose and wrapped her housecoat around her and walked through the bathroom to where Amory slept at the back of the house. She touched his forehead, then moved her fingers to the little hollow behind his ear. His mouth was half open and his arms were thrown back above his head, his hands closed in tiny fists. The way he had always slept since he was a baby. Her lips brushed his eyelashes, and then she smoothed the sheet around his neck. So innocent, so far away from it all. If only she could keep him this way . . .

In the kitchen she opened the icebox, then closed the door and leaned against it. The stove, the enamel-topped table, the matched tins of sugar, flour, tea, coffee, cookies, Cora's aprons and towels. Cool and dead in the moonlight. Was any of this hers? Then down the back steps to the garden awash in moonlight, where as though at the bottom of the sea drifted roses, bachelor buttons, larkspur, forget-me-nots, and hollyhocks at the backyard fence where battered garbage cans leaned sadly together. The swing— no one had remembered the cushions. She bent to turn them up, and then she almost smiled. What did any of it matter now. Just beyond the fence lay something that she had kept at bay for years, a kind of *terrain vague*, some sort of chaos that she had fought against with all her soul the way she had fought with shears and scissors and knives against weeds and blight and rust and corruption. And now she had lost, and it was all about her, pervasive as the moonlight, she standing there alone in the ruins. That was where Andrews had stood so often, there at the corner of the fence, smoking, looking off at the horizon, the way he always stood looking out of the window when he was in the house. He had wanted to go out there, and she had known better, and tried to hold him back.

"And wasn't I right?" she said aloud. "What was it like for the two of you at the end—drunk, coughing in the smoke, fire like a fence around you." Her eyes closed and her knees went weak and she lay down in the swing, cradling her face in her arms. Here where Blair had sat—only days ago—gone, too, gallant in his crumpled way, trying to tell her. *Emily now you listen to me Andrews is heading for terrible trouble if we're lucky you may be able to stop him I can't I've tried and he won't listen he's like a steer in the chute walking head down toward the butcher with the sledge hammer Emily he will bring disaster down on all of us unless he's willing to listen maybe you can make him understand if it's not too late already it's not the way he thinks it is I'm talking about life and death Emily out here life is cheap and death is fast and easy.* She shivered as though dew had fallen cold as rain upon her. Then she got up and walked back through the garden to the driveway, moving like a sleepwalker as gravel ground beneath her feet, past the roads, the bridges, the cars of Amory's miniature city in the dust. Cottonwood branches trailed her hair and above her, filtering the stars, she could see the outlines of the tree house. She stopped for a moment and looked at the front lawn, jeweled where moonlight touched tiny beads of water, strewn with a precision of shadows, and then she went in through the screen door to the living room. It was there in the desk. She had read it once that night, then hidden it, and now it drew her back like some forbidden book from her childhood. She took it from the drawer, then returned to the front porch where she sat down on the steps, wrapping the housecoat tightly under her legs, and sitting there stunned in the moonlight she read those last lonesome desperate defiant words:

My will is made so that I don't have to think about that, thank God. I've got no heart tonight for dividing up the pot. I don't leave anybody but Mary Rose, and that's between me and her. So everything is finished now, Thayer, except for a few words I'm putting down here for you. Not because I care anything about you because I don't. I'm leaving them for your kind, Thayer, you and everything you represent. Partly so that you will know that you didn't have me fooled. I'll admit to having had a little hope—strange thing how hope is the last thing to go, even when you know better. That's why I was at your place this afternoon, just to tell you one more time where you were heading. I even asked your wife to try and stop you. I guess she doesn't want to know, Thayer. I can't say as I blame her. Then she told me that Clay was in jail and I knew you were out of reach. You have decided to ride the tiger— God have mercy on you when you try to get off. That beast has been caged up in this town for quite a few years, and now you've let him loose again. You think you can ride him, and that I was afraid to try. God forgive you in your pride, Thayer; fire and destruction wait upon you, and death at every corner. Because you wanted too much. I was content to keep that beast in his cage and feed him now and then to keep him quiet. You've got to break him. You're going to play St. George and put the sword to him. I never trusted saints, Thayer. Life is too cheap for them.

But then as between you and me, who would ever be ready to take my side. Just the difference in the way we look, you the ascetic, lean and sharp as a sword, bearing the burden of family, tradition, civilization—oh don't be modest, Thayer, it's in your face, the way you talk. Noble as the knight setting out in search of the Beast. As for me, I smell of the pit. I've spent too many years in the rendering factory, wading around in blood and guts, down where the stink is. You smelled it the first day we met—tiger's breath, rotting bones and flesh. But you, you didn't smell. That's the difference. And you figured that nobody else had a right to smell, either. One thing you'd better learn fast is that there's always stink. Unless you can figure out some way to invent a slaughterhouse without blood. Maybe that's what you and the Commissioner have in mind.

The main thing is that I'm worn out with it, just tired to death of fighting on a half a dozen fronts for people who don't really give a damn whether I win or lose, or maybe it's just because they figured it out before I did that you don't end up winning or losing either one but just keeping on. I've done it the way you keep on blocking and tackling when you're thirty points behind. Win, lose, or draw, it's how you play the game—that's one you probably know by heart. Well, it's all right for people who don't have to depend on the game for anything, for whom the whole thing really is a game and not some kind of siege warfare that lasts a lifetime. One of those phony slogans the gentry thought up for itself because it looks so good in needlepoint. Who can afford it? Try telling it to some kid down in Niggertown.

Clay and I broke every rule in the book. You know it, too. You've gone over the accounts with a microscope, you've put your nose into every hole you could find, you have an idea how we worked it out. What you never got through your head was why. You believe it was because we wanted money, don't you? You're wrong. That's something you pennypinching New Englanders think about everybody because you're so goddam mean yourselves. Thrifty, you like to call it. We had cavalry and sabers and land we knew because we lived on it; you had trains and slide rules and factories. You beat us the only time we could ever get you in a shooting war. You keep on beating us with your banks and your Bibles, your laws, the way you keep the books. And we still hate your guts, and don't you ever forget it. Between you and me, Thayer, is a line that won't ever be crossed. Maybe you got God on your side the way I got the Tiger on mine. Yet somehow I never figured God as somebody who put on steel-rimmed spectacles and read the Bible on Sunday, but maybe I got that wrong too, along with so many other things.

But however it is, I'm not giving you the pleasure of waiting around while you batter the walls down and then drag me through the streets in a cage. You've got Clay in there, but you won't get me. I could wait, of course, because you'll get yours, too. You're trying to live by the sword, Thayer, whatever name you put on it, and you will perish by it. There aren't any free rides, even for saints. But probably you don't think of yourself as a saint. You're just honest, thrifty, principled, incorruptible. I say you're a cold, arrogant, soulless prig. I agree that saint is too big a word for that. Yankee is a good enough word for you. You know something? New England didn't make this country. New England stayed on the sea side of the foothills and made money. Give me a Clay Carter every time.

But don't get the idea I'm pulling the trigger because of you. This one's all mine, Thayer. I've lived long enough. I'm tired of lost causes. I don't want to march any further. I had lived a small lifetime before I ever came to Grey Horse. That's something that wouldn't have occurred to you, would it, because for you my life started the day you heard my name. I've lived the way I had to, done what I could the best way I could. I leave no children, nothing but what I managed to do here for quite a few years and I'm not sticking around to see you put the torch to it. I'm moving on, friend, no doubt to Hell, where I sincerely hope not to find your kind, sir. Meeting you has confirmed something that I first observed a long time ago, that occasionally men meet their exact opposites, and then they must find a reason for their hatred. You're mine, all right. I knew it when I saw you getting off that train. I might as well have loaded my gun that very day. Like it was all written down somewhere, when it would happen, how it would happen, who it would be. You're a hound of heaven, Thayer. You'd track me down if it took you the rest of your life. I don't think that Carter means a damn to you. Carter or his wife, and there, buster,

you are really playing with fire. Both of them are just a way of
reaching me, because you need me like you need the air you
breathe. Just make sure nobody lowers the boom on you along
the way.

So show this letter to the Commissioner for me, will you,
Thayer? Tell him thanks from me. Tell him I appreciated his trust.
Tell him I know something about how hot Washington can get in
the summer. Tell him I don't have any intention to be hogtied and
hauled up before some Congressional committee so that you and
he can take the bows. Tell him I don't hold it against him, because
Washington has ground down better men than him. And tell him,
goddammit, not to send a boy to do a man's job. Cause you better
grow up, son. This time you were matched with a tired old puncher
who was through before you ever came. But it won't always be that
way, and if you're really taking on Clay Carter, then you're over-
matched but good.

Well, what the hell. I held the line for a while. They didn't do
too bad with me. As a Southerner, I cared about them, Thayer.
Maybe because they were whipped, too, and God knows we had a
red hand in that one. So I was corrupt and crooked and venal, I
misused the trust put in me, I lied and stole and cut the corners
and threw a hell of a lot of business Carter's way. But between us,
him for his reasons, me for mine, we gave them a pretty good run.
I pity their lost souls when it's left to people like you to take care
of them. Read them the regulations, Thayer. It's worth a laugh or
two when it's a hundred and five in the shade and you're trying to
pry the white men off them like flies digging into a carcass. Anyway, I'm turning in my rubber boots. I waded in it long enough,
too long to be brought to book by the likes of you. I could always
do business with a crook, but God protect me from the righteous.
When your kind starts to take over, it's time for my kind to bow
out.

One last thing. Don't fool around too much with Carter. There's
nothing Dixie about him. He doesn't know what it's like to be
licked. He'll whip your ass right out of town. And as for the lady—
I wouldn't count on it, whatever she says. She travels with a lot of
baggage—you'll be the one to do the carrying. Then, too, and it's a
hell of a note that I should feel like I have to remind you of it,
you've got a wife and son to look after whenever you can take

time off from exercising your soul. Get the hell out of here before
this town sucks you all under. It finally beat me—it and a carload
of booze and a couple of hundred years of history and a long line
of Southern ladies—did you ever wonder why I married Mary
Rose? I was beat before I got here, and knew it, and made up my
mind to go for broke. But you—I like your boy even if you are a
creeping Jesus. Your wife, too, if she could ever get over the fact
that you come from Boston. Get out, because they're going to beat
you the way you beat us, and you won't like that a bit. Go back
where people understand the way you talk. Out here you just don't
make sense.

You'll find the key to my safe in the back of the upper-right-
hand drawer of my desk. The confidential stuff is in there—the
Dalton case and lots more. Sometimes I wonder why I didn't give
it to you in the beginning. It would have saved us all a lot of trou-
ble. The funny thing is, Thayer, that you and I have a lot of history
in common, even if it doesn't make very good reading from my side
of it. But then when push comes to shove, I'll have to take my stand
with Carter. I reckon we're both carpetbaggers as far as he's
concerned.

He must have gone right home and shot himself. Midnight
when Mary Rose had called, and she had gone over and waked
Cora so that she could come and stay with Amory, and then she
had walked through the silent, moonstruck streets to the Agency.
Mary Rose was standing in the door, waiting, dressed in a wool
bathrobe, her hair in braids down her back, her face as it always
was, except with deeper lines when she turned to the light. They
went together along the hall to the back bedroom. The heavy
body was sprawled across the bed, as though he might have fallen
asleep while praying. On the sheet where his head lay there was a
stain dark and ragged as a peony. On the pillow, still clutched in
one hand, the revolver. She looked around, at the U of Virginia
pennant on the wall, the photograph of the fraternity members
against the ivy, a golfing trophy—a college boy's room. On the
night table, an envelope. Andrews Thayer. "I don't know why I
called you," Mary Rose had said. "Because you are not part of it,
I guess."

Not part of it, my God, what does it take? She sat there in the moonlight rocking back and forth, holding herself as tightly as she could with her arms pressed against her breast, weeping for a dead life where fingers just missed touching, where eyes did not meet, where voices spoke but never answered. Hadn't she died enough to make her part of what had happened, or would she have to be buried like the others? So many gone. Death at every corner. Fast and easy, just the way he said.

She replaced the letter in the desk, then found her bed again. On the night table were the pills. She shook them loose in her hand, round and golden, glowing like tiny sunflowers, three, four, five . . . That memory of a sea dark as wine where pine trees came down to the water's edge and light was an element like earth or fire or water and herbs filled the air with their sweet tang and cities clustered around harbors where sailing boats rode the tides and rough bodies collided with cries of love or hatred and laundry flapped like gulls in the winds of narrow streets and voices called back and forth from window to window, answering, answering, like a choir from the ocher hive.

Then she lay down and clung to the edge of the mattress with both hands, staring before her into the blackness until the sea and the pines and the sails and the murmurous cities had faded away, until there was only a small cluster of sandstone buildings in a wind-rippled sea of grass, the valley of the old encampment, blackjack trees dry and shriveled in light that was more fire than water, hawks above the cemetery where a cedar leaned like a spear against the shield of the sky.

One by one she put the pills back in the bottle. And then she slept.

"Simply amazing how hot it is for October." Mr. Thayer removed his panama, wiped his glistening forehead, then gently replaced his hat upon fringes of carefully combed white hair. "Not really a breeze here at all, is there. Just that damned wind, day and night."

She stood with him in a pyramid of shade cast by the long

peaked roof of the station. The dust swirled at their feet, and somewhere a loose sign banged.

"There is a lot of wind," she said. "I suppose one gets used to it. I don't really notice it much any more."

His suit was dark, well tailored, perfectly creased. He carried a thin ebony stick with a gold head. Beside him were two bags, carefully graduated in size, fine leather gone dark gold with age. His shoes had the look of varnished walnut. He drew from his vest pocket a large gold watch, the watch that he had this same morning promised to Amory when they said goodbye.

"I would imagine the trains are pretty well on time out here," he said, peering up the track. "Don't see what could hold up a train in this part of the world."

Andrews had been taller, less precise in his actions, but there was something in the delicate modeling of the face, the thin bones beneath finely flushed skin, the way both their faces lifted when they spoke . . .

"It was kind of you to come," she said. "I'm sure it meant a lot to Amory. He's so fond of you." She could say those things now. She was no longer afraid of him, as though nothing again could hurt or frighten her. Something had gone dead, some source of uncertainty or dread, and in its place was a will as hard as his, as though her soul had turned to stone.

"Amory is a Thayer, Emily. We can't forget that. The image of his father. His eyes . . ." Then he looked at her closely, his face wrinkled against the wind, his own eyes hard as agates. "Maybe after a while things will seem different, Emily. I hope you'll bring him home someday. You really must, you know. He doesn't belong out here. These are not our kind of people. It's not the sort of place for Amory. Not by any stretch of the imagination."

In summer the sun struck like a hammer. Now it burned very lightly, and dust devils roamed along the gleaming strips of track. Two Indians who stood not far from them held their hats and leaned against the wind.

"Andrews is here," she said softly, patiently. "This is our home now."

He stared at her, and his mustache moved like a caterpillar above his mouth, and she wanted suddenly to laugh except she knew that there would be tears, and he wouldn't understand.

"Emily, you have been most courageous. Most courageous. Like everything else, however, courage is best when not indulged in to excess. I don't want to go over it all again, but you must realize that nothing will be gained by your staying here. Andrews would not want it, I'm sure of that. You must think of the boy now. He is the important thing. Now that Andrews is—no longer with us, Amory is the one who counts. You know that I am ready—"

She put her hand on his arm, as though to comfort him.

"You're alone here, Emily. You haven't a friend in the place. What can you do in such a town? The scandal . . . the talk. Amory should grow up as far away as possible from all this."

He tapped his stick against the gravel, querulous now, his face quivering and loose with age. He wiped his forehead again with his handkerchief, and she saw how green the veins were against the bones of his hand.

"We have talked about all that," she said. "It was good of you to come. Amory will write."

"I never understood the boy," he said then, still holding his handkerchief to his face, his eyes suddenly so hopeless, his mouth trembling. "Why, Emily, why? All of it so unnecessary. I used to say to his mother, when he was not much older than Amory— even then always wanting to do everything the hard way . . ." and then he seemed to forget, not the past but the present, and he stood there in the sun, silent, his face working. "Something in her family, perhaps. Something hereditary, like deafness. He never wanted to listen to me. Almost as though he were ashamed," and he shook his head. He looked at her as though he could not remember who she was, and then they heard the whistle, sweeping toward them across the level land.

She found a porter, then helped him to his seat.

"You change at Chicago, over to the other station. There'll be someone to help you. Try to sleep. It's such a long way home."

He nodded, looking up at her with eyes that pleaded, his face suddenly undone as though he had lost his false teeth.

She took his hand and held it for a moment, then bent and touched his forehead with her lips. It was like saying goodbye to a child. And then she went back out into the sun.

She waved to him through the window, and he moved his stick up and down until the train lurched and crashed convulsively and then slid forward. Dust spun upward in a glittering veil, and she could no longer see him, and then the last car faded from sight, glimmering away into the pure emptiness of sunlight like a fading mirage.

And standing there alone in the silence, she felt as though something as irrevocable as death had just happened. The wind still stirred the fallen dust, the shadows thinned and shrank, but it was not the same. She looked up at the sun until her eyes burned, and when at last she turned away she saw around her a world in flames. "He was the one who cried," she whispered fiercely. "I could have told them. It's my turn now."

PART TWO

Is My End

Grey Horse, Oklahoma,
in the Fifties

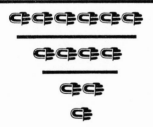

POINT IS THAT THERE ARE SO DAMN MANY THINGS YOU would have to know before it would make any sense to you. Provided it makes any sense at all, that is. I wouldn't swear to it. I wouldn't claim that any more, looking back at it. Man ask me why this, why that, I'd be damned if I could say. Maybe I could say these are the things I've lost. Add it up that way, all the things that were taken away. Joe Don laying dead over there in one of them military graveyards in Holland. Claim it's him, anyway. How do they know when your plane falls out of the sky like a house on fire? Daughter in California. That's where she was, anyway, last time she wanted money. Now you coming in here after it's all down the drain and talking about Amory . . .

Let me tell you something. I remember one night down to the depot in Tulsa. I was putting them on the sleeper to go back to their momma in Dallas. They had been living right here in the hotel with me for a month. Got them a room next to mine with a shower, monthly rates, credit at the coffee shop, swimming laid on at the country club. Didn't have anyplace else to take them to that wouldn't be just as hot and dusty unless it was Colorado Springs. Not that Dallas was all that different—just bigger is all. How the hell do you ever know with kids? They acted like they enjoyed theirselves. Hell, we took it all in. Stomp dances and steer roping on the Fourth, more malts and barbecued pigs than you could shake a stick at, and handmade boots thrown in, tooled real fine with their initials and all. I guess it's mainly buying when you get right down to it, buying and eating and laughing at yourself so they won't take you too serious because that would sure as hell have scared me half to death if anybody had ever just shut up. Talking it up in the infield so nobody gets too tight is what I mean. Chatter. And you don't only got to manage the whole goddam deal, you got to pitch nine innings every day with a double-header on Sundays. And knowing you're bound to finish last before the season ever starts. So I couldn't tell you whether anybody had any fun out of it or not. What I mean to say is that when it's one month a year that you're together, it's kind of what I would figure the World Series to be. There's too much riding on every pitch, and you have to work at it so damned careful. You've been keeping the ball down and getting the good hops and reading the other club's signs and then all of a sudden you lay one in there high and hard and a little on the outside and that's all she wrote for another year. So you got to stay loose and work the corners. And after you've been working the corners for a month you start to get edgy-like.

The way I was when I put them on that train to send them back home. That little old kid boy of mine, I named him Joe Don after his granddaddy, he was laying up there on that top bunk grinning down at me like an ape, and the girl, Norma Faye, she's the older one, never did talk much, had more to her than the boy, I guess, keeping it to herself the way girls do from the time they're big enough to see in a mirror, she was standing there where she could look into that little piece of glass and fool with her hair. I was slouched against the door like I didn't know whether to go in or get out, trying to make it funny the best way I could, still talking it up, pulling it all together like it was a case in court or something, hoping they would remember all the good times and the jokes and who said what and where we went and don't forget and all, just kind of easing it up to where I could say goodbye. Well, every time I would get to where I had it already to say, I just plain choked up—no other word for it—shaking all over like a dog shitting peach seeds and ducking down the corridor for a minute like I had to ask the conductor something and wiping the goddam tears off my face and then coming back laughing like something you'd hear in a swamp somewhere. I mean running around there like a chicken with his head off and people

staring at me and all. Well, I never made it. I mean I just couldn't
say it. Then the conductor started to holler and I grabbed them
kids and made some kind of a noise that sure as hell didn't have
any sense in it and then I beat it on out to the platform where
they couldn't see me so good and I could pretend I was making
faces. I wonder if they noticed anything. And if they felt sorry
for me or what. And then when the train started to pull out I
felt so damned bad I just took off down that platform, knocking
people out of my way and keeping even with that window, trying
like hell to holler something, anything, just their names even. I
never did get it out. Kept on waving until they were out of sight
and gone. Felt too bad even to get drunk. Just tired all of a
sudden—dog-tired. Drove all the way back to Grey Horse crying
so hard I couldn't hardly see the road, mad at everything and
everybody, wondering how come it was that they were so much
braver than me, if brave was the word for it.

So that was the way it would be when I saw them, and then
there would be a kind of hangover for a while, and then just one
hell of a big empty feeling, or more like one big ache, maybe. Just
nothing, not caring, not giving a damn until I'd see a kid on the
street about the size of one of mine and then I'd just go all to
pieces, unravel like a baseball somebody's knocked the cover off
of. Waiting for the letters—God Almighty. For a long time I
wrote every week—stuff I'd copy out of newspapers, stories I'd
heard, anything to fill out two pages. There wasn't anything happening to me that would make sense to them, so I had to make it
all up, and not really letters at all in the normal way. Every
evening stopping by the post office—I gave them a P.O. box
instead of the hotel. Like maybe a man just wasn't supposed to
live in a hotel, I don't know. I didn't hardly ever get any answers.
I kept it up for God knows how many years. Looking back at it
now I don't rightly know how I did it. You may not believe this
but for the first two years I cried every time I sat down to make
up one of those damned things. I cried every time I saw somebody
I knew with his boy, playing ball or whatever. I don't guess I
ever cried in my whole life before then—everybody always said I
was born looking about as ornery as I do now and didn't ever

change—but I mean to tell you I made up for it. The thing is that when people get together they talk a hell of a lot about their kids. I would set and listen, not saying anything, nobody asking me about mine, like they was dead or something. It took two years more or less before I got to the point where I could handle it, and then it was sort of like something somewhere had just quit. Battery gone down, run out of gas, I don't know.

Emily said it to me one day. You know, Amory's mother. No, that was her name. Emily. Indian? Emily wasn't no more Indian than I am. Wasn't anybody could be less Indian than Emily. You got it mixed up, I guess. Anyway, I had said something about my kids, something to the effect that they were all I had. And she just said real quiet, Why, Jack, don't you realize, you don't have them any more, you haven't had them for years. Like she'd pushed a dose of smelling salts up under my nose. I don't guess I cried any more after that. Well, she was a fine lady, Emily Thayer was. Had no business being in a town like Grey Horse but you couldn't have drug her out of here with a team of mules. Hated the place even more than I did.

Course I really didn't hate it when you come right down to it. With me it was just that I plain didn't give a damn any more. Hell, I took every criminal case that came along and got the sons of bitches off. Take the Red Hawk case, where it all started. Old Shoat Dalton was as guilty as he could be. You ever read about that? Too young, I guess. That even made the New York papers. I got him off. Him and lots of others. It was years there I didn't lose a case. Until the big one, that is. Emily was where I lost. All the way around. Made plenty of money before that Crash and after, sent it all down to Dallas for the kids. Where it went I couldn't tell you. Joe Don sure never touched it, went into the military and over across and got hisself shot down. Norma Faye was still writing me for money up until a few years ago. Their mother inherited a potato-chip business—she never needed money. I guess that's why she figured she married beneath her. Anyway, it was all I could do. People figured me for rich and I didn't have a pot to piss in. Lived here at the hotel like I do now, same room, all my meals at the coffee shop, I had nothing to

spend money on. Once I thought about buying a house—no, goddammit, twice. First time was when Amory was going off to
school and I kind of jumped my tracks and asked Emily to marry
me. Then when old Clay died and left that big house up on
Cedarvale Hill, I thought I'd like to buy it. Don't ask me why.
Just to be mean. Cause I hated that son of a bitch so much,
maybe. Turned out he left it to the Catholic Church in his will.
The four-flushing bastard. Trying to buy his way in, right to the
end. What I couldn't tell you about him, but then it wouldn't
mean anything to you. Just to say his name makes me mad. No, I
was better off sending the money to the kids. The thing of it was,
don't you see, that I just walked out one day, leaving them all
sitting there in Dallas in that new house with a new car out in
front and my name on the door right next to her daddy's down at
the plant where we cooked all those goddam spuds. Man, I
haven't looked a potato in the face since. He wore a ten-gallon
Stetson and Justin boots and pushed those chips like there wasn't
nothing else to eat in the whole state of Texas but dust. I had been
a pretty fair Texas League catcher—even caught batting practice
with the Cards for a year—and put myself through law school
and had the kind of contacts he liked. Concessions in the ball
parks, that type of deal. Trouble was I never got over Arkansas
and that tribe of fox-hunting ball players that gave me what little
I had for the first eighteen years of my life. I mean I can't hardly
remember eating at the table with women before I got married.
They always did the cooking and served and waited until we
were done and then ate after we had divided up into those that
were going to sleep on the daybed or the swing and those that
would play catch the rest of the afternoon.

This woman, her name was Maxine, she knew how she wanted
it to go and where I was supposed to fit in. I guess she liked me
because I was stubborn, or for what she thought she could make
out of me. Fair enough. She kept the place too goddam clean for
one thing. Then she didn't like it that I kept hounds out in the
back in that kind of a residential neighborhood. Nor the fact that
I would have ball players coming home to dinner and maybe to
spend the night without telling her. And then I never did give a

shit for bridge. I could have gone along all right just by not paying any attention to her—that was the only way I ever saw anybody get along, anyhow. But she was on me to the point where I started taking it out on my kids and my dogs, and then I figured that what she was looking for was someone who'd gotten a hell of a lot more used to women than I ever did. She had a right to it, I guess. But that's what I mean about the money. I couldn't have explained it to anybody then. I sent her the money to look after the kids and the dogs and then when the kids were gone and the dogs dead, probably, I cut back some and the money just piled up in the bank and twice, like I'm telling you, I had the thought to buy something. I guess I just wasn't meant to settle down. Wasn't much sense in any of it, of course. I had no business at all buying that castle of Clay's, just because I hated the son of a bitch.

Emily was different. Did I tell you I asked her to marry me? We were standing there in the jail—I mean it—right there in the county jail, and I hadn't been so excited since I got off the train in St. Louis and asked the first redcap I saw where Sportsman's Park was at. Well, it didn't last long. Either time. You'll probably say it didn't take much, but Emily had me fooled. Amory's mother. She had everybody fooled as far as that goes. I kind of had us down for two of a kind. In a way, see, it was like we didn't live here at all, either one of us. I never could figure out why she stayed, unless it was just that she didn't have anyplace else to go. With me it was a place to make money—no criminal lawyer ever had a shortage of business in Grey Horse—and I didn't have nothing better to do because after I got over losing my kids I didn't figure anything else could ever matter to me much. Turned out I was wrong about that, too, but that was the way I felt. She always said she stayed because of her husband—that was Amory's dad, name of Andrews, he's probably told you about him—because he was buried here, and she wanted the boy to have a father, and so on like that. I never followed any of it real good, to tell you the honest truth. It didn't make a whole lot of sense to me. But she stayed, and got herself a job down at the City Light and Electric and that made her like everybody else around here except the

Chetopa and maybe the Agency people. We were all of us just eating high on the hog until the Crash and then it was just crumbs but no place else the hell to go to. I mean you just held onto what you had, and thanked the Lord you had it, whatever it was.

The point of it was, though, that Emily wasn't like the rest of us. Nor the boy, either. Amory, I mean. Special they were, the way they looked and talked. Part of it was Eastern. But in her there was something just a little bit harder and then, goddammit, at the same time, just a little bit softer than what you would normally run into out here. Like a diamond in a velvet box. Sometimes she made me afraid to look her in the face. She was like what in Sunday school they called one of them there avenging angels, carrying a sword and all. One of them people who never forgets a thing and never lets you forget, either. Her hair turned a touch grey after Andrews died, and she got a little thinner, and she had that skin that always made her seem like she had a tan, like she had been in the sun most of her life, and when she looked at you she didn't smile. Lived up on the hill in a little white house, walked to work and back every day, took care of her flowers, raised that boy. Never visited anybody or had anybody in her home that I know of, outside of myself. A real lady, Emily was. She hated the place so much that she never even talked about it, just like it wasn't even there. Maybe people were ashamed of what had happened, although if that's what it was they sure as hell got a late start. God knows there was a whole lot to be ashamed of, and she wasn't about to let them forget it. Just the sight of her, strong and straight and kind of fierce-looking, walking back and forth to work through all those years—well, I think it did something to everybody.

It was like what happened to the town. All those crazy years after the war, right up to the Crash. Money laying all over the pavement, Clear Creek overflowing with bathtub gin, polo and Stutz Bearcats and drunk Indians and Cadillac hearses and the country club set renting Pullman cars to go to Dallas for the weekend of the O.U.-Texas game. You could smell that it was rotten even before it busted—too many lawyers, too many guardians looking after somebody else's money, shootings and liquor poisoning and dope and murder and suicide—every goddam thing in the book and somebody making money out of it whatever it was. Just take those Red Hawk killings. Like some kind of tumor that won't stop spreading until it's all over everything like a big old black tarantula. I got Shoat off and that just made it worse and then right in the middle of it comes this Harvard preacher who's going to clean it all up. Well, he got sucked under along with the rest of us. The whole thing spinning around like a tilt-a-whirl out of control until the day in '29 when half the town's lawyers jumped off the Triangle building and the other half hit the road like it was the opening of the Cherokee Strip all over again. And after that it got real still around here, the whole town about like some old boy you've pulled through the D.T.'s and he's still breathing all right, but barely—nothing but a hollow goddam shell is what I mean.

So she waded through the mud and came out like Joan of Arc. Emily, I'm talking about. Like nothing had got on her from all that mess but just the blood, and she wanted that to show. And it showed, all right. There wasn't no chance for anybody to forget anything as long as she was there, hung around our necks like a stone.

And the boy, Amory, the one you asked about. He had a wonderful pair of hands, that kid. And quick? Just like greased lightning. You could see he was going to be tall, and he had that easy way of moving, everything flowing along together like he was on ball bearings or something. He was a natural. I could see it by the time he was eight or nine and I used to come up to visit in summer and pitch to him in the backyard of that little white house. Pretty soon we started going down to the Legion diamond and I had him shagging flies by the hour. I didn't hardly want to believe it, but I knew just the same. I hadn't spent the best years of my life squatted down behind the plate for nothing. My God, he was even a switch-hitter, as if all the rest of it wasn't enough. The only thing I ever wondered about at all was how much heart he had. You know, fire. Pepper Martin stuff. Run all over you if you got in his way. Maybe it was just the way he went about it. He made it all look so easy, like the best ones always do. He was working out with the Legion team by the time he was twelve. He was quiet, that kid. Didn't talk like the others, or look like them, or act like them, or even think like them. They knew he was different, too, but they didn't bother him any. For one thing I made it my business to be around, and then it didn't take any sense at all to see what a hell of a ball player he was going to be.

So it went along like that. We sat there through the years, watching the town go from boom to bust, living more or less on the margin. I don't know just how to tell you. I had plenty to do and so did she, but we were there in some funny way like we were just passing through, like when you're drumming some product or other and you're always ready to throw your stuff in the back and head out once you're finished. But all the same she looked after that house real good, or Cora did anyway. I couldn't say just how it got started. She sure as hell didn't like me any more than she liked anybody else around here in the beginning—maybe she never did, when you look at it from where it ended up. It must have been Amory. It must have been when I was coaching that grade-school team. That's how it was. I took to driving him home, little old kid with his daddy dead and all. I knew the story, you see. I did if anybody did, along with Clay and that circus freak Cody, and there would have been parts even they couldn't understand. So you can more or less see how it was. Joe Don just a picture in my wallet, not seeing him at all any more by that time because his mother didn't like to have him in this hotel where she thought he saw and heard too much and I was too dumb proud to go back to Dallas after I had once walked out of the place like that. What brought us together was that boy, Amory. She had her dreams all right. I learned that the hard way. And I guess come to think of it, they've sort of worked out. I had mine too, but since when did a man play professional ball with a name like that? Amory Thayer. She made that plain enough, too, that baseball was all right for Grey Horse but that he wouldn't really need it where he was going.

Point is that she had gotten it into her mind to send him off to school. I didn't listen to that much because it didn't make any sense to me. Who's going to send a fifteen-year-old boy away unless it's to reform school? And what she couldn't see, and I wouldn't tell her, and maybe that's where I made my mistake, was that the kid loved this town. He was home—this was where he came from, and that little white house with the red tile roof was his home place. Whatever it was to her, to him it was as big as the whole world. He was on all the teams and top of his class and when he started going with girls, well, he was hard to beat in that department, too. I don't guess either one of us knew how he really felt about it, and I don't suppose we ever asked him. I know goddam well we didn't, looking at the town the way we did. And by the time he turned fifteen Emily couldn't talk about anything else but Amory going away. She got in touch with this school back East and he took the tests and all and goddammit if he didn't win. Like they was paying him to come there, if you will. I figured they were getting him cheap, an arm like that and would damn sure hit well over .400 in any schoolboy league you could find. I guess it wasn't until the excitement of it all died down that I began to realize that he would be going away for good. Kid that age leave home, go that far, chances are you're not going to see him much around Grey Horse any more. So this was what she had been working for and saving for and doing without for all these years. Just to send him back where his daddy had come from. I said to her once I figured his grandparents could surely afford to take care of whatever bills there was and she cut me off cold the way she could, saying something like she wasn't going to be paid to be no nurse. All right. So she had to do it the hard way. But all it took was one look and you knew damned well she'd make it one way or another.

Well, like I say, this was what the last ten years of her life had been about. Just to get him the hell out of here once and for all. I couldn't rightly see how she'd stand it once he was gone, but that was another story which she straightened out for me but good later on. As far as I was concerned, I didn't like it a bit, but then who the hell cared how I felt about it. I wasn't the boy's father, even if Emily and me were going around together pretty steady by then. Plus the fact that there was something new in the deal which came pretty close to putting Emily right up the wall. I'll say this to her credit, that she never said a thing about it to the boy, even though it was pretty plain how she felt. And to me she didn't have to say word one. I knew what was going on in her mind and that she would move heaven and earth to get that boy out of this town. Point of it was that Clay Carter—man that had that house I told you about—Clay had a daughter name of Rona. Rita's girl. Well, it's a complicated story and none of it nice and I'm not sure you'd understand it all any better if I told you. Just leave it at that, that she couldn't have hated Clay's guts any more if he had gunned her husband down right in front of the house with her and the boy watching. I mean whatever her reasons, and she had them, she could smell old Clay ten miles against the wind, and what she smelled spelled skunk.

So wouldn't you know that when the time came for him to get hisself a girl, that boy couldn't do nothing better than start in after Rona Carter. I reckon everybody in town was holding his breath, just like I was. You start playing pepper with nitroglycerin, somebody's liable to end up dead. And it went on like that to the point where I got awful edgy about what Emily might do, knowing how she felt about Carter and all. We got a hot climate here, and all that kind of stuff gets to working around pretty early, and God knows what Emily was thinking—Rona Carter pregnant or something, the whole goddam thing all over again. Because the kids were really stuck on each other, anybody could see that, and plenty old enough to do a lot more than just play house. Out every night together that summer while Emily and I sat in the backyard, me talking and running through one pack of cigarettes after another while she just sat there cool and hard like somebody had chopped her out of ice. Every car that went by out front she'd raise her head and listen like a bird dog sniffing the wind. Point is that she had planned it all out for so long, every last little detail, and now one false move and the show was over. It was the World Series business all over again, working the corners, the whole goddam season run through right down to the end with just a couple of innings to get past if you could last. And then the son-of-a-bitching roof fell in all over the place.

I remember that summer because of the dust storms. Sky

would turn all dark and the sun looked like a piece of red-hot iron. Every once in a while it would take a notion to rain and then goddammit if it didn't rain mud. Fact. And then it was hot, up over a hundred every day, and worse if the wind was blowing. The kind of summer where everybody just sat around with their tongues out, fanning theirselves, drinking ice tea or Coke from breakfast right on through. Out here if you don't like the weather you just got to wait a minute, but that son of a bitch wouldn't move. Weeks and months of it until there wasn't much a man could do except rent himself a locker in the icehouse or sit in the picture show all day long.

So that night we had been to the show—it was more or less air-conditioned—something about the Royal Canadian Mounties, I remember, with what's-her-name there, Jeannette MacDonald, and old Nelson Eddy. It was cooler than outside and she liked all that singing, so all right. I ate popcorn and looked at the horses and took in the scenery and kind of turned down my aid when they opened up with the music. Come home about nine thirty with some ice cream for Amory. Poor kid was working on Latin and algebra that summer to get ready for that school where he was going. Plugged away at it pretty good, I'll say that for him, even when the kids come by in their cars and honked and all. You couldn't tell what he was thinking, whether he was mad or not. I would have been if I was him, but then there wasn't anything about us the same, unless it was the way it felt to lay some good wood on a ball.

So we come in the house and she calls out his name and nobody answers. She calls again, then gives me a quick look and heads for his room. When she comes out she's got a note in her hand and she looks like she's gone to hell and back between the time she went in that door and the time she come out.

"He's gone," she said to me, and I thought she'd hit the floor before I could get to her. "I knew something would go wrong—I knew they'd find a way to get him."

That's what she said, something like that, looking right at me and not seeing me either, just kind of staring off somewhere like I remember her doing there for a while after her husband died.

"Take it easy," I say to her, just to say something, but when I put my hand on her she jumps like I've touched her with a live wire.

"Stay away from me."

She looked awful, all bunched up like a cat in a corner, scared and mad and ready to spit if I touched her again.

I called her name, then. "Emily," I said, "look, this is me, this is Jack," but she wasn't having any.

"I shouldn't have trusted you. I remember the day you came and told me to leave."

She went on like that, I don't remember exactly, except that I knew that she was past the point where she could cry and I didn't like it at all, and she was asking me to take her to Clay and I sure as hell didn't like that.

"Where's he gone to?" I asked her. I wanted to kind of sight in on the main event right in the here and now, but goddammit if she hadn't jumped back ten years and there we were all over again just like that morning when I drove up to the house and got her and she made me take her out to see what was left of the ranch house while it was still smoking. I hadn't been able to stop her then and I wasn't doing a damned bit better this time.

So we went back out and got in the car and all the way up to Clay's I was trying to think just a little ahead of the game, knowing that it had to be tied in some way or other with Rona but hoping like hell that Emily wasn't jumping the gun. Because Clay didn't exactly blow first trumpet in the Salvation Army. He didn't owe Emily a damned thing. If I'm right about what happened out at the ranch house that night, then he had reason to be afraid of her, and when Clay's afraid he takes out insurance. He protects himself. Which means he's been holding back a pinch-hitter for the late innings just in case. And then there was his side of it too. He'd had his ass thrown in jail, and lost his wife, and his ranch burned down, all because of some tin soldier out of Boston walking around with a sword and a Bible trying to make something right that was wrong before he ever got himself born. And now his daughter, all he had left . . . But how could I say any of that to Emily. I tell you for a fact I would have liked to take a quick look at her pocketbook. It wouldn't have surprised me a damn bit if there was a pistol in there. She was like her husband that way—she figured that she knew right from wrong and bad from good to the point that she was ready to kill off everybody in sight to make her point. And doing it, by God, in a kind of merciful way, careful and clean, and expecting you to be more or less grateful for having had God's will work out that way, even if it was a kind of jackass-type justice and you were on the receiving end of the kick. What I'm saying is that she would have gunned him down and figured she was doing him and everybody else a favor. I say it comes from too much Bible reading, but what the hell. Maybe she never looked at a Bible in her life.

Anyway, there we were in the driveway to that big old Spanish-type place and I could see the lights of town down below and I was asking myself where we'd be by the time this night was over. I hadn't hardly cut the motor before Emily was out of the car and up on the porch and through the door without so much as ringing the bell. I thought sure as hell then that she had a gun and that it would all be over before I could stop her so I jammed the brake and took the steps all at a bunch like I was hot-assing it down to first on a not too good bunt and me running about like most catchers. I sailed through the screen door and there they were just staring at each other, Clay in some kind of a lacy shirt that showed up white in what little light came through those leather-looking lampshades, his arms folded across his chest, standing there tall and mean-looking as ever, hair about the color of sleet and cut down real close to his head, and damned if the son of a bitch didn't have his mouth open like he was laughing that laugh that you can't really hear, like he'd been standing there waiting for us all evening, just laughing to himself. When he spoke it was me he was talking to, but he never took his eyes off Emily, like maybe he too figured her for a gun.

"You seem like you're in a hurry, Jack. I always had you down for a man who took his time. Live longer that way."

He had a nasty way of talking, Clay did. Like every time he said something to you he hit you in the face. Like he was born knowing so goddam much more than you would ever know.

Something like that. Like he hated your guts for putting him to the trouble to speak to you. Well, usually I spiked him right back, but he had me in a hole this time and besides, I was ever damned bit as worried as he was about what she was likely to do. But she was just looking at him, staring him down, one of those slim, hard little bullfighters right in front of a Texas longhorn.

"I want my son, Clay."

I think I let my breath out then because I knew she wasn't going to shoot. She was the type if she was going to pull the trigger she would have to do it right now and talk later, provided she would talk at all. But once she was using words, that meant it wouldn't go no further. At least this time.

"It's been a great many years, Mrs. Thayer."

Polite, the son of a bitch. He carried a sword, too, but he didn't bother with the Bible. Wanted you to be nice and relaxed when he put the cutting edge in, but at least he never figured on getting any thanks for the job.

"I've come for my son."

He smiled a little then, if you could call it that. Talking never bothered Clay any. Well, once or twice, maybe. One night down to the county jail—something Cody said to him. That sure as hell hit him where it hurt, whatever it was that freak was putting out. And then, goddammit, yes, this time, too, because she had him by the short hairs.

"Look around, Mrs. Thayer. If you think I've got him hidden here somewhere."

I doubt that she even heard him.

"You ought to keep that little slut of yours on a chain, Clay."

Well, sir, I can hear it as plain as though she just got through saying it. My God, I'd never heard her talk like that.

"They've run off together. Amory left me a note. Either you find them quick or it's on your head. And if she comes back pregnant, then you better look for a knife. I'd kill her before I'd let her marry Amory. And if they don't come back at all, then I'll kill you. That's a promise, Clay. I would have killed you ten years ago if it hadn't been for the boy. If he's gone, I won't have any reason to hold back."

That was it, more or less, hitting him with it like she was slapping him back and forth across the mouth. I could see the color coming up along his neck so that instead of being red like he normally was he was pretty close to purple. Swelling up like a turkey cock, the blood in his face and all—I didn't want him to slug her so I moved to get in between them.

"Stay out of it, Jack."

He looked mean but his voice was soft, and yet a little too soft to suit me.

"In the first place, Mrs. Thayer, don't call me Clay. Only my friends call me by my first name. I don't even know you, and I don't want to know you. And watch who you're calling a slut. I don't need any lessons from you or your family on getting in behind what belongs to somebody else. If your boy has taken off with my daughter, I guess we can claim some previous experience in that direction, too. What's your proof?"

She held out the note to me and I passed it on to Clay. He studied it for a minute, handed it back, and then looked at me.

"What about it, Jack?"

I told him I didn't know any more than what it said in the note. I wanted to stall, buy a little time, get them both to the point where they could talk without throwing dusters at each other. But she wasn't having any.

"You killed my husband, Clay, because you were afraid of what he had on you. I let it pass because I knew you would go after me if I made a move, and I had the boy to think of. Now you're taking him away from me, using that little slut of yours for bait. You do that and there won't be anything this side of hell can stop me."

He looked at me for a minute and I could see his hands moving.

"You use that word again and there won't be enough of you left to stop anybody. Nobody asked you in here tonight. Nobody asked you to come to Grey Horse. He was sniffing around after Rita—that's how he got in trouble. Get down off your high horse, Mrs. Thayer. You aren't the first one it's happened to. Trouble is that husband of yours wanted to make a federal case out of a piece of pussy."

I grabbed her, then, but not before she had spit on him. She was going for his eyes with her nails, and I had ahold of her arms up around the shoulders—it was just like grabbing onto a loose bunch of steel rods. She was trying to say something, call him something, but either she didn't have the words or just couldn't get them out, one.

"Get her off the place, Jack."

Standing there with his legs spread apart, his hands on his hips, his head thrown back in that hard way he had. It took a hell of a lot more than a lace shirt to make that son of a bitch fit for anybody's living room, even his own. On him it would look better in a bull ring.

"You always did have a filthy mouth, Clay," I said to him. "I got another word for it, too, but it'll keep. We'll be back."

He laughed that ugly laugh of his and reached in his pocket for one of those little Mexican cigarillos he smoked.

"Looks like Mrs. Thayer's got a way with lawyers. She's going to need it, too. Nobody in Grey Horse talks that way to me unless he's ready to go to the mat. I don't think you're big enough for that, Jack—or rich enough, either. Too hard on your clothes. So my advice to you, son boy, is to take cover while there's still time."

I could have answered that, too, but whatever I had to say to him could wait because I could feel that she didn't have anything left to fight with. I got her out to the car one way or another and she sat there with her face in her hands, shaking all over like she had a chill. She didn't say anything until I got her home.

"No," she said to me when I started to get out. "I don't want to see you again until you find him. Wherever he is, however he is, I want him back. Tonight, tomorrow, whenever—just as long as he comes back."

Mainly I was just mad as hell at everybody, at Amory first for pulling such a bonehead play, then Clay for going after somebody he knew he could lick with one arm tied behind him and the other sawed off at the elbow. At her, too, for dragging me into something I hadn't wanted any part of, and mostly at myself for letting it happen all over again. The trouble was that all of a sudden I was acting like somebody's husband again, and somebody's father, too. I had been ready to go after Clay no holds barred for talking to her that way, and I had given up protecting women as a general rule about the time they got the vote. And too, I wanted that kid back where I could throw curves at him and watch him hit the breaking stuff with those last-minute wrists of his. I don't know what I had been waiting for. Somebody to jockey me enough to get me mad, I guess. But mad or not, it seemed good to be taking charge again, like getting back down onto the field after too many years in the front office. I was plain excited about it. It made me think of one New Year's Eve when we were sitting in front of that gas stove in her living room, listening to the guns go off outside, and Emily for some reason or other asked me if I was happy, and I realized I hadn't thought about it for as long as I could remember. Well, I was thinking about it now. I felt like I had something again that was mine, and I wanted to stake a claim. And sure as hell the first thing to do was to find that boy and hustle his ass back home.

Maybe it was all because I wanted it so bad. The way I found them, I mean. Man, I was like a fox hound on a June night with just enough wet to hold a scent. I figured they didn't have a car and would have to find wheels some way or other. There were three roads out of town where they could hitchhike, and then the bus. If they had already caught a ride then we were in trouble, because outside of practically setting up road blocks with stuff in the newspapers and all, our chances of picking them up quick were pretty slim. Might as well try the bus station first—somebody would have noticed them there if they had boarded a Trailways for Tulsa or further on.

Somebody had. He hadn't sold them the tickets—they had been bought before, probably so as not to attract attention—but he saw them getting on the bus, partly because he remembered Amory from having seen him play ball and partly because there was somebody else with them who caught his eye.

"That big tall fellow in buckskins, little white goatee beard, you know who I mean . . ."

He couldn't remember the name, and I'll be damned if I could believe it. It sounded so crazy to me I didn't even want to say who I thought it was.

"The one who owns the Curio Shop—old Buffalo Bill what's-his-name."

"You talking about Cody?" I asked him sort of quiet-like, because I still didn't want to believe it.

"Cody," he said. "Sure. He was talking to that boy like he must have been with him. It might have been the Carter girl. I couldn't swear to it. Tulsa was where they went to. Not many stops between here and there. Change in Tulsa and then you can go just about anyplace you want. We could check the schedule—somebody run off or something?"

He was beginning to smell it by then, and I didn't want to do any explaining so I gave him a dollar and cranked up for Tulsa. I didn't like the combination worth a damn. Thayer—Carter—Cody. We'd covered that ground once before and I couldn't see anything good in it for anybody.

I made it in just under two hours and then I started to realize what I was up against. That bus station was packed like a Sunday double-header in St. Louis on the Fourth of July. Kids and old people and babies, black, white, and red, overalls and levis and tennis shoes and chewing gum, most of them having a late dinner or an early breakfast on peanuts and pop. Lines at the ticket counters, lines to the buses, lines at the information window, and one of those short-circuited public address systems putting out a mixture of static and nails on glass that sounded like a chicken yard with a fox in it.

I went around there looking at everybody two or three times to the point where they must have figured me for a G-man or at the very least somebody trying to flush some San Quentin quail. They didn't have anything else to look at and pretty soon they were all looking at me, so I sat down and tried to use my head instead of my feet. They weren't in the station. That much I knew. And nobody had seen them. At least nobody would tell me different. Maybe they were holed up in Tulsa someplace, waiting for a chance to move on. And yet Cody wasn't the type who could take a chance on hiding for very long. There were so damned many different combinations. And there was always the train. I moved fast then, but I didn't really need to. You could have played the Series in that station, and never heard them hollering. It looked that big and empty to me, and there was nobody I knew in sight.

So it was dawn by then and still hot and I wasn't any closer than I had been eight hours ago and I figured I'd better have some coffee and loosen up a little before I got out on the road again. There was a Pullman diner open on First Street. Walking out of the station through the revolving door I could see the neon sign blinking on and off, orange and green, and it was that easy. They were all three sitting there at the counter when I come in. It was Cody all right, that Stetson sticking about a half a foot above his head, eagle-claw necklace hanging down to his belly button over a blue silk shirt, buckskin coat and leggings, and boots you could see in to shave. Rona had her head on her arms, asleep, and Amory was reading a copy of the *Sporting News*. As for Cody, judging by the way that counterman looked, sort of like somebody had just hit him with a hammer or something, I figured he was talking. Old West stuff, you know. Cowboys and Indians. So I just eased onto a stool and asked for coffee and then I turned and looked Cody straight in the face.

"You folks sure as hell look like you missed your train."

Nobody made a sound.

"You want to ride back to Grey Horse with me or you want to take the bus back, the way you come?"

Cody looked over at Amory and stirred his coffee and didn't open his mouth. I was tired and jumpy and ready to put my fist about halfway down his throat, and maybe he knew it.

Amory yawned and gave me a sick sort of smile, the way he would when I fooled him with a change-up. He even looked a little bit relieved, like he wasn't so sure any more just where he was going. But he was down in the mouth, too. I could see that. Maybe running off wasn't the answer—he had probably figured that out for hisself before he was halfway down the road to Tulsa. It had all sounded different just talking about it with Rona, and that freak laying it out about how they would all of them go to Navaho country and start another shop with real Indian stuff and not just what these drunk Chetopa still had left to sell. But once they were on their way it probably sounded a whole lot shakier. On the other hand, going away to school halfway across the country where he hadn't never been wasn't the answer either— you couldn't just pull the kid up like a dandelion or something.

"How about you?" I said to Amory.

He didn't answer me right away, until he had looked at Cody and then at Rona and then back at me. "I guess I'll ride," he said.

I got up and got me a newspaper and hid behind the sports page for a little. I didn't want anybody to see how happy I was that he was right there where I could see him and checking averages just like he ought to be, even if he did look a little peaked.

"Breakfast is on me," I said to nobody in particular. "Unless you want to pay," and that I said to Cody. First time in my life I ever saw that monkey with his mouth shut.

Rona she was just mainly asleep, while we ate breakfast and all the way back home. Amory I could see in the rear-vision, looking out the window, holding onto the girl's hand. He used to go quiet on you that way, and it was sort of sad for some reason or other. Anyway it seemed like that then, like he was too young to be so serious. I put it down to his daddy being dead, but then you never know.

Well, they all seemed so beat that I just didn't have the heart to lay the wood on. Cody was the one I blamed, though I didn't know exactly why until later, and how are you going to talk to a freak like that in front of a couple of kids. Belongs in a sideshow, that bastard. I never did get the whole story out of him. By the time the dust had finally settled it didn't seem to matter much any more. He's still got that shop. Just about the only ones left, him and me. You see what you let yourself in for, asking about Amory. But he couldn't tell you anything. He's been crazy for years.

So I dumped Cody at his shop and drove Rona home to Clay's and then the boy and me we come on back to the house. I was ready for a second breakfast, and I wanted to get it all straightened out between Emily and the boy. Does it seem funny to you that just the thought of it made me happy then? It seems pretty funny now, I'll tell you that, if you like that kind of a joke. We pulled up in front of the house and I held onto the car door for a minute.

"I'm not asking you how come you did it. I have my ideas, but I don't have anything to say about it until you're ready to tell me. The main thing in all this is your mother. I don't know what you could have done to hurt her any more than you have. I hope you'll be man enough to tell her you're sorry. Everything she does, no matter what you may think of it, she's doing it for you. Don't you ever forget it. Now let's go on in the house together."

I talked to him that way so he would feel like he had somebody behind him. I reckoned he would need it. But we weren't done yet with that night's surprises. Cora was waiting at the screen door for us, and I have to admit I wasn't half ready for what she had to say. I wasn't ready at all, in fact. Thinking back on it later I could see how Clay had set us up for the one he threw past us. I should have known better—you don't talk to him that way and get home free. He don't play the game that way. He had let us off too easy, standing there with his thumbs hooked in his belt loops and rocking back and forth on his boot heels, actually laughing when he had been as close as that to kicking her teeth in. So I should have been watching for a sucker punch, but I had my hands so full that I wasn't paying any attention to what was going on where I couldn't see it happening. It was such a fine clear morning with the heat waves just beginning to lift up off the pavement and that Pullman-diner breakfast sitting right where it ought to be somewhere between in and out, and I had found the boy and brought him back, and I was running the show again. Looking after somebody besides myself. Doing a little Big Daddy bossing around and liking the feel of it again. It had been the kind of a night when your life can't ever be the same any more, and I knew it, and I mean to tell you that it was a good deal more than just all right. There was something new in the air, like you're a kid and you sneak off before light to watch them unloading the animals off a circus train, and I was every bit as excited as a kid and damn sure meant to keep right on rolling now that I had a lead that I could work with.

"Tell the missus we're home," I hollered to Cora, and then I put my arm around the boy's shoulder and we went on up the walk together to the house. I had kind of figured that my hollering like that would bring Emily to the door, but then again maybe she was sleeping it off. And then I realized that I had almost forgotten what a rough night it had been for her. Now that I look back on it I can see that we must have looked pretty foolish to Cora. Just dumb, like people who never would learn better no matter what happened to them.

Cora had a real hard head, no time for any nonsense, kind of person been making regular payments on her casket and funeral plot since she was old enough to work, and that was a long, long time ago. Never needed to ask do you have trouble but just what trouble have you got. Every time she laughed she looked over her shoulder expecting to get paid back for it in some way or other. Hardheaded, like a mule, and taking no chances when she could help it.

"Wants to see you a minute, Mist Jack."

I had time for everybody that morning. So I gave the boy a squeeze just to let him know I was with him.

"Go on to bed now and get some rest. I'll handle your mother."

It seemed so natural to me to say it just then. To tell you the truth you couldn't have put a hair between what I felt about him and Joe Don. It was all just one and the same.

So then I looked back at Cora and my lead had dropped to one with the tying run on third. She always looked like trouble. This morning she looked like bad news all the way.

"Miss Emily done gone with the law. Come up on the porch while I was fixin' the coffee. Stood out there waitin' for her to get dressed. Sweet Jesus in Heaven they done took her to jail. Trash like that come up here took her away. She said tell Mist Jack."

I could see him standing there, laughing that coyote laugh of his that don't make any noise so it's more like he hurts somewhere.

"What did she say?"

"She said tell Mist Jack. All she said."

"All right," I said to her. "You keep that boy right here. Feed him. Make him lie down. Tell him Miss Emily's gone to work. Anything. I'll be back as soon as I can."

So I jump in my car and get her started and head off for the goddam county jail which was not exactly the place I had in mind for a proposal. Point is, you see, that it hadn't really registered on me. I was like a man discovered gold in the middle of the desert. Jumping around there, whooping his head off, spilling his water and making every kind of noise, letting his mules go running off so he'll have to spend half a day in the sun rounding them up—he don't even notice that there's nobody else to hear and that like as not, he'll never make it back out of that desert, gold or no. And then if on top of it all it turns out to be fool's gold . . . That's what Cora had in mind when she looked back over her shoulder every time she laughed.

Well, in a way, you can't blame me for not noticing it too much. County jail was pretty much like an office to me. Man gets used to his office. Spends half his life there. If I had had a bunk there I could have called it home. That's where I did my business, if you see what I mean. The only two times I could think of when it didn't seem altogether natural for me to be there was one night about ten years before this particular time I'm telling you about when Clay spent his first and last night in jail, and now this one.

She was in jail all right. Emily Thayer. Jailer didn't say a thing, just shook his head and looked a little surprised and a whole lot scared. He went with me and opened the door and she was lying there on the bunk, very straight, her hands real white there against her dress like she was laid out for a funeral or something.

"Well?"

That was all she said. She could have sawed through those bars with that voice.

"Well," I said. "I brought him home."

"Is he all right?"

She hadn't even looked at me, just lying there in the shadows where I couldn't hardly see her. I pulled up the three-legged stool and sat down alongside her where I could see the sky out beyond the bars. Goddammit if it wasn't like that night with Clay all over again. Everything about it was different, but something about it was the same. Like it was all kind of freakish that we were there at all. I halfway expected that sideshow bastard Cody to show up just to make it a full house. But there we were and I didn't have but one thing on my mind, and one of the things that was different was that this time I intended to be on the talking end of the stick.

"I'm asking you to marry me," I said.

"You didn't answer me," just like that. "I asked you if he's all right."

"He couldn't be better," I said to her. "Let me take care of you, Emily."

It was like she didn't hear a word that I was saying.

"Why did he do it?"

"Look," I said to her. "I picked them up in Tulsa. There's a diner down there on First. The kid was asleep, Rona. Cody had this short-order cook by the ear—" but she wouldn't let me finish.

"What do you mean, Cody?"

Point is, it was like quicksand. I couldn't get untracked. Every time I got one leg up the other one sank down deeper. I told her Cody was with them, kind of impatient, you know. Well, goddammit, I was asking the woman to marry me.

"You're lying to me. You lied to me when Andrews died and now you're lying to me again. Every time something really important to me happens you lie about it."

"Now look here, Emily," I said to her. "Something important is happening right now. I'm asking you to marry me. I don't know how to tell you about it. Ever since I lost Joe Don and Norma Faye—all those goddam letters, going to the post office every night, crying like a kid for thirty days when I had them and then just more or less hung over for the rest of the year—even seeing Amory was enough to make me bawl. Then this morning I walked into that diner and he had the *Sporting News* spread out in front of him."

I didn't quite know where I was going then, and I took a quick breather to try and figure it out, and she hadn't even turned her head to look at me, just like I wasn't there at all.

"You might have the courtesy to pay a little bit of attention— I have been up this whole night—" but she cut me off.

"You haven't answered me," she said. "What did he say? Why did he do it? He must have said something."

I just shook my head at her. It was like we were on two different trains going by in opposite directions.

"Wait a minute, Emily. We had breakfast and then I drove them back to Grey Horse. I put the kids in the back and Cody up in the front where I could watch him. I never trusted that freak any further than I could throw him."

"Something's happened to Amory and you're hiding it from me. I don't even have to look at you to know that you're lying. What has happened here to make you all this way? Why is it always me who has to pay the price?"

Well, she went on that way for a while, cursing the town, me included, not raising her voice, talking about sins of pride and corruption and Catholic stuff, more or less like she was talking to God person to person, or at the very least a priest. But I wasn't about to play that game. What in God's name is wrong with me that people feel like they have to tell me their life story? Who asked for it? Who needs it anyway? I didn't say that, of course. I didn't say anything. I just sat and took it for as long as I could stand it and then I got up and walked over to the window and grabbed hold of those bars for all I was worth, like I was Samson or somebody.

"Emily," I said, raising my voice and calling her name over and over and louder each time until finally I had her shut up. Then I turned around and looked at her where she lay stretched out like Joan of Arc or somebody on her coffin.

"I'm going to tell you a few things and you can listen or not and you can like it or not but I'm saying them anyway. Sooner or later we both got to look it in the face. Let's take my side of it first. Nobody in this town's got less than I have. I live in a hotel room and eat in a hash house. I read the sports page with my coffee in the morning, and sometimes at night I go over a handful of letters that don't have any sense in them any more. I've got a half a dozen photographs of what don't belong to me if in fact they ever did. My life has got about as much to go on as last week's newspaper. And whatever they do, and no matter how low down it is—murder, rape, stealing, bad checks, you name it—I get them off and get a little of my own back that way. Like maybe someday I might be able to even the score. The only trouble is that that game was over the day I left Dallas, and I won it and didn't even know it because I had been hit hard and scored on and I've been acting like you can't win unless it's a shutout. Point is it's in the record book—finished. And all along I've been fussing around out there like I was working on a no-hitter and didn't even know it because nobody tells you and that's the way it ought to be. Listen to me, I'm trying to tell you. He looked up at me this morning with that simple-Simon smile on his face like when I've fooled him good and goddammit, what did I care what he'd run off for. All I cared about was that I'd found him. He knew it, too. We didn't even have to talk about it. Like we never talk about anything anyway, except averages and when you call for the hit and run and when to make the cutoff and such. That's enough to cover most things in life. All the dreams I can handle are what that boy has in his hands and his wrists and his arm and just the way he moves. Joe Don may sound more like a ball player, but we can always give him a nickname. So Clay is laying it out a yard wide and all of a sudden I'm ready to hit him in spite of his perfect record for self-defense—the Mexican in the kitchen is what I'm thinking about now that Cody has more or less retired —and then you fold up and I figure it's better if I'm around for a while like a live coward because you're going to need some looking after, and I wasn't so far wrong at that. I mean I was ready to get beat up and didn't care if I did. For somebody who hasn't had much to care about—well, you see what I'm talking about. What I'm saying to you, Emily, is that I won't try to make you happy. I've tried that once and I've learned better. If my being around, ready to take wins and losses both and work out my plays on the percentages, will do it, then I'm your man."

Well, maybe I didn't put it exactly like that, but that was the general idea. More like I was signing on as manager than husband, but what the hell. I kept waiting for her to do something, just make some kind of a sign that she was listening, but she didn't lift a finger. Anyhow, by that time I had worked the count to where there wasn't anything left to do but hit away and pray for the fence.

"You want to know why he did it? Because you've got him living like he was all the time in church or something. You set up his daddy like a little tin saint and both of you are in there lighting candles and incense and God knows what other kind of Catholic stuff. You may think you can live the rest of your life that way, but you got another think coming. You know how he's different from you and me? I'll tell you one way. Because Grey Horse is where he lives. Because he's got a girl here, and he's on the ball team, and people know him and like him and talk to him on the street. Nobody asks him where he's from. Ever think what that means? You haven't thought about anything else for ten years except getting him out of here. Suppose you had planted a tree ten years ago—what would it look like now? You got to wake up, Emily, see it the way it is. Then this business about the boy's daddy. I don't know what you've been telling him all these years, but I've got a pretty good idea. I don't even know what you really believe yourself. But he didn't die any hero, hear? He died a fool. And that's the best thing I can say for him, because if he knew Clay didn't kill any of those Red Hawks, and that's the truth, and I could prove it if I had to, then he's just a son of a bitch plain and simple. I'd a whole lot rather think of him as a fool, like he really believed that Clay was guilty and was doing everything he could to pin it on him. But even then, the part about Rita don't read so good. He was bird-dogging her, and I know it, and you know it, and everybody in town knows it. Hell, you were out at the club that night. I still remember your face when you went by me at the bar, heading for your car. Clay knew it and was mad as hell about it. Mad enough about it, and

about being throwed in jail, to get rid of Andrews by whatever
way came easiest. But not his wife. Clay wouldn't have killed
Rita. He went halfway around the world to get her and he wor-
shipped the ground she walked on. The main reason your husband
died, Emily, was because he was mixed up with Clay's wife. I
can't tell you who killed him, except that it wasn't Clay because I
was with him that night, or even how he died. Maybe they got
careless in bed. That's the way it looked, anyway. Even Cody had
an alibi; as far as anybody knows, he spent the night at the State
Hotel. I saw him myself at the jail that same evening, and before
that he was at the Smoke House and getting his hair cut. But
whatever the hell happened, and I doubt if there's anybody who
knows the whole truth of it, it don't give us anything to live on.
Any more than I can live on some faded snapshots and a half a
dozen lead-penciled letters. Pick up thy bed and walk is what the
Man says. Move on. It's the same thing, Emily. You're trying to
even the score in a game they turned the lights off on ten years
ago. Nobody else playing but you. Nobody cares whether you
win or lose. Except me, goddammit, and I can't tell you why
except whatever it was that happened last night and now here I
am asking you to marry me. But you, Emily. You and the boy,
too. I'm not signing on to look for no holy Catholic grail. And I
don't want it for Amory either. Don't mix his happiness up with
your peace of mind. They're two different games, baseball and
football, anything you want but different. You set up a tin saint,
that boy's going to knock it over someday. Give him something
flesh and blood. That's what he's going to need."

Well, I don't rightly know what I expected her to say. I
suppose I ran on at the mouth like that because I didn't want her
to say anything, like whatever she would say would have to be
bad. I couldn't even tell you how much she heard. She never
looked at me, never blinked an eye. But I had talked myself out all
right, right out into left field. Started off asking her to marry me
and ended up kicking hell out of her dead husband. Real smart. I
had gone ten years without saying a word and then I have to
pick a time like that to lower the boom on him. So I light a
cigarette and go over and look out the window again and what am

I looking at but the goddam Agency Building. It sure as hell wasn't my day. Then I had to strain to hear what she said and I knew from just the sound of it that it was going to be bad. The only thing I didn't know was how bad, but I found that out, too, just the way she started, telling me like she always did, like it was some verse out of the catechism or whatever they call it, that Andrews Thayer was the finest man she had ever known.

"The town killed him—all of you. How it happened doesn't matter any more. Why it happened is something I'm sure you could never understand. It had mainly to do with what he was as a human being. He was the kind of man who can't live among people like you, because you won't let him. He had to die so you could go on living, and in a way he died for you, or for something here that he thought had to be fought for to the very death. Even if it was a lost cause right from the start. Well, I've learned to live with that sacrifice and even to accept it, as long as it's not forgotten. But I won't have it cheapened, Jack. I won't let you, or Clay, or anybody else turn it into something common and sordid. Now I'm going to tell you something else that you're not going to like to hear. I always meant to go with Amory when he left for school in September. To go for good, Jack, and not come back. I needed you for protection right up to the last minute, just in case something went wrong. I wasn't even going to tell you, but now I can't do any different. Just get on the train and go—just like that. There's a town where the school is. I could always get a job. Just walk out of here without a word, like I'd never been here at all. Like none of you had ever been alive as far as I was concerned. Well, I can't do that now. But Amory's got to go just the same. I won't let anything or anybody change the way I've worked out his life for him. There's an account in a Kansas City bank. I'll tell you how to operate it. Enough in it to pay for Amory's education. That's how it was that I could leave this fall. I had everything ready and then Carter came back into my life. You've always done what I asked you, Jack. I've got to ask you again."

"You're talking crazy," I said to her. "I don't know what you're in here for but I'll get you off. Some of Carter's foolishness," but she shook me off.

"I've got to ask you to handle that money and get that boy through school. I've got to ask you to explain it to him. I've got to ask you to take care of him like you were his father."

"Emily, I come up here to ask you to marry me. The past don't matter, and we can settle the future later. Let me look after you, Emily."

That was the only time she budged. Just one little shake of her head. Never even looked at me. Well, she had me beat. I'd said everything I had to say. All of it but the last thing of all, and I just couldn't get it out. Maybe I was trying to say goodbye. I don't know, except that it hurt like hell. That she could just get on the train and take off, not a word, nothing, all those years and the boy and all and she could just leave me flat-ass in the dust like that without even saying goodbye. I felt like I wanted to lay down by myself somewhere and die.

What was she in there for, you say? Oh Christ, I've talked most of the night as it is. I guess you'd have to say she wanted revenge. She thought the town was to blame, and somebody had to pay. Grey Horse wasn't any kind of a place for a lady like Emily. She and her husband—you'd have to say that they were a little better than most. A whole lot better than the kind of trash the wind blew into this place. Trouble with both of them was that they just expected a whole lot more of people than they had any right to expect. I guess we all want people to be a little better than they are, if we got any kind of pride or whatever you want to call it. Point is how far are you willing to go to make people do like you want them to do. You ready to argue, you ready to fight, you ready to kill? Every one of those is different. I'd have to put Emily and Andrews both right there at the end. Maybe that's the way it is when you really believe. I don't guess I ever believed anything that much. That's probably why she married Andrews Thayer and couldn't even work up a yawn when it was me putting the question to her. I don't think you'd want to hear it, you know. It's all over and done with, nobody cares any more, not hardly anybody living even out of all that but me and that carnival freak, Cody. Emily, of course. Don't even know where she is now. Amory, but he was too little. They're all dead, Clay, Rita, old Blair Booth, Andrews, Shoat and Orval. Not to mention most of the Red Hawk family. Maybe it was all Shoat's fault, when you get right down to it. He didn't need all that much money. I guess you get used to the cheers and the champagne and a new town with new girls every month, and then one day it starts to hurt when you get off that horse on the run and the rope won't go where you want it to and the steer is back up on three legs and you've got his head twisted halfway around to China and he's got you beat, and there's some young son of a bitch out of Comanche with a black hat and he can throw and tie 'em before you can get your ass out of the chute and your rope down the way it ought to be. Can't cut the mustard anymore, and it never did feel like you was earning it because who would ever pay you for roping steers faster than anybody else anyway, but you're used to it now and you need it, and somebody's always got an easy way of getting it.

But then maybe Shoat wasn't any more to blame than anybody else. Rita was in and out of bed like a hot-water bottle, and way too big-time for Grey Horse. Maybe Clay was a little too old —Grey Horse was sure as hell too small. When a woman's been around as much as Rita had—and I'm talking about bed, now, and whiskey and you name it—then I don't care how sweet talking she is, you better handle with care. That's one thing Clay never got through his head, as far as I know, anyway. God knows what he had eating on him—he set her up in a doll house, treated her like she was made out of glass, in public anyway, when a whip would probably have suited her better. Blair full of whiskey and good intentions, needing help and protection both and counting on Clay for that and plenty more. Andrews and Emily—what did they need that made them come all this way? This was one party they sure as hell weren't invited to. And then Buffalo Bill. I guess when you get right down to it he would know as much as anybody. There's only one trouble with Cody. He's nuts.

Just like they were all of them there in that cell with us, some dead, some living, half of what had happened forgotten and most of it nobody ever really understood but there it was, something that just wouldn't die no matter what you did to it. Turned us every way but loose and sure as hell wouldn't let go.

But I haven't told you about Amory. That's what you asked me about, wasn't it? Yeah. Well, I had to go back and get him. Somebody had to tell him. Right about then I was wondering how come it had to be me, all the way back to that morning when I come up to the house to tell the lady about her husband. There wasn't any of it had to be done by me. Nobody ever called on me to be a saver of souls, and I sure as hell didn't hear any voices in the night. But once started there just wasn't any way of turning back. I was in it for good even if I didn't know why. So Cora made me some coffee and I sat down there in the bedroom to wait until he woke up. I had been in that bedroom before, arguing with Emily, trying to talk her into getting the hell out of here right after her husband was killed. I lost on that one, too. Come to think of it, I don't think she ever paid the slightest mind to anything I ever said to her. Unless it was to listen and then do the opposite. I've caught pitchers like that. Well, it looks smart as long as you're winning. When they start to hit you it looks right dumb. And Emily was beginning to get hit all over the place. So I leaned back in that little old rocker and got some sleep myself. I had been up the whole night without taking in a nickel, and that has a way of making me tired.

The boy slept all day. I let him go, figuring he would need all the rest he could get for what he was going to hear. He woke up in the late afternoon and Cora fixed a plate for him and he asked a couple of times where Emily was and all I could say was that she wasn't back from work yet. Call it a hit and an error. I had to say something. Then I told him to get his glove and we would go down to the ball field and hit a few flies. Partly I wanted to get him away from Cora who just stood there like she'd taken root, talking to the Lord and about half crying so that she looked like she was getting ready to cash in on that casket insurance, and partly because I wanted to be outdoors with him where I could have a little room. I made him run some down there, but he caught everything I put up in the air and back would come that one-hop throw-in, powerful, right on the button, just like he was rolling it off a reel. I guess that would have made me cry if anything could by this time, so after a while I just said shit and tossed my bat away and waved him in and we sat down on the bench by the water cooler and I let him blow a little before I said anything.

"We haven't talked yet about last night," was how I started.

He was pounding his fist into the pocket of his mitt—it was a new one I gave him when we got the letter about the school and all—and he stopped a minute and then went on.

"You haven't told me yet how come you did it."

He looked up at me then, and going by the look he gave me I would have been hard pressed to say whether he liked me or not.

"I don't see why I have to go away. Nobody else goes away— why do we always have to be different?"

"Well, Amory, your mother and you," and that was about as far as I got. That was one I wasn't yet ready to field. "Whatever she's doing, she's doing it for you and don't you ever forget it," was what I finally came out with, but I had said that before and it didn't take us very far the first time. He just shook his head, stubborn, and went back to working on that mitt. Deal with me is that I'm no good on the question-and-answer. I can make you a speech, a hell of a summing up, lay it in there with plenty of whatever you're calling for, but cat and mouse ain't my game. So I took a deep breath and lit out for home.

"I guess Rona's part of it, right?"

He nodded his head.

"And you can't figure out what your mother's got against her."

He was with me.

"And it matters to you, and to her, enough so that you were ready to run off and hide until your mother gave up and let you have it your way. And Cody got into it some way or other for some half-ass reason of his own and he was going to make it all right."

He looked at me again, and if he still didn't like me, at least he didn't look like he wanted to hit me.

"Cody helped us—we asked him to—it wasn't his fault."

Well, I was ready to talk about a lot of things, but not about that freak. So I just rared back and threw it past him.

"How much do you know about the way your daddy died?" You ever see a pinch-hitter take a called third strike, bases loaded, two outs, then just look down for a minute and turn back toward the bench, dragging that bat behind him? Beat. That was Amory. He took the glove off and just sat there, looking down at the ground. I don't know what he knew, or what people had said to him, sometime or other, the way they will. But whatever it was he knew, he gave it to me the way she had taught him to say it.

"Dad was killed trying to save somebody in a fire. Nobody else was brave enough to try and get her out of there. It was a woman, trapped in a burning house. Dad ran in there where the fire was and the roof caved in and he never came out."

So low I couldn't hardly hear him, just barely more than a whisper.

"Anybody ever tell you who that woman was, and where it was, and so on?"

He didn't answer me.

"Well, son, I'm going to tell you now what maybe you've heard and maybe you haven't. I'm going to tell you what I believe to be the truth even though there may be other people who believe different. I'm telling it to you because you're old enough to know, and because it just don't make sense any other way. It was a woman, all right. That woman was Rona's mother. She and your daddy died together in a fire at the Carter ranch. The whole place burned down, and what little was left was enough to show that the two of them were alone there in the house when she burned. There was a truck parked out in front of the house with whiskey all over the floorboards. Somebody had been drinking. That same afternoon Clay Carter had been put in jail on a murder charge signed by your father. The night your father died a man named Blair Booth committed suicide. He was the Indian Agent here, your daddy's boss. I was Clay Carter's lawyer and I got the charges against him dropped. I hardly knew your mother at the time, but I was the one who arranged for your daddy's funeral and then I tried my best to get your mother to go on back where she came from where there was family and all. I told her what people believed about your dad and what it would be like for her to go on living here, but she wouldn't listen to anything I had to say. Your mother believes that Clay Carter had your father killed because he was the only man in Grey Horse who had guts enough to call Clay's bluff. There were lots of people being killed in Grey Horse in those days, and your daddy thought Clay was behind it. That's why he put Clay in jail, and according to your mother, that's why he was killed. That's why she feels like she does about Rona, son. That's why she wants you to go away from here."

Well, he had tensed up, like he didn't know where the next pitch was coming from, but he stayed with it, I'll give him credit for that.

"Did he? Did Mr. Carter kill my dad."

"Amory, I'm telling you the best I can what I think really happened, and I would have to answer no to that. Your daddy was in that house with Mrs. Carter, probably just to talk to her about the Red Hawk killings and find out what she could tell him. Maybe she was drunk, and one way or another the house caught on fire, and he couldn't get her out and he couldn't leave her and before he knew it he was trapped the way you said."

I was kind of running out of breath, had more or less overrun my base and was scrambling to get back. Once I had said it right out like that it didn't sound so good, and who had asked me to start acting like a Baptist preacher at my age.

"That doesn't exactly make him a hero, does it."

He wasn't asking me, he was telling me, and that made twice in one fairly long day that I had made Andrews look bad. The dumb part of it was that I hadn't meant it that way at all. I won't say I liked him, but I had a kind of respect for him. Well, the truth of it is that I didn't like him worth a shit, but all right, he had been to a law school and not some barber college. I know big league when I see it, and I know bush.

So I just said, "I don't think he would have asked anybody to call him a hero. He didn't come out here for that as far as I know. I don't think that was the kind of language he talked. Man don't have to be a hero to remember him and claim him as your father. He put his pants on one leg at a time like the rest of us, but he had a lot going for him. He was smart, he was honest, he had class. The kind of a man who would go right into the wall if he had to to make the catch. That's enough in my book."

So we sat there for a while and the shade reached on out beyond second base and I was hoping he would want to talk some more about his dad because I had the hardest way yet to go. Point was I couldn't tell what he was thinking. He seemed kind of froze-up-like and I would have given a lot just to be able to call it off then and there. But there wasn't anybody in the bullpen and I had to get out of it the best way I could.

"The deal is," I said to him, "that whatever your mother did was always for you. Personally I never knew anybody so ready to put somebody else first. She hasn't had but one thought for the last ten years, and that was getting you out of here and into a school where you could get the kind of education she wanted you to have. These burr heads here, Amory, hell, they're not going anyplace. Someday you'll thank her for it. Now I'm going to say it again, what I've already told you. Don't ever forget that whatever she's done, it was for you. Maybe your daddy wasn't a hero, but she sure as hell is one. And you and I are going to remember that, and we're not going to let anybody tell us different."

He had that glove on again and was pounding the hell out of it, and I could see the tears falling down there in the dust and I was having hell's own time trying to hang onto myself and get it out. Damned if it wasn't like that night at the train all over again, except I didn't have any place to run to.

"Your mother's up there in the jailhouse, son. I was with her this morning. If there is a way in God's earth to get her out of there, I will do it. But whatever happens, we will just have to carry on the way she would want us to, and believe in her, and be thankful to God for her and all she has done for us. She has asked me to take care about school and I will sure as hell do it. And whatever else needs doing that is in my humble power. I don't claim that I can measure up to her, but I'll do my best."

Well, I went on that way some more like it was some kind of a prayer meeting or other, and I explained it the best I could and mainly just kept on talking the way you do when somebody has been hit so hard he can't do nothing but cry. And he cried there for quite a while, rubbing at his nose with the back of his glove, and then he stopped, all of a sudden, just like that. One minute hanging onto himself and trembling to beat hell, and then just like somebody had given him a horse needle full of morphine. I put my arm around him and it was like I had hold of a stump. Like somebody had brought the bat back and hit him right across the nose.

After a while I got up—it was evening by then—and waited for him to get up too, and then he looked at me and I guess I won't ever forget that. He looked about the way you feel when you've got a face full of novocain. Stunned-like, he was.

"I never asked for anything, Mr. Bird."

Like he hadn't understood anything of what I had told him, or like somebody had taken away from him forever the only thing he had ever really wanted and which nothing else could ever make up for.

"I never asked anybody for anything. I just didn't want to go away, that's all."

Well, I never forgot any of it, like you see. I wonder if he remembers me at all . . .

PART THREE

Wild Geese in Winter

Grey Horse, Oklahoma, in the Sixties

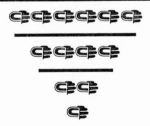

I WOULD GUESS THAT BETWEEN HOLLYWOOD AND NEW YORK there must be ten thousand of them. American gothic gone soft with subsidies; Western classic worn to the bone by loneliness. A two-story business district squatting on its heels under the pitiless purity of a sky too bright to look at. A constellation of frame houses ordered in precise monotony, replete with picture windows, fake Chinese lamps, imitation French-provincial or British-imperial or American-colonial or Danish-modern furniture. Everything is a replica of something else here in a land so flat, so empty, that there seem to be no native forms. Even in the desert, dunes cast the shadows of pyramids, but here it is always high noon and the very shadows are in hiding from the sun or the wind or whatever violence it is that accompanies every season except the burnt-out funeral time of fall.

Cars bask in the empty streets like Gila monsters. They move slowly through the winter sun like something prehistoric, in bluish asphalt prehistoric sludge, and their heavy tires complain like the tired mouths at their windows. Nobody on foot. People stared at me when I walked along those streets swept clean of life. Women, mostly, in slacks and curlers and flat heels, in cars, in stores. All of them staring with the dull, stricken gaze of incurious cattle. Had they recognized me? Heard rumors of my coming? I was afraid of them, and fled their heart-shaped glasses with the glittering chains that draped their withered necks. No doubt in summer they wear shorts. By the time style gets here it has been leveled down to comfort.

The second stories of the buildings are empty. Even in winter the windows of the storefronts are lined with yellow cellophane as a protection against sunlight. Where the vacant windows begin of stores gone out of business is the laundromat, and there I sat and drank Dr. Pepper and washed my socks and underwear amidst twenty-five machines that vibrated against the bolts that fixed them to the floor. I have gone by just before noon, in early evening, and at five in the morning on my way back to the hotel. The laundromat is always open, neon tubes glowing, the pop machine rumbling so that the empties shake in their stacked cases. Cockroaches rush erratically along concrete trails. Like a chapel, it is a place where some sort of spirit dwells, some kind of humming, self-contained malevolence at the heart of so much silence. No one is ever there.

At the several drive-ins cars are biased like the Boeings I saw at the Kennedy Pan-Am when we came through New York. These are the sidewalk cafes of Grey Horse. Early in the morning cattlemen smoke cigars at the counter of the Coffee Shoppe, wearing identical custard-colored straw hats with black bands, high boots with multicolored stitching, and levis that have not been shrunk or bleached the way you see them in the streets of St. Tropez. They have swelling bellies contained by tooled belts and propped up on thin, prancing legs. They are built along the general lines of cattle. For them comfort has gone part of the way at least to style, and though in my books they are tall and lean and leathery, variations on a theme by Cooper (Gary), here they all look like the men you see in a crowd scene in a TV Western when somebody has been shot and the townsfolk rush into the street while the gunfighters are burning leather and heading for the hills. Curiously, they all seem to wear dark glasses now, but I suppose that just goes to show that at least the preference for whiskey hasn't changed. . . .

Yet if there remained something malevolent in all that emptiness, some kind of coyote spirit yellow-eyed and wary, there was no longer any terror that I could see. Why had I thought that our very names would drain the blood from their cheeks so that the skull shone through, ashen as a fire gone dead; imagined that they would have watched us with growing dread as we slowly came on from so far away across that level land, me carrying her back from the desert in my arms, so that finally they would turn and seek the comfort of darkness, afraid to look upon that body, that face that had moved so long among them like the image of some tragic queen? Was it simply that the terror had gone on living only in my mind, and that I had come back to a country of my own imagining that had vanished from the earth? For they were gone, all, disappeared again beneath the shifting dust. I walked those streets which ran through me like the vessels of my blood and wept at every crossing for all of us; for them because they were beyond my reach and for myself because they had left me here alone; letting the great waves of feeling break down upon me and hurl me against the stony truth of what we had all become. Come back from over the water with her in a coffin, to bury her in the only home she had, and me trembling like a lover at her graveside, coming back, coming back, knowing only that if I didn't laugh some kind of laugh or other that I would surely cry. . . .

And if I pretended to see it like ten thousand other towns, trying as best I could to keep it at a distance simply because it would choke me if it came too close, yet I could feel it only as one, the map of my childhood, the single tree in the forest where the honey of my life was stored, the town unique, isolated, indivisible and imperishable where I had reached up from love through pain to a loss I would never finish calculating. An opening in my flesh which would not close, a name I could not speak, a dream I would never understand. That small, one-story white house with the red-tiled roof; the gas heaters I used to light with trembling hands in the dark of winter mornings; a garden full of roses that she tended with something less than love, yet more than duty, the way it would be with someone else's child; uncared for hollyhocks and sunflowers careless and gaudy against the alley fence; the cottonwood among whose branches I nested like some awkward, fledgling mockingbird; the driveway through whose dust I drove the little cars my father brought me. He was the man who told me to ride the pony while standing on its back, and all I could do was to hold out my hands to him, begging him to take me off; and he was the man who ordered me to dive into the deep end of the country club pool, knowing I could not swim, and I just stood there, looking up at him through the tears; and it was he about whom she told me that day when the sun broke the windshield like a lance and I could only hold my breath and then climb into the cottonwood and watch through the branches for his return. So that he stayed forever with me like the memory of some blind man begging in the subway from whom one turned away and then could never forget. But now I had brought her back to him, where he had lain so long alone, and thus perhaps . . .

And all because there was no way to keep her quiet there in that little cemetery in the presqu'île de St. Tropez where I had stood beneath the cypresses in the pale December sun and watched her being lowered into the ground. Somehow or other she knew she wasn't home, and at night I would wake up and know it, too, hearing lost steps in the silent, stony streets of that far-off town, listening to shutters that groaned in the roaming wind.

It was a better place than most to spend eternity. Below her the plain stretched right to the shore, patches of color pieced together in a crazy quilt of rose houses with blue shutters, plowed fields dark brown on beige, green hills and purple sea, vineyards and orchards, all englobed in light which in the summer was like the play of knives in the sun and which now shimmered slowly, lazy as bees in winter. Heavy horses furrowed the earth, and distant figures in blue bent low in the vineyards, and in the dust-muffled avenues between the plane trees of villages redolent with the smoke of pine cones and roots of vines and the branches of olive trees grown grey with age, old men played at boules in a green silence.

But the voices were not hers, and there would be no one beside her to whom she could tell her story down the years, no trees that she could name knowing the music they made in the wind, no birds whose songs she could remember nor flowers whose scent she bore upon her hands like some familiar perfume. And then Christmas was coming, and she was alone, and a long way from anywhere, and I knew I had to take her back, partly for her, partly for me, partly so that all of them could rest in something like peace, wherever they lay. . . .

So I had a glass of wine with the mayor, and we talked about Christmas, and the Americans who had fought their way up from the beach twenty years before, and how everybody had to come from someplace and go back there someday, and how he was going to be buried on his own land no matter what the priest said because ever since they had buried the film star there, the cemetery was just a place where people came to take photographs and break branches from the cypresses to keep as souvenirs, paying no attention to the monument to the war dead which the mayor himself had commissioned, and everybody said . . . And then I stood again in the wind and watched them joking around their cigarettes as they lifted the coffin from earth that still looked raw while red clods rattled under the spades as though her bones were astir. And then I hired a hearse and drove her to Nice, and we changed planes in Paris and then went right on through to Tulsa, and everybody—hostesses and porters and customs officials and fellow passengers—just as nice as they could be when I said that I was taking my mother home for Christmas because she was dead. And then in Tulsa the crew-cut young man from the funeral parlor in Grey Horse was waiting because I had written ahead—I was waiting for him to say something, just my name, but he handled everything with an unctuous silence which made me feel querulous and suddenly very tired, and then too, I somehow resented the fact that on an occasion such as this he was wearing a cowman's hat and a braided thong through a turquoise brooch instead of a plain black tie—and then it was all over in a matter of two days. The drive back to where it had all started through country I scarcely dared to look at, the somber preacher furnished as part of the package, another set of gravediggers just as oblivious as the others to whatever I might be feeling, a sharper wind that made me turn my collar up, a bluer sky that hurt my eyes, and a cedar tree that made me think of cypresses . . .

And now for a week I've been sitting here in the State Hotel, picking away at it all with a geologist's hammer. A week, alone, in a worn-out little cattle town, breaking up the stone of memory, lifting out the chalky fossils which are all that remain of that teeming garden somewhere back in the past. For they are all gone, and there is nobody left to know. Jack would have known, but he's out there under the cedar, too . . . How he sat through those last lonely years in the lobby of the hotel, waiting all day long for someone who never came, dividing the hours between the simulated play-by-play and the box scores, morning and evening, leaning with both hands on his cane, that cane with a serpent which wound around it with two red rubies for eyes, a souvenir of the Los Angeles Olympics in nineteen thirty-two. He always kept his hat on, and his face was mottled and sprinkled with hairs, about halfway between catfish and toad. He wore tan-and-cream perforated shoes, and white socks rolled around the ankle bone. The skin of his legs was a kind of milky blue, like that of a plucked chicken. Always looked as though he might just fizz away to nothing in a hard rain, like an Alka Seltzer tablet. His false teeth clicked like a pair of shears, and he could remember batting averages as far back as . . . Who was it he was waiting for? Who was it who never came? A woman for whom he used every trick in the book and still couldn't get her off, and to whom just for the hell of it he kept his word, as best he could? Or a boy who could throw them out from deep center field on one bounce like he was rolling it off a reel, switch-hitter, fast on the bases, what a man would have to call a natural?

And Cody . . . the Chetopa Museum bought up most of his stuff, and now his Curio Shop is an information center for tourists. Six and a half feet of bone and sinew that you could hardly see when he turned sideways, long white hair that curled up over the buckskin collar of his jacket, leather leggings, crossed gunbelts, a hat that almost scraped the ceiling and boots that looked like they were varnished every morning. He had walked through my boyhood like the ghost of every dime-novel frontiersman I had ever read about, moving like he was held together by baling wire and would one day just collapse into a pile of dust. The way he would lift his nose and then peer out over it while he talked to me, as though it were a gunsight. Can't remember that he ever smiled. People always said that he should have been on sale along with the arrowheads and beaded belts and peace pipes and the rest of the junk. But whenever I came by he would put up his Out to Lunch sign and take me back to where he had his scrapbooks and his gun collection and all those memories. And finally that story that he was always trying to tell me about the Carters and the Thayers and how he had a debt to pay back and how he had decided that the three of us should head out to Navajo Country where maybe there was still something left of the West the way it ought to be, but then Jack found us and brought us back, and after that I never got any further West than St. Louis where Jack came to meet me a couple of times at Easter because St. Louis was a town where he knew the hotels and restaurants around the ball park . . . Eyes like squirrels in a cage, and then they told me how toward the end he tried to set fire to the old folks' home where he lived and they got the jacket on him and took him to Vinita and nobody ever saw him again. Probably buried there at the state asylum, or cremated, whatever they do with you down there when your time comes. And did he sing *The Last Roundup* when he knew it was time to pack it in?

Rona . . . Just a name. Married. Moved away. Never came back. Nothing to come back for. I stood under the dusty black-jack trees in front of the big house on the hill and heard the nuns murmuring like pigeons on the porch. Behind me, down below, was the town where we had been so afraid, and loved each other anyway, in the grass, in parked cars, wherever there was starlight and silence enough to hide us from all the eyes and ears. Just a name, and a face, and dreams that ached like memories. Clay was gone, too, and maybe that was why the valley seemed so lost, empty now even of terror, the days of passion buried beneath the drifting leaves in some final burnt-out fall. . . .

And then at last—because I was afraid most of all of her—the county clerk. I took her out to lunch, passing myself off as a writer of Westerns looking for material, relieved and yet somehow melancholy that she had not recognized me. But she knew the story, all right, and I was the listener she had been waiting for. Soft and saggy as a sack of flour. Eyes that pecked at me like starved birds while her chubby hands languidly applied butter to the bread. Violence and corruption recollected in the tranquillity of ceiling fans and iced tea. Yes, she remembered it all. In the neighborhood of thirty thousand dollars. Seems like the city couldn't afford a detailed audit, so it went along like that for years. That was the excuse, anyway. The city manager then was one of Clay Carter's boys, the way they called them in those days. Yes, some said so, that Carter—he's dead now—knew about it and held it like the ace of trumps until he was ready to play it. I don't know. I was the court stenographer and I took it all down and that certainly wasn't mentioned. Honey, the way it was done was that the non-add key had been filed off so that when you hit it and it registered there wasn't any mark made on your stub. That way nobody could see that the non-add key had been used at all. Now that would mean, don't you see, that in a given column of figures you could non-add a certain number of items every day or week or whatever and put the total of those items in your pocket. When the overall totals were audited—and there wasn't any deeper checking—then the totals would prove out and the error wouldn't show. Right cute. She wasn't what you'd call liked around here. A whole lot too high-hat for these parts. Got what was coming to her. As for her husband, well, that's another story . . .

The meal wasn't much, but it was her giggling that left a bad taste in my mouth. All neat and simple, like a rattlesnake. And after that I thought better of Spence and all the others for not having thrown it in my face when I was blowing off about my Indian mother and maiden aunt and the rest of that phony story that wouldn't have been good enough for the *True Westerns* I used to read under the covers with a flashlight . . . as though my story wasn't good enough as it was. Mr. and Mrs. Andrews Amory Thayer, he the hero who had died drunk in Rona's mother's bed, the two of them burned there where they lay after they had framed Clay into jail, and then Emily, who got sent to the State Prison for Women in McAlester and stayed there until she got out on good behavior during the war and went to work in a defense plant and then just stayed on and opened a shop where she sold odds and ends made by her fellow prisoners. Some kind of social work, was what she had always said in her letters . . .

I'm not sure that I understand it any better now than I ever did. The years go by. More happens, and yet so much remains unchanged. And perhaps the time has come to give up trying to understand the why of it all. I think I would be satisfied if I could just get to the point where I could say: This is what happened. This is the way it really was.

But I am here, after all, midpoint between Hollywood and New York, and I have questioned the natives and examined shards and artifacts and consulted records and survivors and strained my eyes over hieroglyphs and frescoes, and all in spite of a pain which eats at me like leprosy. I don't even know who I'm writing it for. Maybe for you, Andrews. Or you, Emily. Or Jack—maybe you were the only one who really cared. You or Cody in his crazy way. Would it matter to my children? Certainly not to Diane. I'm not sure any more. I just don't know. But then maybe, when all is said and done, it's for me. Because it is Christmas and I am still alone, in the very heart of the only place I thought belonged to me. And now I find that these streets are cold and empty, and the voices full of doubt, and the roads run to the horizon and disappear. And yet maybe it is better that way. Thirty years is a long time to go on pretending. I am like a deserter from life coming back into the light after decades of hiding in the cellar of my own home.

Sometime, somewhere, time out of mind, I had jotted it down and folded it up and stuck it in my wallet. Words I hadn't really understood at the time. It was a habit I had had for years, so that opening that wallet was like biting into a Chinese fortune cookie.

The years, after all, have a kind of emptiness when we spend too many of them on a foreign shore. We defer the reality of life in such cases until a future moment, when we shall again breathe our native air; but by and by, there are no future moments, or, if we do return we find the native air has lost its invigorating quality and that life has shifted its reality to the spot where we have deemed ourselves only temporary residents. Thus between two countries, we have none at all, or only that little space of either in which we lay down our discontented bones.

My bones were discontented, all right, and my years seemed more than ever now to have a strange kind of emptiness. Some essential reality had been too long deferred, and I seemed to have no native air anywhere to breathe. My life had had its source for so long in a spot where I thought I could never go again, and now some kind of dream, too long deferred, was gone forever, because we had come back. Some kind of dream, some kind of image of myself, had been laid to rest for good, and I had none at all; nothing but memories like old wounds and above all a sense of cheap betrayal which our return had only deepened. Was it I who had been betrayed, or had I betrayed them and all their hopes and sacrifices? Because I had loved her, just as I had loved them all, and I had wanted no more than some home place for bones that had ached for far too many years. It seemed to me that I had asked so little, just some kind of native air to breathe, even if all the rest was taken away. Air to breathe, and stones for a barrow on a shore which these bones would never have to leave again . . .

His telegram had come as I was starting on my second *café crème*. It was October then, just three short months ago in spite of all that has happened since. The sun was still warm on the terrace and Henri stood splay-footed alongside our table in the felt slippers he wore winter and summer. He was talking about the weather, I suppose. I never listened to him very carefully, but then he never really ventured very far from the roads he had walked all his life. The directions of the wind, whether it would rain, that kind of thing. I always had a feeling that he thought I expected it, and that he gave it to me the way I gave him his tips. But I was probably wrong about that, too. I was once again in one of those periods when I was discovering that I had been wrong on just about everything. So I let Cynthia do the nodding and went on looking at pictures of policemen in *Nice Matin*. In bathing suits, playing boules, a hairy group of footballers—everything but in uniform. Just as though they were civilians like everybody else. Stories about dances, promotions, transfers, their athletic leagues—a kind of flic house organ about a world that was trying to act like mine. They had never seemed like everybody else to me, but then the Midi made a point of being a rather special place. Parisians always speak of it as picturesque, and droll, and so amusing—all words that I have never particularly liked. I couldn't really say why. Maybe because that's the way money sounds when it talks.

Anyway, it was only when I heard that Henri wasn't talking any more that I looked up. The old lady who delivers the mail had spotted us across the square and brought the telegram to our table. Cynthia hadn't started out well that morning, and now she looked worse. Goggle sunglasses pushed up against bleached hair, her arms crossed over those hard little breasts that you could almost see through the peek-a-boo blouse, her mouth tight and twisted the way it was when she smoked her first cigarette before breakfast or when she thought people weren't paying enough attention to what she was saying. Or if I left her alone at a party where she had to pretend to speak French, or even when she had to go to a movie by herself. She wasn't much on being alone, and just a letter addressed to me, much less a telegram, was enough to freeze her up for the day.

"It's from Spencer Platt," I said, more surprised than anything else.

Henri rolled the cigarette in his teeth and nodded as though he understood. Cynthia crossed her tanned and shining legs and leaned forward over her coffee. "Who's Spencer Platt?" she asked sullenly, as though an old girl friend had come up to say hello and I hadn't introduced her.

"Please call me Paris EUR 64-17 anytime before close of business Tuesday Urgent." I turned it over as though there might be something written on the other side. "That's all it says."

"Who's Spencer Platt?"

"Just a friend, duck. A very old friend. From way, way back."

"I don't like telegrams."

"You never get them."

"I used to. Don't kid yourself."

"Before you met me?"

"Before I met you. How did he know you were down here with me?"

Up to a certain point it's all right. Summer when you can sleep on the beach and throw a ball and dance most of the night with a skinful of local rosé and then make love at dawn, on the beach again or at somebody's party or even at home if you get that far before you run out of laughs. Especially when you haven't made it like this for years and her legs are very slim and hard and she's jealous as hell and everybody keeps telling you how much you've changed and how young you look. Those last days of sun in September always have a kind of hope about them, like maybe the resurrection was for real. Then it's October and all the others have gone and you take it easy on the rosé because you have to get in three good hours before lunch and the advance is almost finished and when you're on your sixth horse opera its easy to lose track of what's going on back at the ranch. And then at last, inevitably, you start looking for the exit, because this is a summertime girl, even if you did leave Diane and the kids back at Hackberry Bucks and head south to the sun with her. Not *for* her. *With* her. There's a difference, and October is the kind of month when you start to find it out. When the tubes of Royal Bronze are empty, and everybody's losing his tan, and you begin to count how many Octobers you've got left.

"Where are you going now?" She had pushed the goggles down onto her nose, almost as though she felt like hiding so that I would have to come looking for her.

"Make a phone call. Like it says in the telegram. You tell Henri about the weather in Yorkshire while I'm gone."

I placed the call and brought her back a copy of *Elle*, which was the best available antifreeze in that cafe where the only ladies you saw were summertime girls no matter what their age, if you could call them ladies. Then I picked up with Henri where I had left off the day before on the subject of the exact degree of alcohol in the local wine. He came from thirty kilometers away, and maintained that the stuff around here was doped. He looked as though he had drunk enough to know. She hated it when I spoke French, of course. It didn't matter to her that I had lived long enough in the bloody country to handle the language with a certain amount of ease. She was sure that I spoke French only to show off, and mainly because she didn't understand it. All of my actions were similarly reduced to some function of her personality. Which was partly true, I suppose, because talking to Henri left me free to think about what was really on my mind.

Spence. Spencer Platt. Everybody's All-American, Wyoming and the rest of it. I hadn't seen him for a year, the last time he and Nancy were in London and had come down to the Bucks for the day. The usual thing—they missed the early train and got there just in time for lunch which cut me damned short because I had to return to London on the 2:10 express to make a football match I had been talking up all week. In fact I was going in to spend the weekend with Cynthia, and nobody could understand why I didn't just forget the match, and Diane was bugged and Spence and Nancy a little cool and superior and I just said to hell with it and left them there with the geese and the pigeons and the poodles and the children, right in the middle of a sodden English countryside afternoon.

So the telegram was a surprise. We were the kind of friends who went on seeing each other without really knowing why any more, but without having to ask, either, because we had been friends so long. And I knew him well enough to know that he didn't send urgent telegrams except on business. And we didn't have any business that I knew anything about. No, it would have to be Diane. She had waited me out with her kind of stolid English patience, all the more English for the fact that she was half American by blood and had been trying to forget it for most of her life, and then decided that for a forty-five-year-old caper this had lasted long enough. Spence would be the one she would turn to—sober, steady, capable, reliable Spencer Platt.

"It's probably Diane." She had pushed the goggles to the tip of her nose, frowning with concentration at all the eyes and mouths, the colors and the clothes, the casual contortions of the boyish bodies. *Elle* for her was a guidebook for girls, less a publication than a way of life, and she was one of them herself, one of those girl-boys who seems to have stepped right off the pages of a fashion magazine for the very young and whom you meet at, say, a publisher's party, which as a matter of fact was where I met her. She was vaguely in journalism although I had never seen anything she ever wrote. She had one of those open, wistful, full-lipped faces that girls have these days—long, straight, two-tone blond hair, a lean, determined jaw, makeup mainly around the eyes, going slow on cigarettes and whiskey, playing it very shrewd and very cool all the way. And yet the very best thing about her was the way she laughed, which wasn't cool at all. She could laugh the way she could dance, and make love, like she didn't even have to try, like it was all as easy as orange juice and champagne. I had produced five books and four kids and lived all over Europe—as far away from Grey Horse as I could get—but I hadn't learned much about dancing or making love either one, even if I did have a sour sort of laugh that seemed to come more from my liver than anywhere else. Unless it was just an advanced case of cancer of the soul. So I began to spend more and more time in London and less and less at the Bucks, which was where I kept my tweeds and shooter's stick and the rest of the disguise. As much as anything else, the whole thing was like a seven-page spread on contemporary England in some illustrated weekly. All of it, before and after. Hackberry Bucks, Chelsea, country squire by day and a swinger in black leather by night until that spring when we bought the oldest Jaguar we could find and drove through watery English sunshine to Dover and got off the boat in France and kept driving on cognac and coffee until we got to the long beach just outside St. Tropez and it wasn't yet dawn and I woke her up and we ran into the sea in our skivvies, laughing to beat hell.

"Don't panic, love. Spence probably wants a hotel reservation or something. Just like him to come down here off season. He wouldn't want to be here with everybody else."

"Who's Spencer Platt?" She had her nail file out, scraping, sharpening, bringing them to a point. If we sat long enough, she would remove her polish, paint it on again, and then go to work on her toes. That's the way they were, these girls. Nothing seemed to be private any more.

"He's an old friend. A very old friend."

"You said that once."

"Wouldn't interest you. Sells soap or something. Not your type at all. He even has his ties cut to measure. He's a cowboy who went East and just kept on going."

"You never introduce me to your friends. When are we going back to London?"

"Henri is my friend. He would be your friend, too, if you'd let him tell you about the weather."

"You know what I mean."

I probably did, and didn't want to think about it. When summer is over, and there's twenty-five years difference in your ages, there are lots of things you don't really want to think about. And then I had reached the point where I didn't think about much of anything any more, not about her, not about myself, certainly not about what had happened to the last thirty years. At least not when I could help it. And up to now, whenever it had started to eat at me, it was always easier to go and get lost in a Western—I wrote them, still read them by the dozens, went to all the movies—or once in a while in a bar, except for the really bad times, and then there was nothing for it but to get in the car and pull her in beside me—whoever she was at the moment—and cut out for the Midi, where with a good-sized stretch of the imagination, looking at the sun and stone and empty spaces of Provence, I could almost pretend that . . .

Anyway, this time I had gone beyond the point where sun-faded memories could do me any good. So I had put all of that away for a while, the nostalgia and the dread, and just lay in the sun—such a wonderfully illusory way of letting it all go, like listening to the rain or watching snowflakes fall or just the way a fire gives you that sense of something living except that before you really know it there's nothing left but ash—and now the sun was no longer warm enough to do the job.

As for Cynthia and me, maybe all we needed was a good fight. That way you either clear the air or kick it. But the truth was that I didn't care enough, and that was why I had run away in the first place, unless you want to say that there was still something I cared too much about, and yet could never have. So I had come full circle again, and we had run out of sun and laughs both, and that's the way it always crumbles, sooner or later. And if she wanted London she could have it, all by herself. Because I was finished.

But by this time they were calling me to the phone and she stuck out her tongue as I got up and it was the best joke we'd had all morning, so I let it drop.

"I'll get rid of him and then we'll take a walk," and I kissed the back of her neck before I left her. Henri didn't need any English to know what that meant.

The closet where they kept the phone was as smelly and close as a locker room, and his voice seemed to be coming to me through a coffee grinder. But it was Spence all right. Nobody else called me Ames.

"That you, Ames? I wasn't sure the telegram would reach you. Where the hell are you, anyway?"

I told him, wondering what he wanted.

"Ames, I've got something on my mind." All I could hear then was a kind of distant roar, as though I held a seashell to my ear. But the ball was in his court, so I waited, and then he said some more. By the time he took a breath the sweat was in my eyes and there was nothing left to breathe but what remained of yesterday's cigarettes.

"Wait a minute, Spence. You're too late. You've got the wrong man. I'm dressed in red corduroys and a sweat shirt somebody left on the beach. A turtle-necked sweat shirt, of course. Probably cashmere. I'm wearing a kind of Russian forage cap or whatever the hell they call it and I've got enough hair to play for the House of David. All I've got to my name besides that is an extra suit, a beat-up Jaguar, and one typewriter pretty well used. Diane, the kids, the Bucks—all that's gone, Spence. I've been on the beach all summer. Under fire. Pinned down. Out of ammunition."

It was the way we had always talked to each other, but it didn't sound right any more. To either one of us. I had never really thought of Spence as having problems, and he sure as hell wasn't thinking about mine.

"Cut the kidding, Ames. I've got to talk to somebody. I've got to talk to a friend. You know how it is, for God's sake. This isn't my kind of thing. I'm in it, and I don't know how it happened, and I don't know what to do about it. The telephone isn't exactly —look, I'm living in this little hotel in the Place Dauphine. You know? I've got the office, Ames. I can't come down there. I don't know how to handle it. Look, what I really want to ask you is if you'd come up. If there's any problem about money . . . No, I don't mean that. It's just that I've got to talk to somebody. It would mean a hell of a lot. All right, you've been through it. What I mean to say is that this isn't the way I've played the game."

I figured that if I could get him down here for a couple of days where he could watch Cynthia do her nails and read her fashion magazines, he would be back with Nancy in a flash. I didn't exactly see Spence folding his shirts, picking out matching socks and ties, packing his bags and walking out on everything he'd built for himself so deliberately over so many years. But that's exactly what he had done, if what he said was true, and now he was lonely, and when you're drunk who wants to talk to somebody who's stone sober.

"Is there anybody else?" That was the kind of question you didn't ordinarily put to Spence. Spencer Platt was a very cool and careful fellow. But all the same it was fun for once to lay it on the line that way.

"Let's wait until you get here. It's not the kind of thing I like to talk about on the telephone. Yes. Well, I don't know what to say. Yes, very much so, as a matter of fact."

He didn't go to publisher's parties, yet there were always secretaries, or other people's wives, or just a stray you met on an airplane somewhere. None of that seemed like Spencer Platt to me, but then something seems to happen when you cross the great divide. What the hell was I doing in a hill town just back of St. Tropez, crunching sandy pizzas on the beach and growing my hair like a beat gypsy, going around barefooted until my feet looked like hooves and eating my heart out for a town I'd never see again? I had my Cynthia—why shouldn't he have his? And then—well, there it was. Admit it. Spence was down, and I wanted to be there when it happened. That much I knew about myself—it was only really fun when somebody was hurting. I had been that way for a long time, maybe ever since they took it all away from me. Not that I liked it, but then that kind of bitterness is something you have to pass on, like an infectious disease. And now he had been gored, and there was blood in the ring, and he wanted somebody quick to get the bull away from him. He had sure as hell called the wrong man, the way it turned out. Or maybe he knew what he was doing all along.

"O.K.," I said to him. "I don't know when we'll get there, but we'll hit the road this evening. I said we—that's Cynthia. Phones don't bother me. She says I never introduce her to my friends. Besides, we're fresh out of Royal Bronze. Royal Bronze is colorless, hydrating, pro-sun jelly enriched with mink oil. I memorized that. Yeah. Well, make a reservation for two at the Hôtel de la Paix, Quai d'Anjou. They know me there. They don't know Cynthia, but then none of my friends know Cynthia."

Sure enough, she had started on her toes by the time I got back out to the terrace. I told Henri to give us the bill. She didn't look up.

"I don't want to go to London," I said.

"Is that what all the talk was about?" She had a corn on the outside of her little toe, and she massaged it as she spread the silver polish with tiny, precise movements of her brush.

"I'm willing to go to Paris, though."

"Who's in Paris?"

"Spencer Platt."

"Who's Spencer Platt?"

"An old, old friend. He sent me a telegram this morning, asking me to call."

"Does he like girls?" She looked up and gave me her smile for the photographers, the way she did for all the jokes that didn't rate a laugh.

"That's what we're going to Paris for—to find out."

A man ought always to leave a margin of carelessness somewhere in his life. As for me, I had grown more methodical as the years went by. I was the kind who thought of everything. I double-checked all arrangements, and tried every lock repeatedly, and turned switches on and off and on and off again, just to be sure. Finally it gets to be a way of life if you carry it far enough, a way of thinking of nothing that really matters. Just the way I left my forwarding address at the post office, automatically, though I had no intention of being gone for more than a few days. Otherwise, the letter would not have been sent on, and—who knows—with enough carelessness here and there, it might all have turned out quite differently. It's ironic to think so, anyway . . .

Anyway . . . the sky behind the mountains was the color of flamingo as we left the coast and headed north to Paris. We had spent the whole day getting ready—packing, making sandwiches, cleaning the little house, dragging it out as though we were both afraid of something which neither of us dared to name. Silently Cynthia packed all her things, right down to the last hairpin, and I let it go as though I didn't notice. I rolled up some laundry to leave with the woman who did our wash, but all of Cynthia's clothes appeared to be clean. In any case she obviously had no intention of leaving anything behind.

Then we took a last swim off the rocks, away from the beach, away from the places where there might be people we knew. It was like that all day long—saying goodbye in a way. Cynthia got tar on her foot and sat rubbing at it with sand while I swam methodically, deliberately, as though I were merely taking exercise. In the crevices of the rocks were empty bottles, rusty cans, limp tubes of suntan cream, dead stalks of some kind of seaweed —the debris of one more lost summer. As we walked back I tried to smell the herbs but the earth wasn't warm enough any more. I noticed that the backs of Cynthia's legs were creased and red where the stone had stamped its surface on her flesh.

Night came swiftly: pink, then purple, then black and soft with stars. Cynthia had made a pillow with a sweater, and slept against the door. Maybe she just didn't want to talk, which was fine by me. It wasn't the way I had planned to end the summer, but nothing about this summer had been the way that I had planned it. Not Cynthia or St. Tropez or the abortion that was performed by the chic, mustachioed doctor in Nice for a price that was much too high in every way . . . She was in bed for several days and I sat in the sun and drank Americanos and watched the French girls going by and thought that they would either know how to take care of themselves or would keep the child, one of the two. But that was probably being too hard on Cynthia. What was there to be romantic about? Nobody wanted the child. I had four already and was throwing in my hand, and Cynthia was too damned selfish and why not at barely twenty? It was just that the French girls seemed so tough and courageous in a way, ready to take their lumps if they had to without that tight-lipped resentment I had come to know so well. Maybe trying to make it with French men was what gave them that special sort of look—they had to be rugged to survive, and since they had never expected anything anyway . . . And then above all, not the letter to Emily, which by itself should have been enough to warn me that things had begun to fall apart but good. I couldn't remember it in detail, of course, and didn't want to after I had sobered up. Because if there was anything I was careful about it was Emily. I always wrote my letters to her in draft and then copied them again, each as precise and orderly and smiling as those photographic Christmas cards of families growing bigger, better, happier year by year. I sent them off like regular payments on a debt and her replies came back like so many stamped receipts, noting with satisfaction the regularity of my transmittals. And then all of a sudden, quite unexpectedly, it was as though I had decided to pay her off in one lump sum and be done with it, only to discover that all that I had been paying up to now was merely interest. . . .

Oh, that letter was full of what drunks like to call the honest truth, about a life so quietly desperate that it had become a substitute for suicide, and now suddenly from someplace (and from where if not from her example) had come fresh currents of courage which had borne me far out upon a soft and shining sea where everything was new and possible again. I suppose I spoke of Cynthia, and sun and wine, and the new book (she liked poetry herself, French poetry of all things, and the fact that my books were only simple Westerns was a source of comfort to her), and a new life, and my great gratitude for all that she had done and been for me, and finally how this landscape, so very different, yet had a way of making me look toward home again. Thinking back on it, it must have been that word home more than anything else. The rest she might possibly have lived with, but when I spoke of Grey Horse . . . We hadn't mentioned it more than once or twice in thirty years, and never, never as home.

I even gave her my address, and urged her to write and tell me what she thought, which in itself was enough to make me break out in a cold sweat, lying on the beach next day, soothing my aching head, recalling how Cynthia and I had made a kind of ritual of it, driving down to St. Tropez at midnight and posting it at the port in the midst of all those long brown legs and tangled hair. Remembering so much else, too, and wondering if she would show up with a gun. And I knew how wrong it was long before morning came, because I had the dreams that night, and woke up freezing, and by then it was too late . . . Except that weeks, then months went by without an answer until at last I felt no more than a slightly stupid sense of gratification, as though I had narrowly escaped death without really knowing how or why. And yet her silence was present in a way beyond all letters, and I knew that someday, sooner or later, in one way or another . . . So that, too, was part of what I put away, lying in the sun, waiting for that new life to come up and take me by the hand, until finally everyone was gone and it was October again. . . .

No, I don't think I would have gone to Paris for anyone else. Not just then, anyway. I had a battle of my own, and I was losing it, and I had made up my mind that when you were as far behind as I was, it was better to stand and fight because like the man said, maybe I could run but I couldn't hide. Not any more. And then Spencer Platt calls my name and I'm off like a shot because he's in some kind of trouble.

I'm not sure that Spence ever knew what trouble was. I doubt that anything had ever really hurt him; he had always seemed to me as being someone impervious to pain. There was something inevitable, almost luxurious, about the way his luck held out, and if I envied him for it, it was because I seemed to have been born a loser. But since when did I envy Spencer Platt? Maybe it was more jealousy than anything else. Goddammit, I liked him, always had. It was just—well, take baseball. I outhit him by thirty points or so, played all three varsity seasons at Harvard without an error, and even got an invitation to spring training from the Cards (I suppose Jack had a hand in that), but Spence was everybody's All-American. He came to that bleak New England boarding school like someone returning home after a long absence, all the way from a one-room schoolhouse in Wyoming, while I pried my way in like a burglar, and stayed there by stealth. He a curious sort of patrician—young Lochinvar out of the West; I a down-at-the-heel Okie out of a New England I could hardly claim. And yet strangely, unaccountably, we recognized each other almost at once. Some extra dimension of shadow that each saw in the other, I don't know. That's very vague, and yet it was this very vagueness in a way that drew us together—some blank spot in my past and in his future. Later, when the way things turned out brought me to think about it more, it seemed to me that Spencer Platt and I were two sides of the same American coin. I suppose that the Thayers, looked at from outside, at least, were people who had made it in a way that to a man like Spence seemed all-important. He probably thought of me as East Coast Establishment as they call it now, which meant the family name, the boarding school, Harvard, all those connections which he couldn't see but knew were there, a *situation acquise* which no temporary exile in Oklahoma could alter. His early friendship with me and then later on, the way he chose his acquaintances, his jobs, his wife— they were all stations on that railroad line which he had boarded in the shadows of the mountains of Wyoming with a tin suitcase in his hand, bound for God knows where.

But I saw the Thayers, and I was one of them in a way, as a peculiarly finished (no irony intended) product of several generations of successful adaptation and struggle, ending in a kind of victory which all too evidently bore within itself the seeds of a kind of defeat. For the problem was that the soil in which the Thayers had put down roots was the struggle itself. Not the land because they were not of the land, because they had bought it and sold it and worked it out but had not yet been claimed by it, perhaps because even now not enough time had passed, sheer generations born and dead so that they might dwell in the earth as well as on it. And not the cities, either, because in all that endless coming and going, the building up and tearing down, the continuous displacement so that everyone there seemed to come from someplace else, the cities changed their very speech and faces every generation or so. So that when the struggle was over, for them at least and at least as far as money was concerned, there was no earth to hold the roots, and family after family—or at least the Thayers—died of inanition.

As for Spence, I suppose I saw him mainly in terms of what I didn't have. Wyoming, that weather-roughened ranch family back in the shadows of the mountains, a place to go home to whenever he felt the need, the kind of Americans who had gone straight to the frontier in flight or in failure or in both and who had taken hold of the land with their fists and stayed with it until it was theirs and who then with all the instinct of migrating birds began the inevitable movement back to conquer that from which their forebears had humbly or in defiance set out into the wilderness. There was something of the proconsul in Spence, a kind of inherent, unthinking imperialism which defined itself in terms of a somewhat indirect form of conquest and rule as compared with the older habits of Empire, and yet which just as remorselessly moved back and laid claim first to the citadels of the East and then to the satrapies of Europe and beyond. He thought I had the keys to the Capitol, and that in part explained his friendship for me, just as my friendship for him had something very much to do with that Wyoming ranch that stood out as clear and hard in the spaces of my mind as the Grand Tetons thrust up against the flawless Western sky. And while I was becalmed in the backwaters of a past I could neither use nor flee, he manned successively the outposts of Empire—Caracas, Brussels, Paris— the frontier again.

Most of this occurred to me in a confused sort of way long afterwards, when I came to know Cecile and saw him playing a kind of Antony to her Cleopatra, but at the time, in those cruel and anxious days of boyhood, it seemed to me quite simply that both of us shared a common need to live very much in the present and leave the past alone. And when we changed it was the past that came to matter most to me, whereas for Spence life lay ever in the future, always out there somewhere like mountain peaks that he must climb.

At Harvard we both made the right clubs through our separate connections—mine were part of a past of sorts while his were already pointing to the future—and went on playing baseball and took out girls together now and then, but I was running with a different crowd by that time. We might have drifted apart—he was already planning his career, or campaigns, to use a better word—and yet he still embodied something important to me, something very Western or maybe American, I don't know, something he probably never even knew he had, something that it seemed to me that I would never have however much I tried in spite of what he thought, and even though about half the time I wasn't really sure whether I wanted it or not. He was innocent of complication, believed without effort in a world that was best described for him by the Headmaster's Chapel sermons, and dealt with life in a noble way all reminiscent of those grand simplifica-

tions of the Old West as we experienced it on Saturday after-
noons at the movies. But was it really innocent? I used to think
Americans were innocent. I'm not so sure any more. In fact . . .
But then that's part of the story, too, in a way.

He finally got too old—or too dignified—to play his favorite
games—baseball, basketball, touch football—but he clung to the
Westerns just as I did. Every time I came through Paris we
would go, Spence and I and his three boys, he for his reasons and
I for mine. I often wondered why he saw so many of the damned
things. I doubt if he missed more than half a dozen during all his
years in Paris. I asked him once, and he mumbled something about
how much he liked seeing the landscapes, looking at me in that
wide-eyed, grave, slightly smiling way of his as though he were
just a little bit ashamed. I never believed that, of course. I think
perhaps he saw himself that way—a man of the West. Hard on
himself, just to everyone else. Worn dignity, touched with a bit
of grey around the temples. He was top gun in that eternal battle
for decency and honor against an unworthy and backsliding
world. Or maybe he just liked watching the good guys win, as
though those celluloid victories somehow reassured him about the
eventual outcome of that battle between right and wrong in
which he so profoundly believed. But more than any of that, it
was a boy's world where there were neither men nor women—
just heroes and villains, good guys and bad, school teachers and
whores. A little faggish, if one can use the same word for heroes
and whores, the way they often are. I know because that's the
way I wrote them, because you start unraveling that ball of yarn
and you end up with Gary Cooper playing Don Quixote and
sending the whole thing up . . .

She lifted her head when I stopped the car and blinked like a
leopard in the green neon shadows.

"Where are we?"

"Just this side of Valence. We're low on gas and they start
closing about this time. I want to be sure we get there by
morning."

"We've got all night," and she tried the phony smile.

"You been sleeping?"

"Just pretending. I was watching you."

"How was it?"

"The way people look in those Westerns of yours. Very Real. Very True. A little hung up. *Angoisse* or constipation or something. It always sounds better in French."

"I was thinking."

"Like what?"

"Like get out the sandwiches and the coffee. Why didn't you ever learn to drive?"

"I had a cousin once who at the age of six refused to learn the alphabet. He said, if I learn that you'll want to teach me something else. *Voilà*."

We pulled off on the shoulder beneath trees stark and still in the moonlight, mutilated like the veterans of all the wars of France. She poured the coffee and I rested my head on the back of the seat, looking through the maimed stubs of limbs to where the stars shone like phosphorus in water.

"He was my best man." Nobody needed it, but I said it anyway.

"Who?"

"Spence. Spencer Platt."

"The friend." She tossed a sandwich in my lap and then leaned back against the door. "The man who's in trouble."

"No," I said. "Spence never had any trouble. He was captain of the Harvard baseball team our senior year, All-American in fact, and best man at my wedding. First lieutenant in the Marines, wounded at Iwo, Silver Star, God knows what-all. He got married right after the war—Nancy whatever her name was. From Philadelphia, very social, one of those blank oval faces and flat chests and nasal voices. Rich as hell and scared to death of showing it, or maybe not scared but just wanting to hold onto the privilege of being different by pretending to be like everybody else. A Puritan version of the Petit Trianon, playing at poverty. So she buys her clothes at rummage sales, drives an old car, that sort of thing. One of those very nice people whom you can neither like nor dislike because you never really know who they are. Liberal in politics, conservative in love. Spence is the same, just more consistent."

"Like liberal in love?"

"No. He admits he's conservative in politics, too. For Spence, Paris really is the Chase Bank and Neuilly and the St. James and Albany, the Jeu de Paume and Harry's and the Travellers. That's the way he thinks, and that's the way he lives. But I'm not putting him down. The difference between us is mainly that I've been pretending for years, and Spence has never had to pretend a day in his life. There was a time when I didn't have to fake it, either, but that was a long time ago. That's the difference."

"All very American, that. Squishy and psychological, like a clam. Here." She handed me the egg and I peeled it and put the shell in my cup.

"He's going through a crisis of belief."

"You should be on the radio Sunday mornings. So send him back to Junction City for a checkup. You've taught me to talk American, like those people in your books, but that doesn't mean I like it. Or clams, either. No pearls—just hepatitis."

"I mean it. Except that his crisis is that he's either got to stop where he is, emotionally speaking, or keep on moving onward and upward. I guess. It's Wyoming, by the way."

"Like where people are always saying things like 'Whoa thar, Ah'm the law in this man's town.' One of your great lines. Did anybody ever say things like that?"

"On Gary Cooper it sounds good."

"Not on Amory Thayer, though. Why do you write that trash?"

"Look, Cynthia. Once in a while something breaks through, a world you couldn't even dream of. I write that trash to keep that world where it is, black and white, as close to one dimension as possible, mono. It's a way of holding onto something that will never again be mine, and yet of keeping it the hell where it belongs so that it doesn't swallow me up. Not that that makes much sense, I grant you."

"You twist everything around so. You always talk about everything like it was dead."

"Maybe. Maybe that's it. He was my best man, you know. Now I think he wants me for a pallbearer. We may be going to a funeral, for all I know."

She yawned and put the sweater back in place and curled up against the door. "Just make sure you know whose funeral it is."

And in her cool and kooky way, she was right.

Just after midnight we bumped across the glistening cobblestones of Lyons. Sometimes Lyons is silver when the light is right, but that night it glittered cold and grey like something frozen in the gutter. Its houses stood along the Rhone like the walls of an abandoned prison, streets deserted, empty of movement save for yellow traffic lights that blinked on and off idiotically through the gloom. Then we hit the autoroute and there was nothing to do but steer along a road that wavered out ahead like a bar of light dissolving in the rain. I could feel the motor's movement in my body, circulating through me like a pulse, and the windshield wipers ticked off the kilometers against the steady slicing of the tires on sloshy pavement. It was like sitting in a bar in a strange town, and there in the soft, sleepy darkness I could almost believe that the emptiness might last. The way it is when you take a trip and you've left it all behind and you haven't yet reached whatever it is that's waiting. Between nothing and nothing there could be a kind of peace. And yet she was still there beside me, sleeping or watching, silent anyway, with her long hair scattered on her shoulder and her bare feet golden in the dark glow of the dash lights. I touched her foot and she shrank into herself like a worm, as though even in her sleep she was afraid of being hurt. Well, pain was better than nothing, except that in some strange way you couldn't remember it. It sank into the swamp along with everything else. Maybe weather was all you really remembered, the way things looked in certain kinds of light. Once in a while a face. The shapes of trees against the sky; the color of the sea. I had given her that, at least, even if I had nothing else to give.

Telling her about Spence was as close as I had ever come to telling her about those parts of my life that lay beyond her view. My war, spent in Washington and then in London, writing propaganda scripts that, for whatever effect they might have had on a distant enemy, sure as hell sapped my morale; my marriage to a rich and historically minded woman, something of a bluestocking in her way but, alas, not a bit of bohemia, by whom I was signed on in a moment of despair to play the patriarch in a do-it-yourself pageant of the England of the landed gentry before the First World War; my childhood, or at least the way I told it, like something out of a dime novel—how my father, he was a Boston Thayer, had gone West to school as a boy (something about tuberculosis, and sometimes the school was in New Mexico and sometimes in Colorado) and got the place in his blood and couldn't rest until he went back out there after he had finished law school and bought himself a ranch (Oklahoma this time; he always had this thing about Indians) and met and married my mother, who was Indian herself. Yes, that's where I get my dark hair from, and the way my skin always looks like I've got a tan. She had been a dancer; traveled all over the world, a very cultivated woman, my aunt always said; and my father met her someplace and they settled down on this ranch in Oklahoma. Just south of the Kansas line. A great big spread. Wonderful grazing land. Bluestem grass. Best there is for cattle, and that's where she came from. My father's sister lived with us then. Aunt Emily. Never married, Aunt Emily. Settled down there and raised me after the fire—she was a mother to me. We were in town that night—she used to take me into the library a couple of times a week—and while we were gone the ranch house caught on fire, and by the time dad got back to the house from whatever part of the range he was on he could hear my mother screaming inside because she was trapped or maybe just afraid to make a run for it, so he went in there after her and neither one of them ever came out. That's the way it happened. Aunt Emily? She's still there. Does some kind of social work. Well, it's a long way to go back; you know how it is. Better part of two days and two nights on the train. My grandmother lives in Boston . . .

That way I really didn't have to talk about it, at least in the beginning when the other boys asked me, and then in some way or other, little by little, I gradually came to believe it myself, or almost, because I wanted to, or because there was nobody around to call me on it, or something. I never really asked myself why. . . .

Cynthia knew only what had flowered on that compost heap: Hackberry Bucks. An eighteenth-century village not far from London, rose brick and apple trees, ponies, pigeons, poodles, children in clamorous profusion. Sheep were scattered across our acres, and we made our own jelly from the apples that lay gently rotting on fields of grass clipped close as lawn by our many beasts. Outdoors the rain was steady and the clay soil held it so that we were always damp; inside eyes watered in the smoke, but it was peat. Central heating was expensive, and we thought of ourselves as subsistence landowners, showing a balky peasantry that it could be done. I wore laced boots and knickers and a grouse shooter's cap, and I carried a stick with a silver and leather handle which folded out into a kind of seat. The children had a tutor, and pony carts, and we rode to the hounds in the fall. In the winter Diane organized charities and ran a mobile lending library and I sat in the beamed attic and typed my sagas, which showed only a slightly better profit than the poultry until I finally sold one to Hollywood. But that side of my life—the literary side as Diane liked to call it, with either a smile or a sneer, depending on the listener—was confined to distant places like London and the States. At the Bucks it was smoky peat and tweed and a bit of cider, and friends down for the weekend. I had smuggled Cynthia in on some pretext or other and she in the languid and wistful and mainly silent way that she affected among the kind of people one was likely to find at the Bucks just adored it, or said she did. Long walks beneath a leaky sky, trees like inkblots against low clouds, birds strange and sudden as the ghostly souls of the ever-present dead. She quoted Wordsworth, and I had her in the attic amidst the manuscripts, and after dinner there was Elizabethan music, madrigals and folk songs, recorders and such. I suppose she knew what I thought of it. There are an awful lot of things you never have to tell certain kinds of women, and even when they seem to be listening they're mainly faking.

But what Cynthia made of me in all that I never really knew. A dark, strangely Latin face anglicized by a soft tweed cap and a curved pipe. Aristocratic manners suitably rude coupled with an American accent suitably democratic. Property and people, good wines and expensive clothes, a slightly slovenly and vaguely romantic kind of wealth from which I maintained a certain distance because, I suppose, it wasn't really mine, and finally, success of sorts in a world to which she aspired even if my books were not reviewed in the little magazines. What's more, I knew who Wordsworth was, and could produce from memory similar bucolic sentiments in French and Italian, if not in Latin. That's what she had to go on, at least until that summer in the sun. . . .

And after all, perhaps some of the pleasure of being with Spence again was that he could give me back a world that he and I alone knew. Before the Bucks, before Diane, a long time before Cynthia. When he was Captain of the Baseball Team and President of the School and My Best Friend, and there was real snow every winter and true green grass in the spring and summers were blue and hot the way summers ought to be, and then in the fall when we all came back from those fitful months of adolescent idleness (I spent them alone on a farm in New Hampshire amidst dog-eared Bibles and yellowing whale bones and cracked and peeling family portraits and one old Irish woman who called me Amy, just like a girl) and the football team would clatter out to practice in a golden drift of leaves . . . When I was searching for something new and running from something old, ashamed of my lies about a father who was dead and a mother who had vanished, and of the letters from Jack, once a week, with his funny writing on the envelopes, and of the fact that there was no place for me to go of my very own at Thanksgiving and Christmas and Easter, and then mainly just my lack of anyplace to call home, anyone to call family any more . . .

If he needed me for a friend, I didn't know it until much later. All I knew then was that I needed him the way I needed someplace to come from the way all the others had. Even if he did call me Ames, and laughed when he got elected captain instead of me, and disappeared in the wrestling room with the blind date I had brought to the senior prom. He was my Westerner, patrician and plainsman and mountain man, too, and some kind of home out there was what I wanted so terribly after too much pain too young, too soon, too much taken away when I had asked for so very little, too many days and nights and weeks and months alone because it was all so far away and there was no road back. He was the one who called me Ames. He named me, and he made me believe for a while that I, too, had someplace to go. . . .

She woke at dawn and lit a cigarette and sat there with her legs curled up beneath her, watching the darkness disappear among the trees. She tried the radio, then switched it off, and stubbed the half-smoked cigarette in the tray.

"You're awfully quiet," she said.

"I'm half-asleep."

"Well, what's the rush, anyway. You act like you just can't wait to get back."

"Back where?"

"Wherever you're going."

"We are going to Paris, to a little hotel on the Quai d'Anjou. Trees that reach to the tops of the highest windows, tiny houseboats in the river, fishermen in canvas coats and rubber shoes, crumbly seventeenth-century architecture."

"Does it have a bath?"

"*Tout confort.*"

"You didn't answer my question."

"You order it, like breakfast."

She examined her nails, then rummaged in her pocketbook for the file. "Is that where you stay with Diane?"

"No."

"You are a bastard, you know."

"With Diane I stay at the St. James and Albany. Convenient for shopping. A charming garden handy to the bar. English spoken. Parking *assuré*. You wouldn't like it."

She shook her head and swung her hair behind her shoulders. "Always thinking of me, aren't you. You're very sweet."

Then she poured the rest of the coffee and sipped it cold, sitting very straight the rest of the way as though she were making up her mind about something of immense importance. Thinking with Cynthia was as physical as making love; whenever her mind worked her body became rigid and apprehensive as though she were listening intently for barely audible voices.

And whatever it was that she was thinking, she kept it to herself all the way into Paris, until at last I switched off the motor and she got out of the car, stretching herself all over like a cat. Then she leaned far over the stone parapet to stare down at the river while I arranged for the room and unloaded the bags and ordered coffee and croissants and two baths. And when I came up beside her she turned her face into my shoulder and I lifted her chin and kissed her.

"It is nice," she said. Her mascara was smudged around the edges of her eyes, and I gave her my handkerchief. "I don't know about the St. James and Albany, but this is nice."

"I told you they reached right to the tops of the windows." I put my arm around her shoulders and she put hers around my waist, and we leaned against each other, smiling a little. "Come on. I want to show you my domain."

The sky had cleared, and along the quais the buildings were rose and gold in the early silence. They were like children's drawings of apartment houses, crooked and crowded and piled one against the other, jumbled all together like construction blocks. We crossed the footbridge to the Île de la Cité, where Notre Dame lay beached on the island like the skeleton of some ancient whale, an intricate arrangement of old bones grey in blue light. As we watched, a whirl of pigeons swung suddenly upward across the arching buttresses and we held our breath and then laughed, looking at each other again as though everything were new in the midst of so much that was so old.

We walked back toward the river without speaking, and then she ran ahead of me and waited on the bridge.

"Back at our hotel," she said when I caught up with her, "there were fishermen and old boats. Blue and yellow, mostly."

I nodded, and took her hand. "This is the loveliest village in the world, one small island like some ocean-going liner moored in the middle of the Seine. We might even belong here some day, if we stayed around long enough. People do sometimes, you know. And behind all that stone are cobbled courtyards and precise little gardens and a most extraordinary silence just for birds."

"I want to order a bath," and then she brushed her lips against my chin, and in the jeweled light of that Paris morning, we walked back along the shadowed streets and climbed the stairs, just as though we were really lovers, and Paris was ours. . . .

I left her asleep in a rumpled bed full of croissant crumbs and newspapers and walked up the Quai to the cafe at the bridge. I had to argue my way through Spence's secretary, and when I finally got him he came through cool and careful.

"Ames. Good to hear you, old man. How's it going?" Just as though we saw each other every day.

"Not bad for somebody who's been on the road all night. Can you talk or what?"

"Look, this is a hell of a day for me. I'm tied up at lunch, and have appointments right through the end of the afternoon."

"You're calling the shots. We left last night and pulled in a couple of hours ago. I'm whipped. Could use some sleep."

"What about dinner? Just the two of us."

"I've got a girl with me. She wouldn't bother us any. She wants to meet my friends. That kind of thing."

"I'd rather not, Ames. Another time if you don't mind."

So he had his own problems, and he wasn't particularly worried about mine. He might have said he was sorry, but then Spence was, as they say, all business.

"Suppose we meet at Harry's, about eight. Without the girl."

"Well, if that's the way it has to be, O.K. She won't like it, but . . . Everything all right?" The way he was talking I figured his secretary had her ear out, but then I had busted my hump getting here and what difference did it make anyway. Unless it was his secretary. I hadn't thought of that.

"Fine."

I waited him out to make him say some more, and then he said it.

"What's the girl's name? I'll send around some flowers."

You son of a bitch, was what I had in mind, but I didn't say it.

"Forget it," I told him. "Flowers always make her think of funerals." Maybe he was in trouble, but he hadn't lost his cool. "I'll see you at Harry's at eight."

There was sunlight in the room when I got back, and Cynthia was sitting up in bed with all of her equipment spread out in her lap. Bottles, brushes, that evil-looking file. The place smelled like a corridor in a hospital.

"The sun woke me up, I guess. So I leaned out the window to look at those marvelous trees again and throw some crumbs to the pigeons. They're all purple and shiny with tiny pink feet and little round red eyes. They walk pigeon-toed, too, really, and run around in circles with their tails in a fan."

"They have draped with their droppings our generals and our poets. Pigeon shit descends upon our heroes like a benediction."

"Don't be so nasty. We're in Paris and the sun is shining and nobody knows our address." She held out her arms. "Come sit over here and I'll do your nails."

"Spencer Platt knows our address. He asked about you."

"Already?"

"I just spoke to him on the phone."

"And?"

"He's fine. Or says he is, anyway. We're having dinner together tonight."

"That's cozy. Our first night here and you have to bring somebody along."

"You don't have to come. He wants to see me alone. That's what we came for, remember? He's in some kind of trouble. He wants to talk to me about it."

She stared at me for a moment with an intensity she reserved for people she didn't like. Mainly other women. Then she went back to work on her nails, very slowly, very deliberately.

"Amory, you are the worst liar in the business. He wants to talk to you about Diane. Why don't you tell me the truth?"

From where I sat I could see myself in the mirror of the armoire. Pipe, shaggy hair that curled around my ears, wrinkled corduroys, desert boots. A green-and-red foulard tucked into an old blue work shirt. A tan that seemed incongruous in the Paris light, and uneven teeth that showed tobacco stain when I tried to smile at her. What I could see in the mirror was bad enough, without going any deeper.

"I'm telling you the truth. I told him I would bring you along. He made it plain that he wanted to talk to me alone. What could I say?"

"It's because you treat me like a mistress or something. You wouldn't be seeing him alone if she were here."

"Maybe you're right. You used to like it when I treated you like a mistress. Now you want to be treated like a wife. You can't have it both ways, Cynthia. He's an old friend. It has nothing to do with Diane."

"Well, it certainly has nothing to do with me. Why all the secrets? What is it you're hiding? Why don't you come right out and say it?"

I looked at her then, at the long blond hair that was dark at the roots, at the blue eyes with the green lids, at the square jaw with pale fuzz along the bone, at the hard little teeth and the hard little breasts and the hands that preened themselves like bantam roosters.

"All right, Cynthia. It's a love affair. Just a couple of middle-aged fags, Spence and me. It all started in boarding school, see. You know how it is in boarding school. They put saltpeter in the mashed potatoes but everybody's horny just the same and there aren't any girls around and one thing leads to another. Some flog the dog too much and get kind of black around the eyes; others discover the glory that was Greece You can read about it in any number of French novels."

"First you lie to me and then you try to get out of it by talking dirty. Life for you is just one big sick joke. I think I'll brush my teeth, if you don't mind."

She may have had a point in her description of my life, but I was tired of her nagging, her narcissism, her nails, her fashion magazines. Tired of the tortuous intricacies that made her a woman, of the endless complications which are so charming when they're new. She was like a bird building a nest that would never be finished, at least not while I was around. Hackberry Bucks was dull as fog, but the sunny chic of St. Tropez could be just as stifling. And anyway, I had forgotten both of them. I was remembering New England, that first fall, the white and black frame houses in a blaze of trees, a distant haze of mountains, the wind from the sea, when I was beginning to understand that I would have to start all over again from scratch . . .

"O.K., so it wasn't funny. I'm tired. You've been on my back. We're low on money, and I've got a deadline. Take it easy. Go to a movie or something. All he probably wants is the address of our abortionist. That's the kind of thing he would think of me for."

"Why not? That's the kind of thing you know about. What I don't like is that you always seem so—oh, I don't know, so cynical, so bitter. The way you run everything and everybody down. Nothing seems to make any difference to you. I doubt if you care any more about Spencer Platt than you do about me. What's the matter, Amory? You want to go back home? Is that what it is?"

I got up and went to the window and looked out at nothing. There were some things she had no right to talk about, even if she didn't know what she was saying.

He looked as though he had stepped out of the Ritz and asked the taxi driver for Sank Roo Doe Noo. Harry's was noisy, crowded with an unlikely mixture of the teen-age sports-car set wearing Edwardian jackets and sideburns and strings of beads and flapper dresses and who just adored what they had heard about the Twenties, and grey-suited, grey-haired traveling types who stood in ranks along the bar, waiting with a kind of sodden hopelessness for a mademoiselle. At the tables in the back amidst dusty pennants and college coats of arms and clippings about Hemingway and the others sat sad-faced froggies in Greek beards and pipes and corduroy suits, accompanied by arrogant, long-haired girls who smoked in silence. A pair of boxing gloves hung above the bar. It was said that they had belonged to Primo Carnera; I doubt if anybody was certain any more, or if anybody cared. Most of the people there had the look of being on hand in case something happened, like a Manifesto or a Famous Face, but they had come too late. The hustling, intellectual and otherwise, had moved to other parts of town.

Yet Harry's was a part of Spence's world, however faded the place might seem to me. I could see that by the way he shook the barman's hand before coming on back to the corner where I sat. He looked right at home among the pennants and the yellowed photographs, very tall and easy in his movements, still young, still handsome in an uneven kind of way, moving through the crowd like DiMaggio, the way he had covered center field. His nose had been broken by a thrown ball, and his dark hair was clipped close to his head and full of grey, particularly along his forehead, which was square and high and smooth as though he never frowned. His eyes were grey or blue, not really one or the other, in a face that was grave, not lined but poised as though he were always sizing you up again no matter how well he knew you, and then suddenly his smile over chipped and irregular but very white teeth was of such contrast that it seemed to draw light down upon him from some invisible source. He was hatless and his topcoat was gabardine, elegant with age the way his clothes always seemed to be, as though he never wore anything either new or old. I remember his shirt—soft, with dark blue stripes on white—and a gold collar pin, and the way he grasped my arm as he shook my hand. I remember, too, that he stood there for a moment before he spoke, just before he smiled, looking at me in a way that was almost puzzled, as though he had not yet made up his mind about just how much he could tell me; and then he was calling my name, laughing a little, thanking me for having come.

"This place all right? Its noisy, but the beer is good, and they serve real hot dogs."

I had a half a dozen restaurants in mind, but what was the point. He wouldn't notice whether the cooking was Chinese or Camargue. I could tell that much from his face. And when you're in love, new and all over again, who needs it anyway.

"Sure. Take off your coat and sit down. How are you, Spence?"

And that was how Cecile came into my life, over beer and hot dogs in Harry's New York Bar.

"What about Nancy?" I asked him, after we had talked for a while. "How's she holding up?"

"It's hard to tell." He looked at me with surprise, as though I were a panhandler who had asked him for a quarter. "I don't honestly know. We haven't discussed it much. She's letting me work it out."

"Why did you marry her in the first place, Spence? If you don't mind my asking."

He was still surprised, but looking through me now as though I were merely an open door into his past. "She was at Bryn Mawr. They had this wonderful home in Philadelphia. I remember the hedges, miles of hedges, it seemed like. Dark green, very precisely trimmed, like fencing around a lawn where the sprinklers were set into the ground. Everything was neat—tremendous order. No loose edges anywhere. She was like that. She always knew exactly what she was doing all the time. A world where everything fitted together so perfectly that you couldn't even see how it was made. Not like Wyoming, Ames. Out there you can still see the trace of the ax on everything. Nothing old but the land, and all of it kind of boom or bust, the way it is with cattle. Nancy was where I was headed ever since I went East. Like she was part of the schools I went to, and a way of life that just kind of happened before I really knew what was going on. Nancy is part of something I wanted then. Looking back on it, the main feeling I have is that we were awfully young. To tell you the truth, Ames, I don't really know."

I lit my pipe and waited, but if there was more he wasn't telling. Or maybe he just couldn't say it, because he had no phrases for it. "And now you fall in love for the first time and you don't know what to do. You want to know what the choices are? I'll name them for you. Number one: separate bedrooms—"

He shook his head impatiently. "Don't put it to me like some goddam marriage counselor. I'm not asking you for that. I told you—there's still so much about Cecile I don't understand, so much that makes me afraid. All those ghosts from the past, and yet at the same time that's what draws me to her. It's just that too much of our lives—hers and mine—seems to be in the past, buried, over with, the way it is when two thirds of your life is gone. I can't believe she loves me—I'm just the guy who can turn off those three-o'clock-in-the-morning phone calls. With one kiss she wakes me up from the sleep of the dead and now I'm supposed to go out and slay dragons and do battle with rivals and stand guard over a treasure that time has already stolen. I'm too old for it, Ames. It happened to me too late."

I was beginning to get a line on him now. All he wanted was everything, to wipe out her past like it was history in chalk on a blackboard, and probably pretend that even her children were his. Besides keeping his own, and Nancy for a governess or something, and then expecting to see in his friends' eyes a tearful, sympathetic appreciation of his extraordinary nobility.

"You've missed the point. What matters most is the chance she's giving you to love somebody for once in your life. But you haven't really told me about her yet—how it happened, who she really is."

He nodded, and then looked around at faces I'm sure he didn't see, and then began, bemused, his eyes a little ironic as though he were surprised himself at the story that he told me. And while he talked he smoked, and made rings on the table with his beer mug, and every so often reached up and felt the gold collar pin at his throat. I sat and watched him as though we were strangers who had met in a train station and were taking a friendly drink together before going on our separate ways. Because it seemed to me that I no longer knew him. Not really. Oh, it was all the same—the tailored flannel suit, the luminous smile, the nose a little too wide and flat at the bridge, dark hair prematurely grey. And yet it was like returning to a house that one has known only to find that someone new is living there. For in all that he said about Cecile there was a kind of total absorption, a loving precision as though the smallest details which he recounted were bathed in a light so total that there could be no shadow. I knew the feeling. I had a story that I could tell in that same way. But it was not of this time, or this place, and maybe that was what made the difference.

Of course it was exaggerated—much too beautiful to be real—and he had a way of narrowing his eyes in wonder at it all, as though it had never happened to anyone else before. I was amazed at how often he used the very word—beautiful. As though he had just discovered what it meant. He was in love, all right, in one fashion or another. The question was whether he loved her or the situation in which he found himself.

"I had gone into this bookstore. Pure chance. It was a Saturday afternoon and I had the boys with me. The Musée de Cluny. Armor and stuff. We nearly always go out like that on the weekend, see a Western, maybe, or there's that wonderful little store in Montmartre where they have any number of electric trains and you can run them yourself, switching, changing directions, anything you want. Anyway, when we were through we walked over toward St. Germain des Prés. We could get our bus there, and the kids needed to stretch their legs after standing around the museum all afternoon. I wanted to pick up some of those post cards of paintings, just for a change. I send a lot of cards, never seem to have time any more for a decent letter. So we went in and looked around a little and I picked out twenty-five or so. I was waiting for someone to help me when she came up. I gave her the cards and asked her how much they were and we smiled at each other. That was the way it started. Smiling at each other for no particular reason in a bookstore that I might have passed a thousand times without ever setting foot in the place."

As for who she was, that, too, came through in a general sort of way. A woman no longer young but not yet middle-aged, in what can be the best years if the bones are right. Children. Earning her own living. Courageous but light-hearted about it, and somewhat ironic about her light-heartedness, as though it had cost her something. A peculiar combination of poverty and elegance that could come from a lot of things but which was probably the result of having lost a lot and then having found and held onto those few things—people, books, a piece of furniture or two— which were essential to her.

To hear him tell it, she was extraordinarily beautiful. He spoke of Botticelli—maybe they went to museums together, the kind of thing you start to do again when you fall in love—though I couldn't be sure just what he meant by that. Perhaps the face of Spring in Botticelli's painting, so mysteriously alive and yet with autumn already in her eyes. Marvelously refined, sophisticated in all the best ways, and yet capable of a kind of earthy directness that would make a man like Spence uncomfortable. The kind of woman who can never pass a mirror or anything else that might reflect the smallest portion of her face without stopping for at least a moment, and yet frighteningly generous as though she had lost so much already in her life that she was ready to give the rest away. He was afraid of her in the beginning, and yet he couldn't forget her either, and there was no way to change that just by being afraid.

"About a week later I called her, half hoping she wouldn't be there. We had had a drink together, and then lunch one day when I was in that part of town, and I was stalling, hoping that one of us could find a reason to say no and then it would just disappear silently into the past, one of those bitter-sweet memories of what might have been. But she said she owed me a lunch and invited me home. She wanted me to see the leaves in the chestnut trees behind Notre Dame before winter set in. Well, O.K., I had never even thought about the chestnut trees behind Notre Dame, winter or summer. So the next day there I am, looking out of her windows not only at the chestnut trees but at the Seine and the back of Notre Dame and right up the left bank to the Pantheon and all the way over to St. Sulpice, all kind of silvery-grey and smoky and looking more like a scale model than anything else. Fantastic. That sudden sense of freedom, of pleasure, and yet, I admit it, it bothered me the way her beauty did. You know how it is—those

Massachusetts graveyards are probably full of preachers named
Thayer and even in Wyoming . . .

"Well, the apartment was unheated, and we stood around the
fireplace and she grilled a steak with some kind of contraption she
had, burning her fingers in the process because she was the
world's most improbable cook and seemed to go about things the
hardest way possible. But we ate avocados and crusty charcoal
steaks—nothing ever tasted better, I can tell you—and looked out
at what seemed half the world and then I don't know, we just sat
and talked about what had happened to us through the years.
Ames, I had a hard time to keep from crying. I know it sounds
stupid, but it was that way. I'm telling you. The place was so
damned beautiful, so elegant and yet so poor at the same time. I
don't mean that I felt bad because she was poor and the place was
bare and all. I loved it that way. I really did. There was something
so fierce about it, goddammit, so hard and courageous and noble
and undefeated. And at the same time so gracious and lovely.
Those were the words that came to my mind in that room that
was cold and spartan and yet rich in the way some kinds of music
can be. And I just wanted to put my head in her lap and cry, like
I had finally come back home or something. Does that make any
sense to you? Look, she only had three or four chairs, but they
were very old, fine chairs, even I could tell that, plus the table
where we ate and a couch that was big enough to be a bed. I
couldn't tell how many other rooms there were, but the place
seemed small. Once I went back to the bathroom and there was a
hose, a green garden hose, running from the kitchen sink to the
tub. I glanced in the kitchen as I went by—a three-burner hot-
plate and a refrigerator that looked like something you'd give a
kid for Christmas. Even the dishes, Ames—cracked, chipped,
broken, but the kind that would have been in the family a long,
long time. Everything about her was that way—she seemed not to
notice, or maybe just not to care. And yet there were flowers on
the mantel, flowers that she had bought herself that morning and
very carefully arranged. No, it was generosity, Ames, a way of
creating beauty from flawed and broken things. She was like that
herself. Flawed, certainly; broken, too, in a way. Maybe she had

cared once about perfection and then figured the price was too
high. Maybe she had reached the point where she couldn't afford
it and so forgot about it. I don't know. What I do know is that so
much of the beauty of it all, of Cecile and the way she lived, lay
in that peculiar combination of careless poverty and casual ex-
travagance. Cecile was the kind of person who would always be
rich, no matter how little she had in her bank account."

That wasn't exactly the way he said it, of course. I write it
down that way because that's what I mainly remember, recollections of what he said inevitably mingled with other memories of
my own, how he came on all at once, in a rush, with so many
different things to tell me that he hardly knew where he was
going, talking to me in a language which was as new to him as the
feelings he described. And then I suppose that I was the only
person to whom he had talked about her. There was something
quite unconditional in the way he spoke that made it seem that he,
too, were hearing it for the first time, and marveling in his turn at
the strangeness of it all. And not the least of what was strange in
the telling was that he spoke of her so often in the past tense, as
though it were already over, just something to dream about. In
another way, of course, it wasn't strange at all. Two people meet
casually, fall in love, and live unhappily ever after. The difference
was, as Spence said, that this wasn't his type of thing. But then
again, whether he knew it or not, maybe it was hers.

"You haven't said anything about the husband." The way he
had described her, there had to be a man in the story somewhere.
Or men, most likely. Besides, he had mentioned children. He
rolled with the punch, but I could tell that it hurt him. With me
it wouldn't have mattered, but I figured Spence for the kind of
man who would be retroactively jealous. As a lover, he was probably like some power-drunk pharaoh, chiseling away the hieroglyphs of those who had ruled before him, while I had long ago
become a willing and wily Odysseus, always willing to negotiate
as long as I made it home.

"Cecile is a widow. Her husband was killed in Indochina, just before Dienbienphu happened. He was St. Cyr, traditional military family, that sort of thing. Almost ten years ago. Her son was just at the age to start school—the daughter was a little younger. Cecile was so young then—I've seen pictures of her. I mean that she was young in the sense of being very intelligent and yet having almost no experience of life. Innocent, maybe, rather than young, although in the long run that may be a choice that one makes. I just don't know any more. In a way she's everything that the very word Paris can evoke for people like you and me, and at the same time there's something of the country about her. Not provincial, of course, not at all, but with a kind of unshakable honesty, a way of being natural that women lose in a city like this.

"She grew up in Burgundy, an aristocratic family living on the land, and didn't come to Paris at all until after the war. She was exceptionally beautiful—I know I've already said it, but there's no other way to understand it. You know how they are, Ames. Paris is a place where people look at each other endlessly. *Elle est belle, elle est laide*, right away, about everybody. There always seems to me a kind of frivolity in an attitude so purely visual, almost as though the monarchy and particularly its manners, far from being destroyed, had actually swallowed up the whole society. And maybe its a good thing, too, in a way; Americans are so damned ashamed of really taking a good look. Anyway, she was known for her beauty, and that's saying a lot in a town as critical as this one. I say this so that you can understand how it was for her when her husband died. Alone, two children, no money to speak of, celebrated in her way—that's a story in itself."

"She couldn't have been alone for very long. Not the way you describe her." This was the exposed nerve, all right, and I knew it. That is, if you were like Spence, who had always been very old-fashioned where the honor of women was concerned. With the kind of women I knew, I was usually inclined to take the cash and let the credit go.

"The family was well off, of course. But there was no question of giving her money. They were people of a much older generation, and there was so much they knew nothing about. Jobs.

What things cost. Renting apartments. Raising children when you had to work and had no governess. Just the things we live with every day. They expected her to remarry as soon as possible, and held it against her when she didn't. Someone of her own class, naturally. A widower with money, let's say. Money was important, although religion, politics, previous marital status, family . . . it all goes together."

"And so she bucked the system. Threw away the rule book. Slept with men when she wanted to. Earned her own living, lived her own life."

He stared at me for a moment, hard, rubbed his hand against his chin and then continued.

"The bookstore was later on, after real estate and modeling and public relations and God knows what-all. And then she was alone, except for the children, and she was never meant to live alone."

"So men came and went. Why not? What difference does it make?"

There was something dogged about the way he stayed with it, not wanting to call a spade a spade and yet coming on almost grimly, for all the world like it was the Alamo or Iwo Jima all over again. My God, we weren't back in Chapel. This was Paris and she was French and on the whole French girls play it straight and are ready to win one day and lose the next if there's a little tenderness thrown in. But there was this code of his—Teddy Roosevelt and Gary Cooper and Albert Payson Terhune in equal portions.

"She was a special kind of woman, and she was alone. That was the main thing. It wasn't just being bohemian or on the make. She's not wild, don't get the wrong idea. Look, beautiful women don't have it all that easy. What it means more than anything else is endless pressure, moths around the flame, somebody after you all the time. Being stopped in the street, followed home, called in the middle of the night and when you answer there's either just somebody breathing at the other end or a sick son of a bitch talking dirty or some hysterical woman saying you're stealing her husband because she saw you talking to him at a party and the bastard hasn't slept with her in years, anyway. And parties where there's always someone who wants to take you home and won't let you say no. Gossip and bitchiness because a beautiful woman alone sets off everybody's early-warning system. A flood of casual invitations, and then on Christmas, New Year's, the important days, nothing because everyone is sure you're somewhere else and anyway, they're at home. O.K., like you say, there were men in her life. She was lonely, and they were always around."

"Well, you like what she is, and what she is is the result of everything that's happened. All of it—good, bad, indifferent. You've got to take the past *en bloc*—there's no way of picking and choosing."

"No, Ames, it's not just the other men. I'm jealous, O.K., that's true. I worship her, for God's sake, what do you expect. But what did you call it? Yes, the past, *en bloc*. That's her life, Ames; her husband, her lovers if that's what they were, her children, her family, so goddam much history that I had no part in. I'm somebody she can tell her stories to. That's her life. I've got to have something of my own. A life that's mine. Those boys— what the hell else have I got?"

"You're selling yourself short. You can make her forget all that."

"No. No, you're wrong there. It might have been that way if I had met her seven or eight years ago. Just after her husband died. I would have had a chance."

"A chance at what?" I was beginning to get tired of it by now because he was playing it too damned cagey. Every time I played a king, he had an ace. And saying all the time what a lousy hand he had.

"A chance that she could love me, could see me as something other than mere security for herself and her children. She can't love me that way, Ames; not the way I feel about her. Too much has happened."

"Come on, Spence. You should never believe anything you hear about a beautiful woman. About a plain woman, maybe. But beauty launches lies the way Helen launched a thousand ships."

He wasn't listening. He was telling me why it was impossible, in spite of love, in spite of everything. He was trying to convince himself, and I was supposed to listen and agree. So that was why he had wanted me to come—just to get him off the hook in a way that wouldn't make him sick when he looked in the mirror again after it was all over. But judging by what I had heard so far, I wasn't ready to play.

"Ames, you keep trying to turn it into a simple question of jealousy. The point of it is that the balance of her life lies somewhere else, and I'm not there. Look, too much has happened, goddammit. Tragedy wherever you turn. Most of her family dead—I don't know how many uncles and cousins, not to speak of immediate family, killed in all the wars. Kids at the time, most of them, or much too old to be out in the rain and the wind all night. Her husband was booby-trapped all to hell and gone in Indochina; her younger brother got his in Algeria. Most of the money down the drain because they hung on where the flag was flying, because they had built something and they thought they belonged there and they just couldn't believe it was over. They could have sold out, scuttled—a lot of others did—but they were proud and foolish and they stayed until it was too late and then they never knew what hit them. No, wait a minute, just a minute, O.K., I don't claim to know much about politics, but let me tell you just one story. Not about that, exactly, but just to give you an idea of what I mean when I say that too much has happened."

I knew his political views, if you could call them that. He had sold his soap in Venezuela before he came to Paris, during the gaudy days of Pérez Jiménez, and he had greatly admired the new highways, the building boom, the surface stability which made it possible to earn an honest Yankee dollar in peace. He was sure he knew his Latin people, too. According to Spence, what they needed was a man on horseback who could use all the big words and make them sound like they meant something. Franco, De Gaulle, Mussolini, Jiménez—for Spence they were all out of the same stable and to him they looked like winners. And whatever he may have thought, his story was about politics insofar as politics is also the way it is for people who have to go on living in a place after the big battles are over and the generals and the journalists have come and gone.

But it was about something else, too, and the more he talked, the less I wanted to listen. I suppose he could see that. I shook my head and bit my pipe and turned sideways in my chair as though I were getting ready to leave any minute. Yet I kept on listening, knowing how much it revealed about his desire for tradition and permanence and nobility, all of those things he felt he needed now that he had built himself a base, and how much it reminded me of memories that had no place in the world I inhabited or in that other world that in some fatal way would never let me go.

"Her father's family lived in Burgundy—wine and a lot of other things. They had this family place, the Château d'Ardières, big, with all sorts of outbuildings and formal gardens, apple trees like Jewish candelabra and the little ones they clip like poodles' tails. Everywhere you looked, all over the place, were vines. There was this straight road up to the château between two lines of trees, and then the château itself with the gardens on the right as you faced it and buildings for the servants on the left and a big cobbled court in the front. There had been additions and the proportions had been thrown off some, but still there was this mass of stone like weathered ivory in the midst of a wonderful great stillness, and the rolling country all around absolutely covered with vineyards. Unbelievable. I know because we drove down there one weekend. It rained the whole time, and it was like we were seeing the place through silk curtains, those miles of vineyards, the château, the blurred lines of trees. There was a cafe in the village—we ate downstairs and there were a half a dozen rooms above. Beaujolais, *saucissons*, getting our shoes muddy in the rain, talking for hours about Burgundy and Wyoming. I knew then that I was in love with her in a way so absolute . . .

"I think the wine was Morgon; I'm not sure. Her father had grown up there, and his father, and others before them. Most of them were buried there, so that it wasn't like mere ownership any more but simply that particular part of the earth where they belonged. Life was simple, more or less medieval, and about as regular as the seasons, I suppose. At least that's the way it seemed to her as a child, the way she told me about it—the long, still summers, harvest time, winter and school and pruning the vines, grapes turning red in the sun. That was the way she told it to me, and I knew what she meant because I lived some long country summers myself, once, don't forget."

And she had told him a lot more, because he held me there, telling it to me as though it were all new, something that had just happened, history that for him had suddenly become his own and not just a series of crowded maps and monuments to the dead. About the coming of the Second War, and Cecile's father being called up and sent to the front, wherever the hell he could find it. His brother who was pushing sixty was killed at Dunkerque. Others, too—Spence didn't know how many; men who had somehow survived the slaughter twenty-five years before. And then one day he came back home, still in uniform, and they found him where he had put his bag down in the courtyard, just standing there looking around him and crying because the Armistice had been signed and it was all over. He was a man who had been against just about everything all his life—it was a habit of his class and he was no different from the others. The only thing he was for was France, some confused, vague notion comprising textbook versions of past glories, the overheated editorials of the press he read, the land he lived on, the people he hunted with, those who worked the place. He never really got over it, the utter, total, catastrophic rout not only of an army but of a class, a whole generation, a way of life which not even the First War had been able to finish off. For him, as for so many of his kind, the army, along with the church and those whose names were listed in the *Bottin Mondain*, was France, and the Resistance was merely disorderly skirmishing by irregulars. And so he took no notice of it, in spite of the fact that his eldest son was in the Resistance from the beginning. Something had been broken so that he just didn't care any more; the old order was gone and in its place had come a life reduced to petty peasant stealth—riding over his domain on a bicycle, his days dealt out in bribes for an extra sack of flour. So gradually he withdrew and slowly starved himself to death—a form of suicide of sorts—and that's why all of it happened the way it did.

From the way Spence told it, I gathered that Cecile's family—parents, her grandfather, her brothers and sisters and her father's brother's wife and this woman's several children, plus all of the dependents or at least those that the Germans hadn't carted off—were all holed up together in that château and the neighboring village, watching each other eat or not eat, as the case might be. Wild animals in a blizzard, fighting over a buffalo corpse that just wasn't enough to keep them all going. It turned out that the strongest and the meanest of the lot was a woman, the aunt by marriage, one of those imposing, indomitable, immovable, massively material French females whom one sees behind the *caisse* in a cafe, whose idea of charity was that it not only began but ended at home, or more precisely, among her immediate own, for whom she regularly produced as though by miracle the local equivalent of loaves and fishes while all around her there was only misery. The rest of the family, the servants, the women and the children and the aged men of the nearby village looked on at first with ferocity and then despair as their stomachs shrank, and accused her of dealing with *les boches*, who in the manner of occupation soldiers spent most of their time on business of one kind or another. And their business with her turned out to be a fairly primitive kind of barter in matters of murder.

It would seem that one day there appeared a group of maquisards from a neighboring region, and the word went out to the local Resistance group to gather at the château to break what bread there was with their brothers-in-arms. The preparations were festive in a clandestine sort of way, nor did the aunt's miraculous touch forsake her. From the very stones she struck fowls, wheat, suckling pig, fruits, and dusty, long-concealed bottles. They all sat long in the great dining room, and it was Cecile's brother, he who had been a *résistant* from the earliest days after the defeat, who proposed the toast of welcome. And then, like fatted calves, not heroes but merely farmboys and students and masons and carpenters with homemade explosives and patched-up weapons, these sons and husbands and uncles and cousins of the people who lived on this land went laughing into the courtyard and were there shot dead, every one, by a truckload of German soldiers, while the neighboring maquisards—in fact disguised *miliciens*, a kind of parallel police indirectly in the service of the Germans—stood to the side smoking, belching contentedly now and then because, *mon vieux*, that was a meal one didn't forget. And then, still trembling, oozing blood, some moaning even, they were dragged by the boots across the cobblestones and dumped into a common grave while the powder burned in the cold air and the women put their aprons to their eyes.

But the aunt—yes, she was taken by the Germans to Lyons, and charged with harboring Resistance fighters. A week later she was back, the charges dropped, and her children continued to thrive while the broken voices in the cold kitchens mumbled her name in hatred. There was no proof, of course, and the family in a crippled sort of way defended her as best they could. But at the Liberation she fled the country and was sentenced in absentia, and then the Château d'Ardières was quietly sold and the family moved away from their living and their dead.

"Well," I said when he was through, "they probably took a hell of a beating on the price." It was a dirty way to put it, but I didn't want any tragedy. I had put tragedy away from me a long time ago, and Harry's Bar was not the place I would have chosen to take it on again.

"They did what they thought they had to do." His voice had all of a sudden gone hard. We might have been sitting in his office, facing one another across his desk. "They stayed and defended her as long as they could, as long as the name of the family was at stake. They stood their ground until there wasn't anyplace left to stand, and then they pulled back in good order. They thought that living on the land and working it and burying your people in it made you belong—in Indochina, in Algeria, even in Burgundy. You put them down too easy."

"No," I said. "You're talking about a class, not a family. You said it yourself—they never knew what hit them. Nobody has the right to be that unconscious. I've heard it all before, Spence. The family bit during the Occupation is not very pleasant, I grant you, but don't tell me about Algeria. And what the devil does any of it have to do with you and Cecile? How many people are in this love affair?" Because I had heard too much as it was, and there was nothing good for me in any of it.

He stared at me then as though he were looking at someone whose face he knew but could not remember. "You make a joke of everything, Ames. You turn people inside out and then laugh because they seem ridiculous. You work it around until it sounds melodramatic, or merely sentimental, like something out of one of your Westerns. It's too easy, the way snobbery and cynicism always are. Doesn't it mean anything to you, the horror of it, that kind of cold betrayal, all those people dead, and then the family staying on, trying to make it right or at least clear their name until there was nothing left but to cut their losses and leave? Maybe it was doomed, but to me it was noble, tragic, heroic even. So many dead, a family under a curse, a whole town full of people involved in something they could never forget, a generation smeared with blood. Laugh. Go ahead. I mean it. But this was something I thought you would understand. Why is it so different from Grey Horse, after all? Do you laugh about Grey Horse, Amory? I asked you to come because you were the only person I knew who might see what I'm driving at. I mean how I can love her the way I do and yet be afraid to go any further. Because all that past that she carries with her is more than I can handle."

I listened, then, as though someone long dead had suddenly called my name. All around me were the pennants and the beer, the arrogant girls draped in smoke, the coats of arms and newspaper clippings and the gloves that Carnera wore, but all I could hear was that high humming silence of the Southwestern plains, keening again in my ears. "What does any of this have to do with Grey Horse?" I had moved away from him, but he reached over and took my shoulder as though he were setting me up for a punch.

"What is happening to you, Ames? What in hell have you been doing all these years? Somebody kicked the wind out of you—or heart maybe, or soul, or whatever you want to call it— and you never got up again. Let me tell you something. It must have been four—no, five years ago. I went to Grey Horse. Shut up, I'm telling you."

His head was high as though he were looking at me from the back of a horse.

"Because I wanted to know who you were. What you were. Why you were that way. Because you were my best friend, whether you ever knew it or not. The Boston Tea Party and the Declaration of Independence—hell, *The Star-Spangled Banner* and Custer's Last Stand—all of it. So once on my way back to Wyoming I cut south and went to that little town and walked the streets and talked to Jack Bird, or got talked to, mainly, and what was his name, the crazy one—Cody. I know all about what happened, and what's more, I don't give a damn."

"You had no right to do it, Spence. Nobody asked you to do that. You were looking for trouble. You were after dirt." I couldn't see him clearly now. My eyes burned in the smoke, and my words came slowly, one by one, as though I were underwater. I could scarcely breathe; a kind of terror held me by the throat, and all I wanted was to get away as fast as I could.

"Ames. Listen to what I'm trying to tell you. You say her past doesn't matter, that if she's the way I say she is, then it took that kind of past to make her that way. You say that I should just accept it, that I could change it all. That the past is all of a piece, and you can't keep the good and leave out the bad. Well, what about you? Did you ever accept your own past—all of it, I mean, and not just part? I'm talking about Grey Horse now. Look at what it did to you. You got hung up on it, Ames. They took you away from the only thing you ever cared about and after that it didn't matter any more and now all of your friends, everybody who cares about you, have got to go on for the rest of their lives trying to make good the loss."

"What did Jack tell you? What did you go there for?"

"It doesn't matter that much, Ames. Let's get back to what we were talking about before. The least you can do is to listen to a man's story without laughing in his face. You're so superior about it, as though all those memories you carry around give you the right to sneer at everybody. Well, there's nothing left of all that. I was there. Nothing but an old drunk leaning on his cane in the lobby of that sad hotel, and Cody—well, he ought to have been committed long ago. Ames, you talk about Cecile as though the problem were simply one of too many beds. That's your way of looking at it, not mine. I'm talking about something else, about where the felt weight of her life is, and I asked you to come so that I could say it out loud to someone, just to see if it made any sense."

"You go to see my mother, too?" I was choking now, and every word was a gasp of pain.

"I don't even know where she is. Ames, look it in the face. Listen to what I'm saying. I'm not laughing at any of that. I even think maybe I understand it. In its own way it was just as noble and tragic and heroic—I admired her for it, Ames. All I'm asking for you to do is to understand—"

But I was already on my feet and walking away fast, my eyes a blur of tears, my hands clenched into fists.

"What's the matter with you?" and then he called my name, but I never looked back. I went through the swinging doors just like it was the Smoke House or the Last Chance Saloon. All I could think about was Jack sitting there that day with me on the bench, telling it to me in that slow way of his, saying that everything was finished forever . . .

Somehow or other I found a cab, because I was in a hurry, and I didn't seem able to get my breath again until I had closed those heavy, muffled doors behind me. Nothing had changed. Soft lights, thick carpets, heavy drapes covering the windows. A rich and mellow silence where the only sounds were of ice and spoons and Madame Germaine talking to her clients and her girls on the phone. She gave me a cool look and held out a cold and muscular hand.

"I thought I told you to find a *petite amie*. You're too good-looking to pay these prices."

"I found one."

"*Alors?*"

"We spent the summer in St. Tropez, but you know how it is."

"Well, I have a young married woman—sensational—bored, burning up, you know the kind. I have a model from one of the collections, very chic. A doctor from Madrid—female, of course —who spends her vacations with us. Enjoys a change, she says. One of the movie girls—what was the name of that film—and a wonderful *noire* from Senegal. Look at the photos. Take your time."

"No," I said. "I'm looking for something different."

"Virgin? That's something different."

"Yes, she was virgin."

"Who? One of my girls?"

"We were on our way to Navajo country. We never made it."

"I don't like for my girls to go on trips unless the price is right."

"We grew up together, might have been brother and sister— my father, her mother—the way it was, the families hated each other. Everything began with her—one night we walked down the alley until we came to the garage, and the car was open . . ."

"That kind you got to get for free," she said drily, wiping drops of water from the tiny bar. "It's not for sale. Not here, anyway."

"How about a room."

"You're crazy."

"I mean it. Someplace to sleep. I don't want to be alone to-night."

She appraised me coldly from behind that vivid mask of oil and powder and silver lipstick and orange rouge and a wiry mass of hennaed hair as tangled as a crow's nest.

"You'll have to pay."

Among all the variations, that was the constant. Suspiciously, as though sleeping alone, at least in this place, was an aberration so extraordinary that one should really pay double.

"I'm doing you a favor because I like you. You'll be taking up space, and that bed won't change partners all night, even though I need it."

"I'll pay you for it. And for coffee and croissants tomorrow morning. You can save your champagne for the people having fun."

The next morning I lay half-emerged from sleep, wishing that I had brought my suitcase and typewriter along. The bed was large and soft like a middle-aged bosom; the sheets had a faintly grainy texture, pleasantly abrasive to the skin. Here behind plum-colored velvet drapes perpetually drawn, it was always night, lit only by a lamp just strong enough to illuminate the multitudinous mirrors. Here was the quiet, the intimate comfort, the stillness of the womb. Living in that house I could have been as happy as a monk.

Yet this sprawled, luxurious sense of peace lasted little beyond the final swallow of the crumb-clogged *café au lait*. Certainly by the time that I was washing in the tiny bathroom dominated by the bidet, I was chiefly aware of the blotchy pallor of that face emerging from the scented towel, as lifeless as a landed fish. On the plus side I had nothing left to lose, which made for a jittery kind of insouciance I had felt before when walking out of a casino at dawn with just enough in my pockets to get me through breakfast. But then that was only money, and this time I had gambled away the Bucks, Cynthia, Spence, God knows what else. Not merely income, but capital. In short, just about everything I had. I felt as though I had been driving furiously for years over a vast continent, relying on hunch and intuition and a road map whose infinitude of symbols I scarcely understood, and now here at last was where all those forks and detours and zigzags and impasses and thruways and cutoffs had led—to a night spent in a whorehouse without even getting laid. Spence had hit below the belt, and it still hurt.

And all the way back to the hotel, down the smoky glitter of the Champs-Élysées, through the Tuileries full of donkeys and sailboats and knitting needles and white-shoed toddlers whose mothers stared at each other stonily beneath the statuary, amidst mythic posturings in concrete and gardens of pure reason and the dingy debris of history where pigeons perched, and at last along the quais whose trees leaned listlessly as exiled ladies-in-waiting above the savageries of traffic, I was aware of a certain grim, aghast, burnt-out desperation, as though I walked as a lone survivor through some Pompeii where death had forked out the snaily spirit and left the shell. I floated with a kind of weightlessness, and people seemed to stare right through me as though I were not there. Some source of blood had been cauterized, some fragile vein that lay somewhere near my heart, and I was left in a world that seemed no longer to exist because I no longer felt it.

And even Cynthia's note—well, when the enemy is at the very gates, the news of the fall of an isolated garrison is merely confirmation of a grief grown too great to be felt in detail. Because there was a letter with it, forwarded from my hill town back of St. Tropez. All Cynthia had left was a scribble of disgust: "Tired of the mini-life. Tweeds and cider suit you better. I'm going home. Suggest you do the same."

But the letter was something else again.

MY DEAR AMORY,

I have read and reread your letter, trying to understand what has come over you. And though I have wanted not to think about them, certain things have come back to my mind with too much pain to be ignored.

I have sheltered you for many years from much of the truth about yourself. Perhaps this has been a mistake, though you know that everything I have done has been for you.

I cannot allow you to destroy yourself this way. I have lived through such self-destruction once, and cannot now stand by and watch it happen to me again.

I am sure that you do not want me to come back into your life at this point, but you have left me no choice. Because if your life is no longer precious to you, it remains so to me. I have built my own life around it, around you and what I have helped you to become, and I won't let her destroy it, whoever she is.

I shall be arriving in Paris on TWA at 12 noon on Saturday,

the eighth of this month, which is eight days from now. I shall expect you to meet me. I am leaving no time for a reply, because I don't want one. I shall be staying at the hotel Oxford and Cambridge, which is your father's old hotel. And if you do not meet me, or leave word at the hotel, I shall know what conclusions to draw and will make my plans accordingly.

I am no longer a young woman, Amory. I have changed in many ways. But one thing in me will never change, and that is my conviction that far too much has happened to far too many people for you to throw away your life so thoughtlessly.

I love you,

EMILY

I was packing when I looked up and saw him in the doorway, tweed jacket and impeccable flannels, a tie striped red and black, his hair more silver than grey and his eyes a puzzled blue.

"Ames, I want you to know that I'm sorry about last night. I paid up and drove over here and waited for you until I finally went to sleep in the car. I was worried. I know you've got your troubles, too."

"Forget it." I was rolling up my clothes as fast as I could, keeping my mind on my business and my back to him as much as possible. I imagined that this must be what a man feels after he's caught his best friend in bed with his wife. "I don't want to talk about it."

"About what?"

"Any of it. I'm shoving off."

"Where?"

"Back to my village. Life is simple there."

"But why, for God's sake? You can't walk out on me now. Good Lord, Ames—"

"Good Lord yourself. What is there left for me to do? You're in love with her and yet you talk like you're trying to give her up. You want me to change your mind for you, or just agree with everything you say? You knew what you were going to do before you ever sent that telegram. So you call it walking out. Well,

I've given you quite a bit as it is. My girl's run off, I'll end up blowing a week that I can't afford to lose, my life is in just as big a mess as yours—worse as a matter of fact. You don't need me here to hold your hand."

I didn't want to mention Emily. And I was packing because it was all over. In three days' time I would be back at the Bucks, and Emily would be there with me, and the interval I would spend at the Oxford and Cambridge, with Emily and Andrews.

"Who's asking for that? What's eating on you, anyway?"

"Me?" If I ever wanted to slug him it was then. I just stared at him and then dumped the rest of my books in the suitcase.

"Look. You're holding it against me because I went to that town. Right? I told you why I went there—because you were the best friend I ever had, and because you had always made a kind of mystery out of that part of your life, and I wanted to know about it. Not because it was secret or because I was looking for dirt but because I cared about what happened to you. And because I know that something is eating at you, right down to the bone, and it has something to do with that place, and I wanted to find a way to help if I could because of all the things you did for me."

"I never did anything for you. What are you talking about?" I lit a cigarette and walked over to the window. My hands were trembling, and there was something wrong with my mouth. I hadn't known until then how scared I was.

"I don't think I would have made it without you, Ames. I wonder if you can imagine how lonely it was for me in the beginning, just to be that far away from home. You were the only one that I could even talk to. Then later on, when I knew you were holding back on me—I suppose I thought I could help. I owed you that much. I still do."

"You don't owe me anything, Spence. Let it go. Anyway, I didn't come to Paris because of you. My mother is flying in tomorrow. Emily. Good old Aunt Emily. I guess you found out about that, too."

I heard him sit down, and I knew that I could look at him then because I had said it, and now whatever there was that was left to me of hope was gone, and I no longer had to care.

"I heard stories. All different, depending on who was doing the telling. All of us are hiding things most of the time, anyway. What I wanted to tell you was that it only helped me understand you better, made me appreciate what you had been through and why you didn't want to talk about it. I think if I were you, Ames, I would be proud . . ."

But his voice had faded out, and I sat down by the window because I couldn't stand up any longer. Proud, he had said. Great God Almighty. I was so proud that just the sound of her name was enough to bring tears to my eyes. Wasn't that all I had ever asked for—just the chance to be proud, and say so, and belong, and be proud of belonging, and talk about it all the way it was, instead of counting it over and over in the dark like a miser with a flashlight? And had he really seen it all? The white house with the red tile roof and columns out in front; a grid of silent streets smoldering in the sun; an empty baseball diamond with shadows moving across it like the crowd after a game, and Jack Bird talking, talking . . .

"I always see her in my mind like that statue of the Pioneer Woman, staring off across the prairie toward the future. All the years she's spent alone. The letters came every week, money at Christmas and on my birthday, cards for the children, like a clock ticking away in an empty house. They sounded just the way I remember her talking—always very serious, very grave, in a way that always made me feel I'd done something wrong—God, how many years ago. She's coming to the hotel where she and my father stayed when they visited Paris. I'm moving over there to wait for her. Maybe she'll want to walk around the streets and see the sights and tell me about the French poets she studied in college and visit Notre Dame and sip a little wine in some cafe. She'll tell me about the letters I used to write her when she needed letters more than she does now, about how she's saved every piece of paper I ever sent her and what a record it will make for the children someday . . . All my arguments, all the things I wanted to tell her about my life now, starting out again, finding my way back home—well, she won't have to argue with me. I'll see her standing there in the passport line and look at that face and think of everything I owe her—and then in a couple of days we'll go back to the Bucks and she'll meet her grandchildren, and they will be the embodiment of what she gave up her life for, her vindication, her peace . . ."

"Tell her she got what she paid for—that you're grown up and that you know how you want to live your own life and that you're on your own."

He was talking tough, but it was hopeless. I had driven all the way to Paris just to watch him suffer, hoping maybe that way to kick it myself, and now it was turned around and he was throwing me a lifeline I didn't have the strength to catch.

"So what does she want, anyway?"

"She wants to pretend that none of it ever happened, and make damned sure that it never happens again. The summer, the girl who just walked out on me, a drunken letter I sent her telling her that I was cutting out."

"Does it take coming all the way over here for that?"

"Oh, she'll never say that that's what she came for. She's coming for a visit to the family. Time we all got acquainted. I haven't seen her since I was fifteen and suddenly she decides the time has come. Just like that." Because whatever else I said, the letter was something I could never show him.

"And the girl? Cynthia?"

"Cynthia doesn't matter. She knows that. She won't even mention her. Rising above it was the way she always put it. For Emily, Cynthia does not exist. Hence the problem does not exist, at least not in those terms. Men have too much imagination; all of them break out in a rash of dreams from time to time. Its all in the head. Ignore them and they go away. That's Emily. Except she never leaves anything to chance."

"She's your mother, but if I were you I'd tell her off. What the hell, Ames. You've paid her back in full. With your marriage, your life, all of it. You don't have to go on paying interest forever. Cut the cord, man. You've got to sooner or later."

"She won't listen to me. I could pull a gun on her and she wouldn't bat an eye."

"Who's she going to listen to, then?"

I didn't have an answer. As far as I knew, she had never listened to anybody, and I couldn't see her starting now. And how could I explain that if she had decided to fly to Paris to see me, it wasn't so much Cynthia, or Diane, or even the children. It was the town, as though she had sat beside me in the night and watched my dreams.

"So that's why I'm packing," I said. "I'm not walking out on you. I just don't have any choice."

"Will you meet her before you go?"

"Who?"

"Cecile."

I shrugged, and smiled at him wearily. "Would it mean that much to you?"

"I have to have dinner with Nancy tonight, at home. We're keeping up appearances for the sake of the children. I've told Cecile about you. She wants to meet you. We've been outlaws for too damned long—in hiding, practically. It will do her good to talk to someone about it. Tell her I'm doing my best, Ames. Maybe you can make her understand what it is that worries me. You were right last night. The past doesn't count that much. I want to make the break. She's what I've wanted all my life. I'm grateful to you for making me say it out loud."

"Is that why you asked me to come?"

"I don't know. I don't really know. But seeing you has made me realize—well, what the past can do to a man if he doesn't come to terms with it one way or another."

That was clumsy as hell and meant for me, but I didn't pick it up. My mind was already on the future—Emily, Diane, putting it all back together. And seeing Cecile would be a way of rounding off the summer, a favor for a friend so that the trip to Paris wouldn't be a total loss.

I had bought a bottle of champagne on the way to the apartment just as though it were a kind of celebration, but when she opened the door, standing there with those deep, dark lines beneath her eyes, her hand vaguely smoothing the chestnut hair at her temple, I knew that I had jumped the gun a little.

"Cecile?"

"You're Amory." Her voice went up and down in the wrong places when she said my name, and the hand she gave me was very small. "Thank you for coming."

And for a very long moment I said nothing whatsoever, simply staring at that face that seemed all of a sudden to have emerged from the mists of a long-forgotten dream, or perhaps from the flickering lights and shadows of some old film seen years before. Ghostly in a way because I seemed to have known her all my life; the kind of face that had in some strange way gathered to itself so much of what I had wanted for so long. I saw her with great distinctness—large eyes set wide apart above high cheekbones, a small, bow-shaped mouth, a fringe of tawny hair that hung down to her eyebrows. Spence had mentioned Botticelli, and I saw that, too; the long, very straight nose, the extraordinary architecture of her bones, and all somehow soft and rounded in spite of the severe geometry of so many clear, clean lines.

"Come in. Please."

I mumbled some sort of thanks and then abruptly thrust the champagne at her as though I were putting a pistol in her ribs. For I could scarcely face those poignant eyes, that strangely broken beauty, and in a moment bewilderingly compounded of pain and gratitude, my casual cynicisms fled me like so many rats. I floundered awkwardly there on her doorstep like a sinking ship, and when I entered the apartment I sank to even greater depths, into some subaqueous calm of soft light from pale lamps reflecting off whitewashed walls. There was light, too, in little puddles along the waxed wood of the floor, on door handles and mirrors and an ancient brass telephone that squatted like a tropic bird on the polished coffee table; vague light that filtered through the watery shadows cast by the flames that filled the fireplace at the end of the room.

She had gone to get some ice for the champagne and I lit a cigarette and wandered from window to window, looking out at the lights of what seemed half of Paris. The curving quais of the Île St. Louis, the enormous weeping willow just beyond the footbridge, the great grey bones of Notre Dame, green benches where I had sat in the sun, silent streets where I had walked beneath the rain—it was as though I looked down upon a map of all that I would have to leave behind.

"What a funny idea," she said, and then I turned and saw her leaning against the fireplace, staring at me with that catlike concentration that I came to know so well. "Champagne. Who is it for, this champagne?"

"For you and Spence. Who else?"

She tilted her head to one side so that her hair moved along her shoulder and smiled a crooked little smile, elegant with irony.

"We have something to celebrate, Spence and I?"

"I think so. I hope so, anyway."

"Then let us drink champagne. After it is cold. We can wait for a while and you can tell me about yourself and then we will have dinner here, unless you want to go out."

"No, I would like to stay here, if it's no trouble for you. This is such a beautiful place," and I gestured toward the windows at the view. I couldn't have told her then how it had overwhelmed me, the bare simplicity of this room, old chairs painted white and upholstered in blue velvet, the low table with a scattering of books before the fire, glowing wood whose color seemed to come from age, all in a kind of absolute stillness charged with life and movement, as in the river which I could see beyond the window. It was so many things at once, but most of all a kind of temple, pagan, open to the sky, sacred somehow, even terrifying because every inch of that room was instinct with an honesty as absolute as stone. The honesty of inanimate things, perhaps—the sea, the sun, the earth and its elements. I had been living in a kind of polar night, long familiar with the shifts and subterfuges of darkness, and here someone had turned on a sun that had never shone on me before.

"I moved here when my husband died. I was lucky to find it, and then lucky to move in at all. I had made an exchange with the man who was renting it—he needed a bigger place so he took my apartment—and the owner here was furious. When I arrived with my children and my furniture he refused to let me in. I had to get the police."

"But you made it finally."

"Oh, yes. He hated me, poor man. As soon as he saw me. Those things are always happening to me. Something about the way I look, I suppose."

Not bitterly, the way Cynthia would have said it. Just an observation on the way beauty or nobility of any kind so often provoked something close to hatred.

"So you're Amory Thayer. That's an English name, isn't it? It doesn't sound American."

"Doesn't it? I always thought of it as very American. I live in England now. That is—"

"And Spence—he said he'd known you since you were boys."

She gave me a glass of champagne then, and I sat down where I could see the fire, and then I began to tell her. About the gypsy years in Europe with Diane and the children, who made their appearances in Paris, in Venice, in Barcelona and Geneva until at last we settled down at the Bucks. About a multilingual variety of tutors and governesses, public gardens in their national diversities, wagon-restaurants, pensiones and hotels, the Costa del Sol and the Italian Riviera. The year I spent in a Swiss sanatorium, recovering from tuberculosis and writing my first book while Diane went on painting in Positano. The bit part I had in an Italian movie about the adversities of an English family on the Continent. Schools in Paris, Zurich, Oxford, summers in Brittany and the Italian Alps. The sailboat that no one ever used, the wine labels I collected in the beginning before we started coming back to the same places the second time around, the hill town back of St. Tropez where I went to write my Westerns, my summers in the sun. About the Leaning Tower and Windsor Castle and Carcassonne. As though that were my history, at least the part that would interest her most, and not a mere scrap heap of fragments that no one would ever be able to piece together.

"But you knew Spence long before that."

By this time we were in the kitchen and she was cooking spaghetti and I was most of the way through the bottle of champagne and crying over the onions or something. And then through dinner I just kept right on going—playing football in the snow, Clint Frank and Larry Kelley, the weekends on the Cape, memorizing Latin verbs in Chapel, and the war and the Bucks and the poodles and the pigeons and even Cynthia. And by that time the champagne was gone and she had brought out some cognac, and I looked around at the way the room shone in the firelight and said, "How the hell did I ever get started on all that?"

"Because I asked you about Spence."

"Well, I guess I told you."

"No. You didn't mention his name."

She smiled at me, and I looked at her then in a way that I had been scared to do at first. I was beginning to know her, the way you can recognize a land whose maps you have studied for a long, long time. Her beauty was a little battered, but like the Venus de Milo, she seemed more perfect for her imperfections. I preferred her that way, life's scars showing on her face. In spite of all the bombing, she had somehow escaped a direct hit. For a moment I wanted to reach over and take her hand, and then I took a cigarette instead.

"My God, do you mean to tell me that I've been sitting here talking about myself all this time? How absurd—"

And then it was she who all of a sudden took my hand. I turned my face away and stood up, as though I hadn't noticed. Something had turned over inside me, and I wasn't ready for that yet.

"No. Spence has always talked about you but you have told me much, much more. You're his best friend—that's what he calls you."

"You're very sweet," and I suppose I couldn't help being just a bit abrupt. "What you really want to know is how it's going to work out. You know where he is tonight, of course."

"Tonight. All the other nights. Yes, I know," and she looked at her watch. "Right now he will be saying good night to the youngest of the children. Why won't she let him go?"

I had had too much champagne to be sober, and not quite enough to be drunk. I had a flat taste in my mouth and a hole somewhere in the region of my stomach. I had gone up too far, and then come down too fast. I had been playing my tunes on a penny whistle for the pretty lady, and now she had given me my nickel and gone away.

"Nancy? Maybe he hasn't told her yet what he wants." I hadn't used that tone with her up to now. I hadn't wanted to.

She watched me, waiting, and then she shook her head. "I don't understand."

"What can she do except sit there and wait for him to make up his mind?"

She shook her head again. "I don't understand you. Isn't it plain to her how he feels? None of us can go on living like this much longer. It's wrong, for all of us."

"Yes. I know that. But Spence has not yet reached the point where he can give any of it up. He looks at your life, the way it's been, and wonders what kind of a place there could ever be in it for him."

"I don't understand that, either. I love him. He knows it. What is there to remember?"

"I don't say it makes any sense. But that's the way it is."

She went on watching me, spelling it out like I was the one she had to convince. "But if he loves me, and she wants him to be happy, and he tells it to her that way . . . Maybe he hasn't told her. She won't believe it until he says it just like that, and even then . . . sometimes it seems so hopeless."

"Is that what you believe?"

She got up then and went to the window so that her back was to me.

"I don't know what I believe any more. But why should she want to keep him if he doesn't want to stay? And why should it matter that much to him what she thinks? He's never loved her. He told me that himself. And is that what love is—the way she acts? Love is a lot of things, but never ownership." Then she turned around and looked at me, almost as though she knew that that way I couldn't lie to her. "What do you believe?"

"How much do you know about Spence? The kind of American he is. What he wants."

"I asked you a question. What do you believe?"

Well, I had come to do a favor for a friend. So I raised the flag and dared her to shoot it down. "That he's going to tell her the truth. That he intends to make his life with you, and that if she thinks she can wait him out or blackmail him with the children, then she's wasting her time."

"Is that what you believe, Amory?"

And her smile was the kind you only learn to make when you've been kicked down so far that there's no place left to go but up.

"That's what he told me."

"And do you believe it?"

She had asked me once too often. She had me against the ropes, and I could either come back punching or try to duck under and out.

"I don't know what I believe," I said, and that didn't take me anywhere. Except, as it turned out, down a road that I hadn't planned to take.

"I believed everything he told me, right from the start." She was standing in profile, staring at a view she must have seen a thousand times. Right now there was nothing out there for her but night. Her throat was long and arched, and her nose broke just a little at the bridge. I wondered if she ever cried. "Now something tells me he's going back. He says he loves me, but what kind of love is that? What difference does it make in the end?"

"He means it, Cecile." I poured myself some cognac like it was scotch. "But love is only part of it."

"Is it?" She came and stood beside me at the fireplace, then knelt down and poked the logs. "Not for me. When I told him I loved him I meant I was ready to go with him, however, whenever he wanted. Married, not married. Any way it had to be for him. But together in some way or other."

"He was swept off his feet. You, all this," and I gestured at the room. "My God, Cecile. He told you what he felt, and he believed every word of it. He still believes it. What he can do about it is another thing."

"No." She looked at me and shook her head very slowly. "It's too easy that way. There are certain responsibilities to oneself in love. In love more than ever."

"Life isn't that simple, Cecile. What do you know about Spence? Why do you think it matters to him so, this business about your family, the life you've lived up to now? Why he wants it for himself, and why he's afraid to touch it?"

She sat down then and curled into the chair, watching the flames that spluttered blue and yellow along the bark. "What is there to know about Spence? He's American, comes from someplace in the West, went to fine schools, married young and made a career. I didn't break up his marriage if that's what you're thinking. Nobody ever breaks up a marriage that isn't ready to fall apart anyway."

"But Spence?"

"I love him."

"But you don't understand him."

"Perhaps he is more American than I thought. More Puritan, I mean. More conventional. He's refined, he has a certain class, he's lived abroad. I thought that would make a difference."

"You don't understand because you grew up in another world. I know that world, you see—I grew up in it, too, in a way. And it's a world Spence will never really understand, just as he will never really understand either one of us. We're what he wants, but wanting is not enough. And then because he doesn't really understand, he's afraid. Spence never did know what he really wanted; he was always too busy figuring out what he ought to want."

"You tell me that life is not so simple as I think it is, and yet it seems to me that you make it far too complicated. And what do we have in common, you and I—our worlds, as you call them?"

I sat down on the floor beside her chair and put the bottle of cognac in easy reach. I had so much all of a sudden that I wanted to say to her, and it all lay down that road I had taken so carelessly. Hours of it—too drunk to make sense, and not drunk enough to stop. I killed the bottle and went on talking as though I had to make her understand before Spence came back. About so many dead, a family under a curse, a whole town full of people involved in something they could never forget, a generation smeared with blood. About nobility and tragedy and heroism.

About the white house with the red tile roof, and a cottonwood tree in front, and catbirds and mockingbirds and hollyhocks in the alley, and streets which ran through me like the vessels of my blood, and pride, and sitting and crying beside an empty baseball diamond with shadows moving across it like a crowd after the game, and Jack talking, talking about a mother vanished and a father dead, and then there was no place left to stand so they went away . . .

The windows were going from grey to silver when I finally realized that she was asleep. She had been sitting there in silence watching me, her eyes wide and concentrated in that catlike look, like probably she didn't trust me, or maybe trusted everybody and just couldn't make me out. I don't recall a word she said, if she said anything at all. And then I stopped talking and right away I was sobbing in a way I couldn't control, the way I could remember crying once before. Maybe it was at my father's funeral. It was like that. But she was sleeping, and I didn't wake her up, and dawn had turned into day by the time I had somehow or other made it back across the empty streets of Paris to my hotel.

I staggered up about ten with a fur-lined stomach and a head like a rock and felt my way along the street to the cafe at the corner. I could have used a white cane or a seeing-eye dog or both. It was that bad. Then over coffee and croissants I muttered nonsense to myself, trying to stitch back together an evening that had come apart at the seams, trying to talk myself out of trouble I didn't need. "She's no goddess of truth, and she didn't spring full-blown from the forehead of Athena. And she didn't rise from one of Botticelli's seas all pearly in the dawn, and she's no goddam wood nymph, either, with flowers in her hair and the mark of the beast in her eyes. She's shopworn, damaged goods, overexposed, a woman with too much past and not enough future, just the way Spence said."

And then on the way to Orly and afterwards, slumped against the plastic sofas in the listless atmosphere of expectation of the waiting room, I made the worst case I could against Cecile. It was a case that Diane or Cynthia or Emily or almost any woman would have liked to recognize as true, which wasn't saying much of anything, and that someone like Spence would have winced away from, preferring to put it in other terms. But I wanted to say it all, to turn her inside out and laugh at her, as Spence had said, and then see if anything was left when that sour laugh of mine had died away.

Well, to begin with, too many one-night stands, too many hopeless dinners with undeclared fags or tired old men or gay young husbands where she went through her little routines again and told her stories that made them laugh because living alone is damned hard and sometimes you need other people so much that it's worth the effort to go through with it all again for the thousandth time. Too many faded hopes and wasted years, abortions, bad debts, misplaced trust, frustration ante portas which only means that nothing ever worked when the big chance came. It was all there in her face for anyone to read, that eagerness as she watched the reactions she inspired, drugged by the admiration of other people the way another woman would be by drink or dope. Always the pleasure of making the heads turn, hearing the excited voices, and then the void. Parties where there would always be someone who listened longest, laughed with more and more complicity, who would as the evening wore on suggest that if she didn't have a ride . . . That way the brilliance lasted a little longer, even if the crowd of idolators had shrunk to one, until the clothes unwrapped her loneliness, and the lights went out, and then the void was there again, smothering like a cat in a crib, even before he had gone. They always left so quickly, a little dazed, almost afraid, as though they had felt the breath of the cat, as though they had slept with a goddess. On sale, always out of season, keeping up. A broken-hearted good-time girl, neither hard nor soft enough, too fine to have fun with, not fine enough to share a life. A collector of trophies, like Will Rogers—I never met a man I couldn't lay.

Well, she had met one. She had set me up last night with the view and the woodsmoke and the casual spaghetti and that face of hers that brought back memories I didn't know I had. I had walked right in and let her sink me with the first shot. Almost. Because I could still get out if I moved fast enough. She could find plenty of others—rich American art dealers on their annual giggle in Paris, writers between ladies to live on, out-of-bed philosophers, round-faced men in Jaguars who had made it big since the war in real estate, skirt- or trouser-chasing pundits of the chic left. St. Germain des Prés was always ready to lie down and roll over. She had only to keep on lunching at the Flore, conspicuous and unmolested among the pretty boys until somebody came along and picked up the check . . .

And anyway, she was Spence's girl. Had I forgotten it so soon? Someone had probably said at one time or another that Cecile had been in too many beds, and that would be enough to give ulcers to Spencer Platt. Old-fashioned ideas regarding a woman's reputation, concern for what people might say, suspicions about being taken for a ride, afraid to make up his mind about what he really wanted and unable to make the deal in any case unless he thought he was getting a bargain. In short, a Yankee, no matter what part of America he came from. And then worst of all, that tiresome obsession with his own destiny, as though it really mattered that much to anyone else. And still . . . she was Spence's girl. I had thrown her everything in the book, and she just sat there and went to sleep.

As for me—well, I had been ducking in and out of bordellos all my life, in a manner of speaking, and I couldn't care less what she had done before last night as long as she would be doing it with me from now on. She had sat there and looked at me and I had told her about myself just as long as she would listen. All the absurd trivia we drag around in our memories—I hadn't realized how much old furniture I had stored away. And the truth was that I was ready to take on the whole show: husbands, brothers, uncles, lovers, children, living or dead: name dropping, skirt dropping, bed hopping, call it what you will.

Because the case that I had made was wrong from start to finish. What really mattered was not some Puritan epic of her life replete with a catalogue of sins, but what everything about her told me of how she had survived. In some important way it was finally a question of style, not what but how, and in everything that she had gathered around her, in that face that was not the mask that she offered to the world but a tapestry wherein was woven the story of her journeying, in her furniture, her books, her flowers, in the very timbre of that voice so light and yet so grave, there was courage and honesty and humor and a certain splendid hardness that stood like granite, unyielding before the sea of tears that beat upon her.

All of which meant, perhaps, that I was in love with her. Love is disdainful of time, and hours are enough, and there was something about her loneliness, about what she had lost, that could have been the story of my life if that tapestry were turned around. If I loved her, it was not for what she had but for all that was gone—the place where she had come from, the green garden of childhood, youth and beauty, hope not yet eroded by time. It was her special kind of loneliness which drew me to her, perfume composed of all the flowers of my past, a cachet of lilac, of hollyhocks, or roses, redolent of memories this very loneliness would help to keep alive.

And yet here I was at Orly, nursing a hangover which was the least of what was wrong with me, ready to gamble what little I had left on a woman who was probably in love with my best friend, and waiting for Emily before whom all else would simply vanish like desert flowers born with the rain and dead in the hot winds that blew the rain away.

But there was a case to be made against Emily, too, and what would be left if I turned her inside out and laughed? Was she one of those taut New England ladies, a cameo at her throat and a chunk of Vermont marble in her breast, perfectly brought up in the genteel tradition of plain living and even plainer thinking, taught chiefly that eternal vigilance was the price of keeping vulgarity at arm's length and virginity intact, and in spite of laces and silks and satiny ribbons and a long-nosed, rabbity kind of flinty femininity, about as gracious and as yielding as the women who burned the witches in early Salem? New England lessons learned all the more impeccably because at second hand. And perhaps by now a tippler, dealing in a smiling way with people just as she used to amuse herself as a girl in summer by trapping flies and pulling off their wings and watching them buzz helplessly around like mechanical toys. Rising above mere things of course, which everybody had anyway, except for money which was in its admittedly grimy way as comfortingly abstract as a Prostestant God and which she squirreled away like so many good deeds, counting it all up every night on her crooked little adding machine, getting her kicks from tabulating angels in her private heaven. To the point that she could get caught with her hand in the till, and do a stretch in the State Prison for Woman, and never for a moment admit the least imperfection in the perfect propriety of her life. And certainly blessed with that arrogant and unshakable certitude of the righteous rich. Because in some way or other she had to be rich—the poor could never afford her kind of stinginess, economically, emotionally, or any other way. Living amidst newspapers in one room with her gold sewed up in a mattress and never coming out. That was the way she made it, with a feeding arrangement by means of a kind of reverse umbilical cord tied tightly to her son, making him repay with interest every drop of blood she ever gave him.

What the years would have done to her was something else— by now she had probably gone to nature like an animal abandoned in the woods. A bit wild-eyed behind careful glasses, hair in perpetual disarray, a purple hatchwork of veins showing through the powder on her face, blunt hands coarsened by every kind of exposure. And could such a woman be persuaded that my life up to now had been a sham? That she had torn me up by the roots and put me in a silver vase and kept me like dried flowers that preserved their colors in an austere sort of way, but from whom the greenness of life had gone forever? That to save my life I must lose it, and that if she lost hers in the process, that it was a price that had to be paid? That I had brought a pair of scissors with which I meant to cut the cord, and that I was prepared to use a hacksaw if necessary, and an ax if I had to?

And yet that was no case, either. Because alone in that town she had feared so much, and all the more because she knew I loved it, she had raised me, made a life for us in all that barrenness because he was buried there, and thus had given me a place in time and space which bore a name, and had a tragic history one could sing, and a terrible beauty that stayed in the mind with all the clarity of a skeleton burned white and clean by a torchlike wind. The flawed beauty of scrub oak and sandstone, and hawks hanging in the sky like some memento mori, and sun and wind that dried the skin against the bone, but still beauty, graven in the heart with the permanence of images in desert temples.

And then suddenly I saw her—I had lost track of time, and the announcement of her flight had been drowned in the general blur of sound which surrounded me like water—and there she was in the line, holding her passport stiffly before her, looking around as though she were not yet sure where she was. I don't know what in particular it was that made me want to cry—whether her pale, wide-eyed sense of wonder in the midst of so much noisy certainty, or her crooked lipstick, or her little round veiled hat on hair that was yellow as ivory, or the slow intent way she came toward me as though she were not used to so much light. I could not see her clearly because so many feelings were in the way. Her clothes seemed somehow dusty, as if she had made a long journey by train, and in that brilliant flutter of birds of paradise she was as plain as a wren. She was smaller than I had remembered, and in some strange way not at all as I had pictured her. And it was not until later on that I recognized the face that I had known, and so much else that the years had brought, and taken away as well.

Then we looked at each other, both waiting as though we were not sure, not saying a word, until finally I took her in my arms, feeling her withered cheek so soft against my own and her body trembling against mine. At last she leaned away from me to look again, all of her aflame with a pride and pain so fierce that I could scarcely meet her eyes.

"I'd know you anywhere, Amory. No matter how many years. You look just the way I wanted you to look. God bless you. I love you so."

I swallowed and smiled the way I had thirty years before, wanting above all to please her, no matter what it cost. "It's been a long time, Mother. I got your letter, and we're together at the Oxford and Cambridge, and in a day or two . . ."

But I could see that she wasn't listening. She was staring at me, her face so radiant that the tears which shone along her cheeks seemed more like drops of light. She didn't want to talk. Not yet, at any rate. And then I took her bag, and she took my arm, and we moved off together through the crowd like some strangely assorted bride and groom.

I took her to Lipp's for dinner just to show her that champagne and roses and candlelight were not what I had in mind. Starched tablecloths and waiters in black and white, politicians and poets, the blue-jowled banker with his wife and mistress, movie people hoping to be seen and the bourgeoisie hoping to see movie people; chic, sparkling, droll, refined, left-wing, right-wing, *le tout Paris*; bejeweled lizards basking in mirrored light that cast no shadow, watching each other with a kind of wary hunger from heavy-lidded eyes, totally and undeviatingly devoted to their lives, their liberties, the pursuit of their own happiness. I found it a suitable port of debarkation for a pilgrim from the other shore.

I had spent the afternoon at Harry's sitting in the back and drinking beer, figuring out my moves while Emily was at the beauty parlor, as she called it. That was her first request, improbable as it might seem, and so I had left her somewhat apprehensively among the gleaming ranks of driers and piles of fashion magazines and the sleek attendants, girls and boys, who took her in hand with a playfulness so hard it froze my blood.

But what I was figuring was that maybe the time had finally come to take a stand. Because the moment of meeting with all its pain and terror and strange exaltation had come and gone, and somewhere in the process thirty years had slipped away, and I saw myself with a kind of horror as one of those child actors who still at middle age carries with him the unmistakable face of boyhood so that he has become a parody of what he was, unable to free himself from what he no longer is.

) 379 (

In that summer's simplicities of sun and sea, my ambitions had gradually been reduced to one. I had decided that I would become my own man, although I was still far from sure as to just what this implied. It had something to do with living the way I most deeply felt, with making sure that I was living my life and not somebody else's, and that somebody else was not living my life in my place, and now I saw that my journey to the sea had been the beginning of a voyage toward where those deepest feelings lay. Not there, of course, not in that sun or in that wind, and not that girl, but there was something in the heat and silence of stone and sea and space that seemed to point the way back . . .

And now . . . my withered life, my debts that I could never liquidate, the tragedies in her past, her heroism, her martyrdom—I could throw them all out one by one like canceled checks. I could play the hardnosed Yankee, too, looking for the main chance, one hand on my pocketbook and the other on my soul, arranging other people's lives to give me peace of mind and calling it happiness. I could make my declaration of independence and be prepared to go to war to back it up. I could send her alone to the Bucks, if it was her grandchildren she was concerned about, and undertake the siege of that apartment that nested in the chestnut trees just back of Notre Dame. But whatever road I took, we had a showdown coming, Emily and I. We had had it coming for thirty years. And there wasn't any point in my running any further, because there was no place left to hide.

So *chez* Lipp we found a table in the back and she sat with her hands clasped before her, her face once again so radiant that as she looked about her she seemed on the verge of tears. And whatever moves I had planned that afternoon, she had made some of her own. Her hair was no longer yellow like old ivory but was blond streaked with silver, ashen wings folded about her face and drawn into a knot behind her head. There were lines of color on her eyelids, and her lipstick was more pink than red. Her skin was still dark the way that I remembered it, except that now her face was entirely covered with a fine veil of wrinkles which her powder tended to bring into relief. She wore turquoise and silver earrings and from the ends of her glasses a chain hung down around her neck. When she took a cigarette from her pocketbook and leaned toward me for the light, I could see that her fingernails shone with a platinum sheen. She still seemed vaguely dusty and a little wrinkled as though she had just got off the bus, but she knew what to do with herself when she got to the city. And the way she was looking around at the other women's clothes, I could guess what she would be doing tomorrow. And then when she looked back at me, I was struck by something childlike in her face, the sly look of a shy child who has seen and heard too much.

She appeared to be entranced by everything, and while I ordered she simply beamed, at the waiter, at the couple next to us, at the bilious regular across the room who glared at us yellowly above the vast expanse of napkin which he had tucked into his collar. Most of all she beamed at me, until I wondered if she had downed a little Private Stock before joining me in the lobby of the hotel.

"I got to Paris a couple of days ago," I said in answer to her question. "You may remember Spencer Platt. I've been visiting him here, waiting for you to arrive."

"The boy from Wyoming. You wrote so often about him in your letters. And now both of you in Paris—how wonderful it all is."

"Yes. Paris has changed a lot since you were here."

"That was so long ago." She said it with an amused little smile, almost ironically, as though she had forgotten and didn't particularly care. "You know, I studied French in college. Everyone seems so young. They wear such colors. My goodness."

I hadn't particularly noticed. Maybe after St. Tropez I was tired of youth and color both, but there was no need to go into that. In fact, it seemed unlikely that I would go into anything because she kept it up all the way to the apple tart—laughter iridescent as soap bubbles, anecdotes of our life together, little sayings she remembered from my boyhood, recollections of letters from school, from college, from most of the cities of Europe, stories that I had written her about my children—all of them worn smooth from constant handling like pebbles upon some sea-washed shore. She was like one of those portraitists at a sidewalk cafe who sits down at your table and does a likeness in five minutes, working rapidly over the years with a fine pencil, laughing away your protests, holding your attention until the payoff. But the payoff was what I was waiting for, so I watched her as she moved along through the past just as though she were revisiting room by room a rambling house where she had spent a glorious childhood. She sounded as though she hadn't talked for years, like maybe they had kept her in solitary. And we might have been a lady of a certain age and her somewhat younger companion, just back from St. Tropez after a season in the sun, keeping up the laughter though summer in every sense was gone. But whatever she was behind her smile, I was grim behind mine. Or trying to be, at least. I had made myself a desperate kind of promise, and I meant to keep it.

The coffee came and I lit a cigarette and she took out her compact and worked at her lipstick a little.

"Spencer Platt told me a funny thing the other night," I said suddenly. "He told me he went to Grey Horse. Just a few years ago."

Nothing had happened to her face. She moved her head around, studying herself in the mirror.

"How interesting. I haven't been back there in longer than I can remember." But something had happened to her voice. Something had dropped shut like a steel grill. And then the lights went out in her eyes, and she was watching me with a kind of armed intensity which I had never seen in her before.

"He talked to some people who used to know us. Jack Bird. Cody. Jack was the one who told him the most."

"I haven't thought of him in years. He took an interest in you—baseball, I think it was. I don't remember."

I waited to see if her memory would improve, but she was silent.

"Jack told me once he asked you to marry him."

"Jack said that to you?" and I thought for a moment she was going to break. But I was ready for that, too. I was already snipping away with the scissors and I had the hacksaw ready just in case, and then there was always the ax . . .

"What else did he tell you?"

She was backing up now, blinking, her guard down, her eyes not focusing very well.

"I saw him twice during Easter vacations from school. In St. Louis. When you were . . . away. Jack thought a lot of you—he was half-drunk most of the time, but he remembered pretty well. I couldn't follow most of it then, but I remembered what he said about you."

"Why did he go, this friend of yours? What business was it of his? Did you ask him to go?"

"He went up to the Court House. That's how he found out."

I had her down and she was hurting, but some kind of instinct made her get back up and stand there, waiting for me to hit her again.

"I don't understand it, Amory. Why would that interest him? It's all so long ago. Aren't they all dead by now?"

"I don't want you to hold it against yourself, Mother. Not telling me, I mean. Something in your letter made me think you had the idea that I didn't know." Because if I could make her believe that I knew the story already and that it didn't matter to me, and that my opening move was one of magnanimity, forgiving her for her silence through the years, then I would have her on the run, with at least an outside chance of keeping her that way. "We're partners, after all."

I ordered a couple of cognacs and waited for her to pull herself together. The tables around us were filling up, but she wasn't looking anyplace but straight ahead. The flesh around her mouth sagged in little tear-shaped lumps, and the lipstick ran crookedly up the side of her face as though she had tried to paint on a smile and hadn't had the courage to finish. She had that look of someone who'd been knifed—surprise, pain, horror, helplessness.

"How much—" and then she drank the cognac and tried again. "How much of this have you discussed with Mr. Platt?"

"All of it. Everything he found out."

"What does he know—what does he tell people?"

I shook my head. "As far as I know, he's never talked about it to anyone but me."

"His wife? Diane's friend, as I recall."

"I very much doubt it."

"So Diane wouldn't know."

"No. I never told her, anyway."

I wanted her to think that she still had a chance, just so I would know the worst if I could bluff her into showing it.

"And this girl of yours—Cynthia?"

"Cecile," I said, just for the hell of it.

"Cynthia—Cecile. It doesn't matter. How much—?"

And I shook my head.

She took one of my cigarettes and watched me while I lit it for her.

"Why do you say we're partners?" and she looked at me through the smoke with a suspicion so profound that I shuddered at how much it had taken to teach her to look at anyone that way.

"Because I think we have the same thing at heart. My best interests, I mean."

She was still frowning at me, but now there was something else in her eyes, something hurt and infinitely gentle, something sadly like a last-chance kind of hope.

"You see," she started, and then she waited as though she couldn't find the words. "Maybe I made a mistake from the beginning. I made up my mind to keep it from you so that you would be free of it all. But then maybe the only way to be free of it would be to know every last little detail by heart so that finally it was just part of you and it wouldn't matter any more. I thought of that, too, after it was too late. I've had a lot of time to think in my life . . ."

She pushed the words forward like so many skirmishers, probing, seeking contact, but I wanted to extend her lines as far as possible before I struck back. At the time I didn't want to think that she might be telling the truth; I was simply watching to see what kind of gambit she would try. Truth mattered less to me now than getting what I thought I wanted. But she fooled me. She came right down the middle.

"When you wrote me during the summer about what was happening, I realized then that I had been waiting for it for years, expecting it in every letter, knowing in some way or other that it was bound to happen. I ignored it at first, as though my very lack of reaction would have the effect I wanted. And then I realized that I was simply repeating the mistake that I had made with your father. That's when I decided to come here, breaking a promise I had made to myself almost thirty years ago. When I went to prison—you know all about that now—and I swore to myself that I would never see you again. And simply because I thought I could do the most for you that way—by staying out of your life forever."

The sadness was still there, but it had been focused to a kind of painful exaltation. Her breath came and went unevenly, and her eyes glistened as she looked up toward the light. Like forgotten children left by themselves to play, her hands went on breaking bread into tiny crumbs.

"I didn't know whether to tell you about it or not. I thought —hoped, rather—that just by seeing me again you would remember what you seem to be forgetting. That's what I had meant my letters to be all those years—a reminder of that world that you must never wholly forget, just as though your present happiness or safety or whatever you want to call it depended on your recalling every day who and what you are. Your father was a very weak man, Amory. I always thought the trouble was that he couldn't live up to his family—the name and all. Even the money. I think he wanted to hide from all the responsibility and at the same time consider himself noble for having done so. He was always that way. Life could have been so simple—just the things that everybody wants. He was always brooding. I don't know. That's why we went to Oklahoma in the first place—he wanted to make his own way, be useful, in a place where the family name or money couldn't help him. Of course the Commissioner was a family friend, and there was always money in one way or another, but that sort of thing Andrews could overlook. He needed to pretend to himself that he was doing something with his own two hands, helping others instead of merely enjoying what he had. All very New England, I suppose. I tried to tell him, of course, and then he met this woman. Did Jack . . ."

I nodded, and swallowed what was left of my cognac. It wasn't really working out as I had planned. Because I had come to fight, and here she was telling me her sad stories in a reminiscent, melancholy kind of way that lulled me the way her voice had all those years that we lived alone together in the little house.

"Striking, I suppose, in a free and easy sort of way. She wasn't so much a whore as just a tramp—trash, to use one of Cora's old expressions. She was a dancer—she had always used her body to get what she wanted—I suppose there didn't seem to be much difference. Andrews for her was a one-way ticket to wherever it was she wanted to go. As for him—well, can any man resist that sort of thing—passion, tears, that careless kind of glamour that men never seem to realize is only on the surface until it's too late? And isn't that your story, when you get right down to it? You need to be protected from yourself, just the way your father did—that's what Diane's up against. My God, that I should have to live through it all again."

And if I hadn't known something of her story, her cool calculations and the ruthless cutting of her losses, I would have taken the sucker punch right then and there. Her face was grey and lopsided with what looked for all the world like suffering, but then five years of prison must have taught her all that she would ever need to know about the arts of camouflage. So I motioned to the waiter for more cognac, and turned my eyes away.

"I might have been able to stop him, I don't know. The whole place had come as such a shock to me. Violence; horrible, sickening violence—that was the atmosphere. Even the weather—bitter cold in winter, and in summer so hot you couldn't breathe. All the murders—this whole Indian family—the easy money. I never understood it, didn't want to, even to talk about. We had no business there was all I knew. Andrews never had a chance. Maybe I could have helped him, but we were so young, so different from the others. We were still playing the game by rules that everyone else had given up, those who had ever learned them at all. I suppose everybody in that town knew what was going on. I only knew what was happening to Andrews, and there wasn't any way that I could stop it. People talk about doom, fate, God's will—that's the way it was. Just sitting there day after day in that little house, trying to keep from breaking down, watching him get closer and closer to the fire, not even anyone to talk to. It all had to do with Clay and Rita Carter—Rona's parents; you remember them—and the gradual killing off of her family, and there was a man named Shoat Dalton and the Lord knows who else involved in it all the way up to Washington until somebody had to be sent into that jungle just to make it look like they were trying. Andrews was the right man for it, I suppose—he was the kind of a man who was ready to be burned at the stake for what he believed. Sometimes I think he never really wanted to come back out alive, and maybe that's why I knew all along that I couldn't help him. And then the woman—it might have been different if it hadn't been for her. Maybe they needed each other, I don't know."

She lifted the little glass of cognac, sniffed it, held it to the light, then put it back on the table in front of me.

"What I do know is that they were lovers and that she was pushing him as hard as she could push. Maybe they planned to leave town together in a hurry—maybe that's why Andrews put Clay Carter in jail. I think Rita Carter wanted him there more than anybody else, and maybe she had her reasons. I don't think anyone ever knew, unless it was Jack, and Jack's mind had so many turns and twists in it that he didn't even know himself when he was lying and when he was telling the truth. Anyway, it wasn't but hours after Carter went into that jail that Andrews and Rita were dead, burned to death out at the ranch house, everything lost. That wasn't any accident. Maybe they were out there looking for money, packing, getting ready to leave—maybe they were just taking the first real chance they'd had to be together with Carter out of the way. Whatever it was, they were dead before that fire got started, that I'm sure of. Somebody killed them, somebody Carter sent to do the job. People said he always had men around for that kind of thing—I didn't have to look any further than Cody. Your friend talked with him, too, I suppose."

"Listened to him would be more like it. Cody never was an easy man to talk with. I don't really see him with a gun, unless it was loaded with blanks."

She shrugged her shoulders and looked at me in a far-off sort of way as though I could never understand.

"Sometimes killers come that way—clear-eyed, pink-cheeked, smiling, just like your next-door neighbor. You'd be surprised. I was. I never got over it. But however it happened, it was all so ugly and vicious that I knew I could never tell you the truth. And even if I had wanted to tell you, who would there be to back me up? Nobody was talking. Not even Jack. And Jack was the only one who cared. So we made our own truth about it, Amory. We made it the way it had to be. It was as good as any other way, after all, as long as it protected you, gave you a chance to grow up before somebody, someday, pulled it on you like a gun. Has anyone ever done that?" She smiled at me then as though she were telling me goodbye on visitor's day. Not really a smile at all. "It didn't happen as long as we were together, at least as far as I know. Did Jack—just before you went away?"

I shook my head, and her eyes flared up and then died away again.

"Carter never framed me, whatever Jack may have told you. I stole the money, and that money put you through school. Grey Horse money. I wanted it that way. Carter learned about it from the city manager, and held it back until he needed it. He got even in his way, I suppose, just as I did. I spent five years in a women's prison," and then her teeth clamped into a kind of lockjaw and the words wouldn't come and her eyes were shining again up toward the light and I wondered if I would really have the guts to push the plunger.

So I lit a cigarette for her and threw what was left of the cognac down my throat. "And that's why I have to go back to Diane. That's what you've come here to tell me."

She looked at me and then nodded very slowly. "That's why

all this foolishness has got to stop. You haven't got the right. Too many people have paid too much just to have it happen all over again."

I nodded, and then waited, counting the way you do when you've pulled the pin from a grenade.

"Look. All your stories. They don't really matter any more. They haven't for a long time, because after Jack told me as much as he did, and especially after I went away . . . Well, I made up my own version of it all, and I got by that way. At least as far as your Grey Horse was concerned. Because mine was different. Mine was the town I grew up in, playing tennis in that abandoned garage on Main, the show on Saturday afternoon, baseball about half the year and football and basketball the rest; the way the town sat there in that little valley, surrounded by grass as far as I could see; Indians and cattlemen, Negroes, Mexicans, Jack and Cora and Cody, and Rona Carter. That was my childhood, which was all I ever really had to go on, once I left. Would you believe me if I told you that I still dream about those people? That nothing on the surface of the earth is as clear in my mind as that little town? That I've spent thirty years trying to get away from it and trying to get back? It was the last time I saw you, when Jack brought me to visit just before I left, and all you said was "You're leaving now. I got you out in spite of everything. Promise me you'll never come back." All right. I kept my promise. You paid your price, but I've paid mine. I've been flopping around like a chicken with his head off for thirty years, and I can't stop bleeding. It's all been a sham, mother. I built it up for you more than anything else, just the way you built your life for me. There was nothing of mine in it. And I kept running away, and coming back, and running away again, until this summer when I wrote you because I thought I had made it over the wall for good. But now something has happened that I never even asked for because all I was ever really looking for was a place of my own. I've fallen in love. With a woman just as lonely as I am. Who has lost just as much as I have, and probably more. I can't give her up. I'm not going to. That is, if I have anything to say about it. Because whether she can love me or not is another question."

She stirred and looked away, at that room so full of all the life she must have dreamed of once. Then she looked at me again, her eyes bleak, her face without feeling, as though I had made my bet and she was thinking it over, wondering whether to call me or raise the ante.

"I kept you away from that town because there was nothing there for people like us, Amory. That town killed your father. It would have gotten you sooner or later. My only regret is that I left your father there, but then there didn't seem to be much point—he burned to death, and he was there forever, whether I wanted him to be or not. But all right. It's over, everybody dead now, I suppose. No reason to carry it around like a cross the rest of our lives. But I didn't come here just to tell you those stories all over again. I've been afraid for a long time, Amory. I know you, just the way I knew your father. He wanted to die in some way or other, and so do you. You call it taking off, but you go further out every time. You letters—they were always a little too perfect, like something you made up every time you sat down and wrote. I'm your mother, Amory—I know things about you, feel what's happening to you, no matter how far away I am. No, I came with something else in mind. I'm not going to ask you to go back, now that I see how you feel. Your letter really put that out of my mind. I've known something about your loneliness. You will admit that I've had my share of it, too. I had a little business there in the town where the prison is. I've sold it, Amory. I've come with everything I have. And I can help you now, the way I always have, the way I always will. Paris doesn't matter to me. We can go south to that hill town you wrote me about. So many years have gone by, Amory, but there's still time. Because I know you, and love you . . ."

I sat there staring at her, trying to hang on, trying to find a way to say it that wouldn't make her burst into tears. Because that terrible radiance was in her face again, some intense coupling of hope and hunger before which speech withered into awe-struck silence.

"I'm in love with a woman named Cecile. Cecile de Fleurie. She is French, just about my age, with children of her own. She has raised those children alone because her husband died a good many years ago. Most of the things that came to her from her family or her marriage have been lost. What she has left is her children, part of her beauty, all of her courage. I thought that perhaps if you met her, that you would recognize something—"

But the radiance had faded, and she seemed to be studying me again, getting ready to call my bluff, if bluff was what it was.

"My marriage was destroyed by the kind of woman men call beautiful. I've seen women of that kind. Ready to sacrifice anybody else just to get what they want. I've been through it once. I'm asking you to give her up, to quit playing with fire, to come to your senses before its too late. My God, how many times does it have to happen."

"And if I don't?"

"Then I'll find her, and tell her who you are. And I'll go to Diane, and to your children, and do the same. The whole story, all of it. Where you really come from. What it was like in Cell Block Number Six. All the lies you've told them all these years."

It couldn't have been a laugh, but I must have smiled, because I saw its shadow move across her face. "Do you think it would really matter? To them or anyone else? Nobody cares any more. These things are important to you, but nobody else wants them. Everybody's dead. Well, let them stay that way. What appalls me is that you would even think of that kind of black-mail—"

But she wasn't looking at me any more. She was folding her napkin very slowly, and brushing the crumbs from her lap. Then she rose, not saying anything, looking straight ahead of her as though she saw a friend at the other end of the room. Tired, a little grey and dusty in spite of the ashen hair, walking a little crooked like a punch-drunk fighter but still on her feet, carrying her bravery before her like a banner. And I had to hold onto my chair to keep from going after her, as though we were still bound together by those filaments of pain which I had done my best to cut.

The threesome at the next table—man, woman, and dog—kept

staring at me and muttering between mouthfuls about Americans, so after a while I paid the bill and got out on the street. I walked blindly then, bumping into people, not sure where I was going until I found myself by the weeping willow beneath Cecile's apartment. Above me her lights still burned. Spence was probably there and it was foolish to take a chance, but by now it was too late to worry. For back along the road that I had traveled I could see my bridges collapsing in flames, and she was up there waiting just as she had been for the last ten years. Waiting for someone who was mean enough not to give a damn and big enough to stay. I figured I could qualify for the first part if beating up old ladies was any kind of a test, and as for the second—well, I had made my mind up and all but told her so, and now it was up to her.

So I rode to the top floor in the little triangular cage that passed for an elevator. She must have been standing at the door when I pushed the button, because it opened almost at once and she was there in a long white housecoat and her hair hanging loose over one eye and her face somewhere between surprise and disappointment.

"I saw your lights—I thought Spence might be here."

She let me in and took my coat in silence.

"Look—I don't want to bother you. I was on my way to the hotel . . ."

"I'll get you some whiskey."

"Really, Cecile—I didn't mean . . . Just one then. Very light."

I watched her fix the drink, her tiny hands, the way her hair fell forward, the severe serenity of her face. In the strange hush of that apartment I heard a burry, bitter trumpet coming from the radio, Miles Davis or somebody, and I stared at the banged-up beauty of it all and wanted it so much that I was afraid to say a word.

"I understand that your mother is in Paris. Spence called and mentioned that you were having dinner with her."

I let the scotch burn my tongue for a moment and then sat down.

"Yes, she's here. She's playing for keeps. She intends to win."

"Win what?"

"Nothing. It doesn't matter."

"Spence thought it mattered. That's the way he talked about it anyway. I didn't really understand. What is there to win?"

"It's mainly what there is to lose," I said, and looked at her through the glass. "She wants me the way she thinks I am—no changes. About forty years ago she drew up a blueprint for the future. No additions, no alterations, no extra room for anybody else."

"Say it in plain English."

"I've had it."

"Say it in French."

"*Elle se fout de ma gueule. Je ne suis plus dans la course.*"

"And who decided this?"

"She has. She's the only one who can. I owe her everything. Ask her."

"What you are saying both in English and in French is that you are going back to England."

"That's about it."

"*Bien.*"

Her mouth had twisted just a little and her eyes burned a bit more fiercely, but otherwise she hadn't moved a muscle.

"I had hoped that you would stay and help. I don't know why—I just thought you would. Now I suppose that he will be the next one to go."

Like some petite Athena, her hair like a helmet around her head, every bone of that extraordinary face chiseled by love and honesty to a clarity that I could scarcely stand.

"I can't help you. If I helped you I'd help myself. That's why she came. So there wouldn't be the kind of changes that left her out."

"He won't ever make it. I would have had more hope if you had held out. I don't understand either one of you."

"No. Probably not. But I suppose that in a way a man gets the fate he deserves. He's had more than his share of luck."

"You think so?"

"More than ever."

"Meaning what?"

"Meaning you."

She turned away and walked to the window, but the flood-lights were off and Notre Dame was in darkness. But maybe it was something else she looked at—the river, the funny pointed houses on the other side, the red streaks of taillights like tracer bullets along the quai.

"I told you the other night, but you went to sleep on me. Listen to me, Cecile. My father was killed years ago, in bed with another woman. My mother kept it from me, made him into some kind of household god, an icon in the corner somewhere, candles, incense, the works. Then she got caught stealing money and went to prison—prison, that's what I said—and I was sent away to school. Between my father's mother and a worn-out old Oklahoma criminal lawyer, I got all the family life I ever had from fifteen on. I was given to understand that my mother had been framed and that like my father, she was innocent, a hero, a martyred saint if you will. I never knew the real story until tonight, to the extent that I know it even now. Maybe I was always afraid to take too close a look. Anyway, I've been living up to all that phony heroism and paying back bad debts and now I want to change. As for Spence—he meant those things he told you. Spence is not a liar. He just didn't tell you enough. He's part of a system that I'm not sure you understand. I'm not at all sure that he understands it either, for that matter. Because he's part of the American century, Cecile. Part of its health, part of its sickness. Very attractive from the outside, like photographs of New York City by night from the air. Just don't get any closer."

Her eyes were hard as agate when she looked around at me. She came back to the table and poured herself two fingers of scotch, neat.

"I got close," she said, her eyebrows raised for a pensive, fleeting moment. "I understand him. It's hard for him to accept what other people scarcely notice. He's hard on himself and hard on me. He wants something more of me than I've given for a very long time. Maybe never, because nobody ever asked. Maybe that's what people mean by innocence. The quality and kind of expectation."

"All right. Let's say you understand him. And that you knew all along that he wouldn't make the break, which is what you told me. But even if you were wrong about that, how much does he understand you?"

"There's not so much to understand. I've told him about my life. I've never hidden anything."

"It might have been better if you had. Spence is very old-fashioned in that way. Believes that people should be in love if they're going to sleep together. And if they're in love, they ought to get married, circumstances permitting, of course. The casual affair, the friendly liaison—all that is outside what he can accept. He's a romantic, you know—about as far removed from French realism in these matters as one can get. He believes people should be faithful, not on principle but because they want to be, as though there were something intrinsically important about it. Jealous as hell of every man you ever talked to, let alone slept with. Possessive beyond all reason, not at all disposed to play the games we all play from time to time, out of loneliness, out of desire, from simple curiosity. Curiously devoid of sympathy, like most Puritans, as though it were a weakness. Has he ever asked himself what it must have been like for you all those years? How lonely you were, how often you were tempted to try just one more time, on the off chance that at last . . . Has he ever wondered about the choice between the convent and the cafe, and what follows from the decision that you have to make over and over again? Your past haunts him more than you can imagine. The time your brother was killed at the château, the way your family had to leave their land as though a curse had attached itself to your name. Your husband, your younger brother, so many uncles, cousins, dead in wars they never understood. Most of the family money lost because of misplaced, outdated loyalties. He sees the hand of the Lord in all that, Cecile. He comes from a long line of American Protestants; he believes that the damned, like the elect, will be known by their lives. He's

afraid of you because you're doomed, the way Emily is afraid of
you because you're the same temptress who damned my father,
and I am the man to whom the Lord gave another chance because
my mother was willing to die that I might live. It's sick the way
the Bible is sick—full of blood and vengeance and sacrifice and
primitive morality and renunciation. Fear and hate for what one
loves. Love is a form of suffering for Spence. Joy has no place in
his life. That's his kind of American."

At least this time she listened. She filled my glass again and
curled up tight inside her housecoat and stared out at me from the
tawny, tangled thicket of her hair.

"But you're American, too, and yet you seem to think you
understand me."

"Yes, think I understand you, Cecile. Maybe its because I'm
not really American any more. I think I know why you've lived
the way you have. Beauty is just as much a curse as it is a blessing
—you've lived with it the way people live with money, or fame.
You've seen yourself in a mirror all your life. You were made for
pleasure, not to live alone. When your husband died, you threw
the book away—everything you had been taught. Out of grief,
loneliness, bitterness, something. You tried to figure it out all by
yourself, making it new, one truth after another like bricks in the
wall of a place where you could live. You did it the hard way, and
you made mistakes, and you had to pay. And then you reached
the stage where you wanted to make something finer and more
enduring out of all that you had lived, a mosaic perhaps, very
formally composed in the style of those old Roman mosaics where
one sees, say, a Roman lady in her garden, ornamentally surrounded by flowers and pigeons, fish and ducks, and sometimes
round little babies. By now you had all the elements—a place
in Provence, the Île St. Louis, beauty which seemed beyond
the reach of time, your flowers, your bridges and barges, thyme
and boulders by the sea and little inlets where sunlight filtered
through water traced wavy geometry in gold on the fine sand at
the bottom. Everything except peace. It would take a man to
bring you that. A man, or somebody who was willing to try and
become a man, if he could make it. But by that time you had

learned such a hell of a lot that it would take a very special man indeed . . ."

I ran out of breath and she laughed and threw back her head and shook the light from her hair.

"You want to know what I learned?"

It was more like a threat than a promise, but I had no choice.

"That if you're not in love and you sleep together, its mostly sad, and you end up lonelier than you were before. Because being lonely with somebody is worse than being lonely by yourself, and that trying to make it with someone who is lonely in the same way is the loneliest thing of all. That casual affairs are like a steady diet of spaghetti—simple to fix, easy to eat, and not at all *nourrissant*. That I wanted to get married again because I have children and I wanted a man's name and his public presence and security for them, and if I was not quite ready to die so that they might live, I was ready to sacrifice a lot. But finally, that love was more important to me than anything else because nothing was really any good without it. Which meant that I was a romantic like a great many other French people who are not at all the realists you foreigners take them for. I don't mean sentimentalism, which is just the other face the cynic wears. No, *la fleur bleue*—the *midinette* in her rented maid's room looking out at the moon, crying at the sound the accordion makes down in the street. That I wanted to be faithful because I felt that way—and the same for him. Without thinking about principles, I mean. That I wanted someone who hated every day of his life that he had spent without me. Who expected the impossible, more than I had ever been able to give to anybody. Who was moody, and severe, and impossibly jealous because I meant as much to him as he meant to me. Who was ready to take the suffering with the rest, and be there with me when it happened, and who might in the end even give me up because he loved me too much to bring me the kind of suffering he would endure if he were forced to give up everything else he had, when so many years have already gone by and maybe, just maybe, it's too late. He is a very special man, I agree. And if being American has something to do with it . . ." and her smile was very French.

I got up then, and put on my coat and buttoned it and pulled it up on my shoulders, stalling, hoping there might be something else. If there was, it wasn't for me. We didn't even say good-bye.

It was early afternoon by the time I had cut my way through the grey tentacles of the Paris suburbs, and once on the road I just rocked along, not pushing it, not in a hurry because when you got right down to it I had no special place to go. I had made up my mind that from now on it would be one day at a time, taking them as they came, and for the moment that meant a pad for the night. Like I was on the run again, except that there was nobody to come after me. Nobody cared enough for that. Except Emily, and she was here.

We had met for breakfast that morning just as though nothing had happened the night before. Emily read the funnies over coffee while I elaborately cleaned my pipe, and finally I asked her if there was anything special she would like to do today.

"Do you want to know the truth?" and all of a sudden the sly, corrupted child peered out at me through the net of wrinkles. "I'd like to get out of the city. Just drive until we find someplace that makes us happy. You've seen so much. I know nothing of France outside of Paris. Someplace where we can have a quiet dinner and talk."

She couldn't see my eyes because I was wearing dark glasses. For one thing, I was beat. I had been living on alcohol and coffee for longer than I cared to think. And then I had decided that since I was on the run, I might as well find a place to hide after all.

"You mean with the bags and everything?"

"Just throw it all in the back and take off. That's what I mean. I couldn't tell you when I had a vacation last. I've been thinking for the longest about the day when I'd just up and sell out and head for the hills," and she giggled a little, running her fingers along an ashen wing of hair.

"I'm game," I said. "But what about the Bucks?"

"Are they expecting us?"

"Not that I know of." I was being truthful for a change, about everything but Cecile. She hadn't asked about Cecile. I suppose she just took it for granted that the blackmail had worked.

"Well, what does it matter. They can wait a little longer. I've waited thirty years for this and I don't want to lose a single precious minute of it," and she leaned across the table and took my hand in hers.

"Nothing could be easier. You get the bags packed and I'll pay the bill." I could have been asleep and dreaming it, for all the ease with which those words came out. I had said them before so many times, in hotels whose names I could no longer even remember.

"We're going to be happy, Amory. Just you wait and see."

And now here she was beside me in the Jaguar with the map unfolded on her knees, reading out the place names, checking for restaurants in the Guide Michelin. We were headed south, as much by instinct as anything else, and then suddenly I remembered the Château d'Ardières, where Cecile had lived as a girl and where her brother had been dragged head down over wintry cobblestones to a common grave and where her family had finally packed what was left of its honor and headed west, just like any other frontier story. The cafe with the Beaujolais and *saucissons*, and Amory and Cecile listening to the rain on the roof above their bed. Why not? It seemed an appropriate kind of joke for a fading afternoon in late October, driving back toward St. Tropez with someone who was neither Cynthia nor Cecile.

"Just this side of Lyons would be about right for dinner." And then I casually named the place and felt the grief swell into my throat when she noted with disappointment that there were no starred restaurants there at all, and thanked God for my dark glasses because the way I looked at her then was too close to hatred to be of use to anybody.

I lost my way somehow, and asked directions of small-eyed peasants with purple noses, and drove up and around and over vineyards until the whole place seemed like one vast graveyard in the military style, each dream marked by a small deformed black cross. For a while I had hopes that they didn't exist at all, the idyllic village at the crossroads, that château looming above the hill and just below the woods. But Emily kept insisting, and then as the last of the light went underground I found them, the château diffused into an evanescent, mauve approximation of itself in the autumnal twilight, the cafe cheerful in a liverish sort of way inside its dense encrusted coats of heavy yellow varnish. I suppose it was the same cafe—there were half a dozen rooms upstairs and plenty of Morgon and *saucissons*, not to speak of steak and cheese and salad and some kind of chocolate cake. All of which she ate with gusto while I drank, a Kir, then wine, then eau-de-vie, while she told me about my father, showing me old photographs that she produced one by one from her voluminous pocketbook. Andrews in his lieutenant's uniform, the two of them on the day of their marriage . . . Somehow or other I recognized him and tried to identify that face with what I felt about him, but tonight it was just another grief too many. So finally I left her talking with the *patron* and lurched up the winding steps, bulging at the temples, sweating in spite of the damp October chill, my heart as black and twisted as the dried out roots of vines that I had seen along the road. I sank into my lumpy bed and lay there groaning, wondering how it would have been had I been the man who came here with Cecile. Some kind of timeless, illuminated moment when both of us stared straight ahead as though peering through a microscope at specimens of our different pasts, and all of a sudden recognizing that same underlying cellular network of rivers and bridges, forests and fields, roads and canals, linked together now by love? Horror for horror, death for death, betrayal and suffering, murder and expiation—a dark and tragic country where each in our separate ways must make his peace. I loved her for what had happened to her, and she might have loved me because I understood. At least it could be a kind of dreaming, although my dreams that night were very sad.

But next morning, early, while Emily still slept, I walked around and looked at the crumbling, silvery bulk of the great château through the shining avenue of trees, seeing the gardeners where they clipped among their green geometry, hearing tumults of birds which swept as sudden as arrows across the sky, and I tried to tell myself that the wind which spun the leaves could once again blow cleanly through me and somehow fan my senses back to life. I had wanted to turn that solid stone, the long rolling swells of vines, the hard clarity of the gardens and even the very weather into fantasies that matched my memories. But I had failed, for this was no mere scenery for my traveling magic lantern show, whereas Spence, afraid or not, had wanted it for what it really was, and Cecile had known the difference. And yet that landscape was a mirror of proportion, and what I thought I saw within its chiaroscuro planes was that the château would outlast us all, defeats and victories alike, and the château in its turn would be at last received by earth, this morning an ancient graveyard not merely of dreams but of wars, loves, great ambitions, disappointments, history itself. Perhaps I could find a way to live with it, like so many who had passed this way, like Cecile herself who, in her turn, as with so many others, had also come and gone. . . .

It started raining in Lyons, and the windshield wipers marked time like a metronome all down the valley of the Rhone, through the plane trees and the vineyards and the pines to the coast, time that didn't matter any more. It was a Chinese landscape that I scarcely recognized, the valleys vague with mist, the trees sketched in ink against a violet earth. Along the coast the sea was soft, a cloudy grey, and just before St. Tropez I turned back inland and drove through sprays of peach trees and knobby vines to where the village hung curiously suspended in a cloud of woodsmoke threaded through with rain.

I parked in the square beneath the Sully elm, the steaming hood of the old Jaguar nosed right into the flank of the church, there where they put the platform for the orchestra on the 14th of July. And when I turned the motor off, Emily woke and looked around her in a quick and frightened way.

"Where are we?" she asked.

"I've brought you home, Emily," saying her name to her for

the first time in my life, and then I got out and stretched, and the rain on my face was soft and stinging and cold, just the kind of welcome I might have expected.

"Come on. I want to introduce you to my friends."

Henri was there behind the bar, wiping the zinc counter, rolling a cigarette between teeth startlingly new and white in a face like that of a gargoyle ravaged by all the weathers of history. We shook hands all around and he poured the wine, and the others at the bar lifted their glasses to Emily. Faces full of years of sun and wind, voices flowing swift and passionate while like jugglers they spun the trivia of their days into an evanescent tableau of light and grace. And now they were silent, looking with something like wonder at the starved radiance in Emily's eyes as she slipped her arm through mine and leaned against the bar, shaking her head, saying over and over again to me as though no one else were there: "I never thought I'd live to see this town. Not here, where every time you came I knew you were in trouble. Your girls, the place you write your books, that letter you sent me from here last summer . . . I never thought you'd bring me here. I never thought I'd live to see the place."

"I told you," I said. "I've brought you home. If home is the kind of place where you can be alone," and then we shook hands again all around and went back out into the rain and down the winding, empty streets of stone, and the wind met us at the corner and we put our heads down and I wasn't sure whether Emily was laughing or crying or just trying to tell me something. And then I unlocked the door and we stepped into that cold silence—empty rooms, an empty fireplace, the melancholy sound of water dripping from the eaves—for all the world like the silence of a tomb. I put the suitcases down and all my carefully nurtured bravery went out like a low flame caught in a sudden wind. I reached for my wallet to see if I had enough to pay for a long night's drinking in St. Tropez, and then I saw the shopping basket, leaning against the stove, full right to the top with pine cones and gnarled roots of vines. It was a love letter of sorts from an aged, arthritic angel; that blessed cleaning lady had somehow bothered to think of me, and was shrewd enough to know that when I came back I would no doubt be alone and would probably want a fire. It wasn't much, but something that felt like hope took hold of my hand and made me put the wallet back, and then in a furious, tearful, exalted half hour I had a surging fire and the table set and the canned soup on the stove while Emily unpacked the bags and made the beds.

The funny thing was that when you added it up you got a minus number, but hope seems somehow synchronized with the heart and lasts just about as long. I was back in the place where I had started a week ago; I had lost my girl and betrayed my best friend and all I had to show for it was a heartache named Cecile. Except, of course, for Emily. I didn't know about Emily yet. I didn't know how much more she wanted to take away from me. I didn't even know whether what I felt for her was love or hate, and I was afraid to work too hard at finding out. And yet I sat and drank and hummed old cowboy songs and brought tears to my eyes with scraps of verse remembered from school and with a generosity that grew more gratifying with each tumblerful of local rosé, long on alcohol, I conceded to myself that the fault was entirely mine. I had treated all of them as one-dimensional figures, and they had come to life and blown my plot right off the page. No wonder Cecile had seen through me the way she did. Maybe I had been writing Westerns for so long that now my life was nothing but stock characters and phony sets—no people, no trees, no gardens or castles, no tragedy or heroism. Just painted landscapes and mummers in a worn-out morality play. And now Spence and Cecile had each other, and all that was left for me to do was to ride off into the sunset. Somebody always had to die or disappear at the final fadeout. It was usually the guy who didn't get the girl.

"Soup's getting cold," I called to her upstairs.

"Coming," she answered back, trilling it a little, and when she sat down I could see that she had touched up her lipstick and brushed her hair and pinned a brooch to her blouse—a ballet dancer in silver. Then she took my hand and leaned close to look at me and then nodded, her eyes brimming again with that light that seemed to swell and fade inside her like the movement of the sun.

"You couldn't have done anything nicer for me, Amory," she said. "What I said the other night—I hope you'll just forget it. All of that is behind us now, and we're here together, and you're going to do your work, and we'll just see about that new life you spoke of in your letter. O.K.?"

And then before I could answer she was blowing on her soup and telling me about the trip we had made once upon a time, halfway across the country on the train, the first time we came to Grey Horse.

For an unbroken month I lived in the peace of total failure. Beyond my window was a wind-ruffled sweep of prairie, followed by buttes and badlands, canyons and arroyos, gorges, passes, waterholes, and deserts. Lean Indians, some with headdresses, all breechclouted, riding bareback, followed like jackals the West-bound wagon train wherein were bonneted and stalwart pioneer women and sturdy youngsters who knew how to use a rifle. Buckskinned plainsmen watched over them like hawks, fanning out ahead in scouting parties to clear the trail, riding shotgun, talking big, goodhearted as all get out. One woman drove her team alone—a pretty Widow with young children who was head-ing West to claim her husband's stake—and she was much ad-mired by the young Confederate Captain who, it was later learned, had come West to forget and find his fortune, following the bitter defeat of his gallant land and the loss of all his loved ones. He had a sidekick, fellow played a gui-tar, a Rebel, too, with a jug and a horse that was about half mule. And then the Plains-man himself, the Leader, given to drink and dark thoughts and somber looks, a former Major in the Victorious Union Army who, it was later learned, had been drummed out for brutality to his troops. He liked the Widow, too, in a silent, glaring sort of way, and sooner or later there had to be a showdown. Stripped to the waist in the sun, bare knucks, except the Plainsman had stuck a knife in his boot and if it hadn't been for the sidekick who shot it out of his hand at thirty yards . . .

It was an out-of-season life, empty as the beach along which I ran in early evening, a time when the year moved toward its end, the harvest done, the summer people gone, winter in the air. Occasionally a dog would rollick along beside me on the sand; birds I rarely saw save for one tiny feathered skeleton rolling a little in the wind. There was a misty, smoky loneliness upon the land, and driving back from the beach as night moved in across the plain, I saw around me the glow of fires, dead vines being burned in the fields, like the bivouac of some conquering army camped in siege around our little town. I read and slept and typed and fiddled with the car, and after dinner I sat by the fire and listened to Emily as she meandered through the years. Then after she had gone to bed I had a nightcap in the loud café and watched the cardplayers as they argued the nights away. Over my wine I sometimes read old newspapers like scraps of papyrus history from some ancient dig. Nobody came to visit. There was no mail.

After Emily had learned to handle the Jaguar, she was on her own. She found slacks and cable sweaters on sale in St. Tropez, and hauled fertilizer for the rock garden in back of the house, and the wind and the sun put color in her face so that after a while the lipstick disappeared. She seemed perfectly content, as though the rhythm by which she lived had become the very substance of her life, and perhaps that, too, was part of the legacy of Cell Block Number Six. Her French improved, and she did all the shopping, and gradually I came to look forward to the dishes she set before me every night—roast chicken stuffed with herbs, rabbit in olives and mushrooms, fish grilled in the fireplace. I suppose we passed with the natives as just one more of those curious couples attracted by the temperate isolation of the coast in winter. They came in every flavor, like a box of assorted chocolates. Sinewy, hipless women whose leathery faces were framed by close-cropped waves of greying hair; middle-aged ladies and boys in their teens; middle-aged boys with ladies in their sixties. We attracted no particular attention as we sat among them in Senequier's, drinking tea at noon along the port and holding our faces up to the sun like so many flowers clinging to the last of the light.

As far as I could tell she had no thought of leaving, for the Bucks or anyplace else, so I began to think about having the older children down for Christmas. I think they liked me in a rough and cheerful sort of way, the way they might have liked a favorite uncle. Probably I counted for little in their lives from day to day; even at home I spent most of my time alone in my attic study, and there was something about the trench warfare between Diane and me which turned the children's world into a kind of no man's land which they traversed at periodic intervals, bearing messages from side to side. But in my painful and abstracted way I loved them, and saw them growing through the years with continually renewed surprise, as though a person as slenderly rooted anywhere as I could scarcely expect to cast a shadow. And somehow I had assumed that for Emily they would be far more important than either Diane or I to that bridge into the future which she had so carefully contrived. Yet she spoke of them rarely, and seemed quite happy to love them at a distance. About Diane she no longer spoke at all.

As for me, there seemed little left worth worrying about now that I had come to rest in the dead tranquillity of late November, so I concentrated on making my money last and hoped I could hold out until I sold the goddam thing. The strange thing is that no matter how far down a man may go, he's always got to draw the line somewhere. And where I drew the line was around her money, because I didn't want it. So she fussed, and called me silly, and gave me things I didn't need, and I counted words and estimated pages and calculated the number of weeks if my luck held and then scotch-taped the schedule above my desk. And then with December coming on I wrapped up what I had finished and air-mailed it to New York. I pleaded poverty and begged for money, admitting that they had given me a lot but telling of the separation and listing the names and ages of my children in descending order. I promised that by Christmas I would have the

Union and the Confederacy reconciled in a sunset marriage scene with the Major as best man. All I had to go was one wagons-in-a-ring and the kidnapping of the Widow by the Indians, then the Captain and the Major in pursuit and seeing who could go longest without drinking the water, and then the Major being saved by the Captain and the Widow being saved by the Major and then one courtship scene (just a look and a promise) when they get to the top of the pass and all of California is at their feet, and then the Widow finding that after all her husband had left her a dandy little place in Apple Valley, and then the marriage ceremony with crossed cavalry swords and the sidekick square dancing with the schoolmarm and fadeout with the Major riding alone through the apple orchard toward where the sun is going down on distant mountains (if it's a color production, that is). I even threw in my suggestions for a cast, and a couple of composers with Russian-type names—you never knew which coin would bring up all the cherries.

I had a letter back inside a week. There was only one trouble with it. It should have been a long, slim envelope postmarked New York City, with my name typed on the front. My name was there, all right, but in ink and in a hand I didn't know. The letter came from Paris. Actually there were three letters, folded up together, but hers was the one I opened first.

DEAR AMORY,

I can only pray that this letter reaches you. There was no way for me to have your address and then I went to the American library and found your books. I wrote to your publisher in New York, who sent me your address in England. No reply. Then I tried your English publisher, and it took two letters and a phone call to London, and I'm still not sure. All of it too sad and silly to write down. But please, Amory, please; if this letter reaches you, write, call, come, something. I wasn't nice at all and you owe me nothing, I know that, but I have nobody else who knows about it, nobody else to ask.

Maybe you already know what I am going to tell you and just don't care. But even if I believed that, I would have to write you anyway because one of us has to do something. We can't just sit around and let him die.

Spence was on his way to Orléans about the divorce. It's a three-lane highway for part of the way and sometimes you can't see on the curves what's coming from the other direction. That's the only way I can explain it. There was a car wreck, and Spence ended up halfway through the fence on the side of the road. The door must have come open, because he was thrown out into the ditch. I don't know why he wasn't killed. He was shocked and cut up—two ribs broken, I think—but all right otherwise. He always told me that he was lucky. Maybe that proves it in a way. But the other driver didn't have Spence's luck; he's dead.

I heard it on the radio and went to Orléans just as fast as I could get there, but I couldn't see him so I talked to his nurse and told her to let him know some way or other where I was. His wife was there, you see, and so I stayed by the phone in the hotel all weekend, but Monday I had to be back at work, and he didn't call. Then later when I tried to phone him he wouldn't answer. Then finally I got his letter. Read it and send it back. I wouldn't have mailed it to you if I didn't need you so much. It's all I've got. It's all I'll ever have now.

It was written in a kind of scrawl, as though he had had trouble holding the pen. Like the writing of a very old man, limping across the page.

Dear Cecile,

I'm sure you know about what has happened.

Once at Ardières, when you told me the story of your brother and his friends, you said that after something like that had happened, nothing and no one could ever be the same again. That there were things a person just had to do after that, whatever it cost. That there wasn't any choice left. I never forgot it, the way you said it.

But because I was in love I tried to forget a lot of things, like maybe there could be a choice after all, and now I have been made to understand in the worst way possible how wrong I was.

I think it was during that same weekend that you showed me a copy of a letter written by one of your ancestors to his wife. For some reason or other I kept it, meaning all the time to give it back. I have now copied it out for myself so that I will have one to keep, and am sending back enclosed the one you gave me.

Dernières volontés et recommendations
d'Etienne de Pradel
Chevalier de St. Louis
Ancien garde de corps de S.H. Le Roi Louis XVI
Capitaine de Cavalerie

À MA FEMME ET MES ENFANTS

Comme mes juges sont des hommes, et qu'ils sont sujets à l'erreur, pardonnez leur; je les absouds sur cette terre que j'habite encore, et Dieu devant lequel j'ai déjà paru, m'a tenu compte du sacrifice que je fais, et que j'ordonne à mon fils et à tous les miens de faire, de toute espèce de vengeance.

Je vous envoie une boucle de mes cheveux, j'espère que cette frêle dépouille ne vous quittera jamais, et qu'elle vous suivra au tombeau où nous serons réunis un jour . . . c'est toute mon espérance.

Je donne ma bénédiction à mes enfants—qu'ils se rappellent combien sont fragiles les biens de ce monde, l'exemple et la leçon du moment en sont la preuve. Je leur recommande la sublime religion de leur père.

Adieu . . . adieu pour toujours

ETIENNE DE PRADEL

Don't blame yourself, Cecile. We did our best. Too much had happened, to both of us. I won't write again.

SPENCE

Unless by some miracle you can help me. Just one more time, at least to try. Because he loves me, Amory. I know he does. He mustn't kill himself this way, just because of a stupid accident and what it means to him in some blind way or other. So please—talk to him for me. Come back and make him listen. I have no way to reach him. There is no one else who could possibly understand but you. I was proud and frightened and I hurt you, but now I am the one who is begging you to help. You came here once for him. Please, please do it for me.

CECILE

The whole thing made me so sick that I didn't know whether to laugh or throw up, but all I managed was a sour sort of smile. I had been right in the beginning—they cast no more shadow than my Widows and Confederate Captains. Old-time movie stuff, capes and camelias, Barrymore and Garbo. But then I was a player, too, in my Wm. S. Hart kind of way, and there we were.

It took me an hour of digging through those ridiculous papers that I carry around with me, folded in my wallet or in packets bound by rubber bands, like so many old bank statements. Credits on one side, debits on the other. Mostly the latter. But finally I found what I was looking for.

I HAVE SAID MANY TIMES BEFORE *and I will say it again, that the knight-errant without a lady is like the tree without leaves, a building without a foundation, or a shadow without the body that casts it . . . God knows whether there is a Dulcinea in this world or if she is a fanciful creation. This is not one of those cases where you can prove a thing conclusively. I have not begotten or given birth to my lady, although I contemplate her as she needs must be . . .*

And what the hell is a man to do when he has that message tattooed on his heart. . . .

So that night I told her that I would have to go to Paris.

"From my agent," I said. "He's going to be in town for a couple of days. He's important to me."

We were sitting by the fire where she had been helping me sort my papers. She had decided that all my clippings should be pasted in a scrapbook, and tonight she was laying them out, fitting them to the pages.

"You want to come?" I was taking a chance, but it wouldn't help at all if she became suspicious.

"No," she said after a moment. "No, I don't think so." She smiled at me and raised her eyebrows just a little. "I'm very happy here, Amory. I feel as though this were the first place in all my life that I could call home, if you want to say it that way. Isn't that strange? I mean all those years in Oklahoma, and I grew up in Massachusetts like your father, but I don't know. Now this noisy little town like some kind of a beehive or anthill or something. I'm happy. Just say it that way. You go on to Paris and see your man and then come on back and finish your book and then we'll see. One day at a time. I've learned that much, at least."

And whatever it was that made her face light up—peace, hope, some kind of fulfillment, I don't know—was so strong that for a moment she seemed almost young. I saw her then as she might once have been: dark-haired, laughing, awkward and impulsive, wanting more than she could name, in love and full of faith because a miracle had happened, and then the long, slow erosion of her joy by so many tears until at last she was the way I had always remembered—a woman who had lived so long with sorrow that finally all that came and went in her face were various shades of grief. I had loved her in a way that I could find no way to utter except in tears, and every time I looked upon her I was afraid. Perhaps because I was afraid of some demonic power she seemed to possess which enabled her to take the things I loved away from me—my father, first, and then my very childhood. And looking at her now, wondering whether the pain I felt was love or fear, I asked myself what else there was that she could take away.

"You know," she said, and touched her fingers lightly to her hair. "If you're going to be talking about your books—oh, its silly. What business do I have . . ."

"What's on your mind?" I was over the hump because she was no longer worried about Cecile. The rest I could take like after-dinner coffee.

"Well," she said slowly, and then I saw again the eyes of that child who had grown up around the prison and heard the screams and the moaning after the lights went out and the talk, all the talk, because there was nothing else to do . . . "Those things that happened at Grey Horse. I knew them all—do you remember Blair Booth? Blair Booth was the Indian Agent when we came there. He committed suicide when your father exposed Clay Carter—he was at our house that same night—he must have gone right home and shot himself. So Clay killed him, too, in a way, just the way he killed the rest of us. Cody wasn't exactly what you could call alive, and Jack—well, old Jack. Jack stayed out of it some way or other. Maybe because all he ever cared about was baseball, because if you cared about money, or women, or justice, not to mention any kind of decency, then Clay had you. Wouldn't it make a story? If there ever was a villain, it was Clay. And then your father for the hero—well . . ."

And so I had my answer, for she went on turning it into one of my Westerns, taking away the very last thing I had. Except to tell the truth, I had a little hope. A tiny secret bit of exultation. Because Cecile had asked me to come, and I would be on my way tomorrow.

"That's a thought," I said, yawning and getting up. "I never looked at it that way."

"The funny thing was that Blair had come specially, to our house, that same afternoon."

She was no longer talking to me, and I stood there and watched the dreams move slowly across her face.

"Almost the very last thing he said—anyway, the thing that stuck in my mind—was that I should take care of you, because somebody ought to remember. Something like that. It had a funny sound, the way he said it, and that's how I remember him. You were sick, and he sat down there in your little back room and propped the lamp up just so and made all these animals and everything on the wall. You know, with his hands. Do you remember?"

"No," I said after a moment. "No, Emily, I don't remember Blair Booth, I guess I don't remember much of it any more."

"He was Southern," she said. "Real Southern, not Texas Southern like Clay. He had manners, and he treated me like a lady. The only one," and then something like wakefulness came back into her face. "Amory," she said, "I never asked for anything. I just sat there and watched it happen—terrible—some kind of awful madness about it like nobody could do anything different even if they wanted to. You're all I ever had—you were the only thing that was really mine. Everything else was taken away but you. That's why I feel like I'm home. I said I'd show them . . ."

Our eyes met and held, and I had something I wanted to say but I didn't know what it was. The way it turned out was that I never did know because I never said it, and now I'll carry it around inside me for the rest of my life, some kind of silence that nobody will ever hear.

"Right up to the last I didn't believe him. Sometimes I think —I don't know, if I had believed enough, had faith enough, maybe . . ."

"Faith is no good against a car wreck. Or let's say against the way Spence took it."

"I was afraid to believe him. It happened to me too often, I suppose—wanting to believe in someone. I just don't have the courage any more."

"You've been in and out of love too many times. That was one of the things that scared Spence. He didn't see why he was any different, why you should love him any more than the others."

Her eyes were very bright, more green than brown in the light that fell upon her face, and the elliptical lines of paint made her seem almost Egyptian, a cat queen, gorgeous Nefertiti.

"No. I've been in and out of loneliness. I loved my husband, at least to the extent that I was capable of loving anybody then. There were others I tried to love because they loved me, or said they did; mostly because I wasn't meant to live alone. Spence made me forget all that."

"You really love him, don't you. To tell you the truth, I was never convinced. That you might need him for one reason or another—all right. But love him—I don't know. There's something cruel about him—and sentimental at the same time. I've been trying to figure him out for twenty-five years. He's not real—he's the man in the iron mask—he's buried himself so deep that he can't get out."

We were sitting in her apartment over orange peels and bits of cheese and crushed walnut shells. It was her champagne this time, golden in the sun, faintly astir with wavering vertical lines of light. Some last whisper of hope had brought me clattering into Paris with pennants streaming, resplendent in chased and shining armor, ready to do battle for my lady. And then in the first terrible clarity of her glance I saw mirrored a comic, sad-faced knight in rusty corduroy who laughed because he didn't want to cry.

"I love him because that's the way he is."

She dipped her sugar in the coffee and nibbled at it, looking at me in a way that made her seem to see somebody else.

"He locked himself up and threw away the key, and then he waited. That way there was something about him that stayed a boy, and yet those years of loneliness made him a man. Both of us like prisoners, tapping on the walls. And then when we met we already knew each other. He's not real to you because you never knew him. Not the way I do. For months he never came here once that he didn't end up crying. It seemed to me that during all that time I scarcely spoke, and he talked and read me things, books he had loved and hadn't looked at for years, so much about his life when he was a boy wherever it was. We had such an awful lot to tell each other—we had been waiting for so long. In some strange way it was more than anything else like we had been brought back together after years of separation. I love him. I don't care whether I marry him or not. I'm past that point now, to the extent that it ever really mattered, and it never really did, of course. I won't ask for much. Just a part of his life, however he can work it out, as long as it's straight. No shame, no hiding, taking it as it comes from day to day until perhaps when the children are grown . . ."

"You're asking me to make him a proposition?"

"I'm asking him to be honest with himself."

I could see what she meant by honesty, just by the way she sat

and looked at me, so erect, so proud, so uncomplicated, so innocent, finally. She made it seem easy, and maybe that's the way it
was when you really believed in love. I couldn't say. I'd never had
the chance to try it out.

"Use the phone?"

I thought she flinched a little then, but maybe she had just
remembered that I was there.

"You want to telephone from here?"

"It's up to you."

For a moment I thought she might back out, and then she
nodded.

Whatever else had happened, the secretary hadn't changed.
And for all I knew, Spence might have left word not to take any
calls from Amory Thayer. Because Spencer Platt was, as they say,
all business.

"It's Jiménez calling. From Venezuela. Very urgent."

"Mr. Platt is in conference. I simply can't disturb—"

"Very urgent. From Venezuela. Jiménez calling."

We could have kept that up for several more laps, but disdain
got the better of her and she put me through.

"Spencer Platt here."

"It's Amory, Spence."

"Who?"

"Ames Thayer. Remember?"

Maybe he was trying to remember. Probably he was trying to
forget. I tried to hear his breathing, and wondered if he had cut
me off.

"What is all this Jiménez nonsense? Where the hell are you?"

He sounded as though he thought I might be calling from the
cafe down below, and had a gun.

"In Paris. I heard the bad news, Spence. I wanted you to know
how sorry I am that things worked out the way they did."

I was leaving it up to him to pick out the news he thought the
worst, but he played it safe.

"Yes, it was rough on everybody. We all did our best. Just
one of those deals where there wasn't any way to do anything
right. Don't blame yourself for any of it."

"I was hoping to see you—just to catch up on things."

"As a matter of fact I'm pretty busy—"

"I'm leaving tonight on the train for London. How about dinner beforehand?" He was bluffing, so I called him and laid down my cards. "I've seen Cecile." He didn't have to show me what he had. I could see the look on his face clear across town.

"How is she?"

"Bad. I've got to talk to you."

"It's all over, Ames. Finished. Nothing left to say on either side."

"You'd hate yourself if anything happened, Spence. If there had been a chance for things to be different. There's been enough of that already. She's in bad shape. She might do something foolish."

The way he caught his breath was louder than the silence, and I knew I had him.

"You know my club. Just off the Rond Point. Seven thirty?"

"I'll be there," and I cut the connection with my thumb, just to beat him to the punch for once.

"You didn't need to put it that way. How did he sound?"

She had her back to the light and I couldn't see her eyes but the sun in her hair was a halo of red and gold. I didn't particularly want to look at her anyway. It had been a long time since I had cried, and the last time had been right here, and I wasn't about to start again.

"Like he didn't know us. Look, Cecile, you don't really think it's going to work?"

"I don't know what I believe any more. I told you the way I felt—maybe if I just had faith enough . . ."

Her hands were very small, and her nails were painted a kind of scratchy Chinese red. At the corner of one cheekbone was a beauty spot.

"Suppose it doesn't work. What then?"

"I don't know. I don't want to think about it. Not until we've tried. What did he say?"

She was fierce and fluffy, and I had never known anyone who listened so hard.

"Say? He said the same thing to me that he wrote in the letter. 'Don't blame yourself.' Hell, we're not to blame for anything."

There was a bar of granulated light along the silk of her calf. Her knees were large and shadowed where they bent beneath her.

"Make him admit that he knows how much I love him. Shake him—wake him up. Tell him he can't do this to himself."

The tears ran along the lines beneath her eyes and down across her cheeks. She didn't seem to notice.

"I'll tell him."

I got my coat in the hall and then came back into the room. She had the knuckle of one finger pressed against her teeth, but she sat there straight and proud, not giving an inch.

"I'm in love with you myself, Cecile, but I'll tell him. I came up here with my guitar to sing outside your window and to do whatever deeds you asked of me. But once I've told him, and if by some chance he doesn't change his mind . . ." But she had already turned her head away.

He was waiting for me in the vestibule when I came in off the street. His face was ruddy as though he had been running in the cold, and his close-cropped hair seemed more blue than grey. Probably he had come straight from the barber shop or maybe the sauna, or maybe he had just put in a hard half hour at the squash courts. In any case, I had never seen him looking better— clear-eyed, square-jawed, lean-bellied, trim—everybody's All-American. I figured he must have had some anxious moments thinking about my corduroy trousers, but I was up to the occasion. I had spent the afternoon acquiring some new French clothes—Tarzan in the shoulders, Mistinguet in the hips. My collar was stiff as cardboard and my shoes were pointed with a little heel. The only thing they hadn't sold me was the mustache.

He looked at me apprehensively as though it were a gag, and then held out his hand in a tentative sort of way.

"It was good of you to call, Ames. I thought that you were back in England. You left so suddenly . . . Mother well? How about a drink?"

"I don't think so. Why don't we go right up to dinner. I've got this train to catch . . ." and I handed him a smile like a business card. I was playing it brisk and to the point tonight; I was only here because she had asked me to come. And as for weeping in my cups because of all that he had suffered, I wasn't buying.

The club appeared to have been ferried over from London stone by stone. The waiters wore white gloves, and the company was distinguished and discreet. A well-known diplomatic correspondent, a former ambassador, a prize-encrusted writer of eighty years who looked like old man Rockefeller and, as a great moralist, was just about as convincing. The correspondent sat alone, but we shared the long table with the other two who whispered and giggled as though they were telling dirty stories, which in fact they were.

"I had swung out to pass—the road rises along there and curves some. I didn't see him coming until he was right on me. I don't remember . . . My reflexes aren't what they used to be, I guess. My mind . . . I was on my way to Orléans. I was thinking about the divorce . . ."

He tried to smile and then looked at me for a moment without speaking, almost as though he thought I would interrupt.

"When I came to I was lying on the side of the road. Seemed like I could still hear the broken glass falling, tinkling the way it does. Like my head was full of sleigh bells or something. The other driver was killed outright. At least he didn't suffer. He had a family . . . I don't know. That's the kind of thing that doesn't have to happen twice."

"I hadn't heard about it," I said, "until Cecile wrote me. She got my address somehow."

"You still down south?"

He buttered his roll with great precision and brushed the crumbs away with his little finger.

"Just got back. Emily's still down there. I'm going to London for a few days to see the children—Diane is sending the two oldest up from the Bucks."

"You must miss them."

"It's pretty bad. There are worse things, I suppose."

He ordered for us in his loud and labored French. White gloves set out porcelain and silver dishes. The wine was a good Bordeaux *en carafe*, bought cheap the way the rich can afford to buy it. I made some remark to that effect, and the writer turned and stared at me for a moment. He seemed to be observing the padding in my suit.

"How is Cecile?"

He ate slowly, and turned the base of his glass between his fingers.

"How would you expect her to be?"

"I haven't been in touch with her."

It seemed obscene, talking about her in hushed tones amidst so much flaking gilt and faded plush. Through the blue perfume of long cigars the dirty stories went on.

"She tried to reach you—why didn't you take the call?"

"Ames, it wouldn't be fair to her to try and keep it going. Letters, phone calls, seeing each other in cafes or cheap hotels—where does any of that lead?"

"Cheap hotels?" I had said it too loud, and sawed at my steak until they went back to their cigars. "Look. Get it straight at least. She loves you. She's not asking you to break up your home. She's letting you set the rules. She wants to see you and be with you as much as she can. That's all."

I had promised to tell him, not persuade him. Somewhere there had to be a goddam limit to all this. And there he sat with a tortured look on his face, pushing his peas and carrots around his plate.

"I want to make a success of my marriage. Damn near everybody I know in our Class has failed. Our whole generation has failed. Somebody has to set the pace."

He sounded like a prisoner of war, reading his text for a propaganda broadcast.

"What do you call a successful marriage?" It was all I could do to keep from beating my fists on the table. "What the Christ, Spence. We're not a bunch of track men. College is over."

"We're going to stay together, old man. We're going to see it through," and he stared stonily down at his plate as though he were alone in the room.

"Spence," I said. "Listen to me. She's in love with you. You know damn well you love her. Who are you doing this for? Don't tell me you're doing it for Nancy. What would she and your boys want with a ball-less old tabby cat padding around the house, yowling at the moon. You never signed on for suicide. When are you going to start living your own life? You don't owe Philadelphia, or Procter and Gamble or whatever the hell you call it, a goddam thing. And if Nancy wants you the way you are, she must be crazy, too."

I don't know that he heard a thing I said. He hardly seemed to breathe, and his face was that handsome, dead perfection of some stone pharaoh sculpted on a casket.

"You were all set to get divorced. Suppose this accident hadn't happened? Why should that change anything? You think God cares that much about you? Cecile, Spence; Cecile. She's waiting for you. She'll wait until the boys are grown. Go talk with her, tell her how it is, work it out between you. All she wants is to be part of your life."

"I love her too much for that," so low I could hardly hear him, but I had heard too much as it was. It was as if in that hospital they had stuck a hypodermic in his heart, and now I was being asked to break the spell.

"No," I said suddenly, getting up and throwing my napkin on the table. "No, you don't love her enough, Platt. You don't love anybody, man. You are a bloody bastard. I always knew you were. Like this phony club of yours—all of it. And you, too, you priggish whoremaster." They both looked apoplectic, although it was the novelist I really had in mind. Whatever else you could say about him, the ambassador didn't look a prig.

Spence had half turned toward me and put an imploring hand on my arm, but I was too far gone.

"No. I don't want to know your bloody history. We all have histories. There's always an explanation. I'm tired of explanations —none of them means a thing to me any more. The only thing that counts is what happens and what you do, like you wouldn't even pick up the phone and let her hear your voice. I don't care why you did it, you gutless bastard. But I've figured out one thing. You're a real, late-model All-American. Just like those faggish Western heroes you love so much. What did you grow up on? *Ranch Romances? Bob, Son of Battle?* The *Official Marine Corps History?* Look, I know. I write the kind of movie you go to see. I always used to think that Americans were innocent, but you've convinced me that I was wrong. The further East you went the more they taught you, and now you're part of it. Not the old dream, but the new. Or maybe it still is the old one, come to think of it—we just ran out of room at home and now people like you are all over the place staking claims to the rest of the world. But if that's what you want you better be ready to pay the price. Don't lose your nerve the way you did with Cecile. And don't go on killing people and telling them it's for their own good. Because that's what you're doing to Cecile—walking out on her and saying it's because you love her too much. She's the one who's innocent, because she knows what she wants and calls it by its name. You're a hypocrite, Platt—you're talking out of both sides of your face at once. You should have been a preacher or a lawyer, one, but then maybe Americans are just naturally a little bit of both without even having to try. There's been too much lying about the past, right from the beginning. Who knows it if I don't? Oh, to hell with you and your Grand Tetons and Custer's Last Stand and the rest of it. The scenery may be great, but you're not a damned bit better than the rest of us."

I left him to sort it out as best as he could and took the stairs two at a time and grabbed my coat and was still running when I hit the street. I felt fifty pounds lighter, like somebody had broken a ball and chain off my leg. I ran most of the way to the Étoile, pointed shoes and all, before I slowed down to a walk. I felt as though I couldn't get my breath, and then I realized that I was laughing like a prisoner right out of solitary who's made it over the wall.

"What are you doing back? Looking for a place to sleep?"

There was nothing really unfriendly about Madame Germaine. She was just short of time, and time was money. So were a lot of other things in her business. I could have hugged her. Some night I would take her to dinner at the club.

"I want to use your phone."

She looked at me hard, waiting for the joke.

"Last time it's a room. Now it's a phone. You crazy Americans."

I shook my head and laughed at her. "Look, I want to call my girl. The kind you can't buy."

"From here?" She turned her mouth down.

"It's the only home I've got. Give me that phone."

She looked like an oversized hen in a Mardi Gras parade, but for some reason she had always liked me. Like maybe it was fun trying to figure out why I was so dumb. Who knows? Maybe I looked like the guy she never married.

"Hello."

"Cecile."

"Amory. Where are you? Are you with Spence?"

Madame Germaine had mixed me a drink and set it in front of me and now she leaned against the wall behind the bar, waiting to see how it turned out. Her mouth was still down—she only played sure things.

"I told him. I gave him hell. I shouted at him in his club. I called him every name in the book. I didn't make it."

"What did he say? Don't talk so fast."

"He said he was going to try and make a success of his marriage. He said it wouldn't be fair to you. He said he loved you too much only to go halfway."

Then I waited for her answer.

"Cecile?"

"Yes."

"It's not true, any of it. Saying it doesn't mean he loves you. Not for real."

Her voice was slow and very small. "I told him that, too. I just don't know any more."

"Cecile. Did you hear what I said to you this afternoon? Does it make any difference? I lost, but I did my best. He doesn't want us. Either one of us."

Her answers came more and more slowly as though she were suddenly very tired.

"It's not your fault, Amory. None of us could help it. Too much had happened. We were lost too long, and by the time we finally found each other . . ."

"I'm talking about you and me, Cecile. Answer me. Let me come over. Give me a chance."

"It wouldn't be fair, Amory. You know how I feel—"

"Look, who's asking you to be fair? It's how I feel that matters to me now . . ."

"*Au revoir*, Amory. You're been very sweet. Give me a call whenever you come through. I love him too much . . . you know that . . ."

The Madame watched me sitting there with the phone dead in my hand, and then she took it from me and handed me my drink.

"I don't understand you Americans. Anybody else comes in here, I know what they want. Or I can find out. You don't know what you want. You want everything."

"I'm not an American," I said. "I'm not a European, either. I've given up trying. I'm a pimp out of work."

"Don't take it so hard. I've got an English girl. She's new—sensational." And she raised her painted eyebrows and ground her hips a little. "You like older women? The doctor from Madrid is still in town. *Muy simpático.*"

She deserved at least a sour smile for trying, but I couldn't make it.

"You can have the room."

"No," I said, reaching in my pocket for some money. "I think I'd rather be alone."

And after that—well, when I think of all the things that I've remembered in my life, and now . . . I seem to see it dimly through a windshield blurred with rain, so that there are only moments of clarity which are immediately washed away. Driving back, for example—I was drinking before I left Paris and I kept at it steady, swigging on the Johnny Walker that I kept in the glove compartment. One way or another I made it all the way—I couldn't even say how long it took, because instead of following the cutoff this side of St. Tropez I kept on rolling until I hit the long beach on the other side of town and drove the car right down onto the sand and then just sat there, nursing the bottle, looking out to where the sea ran grey and white beneath the wind—and sometime later, I'm not sure just when, stumbled down those stony streets to the house. The fire was out, and there was no answer when I called. And then, just like that, I began to cry. Except that crying is not really the word. I was bellowing, beating my fists against those rock walls, howling like the kind of wind that sweeps down from the Alps and tunes the nerves to the breaking point. There was a case of whiskey in my closet, so I kicked it open and got into bed and started drinking for keeps. And through the blur of the next two days I kept it up, even though she was sitting there beside me now, putting cold rags on my forehead, asking me over and over what had happened. I remember the fire—I could see it from my bed, and she kept it going through two days of December rain, going out for hours at a time to pick up pine cones and whatever loose wood was lying about—and I could smell the smoke, which was the only way I had of knowing where I was. Once I woke up and thought the place was on fire, and kept on howling until she gave me some more whiskey and then I went back to sleep. If you could call it sleep, that is. And if that's the way it really happened. Because there were so many voices, all telling me stories, and sometimes it was the same story that they all told at the same time and each in a different way so that I couldn't understand and my head ached and I would smell smoke and open my eyes and there would be the fire again with Emily's face in profile against the flames and the shadows moving on the wall like all the different faces that just the sight of her sitting there brought back to me. I must have cried and called out—God knows what I said—because I remember at some point, or at least I think I remember, that there was somebody holding me down with his knee and in his hand he held a needle.

And then I woke in a cold grey silent dawn, like someone who opens his eyes on the far side of death. I held my breath, and then moved my legs to see if there was pain. I turned my head on the pillow and saw below me in the kitchen what was left of a fire; thin, grey, smoking ash. And then I heard her coughing beside me, the kind of cough that seems to rasp its way up along the spine.

"Where are you going?" she said, coming awake with a jerk as I threw off the blankets and sat up.

I lit a cigarette and then stubbed it out, pushing my fingers across my mouth. "I feel dirty," I said. "All over—inside and out. I'm going down to the beach."

"It's cold," she said. "It's cold and raining."

"That's what I want. I want the rain to wash me off. I don't care how cold it is."

"I'm coming with you, then."

I shrugged and went to brush my teeth and put on my bathing suit. And when I came downstairs she was waiting at the door.

Perhaps the things you don't do are the ones you remember best. I remember that I scarcely looked at her and didn't say a word as we drove across that mist-veiled plain to the sea. I got out of the car and took my clothes off and walked down the pocked and pitted beach to where the sea rushed up and melted upon the glistening sand. The rain burned on my shoulders and the arches of my feet curled up with cold as I splashed along the surf. But the cold was what I wanted after the blankets, and the fire, and the smoke, and the crowds of faces pressed around me for so long.

So I dove and swam hard and came up gasping and swam some more, every pore stabbed by an icy needle, and then I rolled in the water and looked back toward the shore and there she was, standing in the surf up to her hips, her body half-turned away, her arms clasped across her bosom, her hair adrift in the wind and her flesh all drawn and blue.

"Emily," I shouted. "What in the hell are you doing. It's freezing. Get out of the water and get yourself a towel. Hurry."

She seemed to smile, then, and shook her head as though she could not hear me. It was the kind of smile that made me think she might be crying, standing alone there in the cold. Maybe it was the wind, and probably she was frightened by the sea, but by then I didn't care because suddenly I hated her for needing me so much. And so I kept her there by swimming just as long as I could stand it, until at last I came into shore and then we walked up together from the sea to the car, me puffing on a cigarette which I had dug out of my pants and she coughing that rasping kind of cough which made me angry every time I heard it because even that was some kind of appeal, some kind of asking for what I didn't have to give.

So we drove back to the house in silence and I went right upstairs and got into bed. The blankets felt the way I wanted them to feel, and I slept all day, for it was grey again when I awoke but now the kind of funeral grey that comes at the end of afternoon when the year is dying away. The fire had gone out; I could see the dead ashes from my bed. And then I could hear it too, death somewhere in the house, a hoarse rattling sound like a wagon on a rocky road or maybe like a series of muffled, repeated screams . . .

She was sitting by the fire, her hands crossed in her lap, her head fallen to one side. She slept, unless in some way or other she was already dead. Her mouth was open, and the rattle was in her throat, like someone screaming to get out.

I made the clinic in less than a half an hour, but time didn't matter any more. Too much sea, and rain, and cold; too many years of loneliness, perhaps. And what I remember most are all the things I never said.

So now it's getting on toward Easter, and the rains have started. I guess it rains in Oklahoma at the end of March the way it does most everyplace else. I got the advance I asked for—the Civil War is very big just now—but I still haven't finished the book. I did the wagons-in-a-ring and the kidnapping all right, but I can't get the Major and the Captain through that desert, seeing who can go the longest without drinking. I keep thinking about how it turns out, with the Major riding off alone toward those mountains, and then I just don't have the heart for it. I haven't really made up my mind about anything. I don't suppose I can live in the State Hotel forever, and everybody I know here anymore, at least to talk to, is in the graveyard. But then on the other hand I don't really feel up to the poodles and the pigeons and the homemade cider. I wonder if my grouse shooter's cap is still hanging in the hall. I don't know—lately I haven't been giving it much thought.

So that's the way it happened. I couldn't say what there would be in it for anybody else. With hands like that we probably should have thrown them in and dealt the cards one more time around. But that's the kind of thing you never think of until you know that it's already too late.

Once upon a time I had copied a verse out of the Bible for that jackdaw collection of bright sayings that I didn't really understand. I had been moving it around for years like an extra piece in a jigsaw puzzle, and now all of a sudden it seemed to fit.

Let destruction come upon him at unawares; and let his net that he hath hid catch himself; into that very destruction let him fall.

I guess any of us could qualify, one way or another. For we were all of us just wild geese in winter, hell bent for someplace we didn't know, driven by something we couldn't understand, following the seasons of the sun to keep our blood warm, trying to find a country to call home.

A Note on the Type

The text of this book is set in Monticello, a Linotype revival of the original Binny & Ronaldson Roman No. 1, cut by Archibald Binny and cast in 1796 by that Philadelphia type foundry. The face was named Monticello in honor of its use in the monumental fifty-volume *Papers of Thomas Jefferson*, published by Princeton University Press. Monticello is a transitional type design, embodying certain features of Bulmer and Baskerville, but it is a distinguished face in its own right.

This book was designed by Guy Fleming. It was composed, printed and bound by The Haddon Craftsmen Inc., Scranton, Pennsylvania.